AN
INHERITANCE
of HOPE

Hope you enjoy the story (!!

Larissa S.

LA ⦀⦀ ⦀⦀ LF

ISBN 978-1-63575-980-8 (paperback)
ISBN 978-1-63575-981-5 (digital)

Christian Faith Publishing, Inc.
832 Park Avenue
Meadville, PA 16335
www.christianfaithpublishing.com

All the quotes and footnotes 1–6 were taken from The Holy Bible NIV and from The Founder's BIBLE (The Origin of the Dream Freedom New American Standard Bible)

Printed in the United States of America

CHAPTER 1

"The Yellow Fever epidemic in Philadelphia, in 1793, took the lives of four to five thousand people. At the time, they were unaware that the disease came by way of mosquitoes. The Bubonic Plague, also known as the Black Death, in 1347 was spread by fleas and rodents and is said to have killed tens of millions across Europe within a four to five-year period. Smallpox, spanish flu, cholera, typhus, and malaria have all wreaked havoc on the human race and taken the lives of hundreds of millions of people over the centuries. Today, a new virus has introduced itself—'Le Mal Sombre,' dark evil. And as of yet, there is no cure," explained Dr. Dimitri Leroux with the CDC. "When this one is done with the human race, we'll be lucky to have a million people left on the planet."

Waking up at 3:30 this morning so she and the kids could be on the road by four thirty was the norm for Riley when going to see her parents in Park City. It's a twelve-hour drive from Bakersfield, in which more than half of it is nothing but desert. The drive itself wasn't bad, especially now that her son, Landon, and daughter, Annie, were of driving age.

Riley's mind was bouncing back and forth between yesterday's news of the virus in China and her parents. She struggled to stay focused on her parents because they were the only ones she could do anything about. The dilemma she was having with her mother and father was, even though they were both healthy, she didn't like them living in the high altitude. Her father, who was turning eighty-one this year, slept with oxygen at night. A month back, Riley received a call that her mother had missed one of the steps going down the stairs and fell. A twelve-hour drive was nothing on days like this when there wasn't an emergency, but it would be a nightmare if there was. To be honest, she just wanted them living closer to her. She had heard all the reasons why they weren't going to move numerous times. Riley smiled, thinking back to Landon's speech as to why he should move to Park City and live with his grandparents. It had been a very passionate and logical dialogue he had with his father. However, Jackson had a huge difference of opinion, which revolved around Landon going to college. He had another year to go in high school and was adamant about not going to college. This was where Landon and Jackson butted heads.

Landon was a pleaser, which made it very difficult for him to tell his father he had no intention of seeking a higher education. When Landon came up with the idea of moving in with his grandparents after he graduated, Riley actually considered the idea. The more she entertained the thought of him living with her parents, the more she realized it would alleviate a tremendous amount of stress in her life concerning them. But Riley wasn't disillusioned by Landon's desire to move in with her parents. Although she knew he loved his grandparents dearly, she was completely aware of Landon's love for the outdoors and all the activities that the changing seasons brought with it. When Landon was at his grandparents', he and his grandfather spent a great deal of time together outside, be it sunshine or snow. Both loved to hike, fish, bike, and ski together or simply sit outside, talking while drinking their iced tea on the porch, which overlooked downtown Park City.

The sad part about this trip is, it will be the last trip for a while for Riley's oldest daughter, Annie, as she would be starting college in the fall. She was eighteen and excited about going away to school. Unlike Landon, Annie made friends easily; and Riley knew, without a doubt, she would do well away from home. Annie was intelligent, had a great sense of humor, and was drop-dead gorgeous. Annie had the same outdoor fever as her brother and a tremendous love for animals, so much so that she wanted to have a career that surrounded her with them. It was one of the many reasons Annie and Landon got along so well. Annie loved to go hunting with her father and brother, even though they both preferred rifles and she preferred the bow. She was an excellent marksman when it came to her bow. Annie was seven when Jackson introduced her to it, and it quickly became an extension of her.

When they were much younger, Landon would place bets with the neighborhood kids that Annie could make some crazy shot. The one that still made Riley cringe to this day was when Annie shot an arrow through a small hole in their backyard fence while inside their house. It went through the hole, all right, right through the Alvarez's back window and into their brand-new couch. Not the smartest thing to do when one lives in the city. Landon was very proud of the pocket knife he won from the exceptional shot; that was until Mr. Alvarez came over, holding a very pretty pink arrow in his hand. They were eight and nine then. Even now at seventeen and eighteen, the two of them were inseparable. Riley knew it would be hard for them when Annie left for school. For that matter it would be hard on her too.

Thinking about her children as she drove, Riley got a glimpse of her youngest daughter through the rearview mirror. Sara was reading her book, totally ignoring the conversation that was taking place all around her. She was fifteen, temperamental, and not an outdoorsy person at all. Where Annie and Landon loved the outdoors, Sara absolutely hated it. Although she would go to please her father, she didn't care for hikes, and she didn't go until she gave everyone an earful as to why she didn't want to go. She liked to ski, but she would never rush to get ready, which drove Landon crazy. He never understood the need for her to put on makeup and have her hair perfect when all she was going to do was cover it up anyway. Sara never, ever, went hunting. She didn't even want to see the carcass until it was butchered, wrapped, and put in the freezer. Outdoor work was not her thing, either. She made sure all her chores were inside. Sara's only reason for ever going to the mountains, besides seeing her grandparents, was for her grandparents' amazing house and the mountain view it offered. Her favorite place was on the third floor balcony overlooking downtown Park City. This was her little piece of heaven. Sara would always have her tea glass close by and a book in hand.

Another reason was Sara's love of her grandmother. She loved working with grandmother in the kitchen, where they kept busy with canning, baking, and working in the hothouse. Sara once told Riley that she found canning to be relaxing. Riley wrinkled her nose up at the thought of that because it was nothing but work to her. Riley knew it was her mom that made canning so much fun for Sara. They were very close, and the age difference didn't seem to exist between them. They read the same books, loved the same movies, loved to shop, and loved everything healthy.

The most noticeable difference between her kids was their looks. Sara had blonde hair and crystal-blue-eyes, the kind of blue that people claim they could drown in. They were just like her father's. Even at fifteen, men of all ages turned their heads when she passed by. Like Riley, Annie, and Landon both had brown hair and emerald eyes. People often asked if they wore contacts and were surprised when they were told no. Sara was the same height as Riley, five feet seven inches. Annie was blessed with the short genes, coming in at five feet two inches. Annie was more athletic than Sara and had the figure to show it. Landon towered over everyone, even his father, with his six-foot-three-inch frame. He still had his boyish face, Riley thought, but the body of a mythological Greek god. Girls noticed him, but he was oblivious. Just the way Riley liked it. One thing that she was sure of about her kids was that they loved each other very much, which was the main reason that they all got along so great. And at the end of the day, that was all that really mattered.

The trip to Park City had been planned earlier in the year, and everyone was excited to be staying for four weeks. Landon had invited his best friend, Bram, to come with them. Like Annie, Bram was very outgoing and had a great sense of humor. He was of German descent, tall and well built like Landon, but blonde and blue-eyed. His personality was just the opposite of Landon, Riley thought, which is why their relationship worked. Bram was also an outdoor junky and loved coming up to the mountains with Landon whenever he could. This too would be his last trip to Park City for a while. He was turning nineteen in a month and needed to put all his free time into finding a job. His mother, Ursula, was a single mom and had been working hard to support Bram and his sister since their father died. Bram had always been treated like family. Even his mother and sister got sucked in by Riley's family, so much so that Ursula and Riley had become the best of friends.

Bram was so excited about this trip that he couldn't stop talking about it since they left Vegas. There was something about Vegas that didn't seem right, Riley thought, but she couldn't quite put her finger on it. Her thoughts flashed back to their drive through the city. They didn't stop for gas at the state line; for that matter, they hadn't stopped at all. They would get gas in Saint George as they always did. It was odd and a tad creepy, she thought. They've driven through Vegas so many times that the kids weren't excited about seeing all the hotels anymore. Bram was telling Landon something about fishing, and it brought Riley's thoughts back to the trip. She knew her father would keep the boys busy every day with fishing, hiking, or going to the new outdoor shooting range. This would be good for both of the boys, especially Bram, who needed to burn off some of that energy of his.

This year, both boys wanted to try their skills at mountain biking from the top of the mountain in Deer Valley. This made Riley a little uneasy, but she agreed they could do it this year. Annie hadn't decided yet as to whether or not she was going to join the boys on their downhill adventure. Like her sister, she loved to shop; but if it was a choice between doing something outside or shopping, well, "outside" would win just about every time.

Riley and Jackson used to do everything they possibly could when they came up to visit her parents. Of course, that was long before they had children. Jackson was still in great physical shape; however, Riley was not. She let life get in the way of staying fit, or at least that's what she kept telling herself. She suddenly felt every bit of her forty-three years. Maybe this would be a good time to hang out with Landon and Bram—only for the hikes, though, no more biking down the side of a mountain for her. Let the young ones do it, far too many branches and rocks to contend with. She just needed to make sure there was plenty of hydrogen peroxide on hand along with Band-Aids, the big ones.

"I'm hungry, Mom. When are we going to stop to eat?" Landon interrupted Riley's thoughts.

"We're almost to Saint George. We'll get gas first then eat somewhere. No fast food, though, I need some real food."

Still something was nagging at Riley. What was it?

Being a creature of habit, Riley took her usual exit off the Fifteen into Saint George and pulled into a gas station. That uneasy feeling was still with her when she got out of the car and headed into the station's store. As she walked in to pay for the gas with cash, the man behind the counter looked startled. The expression on the man's face sent a chill down Riley's back. It scared her enough to make her turn around and look behind her.

When she turned back to face the man again, she asked, "Is there something wrong?"

"Uh, no, ma'am. Just surprised to see you, that's all. I mean, with everything that has been going on today, not many people out on the road."

"What do you mean?" Riley asked.

At that very moment, it dawned on her what was nagging at her. The traffic had been very light, even through Vegas, and that wasn't normal. Vegas freeways were always busy with every type of vehicle you could imagine. Even the skies were usually filled with planes coming and going. What few cars that were on the road today were hustling, which wasn't that unusual because there were always a few cars pushing beyond the speed limit. But for the most part, all the cars seemed to be in a hurry. Mulling over it now, she didn't recall seeing any planes in the sky, although she hadn't been looking for them either. As she thought more about it she realized, there were long patches of road where her SUV was the only one on the road.

"We've been on the road for the last six hours. I just now realized there weren't a lot of cars on the road. Come to think of it, there weren't very many big rig trucks taking up space on the road either."

The older man didn't look surprised. "Where are you heading to?"

"Park City."

"Surely, you're aware of what's been going on in China and Europe? I mean, it's been all over the news." His tone was a bit harsh, but Riley ignored it. His attitude lightened when he saw the teenagers in the car. "Oh, it must have been music for you all day."

Riley looked out the window and saw Landon coming toward the station's store. "Yes, that and movies. Can you fill me in on what

I've missed so far? I knew the virus in China was bad, but what's been going on in Europe? I thought it had been contained?"

The man ran his big hand into his graying hair at the same time Landon opened the door. The little bells jingled as he walked in.

"What's the holdup, Mom?"

They both ignored him. The man proceeded to speak while he turned up the TV behind him.

"The virus has spread like wildfire, and there seems to be no stopping it. Millions of Chinese have died, and they can't keep up with all the dead bodies. It has spread into some neighboring countries and found its way into Europe. Australia was the first to shut all its ports in and out of the country. They've quarantined any travelers that were in Asia during the last few weeks. Some places in Europe…"

"Wait, what do you mean 'keep up with all the dead bodies'?" Landon asked, a little more excitedly than he intended.

The big man answered in a matter-of-fact voice, "Burn them, of course!"

"Wow!" was all Landon could say. He turned and ran outside to get the others.

Riley watched as her son ran outside then turned back to the man and asked, "It's pretty deserted out there. Is there somewhere we can grab a bite to eat? And of course, I still need gas, if that's possible?"

"Oh, sure. The pumps are still on, so go ahead and fill up. Um, you still have about six hours to go, don't you? I'm not sure what stations will be open from here to Park City. Honestly, I was about to close up myself. Not a lot of people want to be out, just in case the stranger standing next to them is sick with the virus."

Riley's attention went to the TV, and she was no longer listening to the man behind the counter.

"Unless absolutely necessary, stay home. All Utah schools have been closed until further notice, and many businesses have voluntarily closed down. All flights have been canceled into and out of the United States. All domestic flights have been canceled as well."

Riley brought her attention back to the big man. "What's your name?" she asked.

"Norman Wittman."

"I'm Riley Cooper."

The door opened as Riley introduced herself. She and Norman both turned to see all the kids standing just inside the store, looking very nervous. Not one of them spoke a word. Sara was still holding the door open, as if she were sure she would need to make a run for it at any moment. The same fear she saw in each of her kid's faces was welling up inside of her too. Riley released some of the tension by introducing her children.

"Norman, these are my kids, Landon, Annie, Bram, and Sara." They all shook his hands as Riley continued, "You wouldn't happen to have any gas containers, would you? My car should make it up to Park City from here, but it will be close. The extra gas would be a nice bit of security in case it doesn't."

"I have these four spare containers," he said with a grin as he pointed to them behind the counter. "My wife asked me to go buy some for our generator, only we've decided to go stay with my brother in Salt Lake. I went just a little overboard when I bought them. I don't think I'm going to need eight of them."

Riley looked relieved, "Thank you so much, Norman. How much do you want for them?"

Norman smiled, "Because of my good Mormon upbringing, I'll give them to you for nothing. Besides, it's a bit embarrassing to buy so many containers when I have the key to a gas station."

"I hope it doesn't go against your 'good Mormon upbringing' to be helping some Southern Baptist folks," Riley said with a smile.

"Not at all. Here, you boys take these containers and go fill them up, then fill up the car." Norman said as he handed Landon and Bram two containers each. "By the way," Norman continued, "across the road, in the shopping center over there, is a cafeteria that's still open."

Riley looked across to the shopping center and saw a few cars parked in it. "Are you sure?"

"Oh, yeah, I'm sure. My wife is working there today. Her boss wanted to keep it open for anyone who might still be traveling. By the way, where are you coming from?"

Sara spoke up and said, "Bakersfield, California. It's just north of Los Angeles." She too began to calm down with the ease of the conversation.

Riley told Norman thank you. Then she asked Sara if she would call her father and asked Annie to call her grandparents. Once that was taken care of, she headed to the back of the store to grab some water from the store coolers. When she returned to the counter, the girls were talking in rushed voices, saying they weren't getting through. All either of them got was a recording saying "Unable to complete your call at this time." The cell phones were probably jammed due to the high frequency of calls right now.

Riley looked to Norman and asked, "May I impose on your 'good Mormon upbringing' once again and use your landline to make two calls?"

Norman nodded yes then showed her the phone.

Riley asked Annie to make both calls but to call her grandparents first to let them know where they were and that they would be there in about six hours. Annie did as she was asked. Getting through to her grandparents on the third try, she relayed the message her mother had given to her to whomever answered the phone. Riley was listening to Annie but watching the boys through the big window. With all the containers full, they started to fill up the car.

Riley looked at Norman, and her thoughts drifted away from all that was going on around her, taking a detour toward the subject of human nature.

"Norman, I'm not sure what's going to happen today, but humans are unpredictable when they're afraid. Even more so when they think their livelihood is at risk. They'll come out in droves to find supplies and won't care who they have to go through to get them. I'm glad you've decided to go to Salt Lake to stay with family. If you would like, you and your wife can travel up that way with us. We would love the company. It would be safety in numbers, so to speak. We can wait if you need to pack up some things. I have a feeling life is going to take a vicious turn for the worse, if not tomorrow, then in the next few days."

Norman looked at her for a moment, letting what she said sink in before he spoke, "Yes, thank you. We've already packed, and as soon as Agnes is off work, we were going to leave. She gets off at noon. I hope that's not too late."

"No, that works. I need to feed the kids anyway, and you said your wife works at the restaurant we're going to."

Norman looked relieved. He looked around the store then back to Riley. "Do you think your kids could give me a hand loading up a few things in my truck? I would imagine this place will be one of the places hit, so we may as well take what we can."

Annie couldn't get in touch with her father and was about to say that when the boys came in. Riley then directed the kids on what they needed to do, so Annie quickly fell into step with the others, gathering things. She decided she would tell her mother about what her grandfather said and also about not reaching her father when they were eating.

Sara was already in the back of the store, getting more water and anything else she thought would be of some use to them and Norman. Her nerves were calming down considerably as she moved around the store gathering necessities. The boys were the first to join her as they grabbed flashlights, batteries, and a first aid kit that was too small to help anyone. Sara was grateful when Norman came around, handing the kids some small store bags to place the items in. He told the kids just to grab the water and other drinks that were stacked against the wall. As Norman came back to the front of the store, he told Riley not to worry about paying for anything because it was his brother's station.

Riley was surprised but smiled, "Is it also in your brother's 'good Mormon upbringing to help those in need?"

Norman stood to his full height, which had to be six feet seven inches, and said, "Oh, no, ma'am, he's a drunk and a fornicator. This is him paying for his sins!"

Both boys were standing next to Riley and started to laugh. Riley smiled as that was not the answer she was expecting.

It took them only a few minutes to load Norman's truck. The bed of the truck was empty, so they were able to load all the water and other drinks, along with a lot of boxes of unpacked food items, into his truck. The last thing to do was to shut off the pumps and lock up. Not that locking up was going to stop anyone from coming in, but it made Norman feel better.

* * *

They all had their fill of food and drink. Annie told her mother and the others about her conversation with her grandfather. He said to stay out of Salt Lake City, that it was already crazy. People had already started looting grocery stores and that gas stations were backed up for blocks. There had been a shooting at one station with an agitated driver, which in turn caused a small riot. He wasn't sure if it was completely safe but felt going through Provo might be their best bet getting to Park City. Annie said that her grandfather would try to get in touch with her father, which put Riley at ease.

"Oh, no, Lord, no!" someone cried out. "The first case of the virus has made it into the United States!"

Everyone at the table got up quickly moving to the TV. As they did, one of the glasses got knocked over, falling to the floor, its contents spilling everywhere; no one seemed to care. The news anchor was still talking about the case in the United States:

"Craig Blakely, twenty-nine, flew in from China on the eighteenth of this month to San Francisco. He had a two-and-a-half-hour layover before he caught his connecting flight home to Boston. Doctors say he became very ill after he arrived at his home. Two days passed before his roommate finally called 911. Blakely died this morning at 6:47 a.m. at the hospital. Blakely's roommate is also showing symptoms of the virus and is quarantined at this time."

Riley was frustrated, trying to remember what the news said yesterday. She had shut it off around noontime because it was nothing but speculation by so-called experts. Experts of what, she didn't know, as none of them had anything to do with the virus. Her recollection of news reports didn't help much as they were always vague, as if they were trying to play down the seriousness of the virus. The CDC was on top of it. They had an army of scientists and specialists of every kind on this virus. Something was missing, though—a name—they never said the name of the virus. All viruses had names. They were usually letters and numbers, or names that gave some idea where the virus originated, like H1N1, the swine flu, which started with pigs. They used odd names that weren't necessarily scary, but add it to the symptoms, and the name stayed forever. That one name would cause millions of Americans to run to their doctors or nearest pharmacies to get vaccinations. Her kids all had their immunization shots when they were younger; however, they never got the annual flu shot. Riley never got rattled by the flu mainly because she homeschooled her kids. She even ignored the swine flu scare. The more she thought about it, she realized that she hadn't taken her kids to the doctors for anything other than their wellness checkups. Her teens knew and practiced all the common sense things to do like coughing into the arm, not putting their hands around their eyes or mouth, washing hands regularly, and not sharing drinks with their friends. It didn't hurt either that they lived in the desert where the winters were mild and the summers were hot. Not that she thought any of that would matter much with this nasty virus. Without a name, she wasn't even sure if the CDC knew what kind of virus this was or where it came from.

Today's news, however, was a lot more informative.

"Blakely was in San Francisco with a two-and-a-half-hour layover. A lot of people were exposed in that two and a half hours. It's a busy airport, one of the busiest. Another flight and another walk-through of an airport, many more people exposed. He was sick in his home for two days before his roommate called 911. Blakely's roommate was a young man that worked and probably had a nightlife. More people exposed! The eighteenth was four days ago. The media is just now announcing this bit of news, which means they just got it themselves. Four days, and we're just now finding out about Blakely. Four full days of exposure! The virus, whatever its name, hasn't just arrived in the United States. It's been here for four full days!" Riley was talking to herself out loud. "We need to go! Where are the girls?"

Riley was feeling panicked. She needed to calm down. Landon was telling her something…the girls…restroom. She needed to steady herself. She needed to breathe. She felt her heart pounding. She needed to just breathe…in and out…

"Slowly," Riley said to herself.

She was losing control, and she didn't have time for this! Breathe. The kids needed her.

"Come on, Riley, just breathe."

Nothing mattered but her kids! Riley finally felt her breathing slow; it seemed like it took forever, but she could finally breathe at an even pace. Bram was holding one of her arms and Landon the other.

"Mom, what's wrong? Are you okay?" Landon's words broke through Riley's thought.

"Yes…sorry…I'm fine…but we need to go! Where are the girls? Did you say they were in the restroom? I need to go as well. Find Norman and Agnes for me, and I'll be right back."

Both boys let go of Riley and did as she asked.

Norman was helping his wife in the kitchen when the boys walked in. Neither of them had heard the news about the virus being in the United States. Bram explained everything that they heard, then he told them what Riley said about Blakely and the exposure of the virus now in the United States. Landon added the news that his sister received from their grandfather about Salt Lake City. The big man began to tear up. Agnes, his very petite wife, sat down on the stool next to the sink and began to sob uncontrollably. Not knowing what to do, Bram and Landon left to find Riley and the girls.

"They're both in there crying," Bram said. "I think they're not sure what they're going to do. Going to Salt Lake to stay with his brother was probably their only option. I don't think Norman and Agnes have any other family here."

Riley looked in the direction of the kitchen and told the kids to go to the car, that she would get Norman and Agnes. When she opened the kitchen door, she found Norman on his knees, holding Agnes as she sat on the stool. Agnes was tiny compared to Norman's huge frame. It was as if he was holding a tiny child. Riley thought it was a beautiful sight, even knowing where the scene rooted from. It was a sight she didn't want to break up, but knew she must.

"I'm sorry to interrupt you, but I have an idea," Riley spoke softly. "Why don't you both come with us? My folks have a nice-size home with plenty of room. But I'm sorry, we need to leave now."

They both looked up, eyes red and wet from their tears.

"Yes," Norman said, barely audible. "Yes, and thank you," he said, his voice much stronger this time. He turned to Agnes, "We need to go, honey. Here, let me help you."

They both got up. Agnes looked tired, not just from crying but thoroughly exhausted. She moved slowly to the door, turned to Riley, and said thank you. Agnes said good-bye to the other employees who were also packing up to leave. As the three of them walked out, they heard a loud commotion at the other end of the shopping center. They watched a car drive through the front window of some store. Two people got out of the car, ran inside the store, and within seconds, came out with armloads of stuff. The stuff they were getting would serve no purpose if the world was going in the direction Riley felt it would.

Riley whispered, "It begins."

* * *

Getting to Provo was pretty easy. Norman suggested they use the gas containers before they made it into Provo so they wouldn't have to stop where there might be a public to deal with. They could just drive straight through. It turned out to be a good idea as the masses were out, and though it wasn't too chaotic, the load in the bed of Norman's truck could have been tempting to someone. Once past the university and pedestrians, the traffic lightened until the turn off into Park City. Cars were on the move and often didn't care about the rules of the road. Riley wasn't sure what people were doing or where they were going. It was worse than at the end of a ski day when everyone was heading home. She was sure it was fear setting in, and people were moving for lack of something better to do. It was dangerous. The street that they normally would have turned on was backed up with cars trying to get gas. The line was going both ways from the street causing no movement. They continued down to the second light and turned left. It took them almost forty-five minutes to get through the mass of vehicles and pedestrians. The parking lot for the grocery store and the pharmacy was full, with everyone trying to go in and out at the same time. There were two police SUVs on the sidewalk with their lights flashing, but there were no police. However crazy it looked, people were not rioting, and no cars were going through windows. Once past the stores, they moved more quickly making their way up the winding road to her parents' house. Seeing her parents waiting to greet them brought tears to Riley's eyes. The relief was almost too overwhelming. Riley got out of the car and gave them each a big hug as did Annie, Sara, Landon, and Bram. Even their two-year-old Great Dane, Goliath, got a big squeeze from Riley and the teenagers. Norman couldn't help himself and gave Riley's mother a hug that totally engulfed her before he was properly introduced to her.

"Norman and Agnes, these are my parents, Victoria and Ken. Mom, Dad, I told Norman and Agnes they could stay with us as long as they liked. I can have the girls make up the room for them if it's not already done."

"All the rooms are ready, and dinner is waiting whenever you're ready to eat," Victoria announced.

* * *

Having Landon drive the rest of the way to Park City had given Riley time to get her thought process flowing properly again. She made two lists, two very long lists. Riley loved lists, not that they always made it out the door with her, but they helped to organize her thoughts. The first list was simple, just a list of things they would need if they decided to leave Park City quickly. On a second sheet of paper, she wrote the pros and cons for staying put at her parents' house versus getting as far away from Park City and Salt Lake City as possible, or any other city, for that matter. With both papers in hand, she went into her father's office. She hadn't even noticed how beautiful the day was until now. She stood facing the big window that looked over downtown Park City. The day was crystal clear, with a nice breeze rustling the leaves on the trees outside the window. The sun was setting just above the mountains, making its move to leave and let the night take over. Chipmunks and squirrels were running about in their carefree world. If the human race died out tomorrow, this would still remain the same; all this she was seeing would still be here.

Riley, still looking out the window, spoke in a low, soft voice, "They knew and didn't tell anyone for two days. What are we going to do, Dad?" She turned slowly to face her father and repeated the words, "What are we going to do?"

Her father looked up from his chair as he said, "I don't know, but we'll think of something."

CHAPTER 2

During the next several weeks, everything started to really spin out of control. Jackson had been reached on the phone only once, and that was the day of their arrival to Park City. It had been Riley's father that had spoken with Jackson, and he told Riley's father that the possibility of him leaving Bakersfield seemed bleak but that Ursula and Inge, Bram's mother and sister, were with him. He told his father-in-law that he would not stay long if he could help it. Jackson informed him that there were two other families joining him from their church, and he felt they would be okay, unless the virus got them. If that happened, there would be nothing anyone could do. This was killing Riley. She desperately wanted to talk to him. For that matter, she simply wanted to feel his arms around her once again, but clearly, that wasn't going to happen anytime soon. Riley knew Jackson would do everything he could to get to his family. She would leave a note behind, telling him where they were going when the time came.

Everyone in Riley's family got to know Norman and Agnes and came to love them. Norman had been in the Navy for twenty years and met Agnes on one of his port stays in New York. He said it was love at first sight for him, but Agnes had to be convinced. She came around, of course, and they were married on his next leave. Agnes gave birth to a boy seven years after they married, and he had been their miracle child. With five miscarriages, they were told they would never have children, but then Connor came. His birth brought a breath of fresh air into their lives. Connor was twenty-eight years old when he was killed in a car accident. He had been drinking with some friends and could barely walk, but not one of his friends stopped him from getting into his car. That was four years ago. Their faith was all they had to sustain them, but even that at times didn't seem to help. Riley's heart wept for them. She didn't know what she would do if she lost one of her children. From the way things were going, this virus could very well be what killed them all. She was selfish for a moment and hoped she would be the first to go. Then Riley realized that would leave her children alone, and she could never do that to them.

But the virus was, indeed, coming. The map of the world that the news always referred to showed China half in red and Europe scattered with red dots. By the end of the week, you couldn't tell where China's boundaries were as the red bled into India, Myanmar (Burma), Thailand, and Laos. It was reported that with some of the worst living conditions in India, the virus was moving quickly through the shanty towns, killing everyone in its wake. The CDC could not confirm, but they estimated hundreds of millions of people had died in India. The last bit of information had come from Dr. Dimitri Leroux with the CDC and a camera crew a few days before. He relayed to the CDC that as far as the eye could see, there were bodies of the dead. The doctor and camera crew had not been heard from since.

The little red dots on the same map had shown that the deadly virus had made it to the United States, thanks to Craig Blakely. Blakely had entered the United States from China via San Francisco. Within the first few days of his arrival, San Francisco had about a hundred or so cases confirmed. By the end of the same week, there were a thousand or more. The red dots, thin at first, ran down the state of California. Then it got progressively worse by week two, and California was covered with red dots on the map. Oregon and Washington were covered as well. Riley held on to hope that Jackson, Ursula, Inge, and their other friends were safe. There were pockets of white left on the map, and she knew Jackson well enough to know that he would have moved quickly to get out of there. Hopefully, they were in one of those pockets. The East Coast was covered in red. The red dots on the map had covered New York, New Jersey, Rhode Island, Connecticut, Delaware, Massachusetts, DC, Virginia, Maryland, and even Pennsylvania. The other surrounding states were speckled with red, but Riley was sure, with the high-density population that the East Coast had, it wouldn't be long before it was completely covered in red.

By the end of week two, the United States military began bombing Mexico's cities that ran along the United States and the Mexican border. Healthy civilians trying to come across the border were mowed down without a second thought. Those bodies were moved with a bulldozer into a ditch as if they were trash and then covered with dirt. The Mexican government could do nothing. The virus was wreaking havoc well into the interior of Mexico. They needed help, but there was no help to come. People that lived in El Paso were trying to get away from the border but were held back by the United States military and were under quarantine. This caused massive riots and hundreds of Americans were killed, and large parts of the city were on fire. Other towns, be they small or large, if they were close to the border of Mexico were locked down by the United States military. The border between the United States and Mexico border became a hot bed of violence. Canada, our friendly neighbor to the north, wasn't so friendly anymore. The virus had seeped into Canada but was not as widespread yet. Canada had closed all borders to the United States but had not started bombing anyone. For the most part, everyone along the United States and Canadian border stayed where they were; although everyone was sure both sides of the border were ready for whatever the other had to throw their way. Ken, Riley's father, took the boys and went up to the safe, taking out every weapon he had, from his small-caliber handguns to his large ones, his four shotguns, five rifles, and his new AR-15. Ken had a small arsenal, one he was quite proud of. He wanted them to be ready—ready for what, Riley didn't know.

The lists Riley had started now became very important to everyone. When Riley first showed her father both of her lists, he said she was being silly and that her fears would not run them out of his house. Now her father was listening. The list of needed provisions stayed taped to the counter so anyone could add to or scratch off if something better was put in its place. Riley's original first half of the list never got scratched off; everyone just added to it. Riley decided that they would need to take a road trip into Salt Lake City for some supplies. She would not, nor could not, ask anyone to go, so she knew it would have to be her. However, once she told everyone what she was going to do, she knew she wouldn't be alone. She was fearful for herself and for anyone that would go with her, but the trip had to be made. Most of what was on the list could be found in Park City or in neighboring towns but she had some very specific things she needed from Salt Lake City. There were two very large stores that carried everything an outdoorsman could dream of, and that's where she would go.

A separate list was made for those stores: tents; tarps; cots and cot pads (the nice thick ones); a lot of air mattresses, since they came in nice small boxes; sleeping bags; at least two, if not more, camp commodes; a couple of shower tents; fishing gear; three reloader kits or anything else she could find to help make bullets. She was sure there wouldn't be many, if any at all, cartridges left for any guns in the store. She would grab the empty shell bags, and they could load them themselves. Bows and arrows were a must; all the kids used them, even Sara. She would have to find vane kits, quivers, with both practice and broadhead tips. Annie brought all her tips with her; although she mostly had target tips for practice. If there were any compound bows left, she would grab a few along with a couple of bow scales. Annie could set the weight for anyone interested in shooting a bow. No one brought winter wear with them, so whatever she could find in that department, she would take. Her father and Jackson built the most amazing travel wagon for camping and hunting trips, which they called the Chef Wagon. It was like a chuck wagon on steroids. She wouldn't need anything for cooking and not much in the way of first aid. The wagon had it all. Anything they needed to restock, they could do closer to home. A small canoe might be nice, but her dad had a flat-bottom boat he used for fishing, which was big enough for four men. Riley wasn't sure if that would be too big to haul when they needed so many other things. She put the small canoe on the list.

"I know you're going to tell me no, Dad, but I need to make a trip into the city. We can get almost everything here or close by, but the rest will have to come from Salt Lake." Riley then showed her father the list.

"As much as I hate to say it, I think you are right. But I'll go," Ken said, folding the list in half, setting it on the table in front of him.

Riley shook her head and told him, "You can go, but I'm going too, and that's final."

Landon looked at Bram then to his grandfather and added, "Bram and I are going too."

"What would you like for us to do?" Norman asked.

"I have a root cellar where I store my canned goods and other things I need to finish canning. If you wouldn't mind helping me get them out, so I can get them ready to load up, that would be wonderful, Norman," Victoria said. "I do have one request before you go into the city. Would someone go up to the Lammuchi's and see how they are? I couldn't get ahold of them, and I'm concerned."

Riley sighed, "I'll go now before it gets too dark to see if they're okay. I'll also swing by Mr. Miller's to check on him and ask him what he wants to do."

Riley grabbed her keys and headed for the door. Annie was by her side with her bow in hand.

"What are you doing?" Riley inquired.

"I'm going with you," Annie said.

"I'm going to check on them, not shoot them."

Annie replied with a smile, "Well, Mr. Miller could stand to be shot, but I promise not to shoot him until you tell me to."

"Ha-ha, you're funny, Annie."

Mr. Miller could be rude—extremely rude for that matter, Riley thought. She more than once had wished him ill will, but he was alone, and she felt sorry for him.

She opened the front door when Landon and Bram came up behind her, wearing their guns in holsters.

"Really, guys, I'm checking on neighbors, that's all. The hardware isn't necessary!"

"Grandpa heard gunshots late last night," Landon informed her.

Riley turned to her father, "What do you mean you heard gunshots last night? Why didn't you say something?"

"I didn't want you to worry. You have enough on your plate now, and there were only a few shots. They could have been warning shots or someone taking advantage of the lack of law enforcement and were shooting at the wildlife. It could have been anything, really."

"Okay, all of you need to hear me on this. My first priority is my children, and I'm happy to have all of you with me, I truly am. But please don't hide anything from me. I never have too much on my plate when it comes to the safety of my kids. And, Mom, Dad, I get that I'm your daughter and you want to protect me, but I'm too old for that. It's all about your grandkids now. Okay?" Riley was feeling a little bit too riled up but then finished with, "I'm sorry."

"I'm sorry too, Riley, it won't happen again." Her father got up and gave her a hug. "I'll go with you. Miller can be a handful sometimes."

When they arrived at the Lammuchi's house, there was one light on downstairs, which didn't mean much due to the fact it was still light outside. But the house seemed quiet.

Ken rang the bell, then knocked on the door, and yelled, "It's me, Adam, Ken Logan! Carolyn…Carolyn…Adam!"

He knocked harder and called their names again.

There was a voice inside, sobbing and talking at the same time. Coming through the door, it was hard to hear what was being said. Carolyn opened the door. Her eyes were bloodshot and wet. She looked like she had been crying for hours. She fell into Ken's arms, and he held her for some time. Riley motioned to the boys to go in and have a look around. Carolyn just stood there in Ken's embrace and sobbed.

"Carolyn, look at me." Ken's fatherly concern came in a low, soft voice. "What happened? Where's Adam?"

"I don't know. He was freaking out and scaring the kids last night. We got into a huge fight. I took the kids up to our room and had them sleep with me. I woke up this morning, and he was gone, along with some food and all the water bottles we had. The car is gone too. The jerk abandoned his family! What kind of person would do that now with everything that's going on! That stupid, useless excuse of a man! What an idiot! How could he do this?"

Riley had a few other names to call him but kept them to herself.

"Carolyn, let's go pack some bags for you and the kids. You'll come with us."

She touched Carolyn on the back, which made Carolyn turn toward her. Carolyn smiled as she looked at Riley and wiped her eyes with the sleeve of her shirt. Both boys returned and shook their heads, finding nothing unusual inside.

Riley looked to Carolyn again, "Do you mind if we grab what's left in your pantry? The boys can do that while Annie and I help you pack."

Carolyn and Adam had two boys—Mark, nine, and Matt, twelve. They were sweet boys and loved to hang out with Landon and Bram. Riley never did care much for Adam, who was a little too snobby for her taste. He came into money by way of birth and was spoiled. Riley liked Carolyn, though; she too came from money, but she didn't act the part. Once, she told Riley that her parents made her work at the family business, and she had really enjoyed working there. When Matt was born, she quit working for her father to become a full-time mom. That made Adam happy because it meant she would be taking care of him more too. They bought their home in Park City about four years ago. It was only meant to be a summer home, but Adam loved it up here and moved them here full time. Carolyn didn't mind; the schools were good, and the fresh air was a relief from the pollution back east.

Both boys were asleep in the master bedroom. They worked quietly and only grabbed the absolute necessities. Carolyn had gone to Costco earlier in the month and had stocked up on toilet paper, shampoo, toothpaste, and soap. Riley was pleased to see all the items and told Carolyn so. Carolyn looked baffled.

"As long as you're with us, you and the boys will never go hungry, however, toilet paper is now the new gold!"

Both of them laughed, but Riley knew that camping out was going to be hard for Carolyn, even though her boys would think of it as an adventure. Thinking about it now, it was going to be hard on Sara too.

Instead of heading to Mr. Miller's, Ken decided to take Carolyn and the boys to his house first to unload everything. Once Carolyn was in the safety of Ken and Victoria's home, she thanked everyone and seemed in much better spirits. Sara took the boys downstairs to play some games. She was always good with young children, and Riley realized it was children that brought out the soft side of Sara. Carolyn fell in with the other ladies and Norman, doing whatever they asked of her. Riley had no doubt that she was happy to be around people again.

When the five of them arrived at Mr. Miller's house, they found all his lights on. Ken again took the lead, but this time, by only ringing the doorbell. He didn't call out; he just waited for Mr. Miller to answer the door.

When Mr. Miller opened the door and saw the five them, some still armed, his only remark was, "What do you yahoos want? You here to rob me?"

Ken pushed on the door to let himself in. Riley and the kids just stood there.

Mr. Miller stood with the door wide open, looking at Riley and the teenagers and said, "Ken, I don't know what makes your brain-dead bunch of half-wits stupid, but it's working! They're just standing there like I got all day!"

Riley looked at Annie, who was still carrying her bow, and just sighed. Annie smiled as she envisioned an arrow sticking out of his rear end.

Ken explained to Mr. Miller what they were going to do and extended an invitation for him to join them. Mr. Miller informed Ken that they were a bunch of spineless derelicts, and they were acting like all the crazy doomsday preppers. He wasn't going anywhere when it was safe right where he was! Most importantly, he wasn't sleeping outside in some ol' tent when he had a perfectly good house and bed to sleep in! Ken told him they would be leaving by the end of the week to head north, that if he wanted to come, he had until then to decide. With that done, they all found their way out and back to the car.

Annie said what everyone was feeling, "I hope he stays!"

* * *

3:30 in the morning came early to everyone leaving for Salt Lake. Ken and Riley both wanted to be on the road before sun up. Ken felt sure the interstate would be the best way to go, so that was the way they went. They left at four and headed to Interstate Eighty, where they would take the Two Fifteen south to the Fifteen. Both places were right off the freeway, so it would be easy to get off and back on again. Annie decided to come, since she knew exactly what was needed for the bows.

First stop, Utah Outdoors. It was a three-story building that was enormous. They had nothing like this in California as far as the Coopers were aware. In the center of the store was a restaurant completely encompassed by one of the largest aquariums Riley had ever seen. It didn't matter where you were seated; you had the best view of all Utah's native fish swimming around you. For that matter, you could see it from almost anywhere in the store. The second and third floor looked down on it from the center of each floor. As Riley thought about the aquarium, she was sure that all the fish would be dead by now. Hopefully, some dimwit would have thought to catch a few for a barbeque while they were there looting the place. Riley startled herself when she became conscious of the fact that she was about to become one of those dimwits looting the place. She could justify what they were about to do, however, she would make sure they only took what they needed and nothing more.

The freeway wasn't completely clear. There were quite a few vehicle accidents along the freeway that stayed where they had crashed. The few cars that were moving on the road didn't bother them. They were obviously trying desperately to get to wherever they were going. The dark mountains loomed on either side of them. Their giant silhouettes up against the dark sky brought back that eerie feeling Riley had once before in Las Vegas, but this time she knew where that feeling stemmed from. It was still dark when they arrived forty-five minutes later at Utah Outdoors. The parking lot had two cars under the large awning with one of the trunks opened and completely filled with items from the store. There was also a brand-new pickup truck parked close to the entrance but not under the awning. No one was around. Riley's nerves were on edge once again. *Not doing a very good job of keeping your kids safe*, Riley thought, mocking herself.

Well, they were all here now; nothing she could do but push forward with her children by her side. Ken parked the SUV with the trailer hitched to it in front of the door right next to the two cars. Ken knew that whoever was inside the store was ill prepared as they mostly had clothes in the trunk. He couldn't imagine who would need all those clothes. He grabbed his shotgun out of the back of Riley's SUV just in case.

They all moved quietly inside the store. At first the voices were muffled, then they heard a loud scream—a woman's scream. Annie engaged an arrow and crept in low, going around to the right side of where the voices were. There were some deeper voices yelling at someone and then a woman's voice pleading with them. She was crying, and one of the males laughed, but it was labored as if he was out of breath for some reason. Landon and Bram went left, and Riley and her father went straight ahead, following the voices. In the clearing between what once was part of the clothes and the fishing department was a man on the floor and two other men who had apparently been beating the tar out of him. One of the men had the woman on her knees, his hand in her hair with a good solid grip on her. She wasn't going anywhere, but she struggled to free herself anyway. Riley understood why the man was breathless. It took a lot of energy to beat a man as badly as they had beaten this one. One of the men was about to lay into the man on the floor once more.

Riley yelled, "*Stop!*" as she was running toward them, when an arrow zipped past her and right into the thigh of the man with his foot in the gut of the other. Riley almost came to a complete stop when she saw the man go down. She regained her thoughts and picked up speed. With every bit of the 162 pounds of her body, she hit the other man right in his chest, and he went down with a loud crash into an empty clothes rack, taking the woman with him. Riley was about to fall over also, but Landon was there to grab her. The woman stopped crying out of sheer shock and then moved quickly to the man that had been beaten. The man with the arrow in his thigh was wailing in agony, and his friend had Ken's shotgun in his face. He didn't move.

Riley made her way over to the man that had been beaten. The woman had moved next to him and started to cry once more. Riley tried to get a good look at the man; he was breathing but was in bad shape.

"Bram, go get some cable ties to tie up the one tangled in the clothes rack. Landon, we need a cot or something, we'll use it like a stretcher. Look for a first aid kit as well, please."

Bram was back within minutes. With some help from Ken, they had the man's hands tied behind his back. His friend was still in agony and cussing with every foul word in the English language. Once they got the man on the cot, Riley moved over to the man with the arrow in his thigh. Riley looked at Annie and the bow she had in her hand. The arrows in the holder had two different types of tips on them, broadheads and ones for target practice.

"Good shot, but ah, what kind of tip did you use on this arrow?"

"Oops!" Annie said as she looked at the selection of arrows she had with the different tips.

At this, the man looked up to Annie and growled, "*You stupid little bit—*"

Smack! Riley hit him hard in the mouth. "Be quiet!"

He started to say something again, and Riley smacked him harder and again told him, "*Seriously, you need to shut up!*"

At that, the man almost went crazy. Riley then grabbed the arrow in his leg and moved it, causing the man to scream, "*You mother—*"

Riley moved the arrow again, and again he screamed.

"You better listen to her, buddy, or she'll leave that darn thing in there without a second thought," Ken told him.

The man was in agony but didn't say another word. He just glared at Riley as if to kill her with his eyes. Riley was unaffected by him and continued with what she needed to do.

"Okay, we have one of four choices. One, we can leave it and let your buddy here take care of it. Second, we can unscrew the shaft and leave the head in your leg. Three, I can yank it out, or lastly, we can hammer it all the way through your leg and pull it out the other side."

"Just pull the *f*—!" Smack again! "*Stop hitting me, you bi—*"

Riley moved the arrow again; he cried out once more.

"This is going to work only one way, and that is with your mouth shut. Your foul mouth isn't helping. Since I'm the one in charge right now, you need to show me how well educated you are and find some other adjectives." Riley spoke in a calm voice, "I need something to tie around his leg. They have some good first aid kits somewhere around here, did anyone find them?"

Landon handed her a bag, and she took it.

Looking back at the man, she said, "You need to understand, if I pull this arrow out, not knowing what kind of tip is on it, I could rip your flesh out right along with it. If it's a tip used for target practice, it will slip right out. So I'm going to pull on it slowly at first so I can get a feel of what's in there."

The man's eyes went big, but he said nothing and just nodded yes.

Riley slowly pulled on the arrow, and the man flinched but didn't say a word. She could feel it slide out smoothly, so she pulled it hard, and the arrow slipped out easily. The man let out a scream but still said nothing as he held his leg in agony and rolled on the floor.

"You need to be still, and let me bandage it. Hey, you, you need to pay attention on how to care for your friend's leg, or you'll be in this world alone," Riley explained to the other man what he needed to do as she cleaned it, packed it, and wrapped it.

She told him infection was going to be the biggest battle, but if he kept it clean, it should be okay. She told them that she did more for them than she should have after what they did to that poor man and woman. Riley turned to Bram and told him to tie the wounded man's hands as well. Annie went with Landon to grab some chairs for the men to sit in. Again it was more than they should have done for either of them.

Riley turned her attention to the man who was badly beaten lying comfortably on the cot behind her. The woman was sitting on the edge of the cot, doing her best to clean the blood off of his face. Riley walked over to them.

"He took quite a beating. How's he doing?"

The woman looked up at her, eyes red from crying. "I don't know. He's breathing, but that's all I can tell you. He needs a doctor."

"I'm sorry, there's no doctor. We don't want to take him any-where near a hospital right now. We're going to have to do the best we can and take care of him ourselves," Riley informed her.

The woman looked concerned. "I'm Becca. This is Anderson. He was helping me find supplies when those men showed up. They saw us and started yelling at us that this was all theirs and we needed to leave. Anderson told them we only needed a few things, and the big guy just went crazy and hit Anderson with something, knocking him to the ground. The rest, you know."

"Becca, I'm Riley Cooper, and this is my dad, Ken Logan. These are my kid's Landon, Bram, and Annie. Is it just the two of you?"

Becca was somewhat apprehensive but then answered, "No, my sister's kids, Rachel and Timothy, ran and hid when all the fighting began. I saw them upstairs, scared to death."

"You have no reason to fear us, okay?" Riley answered Becca's concerns. Then she looked to her children, "Landon, you and Annie go with Becca please and help her find the kids. Don't come back down empty-handed, either. We need to get moving, get the items we need, and get out of here. I want to be out of here in an hour. Dad, take Bram, he'll help you with whatever you need. I'll stay here and keep an eye on Anderson as well as these two gentlemen. While I'm in this section, I may as well look for some winter clothes."

Riley glanced around the store. The clothes section had nearly been cleaned out. What was left were mostly winter clothes, which was exactly what Riley needed. She guessed no one wanted them since winter was still a way off. She found some nice pullover hoodies, some slickers, a lot of camo pants, and long sleeve shirts in all sizes. She found a bunch of sweats that she set aside for Annie to look at so she could choose for her and Sara. She found some black and camo sweats for the boys. Knowing Landon and Bram wouldn't care, she picked some out and put them aside. She found plenty of long sleeve T-shirts in almost every size, and she grabbed what she needed. She would have to remember the socks. Riley's thoughts were interrupted when she heard the voices of young kids. She turned to find two young teens with Annie and Becca.

"Where's Landon?"

"You said not to come down empty-handed, so he's gathering things on the list. Mom, this is Rachel and her brother, Timothy. Guys, this is my mom, Mrs. Cooper."

"It's nice to meet you both. I just wish it was under better circumstances. I want you to know you don't need to be afraid of us. We're here to help. Becca you said you were trying to find some supplies? Do you have someplace you're heading to?"

"Actually, we were just trying to get out of Salt Lake City. We kind of just bumped into Anderson, and he said he was trying to do the same. Now I'm not sure what we're going to do. Anderson was the one with the plan, I was just happy to be moving."

"Grandpa, this is Rachel and Timothy. Guys, this is my grandpa, Mr. Logan, and our good friend, Bram." Ken and Bram came up to the group. "Rachel and Timothy, do you want to give me a hand? I really could use it. We'll all get out of here faster if you do." They both nodded their heads yes and followed Annie.

Their suspicions were correct on the ammunition. Ken and Bram said all of it had been cleaned out, but the shafts and tips for the arrows were all there. They informed Annie that there were quite a few really nice compound bows still left upstairs. Annie had Rachel and Timothy help her gather what she needed so they were able to move faster. Rachel thought to get a shopping cart and loaded everything they had into it. Annie found the reloading kits and some empty shells. She wasn't sure if they were the right ones, but she grabbed them anyway. Landon, Bram, and Ken were gathering the tents and sleeping bags. They were in the camping section and found the storeroom, which had everything they needed. They even found the commodes that Riley asked for, however, they took more than she had requested.

Becca worked with Riley to help find some clothes for her nephew and niece. Looking for the clothes and shoes took longer than anything else due to the fact everything was tossed all over the place. While they worked, Becca told Riley everything about herself and the kids—how her sister and brother-in-law went to London, Paris, and Amsterdam for a second honeymoon. She came from Chicago, having saved up her vacation time, so she could stay with her niece and nephew while their parents were gone. The last phone call she got from them was four weeks ago, and they were stuck at the airport, not going anywhere. She thought she would head back to Chicago, but after seeing the news, she decided against it. She met Anderson while in line at a gas station. He was from Australia, and once the Australian government closed all access into the country, he was stuck here. He had been in Utah on business, and when no one wanted to work at the hotel he was staying at, he was thrown into the street along with all the other guests. She didn't know why, but she offered him a place to stay, and she hadn't regretted it. He was amazing with the kids, and when things started to look bad, he said they needed to get away from the city and maybe find a campground or a cabin somewhere. That's what brought them here. They had run-ins with other people but didn't have any problems like this with them. Anderson thought for sure that those two men would let them take a few things. Riley saw Becca's body shiver when she recalled that part of the horrible story. She continued telling Riley that Rachel was fourteen and that Timothy was fifteen months younger than his sister but looked older due to his height. However, he was only thirteen. Riley smiled and thought of Annie and Landon.

Becca turned to Riley and said, "Your daughter, Annie, I'm sure she's happy she didn't kill that man. That would have been hard to live with."

Riley smiled, "She hit him right where she meant to hit him."

Becca looked surprised, "Well then, I'm glad she shot him. Maybe he'll think twice before he beats someone again."

Riley looked in the direction of the two men. She doubted it. They were probably bullies their entire lives. This was more than likely the first time anyone had given them a little piece of their own. She was curious about them but not enough to ask them anything. At this point, she didn't even want to know their names. When she left here, she would leave everything about them behind and never think of them again. However, she would do everything she could to help Anderson, Becca, and the kids.

It was 6:45 when they had everything loaded and were ready to go. They had been there almost two hours, an hour longer than they had planned. Becca had her brother-in-law's pickup. It was brand-new and big. Riley asked Becca if she would be okay with Bram and Annie riding with her. Bram would even drive if she liked. Becca was very relieved. Annie rode with them to help keep the kids calm. Ken laid the backseats down in Riley's SUV for Anderson. They put towels, blankets, and pillows all around him to help keep him from rolling around. He woke for a moment and then was out again. When everyone was ready, Riley and her father went back inside to take care of the two men.

Riley stood in front of the one with the bad leg, looking directly at him. Then she glanced at the other one.

"Here's the deal," she said, "I honestly want to tie you both up so tight that you'll starve to death before freeing yourselves…"

The man with the bad leg said with as much venom and hate as he could muster, "*Go screw yourself!*"

"Defiant to the end with that one, Riley," Ken said.

"As I was saying, I'm not going to make anything easy for you. The world is dying, and you're acting like nothing's happening. The two of you have been given a second chance. You better use it with a more positive attitude on what little is left of life on this earth. I'm not going to free you, your friend here is going to have to figure that part out for you. Your cars have four flat tires each. This is my gift to you."

With that, Riley and Ken turned to walk out.

"You stupid woman, you can't leave us here!" Riley heard one of the men say.

"Well, at least, we know they're trainable. Better adjectives, don't you think?" Riley laughed.

"Yeah, well, moving that arrow around in his leg was very motivating, I'm sure." Her father smirked, remembering the moment.

As they were walking out of the building, Riley for the first time noticed the once beautiful aquarium. The water was murky, and the dead fish floated on the top. Riley thought about the beauty that would stay outside her father's office window and realized that not all that was beautiful would last without the touch of human hands. She thought the world would never be the same, even if someone managed to finally get a grip on this deadly disease that was raging war on the human race.

Ken and Riley decided they needed to get back home. With Anderson in the shape he was in, he needed to be somewhere to rest and heal. They had enough supplies to get them settled into a good camp, and if need be, they could make a few runs into some neighboring towns. Ken did want to stop at one place on the way home. It was a gas station off the freeway that wasn't marked by any road signs. He knew the owner and knew how to get some gas even if it was closed. They found seventeen 10-gallon gas containers at the Utah Outdoors store and took them. Ken wanted to fill them all up as well as the two vehicles. If there were any gas containers at the station, they would take them also.

Riley was happy with all that they found. There was one canoe tied on to Becca's truck, and the bed of her truck was completely full of supplies. A Polaris Ranger was on the trailer, which was not on the list, but had everything packed in good and tight around it. She was happy her father had thought of Sam's gas station. With what they got from Utah Outdoors and the gas, they would be set for a while. Her father had a couple of really nice generators and camping solar panels they could set up so they would have some light at night if need be. They were ready for a major camping trip.

They arrived at Sam Goodwin's Minimart and Gas Station about thirty minutes later. Ken found Sam tinkering around in the store, helping some locals find some batteries for their flashlight. Sam looked up and smiled when he saw Ken. Ken noticed how exhausted Sam looked as he walked up, shook hands, and spoke the usual pleasantries to one another.

"Good mornin', Ken, you're out early. What can I do for you?" Sam said with some effort.

Ken smiled, but he was concerned for his friend. "It can wait. Take care of these folks, and we'll talk."

"Sure, just give me a minute then." Sam turned his attention back to his other customers.

Ken looked at Riley. She could tell something was wrong but said nothing and waited with her father. Sam had the other customers taken care of a few minutes later.

"Okay, Ken, what can I do for you?"

Ken's voice was gentle when he asked, "Sam, is everything okay? You don't look so good. Why are you still here? Why aren't you home with Mary?"

Sam's eyes went red as he tried to hold back the tears. "Mary's in Salt Lake with our boy."

"Oh, how are they doing?"

"My boy died last week while Mary was with him. He travels a lot to South America, mostly to Brazil, and came home sick. Mary went to help him out. She was able to get him to the hospital, but he died the next day." Tears now were swelling in Sam's eyes. No amount of effort could stop them. He wiped his eyes and walked over to the counter.

"Was it the virus?" Ken asked with gentle concern.

"They're not saying, but they wanted Mary to stay just in case. Mary told me not to come, that the hospital is filled with a lot of very sick people," Sam said, choking on tears.

Riley gasped but regained control of her emotions immediately. She knew Mary wouldn't be coming back. She glanced at her father, and they both knew that their timetable had just moved up. Anderson would have to mend on the road. Riley looked outside at their group. She wondered if her mother knew or if the news media was in the dark. Or was the local government keeping it quiet to keep the public calm?

Ken continued his conversation, more focused now, "Sam, we need some gas, and I mean a lot of it. We're going to head up to Wyoming, to the cabins where we used to go fishing and hunting. You remember the ones? Why don't you come with us?"

"No, I'm going to wait on Mary. If she's not sick, they'll release her. I need to be here when she comes home. But you can have all the gas you need. Here, come with me. I have something to show you."

Sam led Ken out the back door, and Riley followed.

"Wow! Sam what is this?" Ken was clearly excited with what he was looking at.

Sam was showing them a huge plastic tank on a trailer. Riley had seen them in California before. People used them for mobile car washes. But this one was a bit bigger than the ones she had seen. This one looked like it could hold 500 gallons or more easily. Sam informed them it was a 1000-gallon tank, and the trailer was made specifically for this tank.

"It's yours, Ken. Those boys of yours out there can bring the truck around and hitch it up. You can fill it up and your other containers."

Riley didn't need to be asked. She turned around and took off, running to the others.

The boys worked like a well-oiled machine with Ken and Sam. They hitched the trailer up to Becca's truck and moved it around to the front to begin filling it. It took a long time, even using two gas pumps at the same time. Riley used this time to check on Anderson. The back end of the SUV was open for air. She came in through the back and sat with him. He was awake. His speech was slow and slurred due to a swollen tongue, which made him hard to understand at times. He wanted to talk, though, and Riley sat with him, answering his questions as best she could.

"Hab arb da kibs?"

Riley took that to mean, "How are the kids?"

"Rachel and Timothy are both okay. Becca too. They've been very worried about you. They'll be happy to know you're awake. I'm Riley Cooper. We kind of interrupted the beating you were getting this morning. It didn't seem like you were enjoying it very much. Hope you don't mind?" Riley said with a smile.

He grunted and coughed a bit, which Riley thought might be a laugh.

She continued, "We're heading to Park City to get the rest of our group. We'll be going into Wyoming to a campground with some cabins my dad is familiar with. Becca said you were heading in the same direction, so to speak. So again, I hope you don't mind our taking you along with us?"

"Mo," coughing a bit, but Anderson also managed a, "Pank ew!"

"You know you talk funny for an Aussie." Riley couldn't help herself and smiled. "Just to let you know, my daughter Annie shot the guy who was beating you in the leg with an arrow."

Anderson was smiling as he moved a bit to make some adjustments to his lying position. He gave a very audible laugh this time and then coughed again.

"Beth 'e pith!"

Riley laughed, "He didn't convey it quite in those exact words."

"I beth," he said.

"He really didn't like it when I moved the arrow around in his leg to stop him from talking. And believe it or not, it took me several times before he was completely motivated." Riley was grinning while she spoke.

Anderson's one good eye was opened wide, and through his puffy face, she could see he was shocked by what she said. Riley could only imagine what he was thinking.

"They're both alive. The arrow is out and the leg is bandaged. Not that they deserved any kindness, mind you," Riley said, hoping to ease his thoughts. "However, my boys sliced all the tires on both of their cars. And I didn't untie them, they were going to have to do that themselves."

Anderson relaxed and lay back, looking a bit more comfortable. They sat in silence for a while, watching out the back end at all the people moving about. Rachel and Timothy were laughing at something Annie had said to her brother. The boys were laughing too as they continued to fill the big tank, which was now almost full. Life looked normal for a brief moment.

"Sam, the guy that owns this station, his son died in Salt Lake City last week. His wife, Mary, went to help him a few days before and managed to get him to the hospital, but he died anyway," Riley spoke softly. She peeked over at Anderson, but he kept looking out at the kids. "He hasn't heard from his wife since they kept her for observation. He doesn't know anything, I mean, if she's dead or not. He won't leave until she comes home. Mary told Sam not to come, that the hospital was full of a lot of very sick people. It's killing him not knowing. I can see it in his eyes."

Anderson moved his head up and down, letting her know he had heard her.

"You need to know something else. You're the only man close to my age in our group. My dad, Ken, he's eighty-one, and another man we picked up is in his mid to late sixties. And then we have my two boys—well, only one is really mine, but I claim both of them, they're eighteen and seventeen. There are seven women, including Becca and myself. We end the total sum of our group with four young kids. I just want you to know we're all outdoorsy people, hunters and fishermen. We're quite capable at surviving out in the wild. We may look like we'll die out in the wilderness, but we won't. You can stay with us as long as you like. But you need to know something else, everything

I do, I do for my children. Those kids are always first and foremost in my mind—which means Rachel and Timothy are now part of that motivation that drives me."

When Riley was done speaking, Anderson turned to look at her and simply said, "I'b mever camped a bay in my wife."

"As long as you don't whine, Annie won't shoot you," Riley smirked.

He smiled as best he could. "Pank ew bor the eds up. Mo whining, got it!" In a more serious tone, he said, "Wiley, weally, pank ew for ewerypang!" Anderson said with effort.

Riley, smiling, patted him on the shoulder as she was getting out of the car. "No worries, buddy, no worries. Get some rest. We'll be leaving soon."

* * *

The rest of the journey was uneventful. It took slightly longer to get home due to the loads they were hauling. More cars were on the road this time now that there was daylight. There was a large military convoy on the other side of the freeway, heading into Salt Lake City, moving pretty fast. Ken and Riley said nothing as they watched them go by. They were thinking the same thing, though, that had they done their run into Salt Lake any later, they might not have been able to get in, or possibly out, of the city. They had done well. Someone was watching over them, Riley thought, and she said a silent thank you. Park City itself had calmed down considerably. There were people driving around, but no stores were open or looted. Riley got a glimpse of the pharmacy that was next door to the grocery store, and not one vehicle was in either parking lot. She would have to talk to her dad about the pharmacy when they got home. It was time to stock up on first aid essentials today, if possible. They had taken a few of the first aid bags from Utah Outdoors, but they could never have enough. They would need to find out if anyone was on any medication and, if so, would need to stock up on whatever it was they needed. It wouldn't hurt to grab some vitamins and anything else they thought they could use. Her parents knew the manager, so hopefully, he would be willing to come and let them in. She didn't want to loot the place, but she would if she needed to.

When they arrived home, Victoria told them they needed to come quickly to hear what they were saying on the news. Why they didn't listen to the news in the car, Riley wasn't sure, but her father never put it on, nor did she ask him to. The boys helped Anderson into one of the rooms and laid him on the bed. Norman and Agnes took it upon themselves to get him settled and took care of him while the rest watched the news.

The United States government had declared martial law. Someone in the group asked, "How could they do that?" No one replied.

The map that they had used to show where the virus was wasn't used anymore. They just said the virus was everywhere and that no city, state, or country was immune. It would be best if everyone stayed put. The world news was horrible as they showed film clips of dead bodies everywhere. Some people were walking around, with their mouths covered with cloth, searching for loved ones. There was no more news out of China or India. The Arab nations were taking advantage of the world situation and had attacked Israel. Israel, in turn, attacked them with such fury unlike anything anyone had seen before. There was no help coming from anyone, and Israel knew it. There were uprisings everywhere, which only added to the death toll. Paris was burning throughout the industrial section of the city. There was absolutely no communication coming out of Great Britain or Ireland.

Riley had heard enough and turned to speak to her father.

"Dad, we need to get into the pharmacy." She looked around the group and told him, "If there's anyone that has a prescription, we need to get it filled. And we're going to need a few months' supply."

Ken looked concerned and turned to go into his office. Riley followed him.

"Dad, what are you doing?"

"I'm going to call Frank, maybe he'll let us in. The problem is that he lives out by Kimball Junction, and with the curfew, I'm not sure he'll come." Worry came out in his voice.

"And what if you can't get ahold of him?"

"We'll break in if we have to," he said as a matter of fact.

With that, Riley left the room to ask if anyone was taking any kind of medication. Norman was on high-cholesterol medicine and had packed all that he had. He thanked Riley for thinking about the medication. Riley also thought about the women and teens that had a menstrual cycle; they would also need to stock up on feminine hygiene items. She went back to the ladies and asked what their preferences were. She would make sure she got plenty for them. There is nothing worse than being on your period while camping, and Sara would ruin her life if her supply ran out! By the time Riley got back to her father, she found him with Landon and Bram getting ready to go somewhere. Her father had a holster on this time with his nine-millimeter in it.

Riley ignored it and asked, "Did you get in touch with Frank?"

"No, but I got ahold of Ron, and he said Frank was going to open the store for some customers that needed extra medicine. He was making his calls to them, and we're to meet him at the pharmacy at 3:30 this afternoon," Ken said in much better spirits.

"We have a few hours before we need to go, do you want to check the wagon and see what else we need? If some of the stuff needs to be replaced, we can get it then," she said.

"Can you do it, Riley? The boys and I need to check on a few more neighbors. They live just up the hill from us, and it shouldn't take long. I know you want to leave before first light tomorrow, so this needs to be done now," Ken's voice was rushed.

"Ugh, Mr. Miller," Riley sighed. "Yeah, sure, Annie and Sara can give me a hand. I'll have the list ready by the time you get back."

* * *

The boys, along with Goliath, went back up to see if Adam Lammuchi had second thoughts and returned home. He hadn't. They moved on to the O'Leary's house, which still had lights on. Goliath jumped out of the backseat as Bram got out. They rang the bell, but no one answered. Goliath went bounding around to the back of the house and began to bark viciously. The boys took off running around back but didn't have to go far when they found what was causing Goliath's frenzy. Mrs. O'Leary was sitting in a patio chair, looking out at the view. She had been shot in the back of the head. Mr. O'Leary was sitting next to her with a gunshot wound to his temple. He shot his wife and then himself. The note in his pocket confirmed it.

"All our children are dead, grandchildren too. No need to stay." It was signed, Malcomb O'Leary.

These must have been the gunshots he heard the other night, Ken thought. He turned his attention to Landon and Bram, who shouldn't have been here to see this.

"I'll take you both home."

Landon and Bram shook their heads no. They were going to stay with him.

Bram asked in a low voice, "What should we do with them?"

"Leave them where they are, there's nothing we can do for them now," Ken replied.

The young men were obviously distraught, but both regained their composure and focused on what they needed to do.

"I hate to ask this, Grandpa, but should we go in to see if there is anything we can use? Water or food?" Landon said in a low voice, as if not wanting the O'Learys to hear him.

"They won't mind, and it won't hurt. The back door is open, so let's be quick," Ken said as he was heading into the house.

Landon felt a little uncomfortable walking around the O'Learys' house with them dead outside. If Bram was, Landon didn't sense it from him. He could tell his grandfather was saddened by Mr. O'Leary's decision to end their lives.

He broke the silence by asking, "Grandpa, should we call someone or something? I mean, leaving them out there is…well, it doesn't' seem right."

"I know, son, I'll call the police when we get home, but for now, let's just see what we can use and leave. We have some other people we have to go check on before 3:30. Why don't you and Bram go downstairs. Malcomb has a room that is actually a safe. They put all their valuables in it along with Malcomb's hunting rifles, and I think he has a shotgun. Grab them and any ammunition he might have. I'm sure he didn't lock it when he got the gun out. Be quick, I want to check on the others."

Ken's response was firm but kind. He knew how hard this was for both of the boys. He prayed they wouldn't find anyone else this way. Ken gazed outside at his friends once more and saw Goliath was still there, lying by the chairs that the O'Leary's occupied.

"Goliath, come!" *Even the dog understood*, Ken thought.

The door was open, and the boys found everything Ken had mentioned. There were five boxes of shells for the shotgun and a box of at least a thousand rounds for the rifles. The rifles were old but in great shape. The boys looked around at all the stuff that was there. Jewelry, cash, gold and silver coins, guns and a filing cabinet. There was some art on the walls that must have cost some money for them to be locked up.

Landon and Bram looked at each other when Bram spoke, "I guess none of this stuff is worth anything now."

"No, it's not. Mr. O'Leary worked his whole life to have all this. To pass it on to his kids. Now they're all gone."

Landon grabbed the two rifles and slung them on his shoulder then took the five boxes of shells for the shotgun and headed out. Bram snatched up the other box of cartridges along with the shotgun then followed Landon.

Ken was outside, loading some things in the back end of the Jeep. The boys put everything they had in the back too. Goliath had already taken his spot in the vehicle when the boys got in. They were all relieved to be heading to the next stop. The next house was the Crawfords' house. It was on the way to Deer Valley Resort. A car passed them on their way up the hill in a hurry. Ken didn't recognize the car or the person in it. As they pulled into the drive of the Crawfords' house, the car that had passed them was now pulling in behind them. Ken got out slowly and stood there, waiting for the driver to get out. The driver didn't move; he just stared. Landon and Bram got out and came around to the back of the Jeep. The driver looked scared. Ken waved and smiled but didn't move from where he stood. The driver took a deep breath, opened the door, and got out of the car. He was a young guy—late twenties, early thirties. He looked nervous but said nothing.

Ken cleared his voice and asked, "Are you okay? You look like you've seen a ghost." The man still said nothing, so Ken continued, "These two boys are my grandsons, Landon and Bram. I'm Ken Logan. Is there something we can help you with?"

The man took a few steps toward Ken and held out his hand. Ken stepped forward, taking it.

"I'm Carson Peterson. I'm sorry, I'm so freaked out right now. I left school to come be with my folks, but when I got there, they were both dead." He looked at his hand in Ken's and took it away. "I didn't touch them! I didn't touch anything, for that matter!" He said it like he had just been accused of some wrongdoing. "I never even went in. I saw them through the window." He swallowed hard, trying to fight back the tears. "My dad said he was really sick and that my mom was starting to get sick. He said he thought it was just a cold at first but then realized it must be the virus, but he wasn't sure. He told me not to come to the house right away, just to make sure, and to call first. I tried to call but got nothing. I got here as fast as I could. It normally would take two days to drive here, but the freeways were horrible, and I had to take back roads."

"We're sorry to hear about your loss. Do you have other family?" Ken asked in a calm voice.

"A sister, but she was in Florida with friends. As soon as the problem started happening overseas, my dad told her to start heading this way. She should've been here already."

"Did you check the whole house?" Ken asked.

"No, I saw my parents and freaked. I got in the car and just left." Carson seemed ashamed but continued, "Her car should be there, but it wasn't. I've even tried to call her, but there's been no cell service for a while."

Landon offered, "We can go with you after we check on these people. If she's not there, you can come with us. Leave a note outside on the door, and tell her not to go in and where you are." Looking at his grandfather, "Should we get some markers or spray paint or something to mark the door so people don't go into the house?"

"Let's see if Simon is in, and then we will take care of Carson," his grandfather replied, turning to walk up the drive to the front door.

Ken rang the bell and knocked hard. He continued doing that until Simon came to the door.

"Hold on, I'm coming! Hold on!" Simon's voice was agitated. When he opened the door, he was still talking, "What's the matter with you, give me a chance to get to the…Oh, Ken, it's you, sorry, I was downstairs, packing up some things." Looking at Ken then to the three young men behind him and then down to the gun in Ken's holster, he said, "Ken, what's going on?"

"This young man is Carson Peterson. You wouldn't happen to know his parents by any chance?"

"Why, yes, if you're talking about Jack and Abby Peterson," he answered, a little confused.

"Carson just found them dead in their house. He thinks it's the virus that killed them," Ken spoke in a gentle voice.

"So it's here then," Simon said as a statement rather than a question.

"Yeah, it is. On our way back in from Salt Lake today, we stopped at Sam's place. He said his son died last week, and his wife is stuck in the city at the hospital. They're keeping her for observation. He doesn't know if she is even alive. He won't leave until she comes back," Ken said.

"Holy cow! I'm sorry to hear that. We're packing up, but I'm not sure where we are going. There's just too many people in Park City that travel in and out of the country, and I just want to get my family as far away from here as possible," Simon said in a solemn voice.

Ken understood, "We are too. My daughter and grandkids are here, and all we've been doing is gathering what we need and packing it to go. We're heading to Wyoming, to one of Sam's and my favorite campgrounds where we go hunting and fishing. There's a few cabins up there with an excellent campground by a lake. There will be plenty of food and fresh water. My daughter thinks we need to be gone at least six months, if not longer. I'm inclined to go along with that thinking." He thought of one other thing, "Malcomb O'Leary is dead. Murder suicide."

"*What!*"

"We just found them." Ken sighed. "Look, if you want to come with us, we would love to have you. We are leaving at 4:00 tomorrow morning. Riley wants to get going, but she knows we need to wait until morning. Driving at night is no good, not now. With martial law in effect, we will be taking a chance anyway."

Landon cut in, "Grandpa, it's 2:20 , and we still need to stop at Mr. Miller's."

"Yeah, okay, we have to go. Think about it, Simon. We have a nice-size group, about eighteen. That is, if Carson comes with us." Ken looked in Carson's direction.

He seemed miserable but nodded his head yes. He had nowhere else to go. He would have to go back to the house and leave a note for his sister, just in case, along with a map of some kind. He didn't like leaving, but his sister could be dead too and waiting for her felt like a fool's wait.

He looked at Ken and asked, "Um, are you still going back to my parents' house with me? It's just up the road. I'll leave a note for my sister. It won't take too much time."

Simon said, "Go on. I have my son and his family here. We have my truck, Alice's car, and Marcus drove up in his big Dodge van. We'll pack the vehicles as full as we can get them. We'll be there at 3:30 to help you with any of the last-minute loading. And, Ken, thanks for thinking of us. You've always been a great friend."

"See you tomorrow morning." Ken turned to Carson, "Let's go, I need to be somewhere at 3:30."

They drove to Carson's house, and just as Carson had said, through the window, both of his parents could be seen. Both dead. Landon and Bram went around back to check inside through the back windows. Bram climbed the balcony and looked in the windows. No one else was home. Carson got into the garage via a keypad by one of the garage doors. He found an orange spray can they used to mark poles in the wintertime. The house was nestled on a corner, and Carson said when the snowplow would come around to clear the road, it would hit their wall. His dad put the poles out each winter with the orange tips so they could be seen. It had helped. Now the spray paint would help to warn his sister not to go in—or anyone else, for that matter. Ken made a rough map, giving directions to his house and to the campground just in case. They left it in a place where she would find it taped to the door inside the garage. She would use the keypad to go into the house as he did. Once everything was done, they headed toward Mr. Miller's.

The road led them back past Simon and Alice Crawford's house. They had the garage open and were busy packing their vehicles. Marcus, Simon's son, waved as they passed. It took them approximately five minutes to get to Mr. Miller's. When they arrived, Mr. Miller was outside, putting something in his car. Ken thought it was a suitcase, but he couldn't be sure. As Ken got out of the Jeep, Mr. Miller glanced up.

"Miller, are you going somewhere?" Ken inquired.

"That arrogant, bossy, half-wit of a daughter of yours came up here and told me to get my butt packed, that you were all leaving tomorrow!" Mr. Miller barked.

Ken smiled and said very calmly, "First off, that arrogant, bossy, half-wit daughter of mine would never talk to you like that, and her coming up here before me tells me she cares about you. More importantly, she got that slag tail end of yours moving. We leave at 4:00 a.m. sharp."

He turned and headed back to the car.

Before he got in, he asked, "Do you need help? I can leave my grandsons here to help you."

Landon and Bram cringed when they heard him ask that. They didn't know what they had done to get punished, but if he said yes, they were stuck helping Mr. Miller. Waiting for his answer seemed like a lifetime.

Finally, Mr. Miller said, "No, I don't need any dorky, wet-nose, snotty kids of yours helping me! I am quite…"

Ken shut the door to the Jeep and backed it out before Mr. Miller could finish his sentence. Both boys let out a sigh of relief then laughed. Landon was wondering why his mom came up here to speak with Mr. Miller when she disliked him so much. He would have to ask her when he saw her. He was glad to be heading back home. He was getting hungry again. His grandmother always had something around the house to munch on, but now with them packing everything up, he wasn't sure.

When they arrived back home, Victoria must have read Landon's mind. She had tons of food out buffet-style. It was mostly things that would spoil if they tried to take them. She had ham, chicken taco soup, pork chops cooked in mushroom soup with green beans (which was Landon's favorite), veggies, and biscuits. Landon and Bram were in heaven and went in right away to eat. Ken, Goliath, and Carson came in behind them. Ken shut off the TV and asked everyone to come into the family room for a meeting. He explained everything that they had found and what they had done. He told of Adam not returning home, finding the O'Learys, and about Simon Crawford's family joining them. Ken turned to Carson and introduced him to everyone then proceeded to tell them his story.

Riley was sickened by the news of the O'Learys and the Petersons. She looked over at Landon and Bram through the hall to the kitchen. This would not be the last deaths the boys would see, and that saddened her more than anything. She would talk to all her kids tonight, but for now, she decided to just let the boys eat. For that matter, she would have a conversation with all the kids tonight. Now they needed to focus on the pharmacy and all the treasures they would find there. Becca asked if she could go to the pharmacy to help find what they needed. Riley was glad to have her help. Carolyn also asked if she could join them. Riley was surprised by Carolyn's request but told her she was more than welcome to come. When Ken was done, he quietly left the room to grab a bite to eat. Riley went up to Carson to introduce herself and conveyed her deepest sympathies for the deaths of his parents. She asked if he had eaten and he replied that he hadn't. Riley led him to the kitchen to get him settled with food and drink.

Once Riley was satisfied Carson was okay, she found Becca and Carolyn and asked if their children were situated. Becca told her that Sara and Annie were with them watching a movie. Riley was pleased that her girls didn't mind caring for the younger children and that both Carolyn and Becca were comfortable leaving their kids in her girl's care. With that settled, Riley told them it was time to go. The three of them headed out to the Jeep with the list in hand and two large duffle bags. Ken had finished eating and was waiting in the Jeep for them. He was happy to see all the ladies going. This trip needed a woman's touch, he thought to himself.

When they arrived, there were several vehicles in the parking lot of the pharmacy. It was 3:40 when Ken, Riley, Becca, and Carolyn got out of the Jeep and walked in. Ken saw Frank in the back of the store, helping some customers. None of whom Ken recognized. Frank waved as he saw Ken come in with the girls. Riley and Becca carried the duffel bags in while Carolyn found a shopping cart. The three of them loaded the cart with over-the-counter pain killers, pills and liquids for allergies of every kind, cough and cold medicine for adults and children, eyedrops, nose sprays, hydrogen peroxide, and alcohol. They found ointment for cuts, burns, itching, and rashes. Every aisle they went down, they found something they could use. Carolyn thought to add a few games for the children, which was a great idea. There won't be much in the way of electronics while at the campsite, Riley thought. Becca reminded Riley about the women's needs, so the three of them found the aisle that had the women's feminine hygiene products and took everything they had. Riley was feeling slightly piggish, but they didn't need to run out of this—not out in the woods.

Joining the women, Ken glanced into the shopping cart. "I'm glad you ladies came and didn't leave this to me and the boys." Taking a mental inventory of the store, he continued, "Frank said we could have whatever we needed. You seem to have taken advantage of that a bit on this aisle."

Becca, noticing the empty shelves behind her, laughed. "Well, you did say a six months' supply. Never keep a woman separated from some comforts, especially when it's her time of the month. We're already somewhat psycho during that time, no need to add to the insanity!"

"Speaking of never too much, where's the toilet paper?" Carolyn looked around to see where it might be. "You know, the new gold? There's no way I'm using leaves or recycled cloth! Oh, and more soap. I'll camp, but stinky I won't be."

Ken and Riley eyed one another and smiled. Winter would be hard for Carolyn.

After her first cold shower, she'll be happy to go a few days without one, Riley thought.

Who was she kidding? The summer nights were cold, and the water never really warmed up. Carolyn would quit the daily showers even during the summer months; Riley was sure of it. She liked Carolyn and knew she would survive this for the sake of her boys, if not for herself. Carolyn found the aisle she needed and walked in that direction. Following Carolyn, Becca began to take all the items out of the cart and place them into one of the duffel bags. Riley followed Becca's lead and then helped Carolyn with the other items she wanted. Carolyn grabbed some toilet paper, only to put it back on the shelf, informing Riley and Becca, "Anything but this."

Riley and Becca looked at her a bit baffled. She said Adam insisted on that brand, and both women understood. They grabbed all the other brands and moved on to soap. Again, not the brand Adam liked. There were other people in the store collecting what they thought they would need. However, no one spoke to the other while in their pursuit of their own needs.

What would one say, "Hi, how are you?" or "Have a good day"? Not now, not when life itself looked like it would be over soon for the whole world. Riley also noticed that the people were keeping their distance. Everyone was keeping to their own aisle, only moving into another one if it was clear. Riley wondered if they understood that just being here, sharing the same air, they could catch the virus. Carolyn was oblivious to this and nearly gave a few people a heart attack. She walked right next to someone, said excuse me, took what she needed off the shelf without a care at all. She totally freaked one man out, who couldn't move away from her fast enough. He said something under his breath, but Carolyn never noticed. Ken was intrigued by all of this as he walked around with the women.

Another thing that Riley noticed was that most of the items people put into their cart would never sustain life. One man had a cart full of cigarettes, beer, shaving cream, breath mints, and toilet paper—Adam's brand. It looked like it was just another shopping day for the guy. An older couple wasn't much better. They had their medicine, grabbed a bag of hotdog buns, a few bottles of water, and some juice, shampoo, snacks, and a few movies. Snacks! Riley refocused her attention back on what she needed, collected one of the duffel bags, and went to the candy aisle. She started tossing in bags of candy, not a lot, but she thought every now and then the kids could have some. She found some cans of nuts and tossed them in too. Her mother would kill her, but she also grabbed some cookies off the shelves as well as candy bars, a lot of candy bars.

Becca found Riley and took one look into her bag and grinned. Chuckling, she said, "Ah, what an exquisite choice to complement our supply of feminine hygiene necessities."

Riley laughed when she saw all the candy bars in the bag. "I was honestly thinking of the kids, but I'm sure my subconscious was telling me otherwise."

Ken heard Frank call his name, beckoning him to the back of the store.

"You girls need to remember we came in the Jeep. I can put the duffel bags on the rack, but the rest will have to go in the back end, and it's not that big," Ken reminded them as he started to walk back to Frank.

"Ken, you're up next," Frank called as he was just finishing up with another customer.

When he was done, he went to the back, out of sight from Ken, and came back with several large bags.

"Ken, I'm giving you a lot of antibiotics along with the other medicine you asked for. I'm also giving you the supply bottles for them. Keep them cool, and they will last for quite some time. I wrote on them what they are good for, and the info packet is taped to the containers, and I've given you some powder for liquid antibiotics for the kids. Just follow the mixing directions, and you'll be fine. Make sure you grab the vitamin C on your way out. Make everyone in the group take them, it will help. For that matter, you should take some of the multivitamins too. God forbid, should this virus kill us all, and all this is for nothing. Good luck, and please tell Victoria, I send my best."

One of the customers overheard the conversation between Frank and Ken and asked, "What does he mean? Why is he giving you all that stuff?"

Ken looked at the man and said with as much compassion as possible, "The world is sick. If you are planning to stay here, you'll probably be risking your life and anyone else's life that's with you. Looking at your cart, you don't seem to be taking this seriously enough."

The older couple came around to the counter, hearing what was said. Glancing in their own cart, the woman said in a quiet voice, "They said to stay home. We're away from the city. We're safe here, aren't we?"

Frank and Ken looked at one another in disbelief. Ken appraised them of the Petersons, that he was positive it was the virus. With that, the man left the group and started grabbing things that would be more useful. Ken said good-bye to Frank and wished him the best. Ken saw the girls outside loading up the Jeep. He then headed for the door with all the bags of medicine Frank had given him. Riley was tying down the duffel bags on the rack of the Jeep when he approached. Ken was surprised at how full the back end of the Jeep was. He added his bags to the huge pile already between Becca and Carolyn. Once in the Jeep heading home, Ken shared what happened inside with the other customers.

"You know, I thought it was odd they weren't taking things of more value," Riley said.

"Should we have gotten more water?" There was concern in Carolyn's voice when she asked.

"No, we're good, Carolyn. Where we're going, there's plenty of water. We'll have to boil it and filter it, but we have everything we need in the Chef Wagon for that," Riley answered her.

"The Chef Wagon?" Carolyn was a bit confused.

"Yes, you haven't seen it yet, but it's a chuck wagon on steroids. My dad and my husband, Jackson, built it," Riley told her. Saying her husband's name made Riley choke up some, but she continued, "It has everything that you would need for camping as far as the cooking goes. It has all the medical needs in it too. When I told you that you and your kids would never go hungry, I meant it. And I also meant it when I said the new gold is toilet paper. We'll always have plenty of food and water even during the winter months, but toilet paper, not so much."

Becca and Carolyn were pleased to hear that and were truly grateful. They both had children to think of, and she was sure that, like herself, their main concern would be for them. With the Crawford family coming onboard, that would add three more children to the mix. If human life was ever to continue, it would have to be through the children. Their safety was always going to be first. If they did survive and the world was no longer what it once was, it would be left up to the group to mold these children into something more than just survivors. The day of doing nothing was long over for these kids. They would be caught between a world with twenty-first century technology they couldn't use and the dark ages. Riley was sure a luxury as simple as turning on a light would be gone soon. A generator would be their new best friend, but even that would take gas. The pumps at gas stations wouldn't be working, which would leave people to be creative on how to get it out of the tanks. It would be hard for them, but they would learn to live without and would discover new ways to make things work for themselves.

They were almost home when Riley turned to both ladies and asked, "Do you mind if I have a talk with your kids when I have a talk with my own? What the boys saw today needs to be addressed, and your kids need to know some things for their safety's sake."

Becca agreed right away. Her nephew and niece had already been exposed to some terrible things, and she trusted Riley without question. Carolyn was a bit more hesitant but agreed as long as Riley didn't mind if she sat in. Riley told her she would do well to be there to hear it too. She was going to be out of her comfort zone and needed to understand that just as much as the children did.

When they pulled up, three new cars were parked in the drive. The Logans' driveway was a big one in the shape of a half-moon.

Vehicles of every kind were parked on it and on the grass too. Ken didn't mind about the grass. It would be left to the elements starting tomorrow anyway. Riley didn't recognize any of them, but her father did and said it was the Crawfords'. They unloaded everything so they could pack it better in the Chef Wagon or one of the trailers. The Jeep would be loaded up with tools and other odds and ends that they may need to get to in a hurry. Riley looked at the Crawfords' vehicles that were completely stuffed to the brim. Riley couldn't imagine what they had packed in all of them.

The smell of freshly baked cookies filled the air when they walked into the house, which made Riley's stomach growl. They heard a lot of intense voices coming from the family room. Men and women were talking over each other, trying to tell the same story. All of them fell silent when they saw Riley and Ken walk into the room. Riley saw the concern on all their faces and asked them what was going on.

Simon walked up to Riley with his hand extended, which she accepted. "Mr. Crawford, how are you?"

"Well, we're all alive for the moment," he answered, "but we were wondering if we could just stay here tonight. Our neighbors are…and…well…frankly, we are a little frightened at the moment. I have no idea how long they've been…" he broke off, not being able to say any more.

"Dead?" Riley finished.

"Yes," Simon said, trying to choke back the tears. "They were good friends, and I never thought to check on them. Not once!"

"It will be tight, but we'll manage. All the boys in one room and the girls in another." Riley smiled at Becca and Carolyn and said, "Sorry, ladies, it's a slumber party in what now is going to be a very small room."

They both understood that life was now on the spur of the moment, and they would adjust to those moments accordingly.

"It's getting late, and before the rest of us eat, I need to have a meeting with everyone. So if you don't mind, could everyone gather in this room please? Kids too, thank you," Riley asked.

Everyone did as Riley requested. Kids were sitting on laps of parents; others were sitting on the floor. Some adults had to stand, while others found a place to sit. Riley started taking a head count. There were twenty-three people crammed into the large room. Riley stood facing them; not one who liked to be the center of attention, she now had all eyes on her.

"For those of you who don't know me, I'm Riley, Ken and Victoria's daughter. Tomorrow we leave for a campsite that's very remote. There will be no store to run to if we forget anything. No running water and no electricity. Everyone here will have to pitch in, that means you young kids too. We do have generators and some solar panels for emergencies. The toilets are buckets with a toilet seat attached to them. I don't expect you to clean my poop up any more than you should think I should clean up yours. Everyone will be taught how to take care of the toilets and showers. My family loves the outdoors and is very comfortable living outside. You will not go hungry, nor will we run out of water. But all this takes work, and for this to work as a group, everyone has to do their part. There are some cabins there. Dad, didn't you say there were four?"

"Eh, yes. There are four cabins and one very large kitchen. However, they are hunting cabins, so like Riley said, there will be no indoor plumbing. They are big and warm, even in the winter. The cabins were built to withstand the harsh weather. Families will have to bunk together, though," Ken answered, then turned it back over to Riley.

"All the food will be combined together. Everyone will have jobs that will have to be done daily. If you are on the cooking staff, you will be the ones preparing all the meals. Hunters and fishermen will not only bring the food in but clean it and butcher it. Cleaning up after each meal will be a group effort. Finding wood, washing clothes, and smoking meat all will have to be learned by those of you who have never camped this way before. Preparing a winter garden will mean building a hothouse and a stone heater. You have all just been thrust back in time where appliances are no more." Riley paused for a minute to let everything sink in. "Life there will be secluded and at times miserable, but you will be alive and away from other people. In six months, we'll see where the world is and go from there."

Everyone looked at each other but said nothing.

Becca made her way forward to speak, "Thanks, Riley, for all this. Rachel, Timothy, and I will do whatever you need us to do." She looked at her niece and nephew, "Right, guys?" Both of them nodded yes.

Everyone was in agreement, but they were a little shocked. No running water was a concern for Carolyn, but she kept it to herself as her boys were excited for the adventure. She wouldn't complain about anything, just find a way to be grateful every day.

Riley continued, "Kids, I need you to understand something. Your education will be daily, as you learn about all the natural resources that are available to you while living in the mountains. You will have to learn to shoot a bow, which my daughter Annie will set each one of you up with. You will have to learn about the wildlife and all the safety precautions that come with that wildlife. Life won't be the same, and I'm not sure it ever will be again. The worst thing I can do for you is to not tell you the truth, so honesty will be paramount. You're going to see terrible things, things I wish we could protect you from. But you need to know one thing. Everything we do, every decision that is made, will be made with you kids in mind. You are the future of this world. That will always be first and foremost in our minds. I am very approachable, which means you can ask me anything, and I will answer you truthfully. Okay?"

The kids gave a nod yes almost in unison.

Sara raised her hand as if she were in a classroom.

Riley saw her and said, "Yes, Sara, what is it?"

"Mom, is this the end-times?" she asked nervously.

"Honey, I don't know," Riley spoke softly, seeing the worry in her eyes.

"*End-times*, what does she mean, *end-times*?" Marcus inquired.

"*End-times*, like in a biblical way," Bram told him.

"Wait, you're Christians?" he asked, in a surprised tone.

"Yes, is that going to be a problem for you?" Riley asked.

"Well, yeah, it is, I don't believe in God!" he snapped.

"Marcus, you and Mr. Miller will get along just fine then," she said calmly.

Marcus was confused and eyed his father, who in turn looked to Riley, "Please tell me Miller is *not* coming."

"Sorry, I can't. He has his own car, so no one has to ride with him. However, by the end of the six months, Marcus, you might be wishing you believed in God. Because after spending six months with Mr. Miller, you're going to want some major God intervention," Riley said.

Marcus was still confused. His dad added, "The lightning-bolt kind of intervention."

"In answer to your question, Sara, God does everything in His own time. There have been plagues throughout history. Each time it was so bad that I'm sure everyone at the time thought it was the end of the world. We're going to do what we have to do to survive. If it's our time, then it's our time." Riley articulated her words clearly. "Right now, Marcus, all you need to remember is that every decision I make will be with these kids in mind. That means yours too. We're going to this particular campground because it has nothing. Everyone else will be heading to places that might have all the amenities. How long will they last and how many people will show up there will make all the difference. Most of them will be like some of you, having no outdoor life skills, which is going to put them in a huge bind, making them dangerous. All of you, however, are with people that can survive out in the wilderness for a very long time. Even if you don't share our faith, we'll still be there for you. I promise you."

Marcus understood that right now, his kids were in the same boat as Riley's, and as long as they didn't threaten him or his family with their faith, then he was okay with that. To be honest, he was scared, and these people had a plan that they knew how to implement. His family would listen and learn everything they could from them—even if it meant cleaning out all the toilets. With that settled, he was now wondering who this Miller guy was. He would have to ask his father later. Right now he would offer to help Ken and the two teenage boys with the last bit of loading.

With the meeting over, Riley took a moment to talk to her father, "Hey, Pop, these past two days for us have been nonstop. I just wanted to know how you're doing with all this?"

"I'm turning eighty-one. The world is not how I would like to leave it. I don't like that Jackson isn't here to help you, but none of it can be helped. You have me, and I hope God allows me to stay alive long enough to help you and the kids, at least until Jackson can get to us."

"Oh, Dad," Riley went to her father and gave him a hug, "I love you so much and am so glad to be with you and Mom! And I know that Jackson won't worry because he knows we're here with you."

Ken hugged his daughter back hard and didn't let go for a good minute. When he released her, he spoke gently while pushing the hair out of her eyes, "I love you too, baby girl. You don't need to worry about your mom or me. Okay? Just trust that as long as we're alive, we're here to help you."

Riley smiled with tears in her eyes. "Thank you. I know and really appreciate it. I guess I don't have to bug you anymore about moving, and Landon won't have to fight his dad about moving in with you either."

"Landon wanted to move in with us?" Ken was surprised.

"Yes, he did. He doesn't want to go to college."

"Not that it matters now, but I would have been on Jackson's side for that one. But I have to tell you, Riley, I'm glad he's here now along with Bram. Out of all the people here, those two are going to be worked the hardest. I'm sure Annie will too. We have our hands full with this bunch," Ken said.

She looked into the room where most were still mingling. She smiled again at her father and added, "I think they're motivated and will learn. The winter will be hard, but they'll be okay."

"How about one of those cookies that smells so good?" he asked.

"I'm starving, but I think I need something more than a cookie."

Riley wiped her eyes with her shirt and headed into the kitchen with her father. In the kitchen, Sara was packing up cookies in plastic containers. There was an ice chest on the floor filled with everything needed to make sandwiches. Homemade blueberry muffins were cooling on the counter. Sara told them the banana nut muffins were in the oven. Finding what Riley wanted, she took one of the plates and put some ham along with some of the vegetables on it. She sat down at the counter on a bar stool and began to eat. As she did, she watched Sara working in the kitchen and concluded that Sara would be working just as hard as the boys.

CHAPTER 3

Riley hadn't been able to sleep, so she was on the main floor when the doorbell rang. Riley looked at the clock as she walked toward the front door; it was 2:30. She turned on the outside light and saw two young women and a young man waiting there.

She opened the door. "Yes…can I help you?"

The young redhead stepped forward and introduced herself, "I'm Kelly Peterson. I have a note that said my brother is here."

Riley could see the resemblance. She could also see the woman was clearly exhausted as were the others. To add to Kelly's exhaustion, she had obviously been crying.

"I'm Riley. Yes, your brother's here. Come in, he's been worried sick about you." She stepped aside to let them all in.

"These are my friends, Tony and Keri. I'm sorry to wake you. I didn't know what else to do. Carson said in the note not to go inside the house, but to come here as soon as I got to my parents'."

"You didn't wake me. I'm really sorry about your parents, Kelly."

"Thank you," Kelly replied while fighting back tears.

"You all look like you could stand to eat something. Come on into the kitchen, we have some homemade muffins and juice." Riley showed them the way to the kitchen.

Tony's expression told Riley she was right, that they were indeed hungry. The three of them took a seat on one of the bar stools. Riley set glasses in front of them and then pulled the lid off the muffin container. She let them choose what kind they wanted. As she was getting the juice out, Anderson was standing in the doorway.

"G'mornin', Riley," he spoke clearer, but his face was still swollen.

"'Morning, Anderson. You're sounding much better, but you look horrible," she said with a big smile.

Tony was speechless when he saw Anderson. Keri's eyes grew in size and she spoke without meaning to, "Oh my word! What happened to you?"

Anderson answered her as he moved around the counter to peek in the muffin container and took one out.

"I was at the wrong end of a whacker's boot." Nodding toward Riley, he continued, "The Sheila here saved my life." His Australian accent was obvious now.

Everyone looked at Riley, and she corrected him, "Annie was the one who shot the...'whacker.'"

Keri asked, "Shot him?"

"Ya, with a beauty of a shot to his hind leg with an arrow. I missed it, of course, as I was out cold," Anderson answered.

"Well, I'm glad you're up and moving on your own." She handed him a glass of juice.

Considering his swollen mouth, Riley went to a drawer where the straws were and gave him one. He thanked her with a smile. It dawned on Riley that the straws should be packed, so she tossed them all on the counter.

There was a light knock at the door. Riley spotted the clock over the stove; it was 3:00. Riley looked at the others and then headed for the door. Tony got up and followed her. She could see through the window; it was Mr. Miller. Riley took a deep breath and quickly prepared herself for some early-morning insults.

When she opened the door, Mr. Miller greeted her with a "Good morning" and walked in, totally taking Riley by surprise.

"Good morning, Mr. Miller. Would you like some juice and a homemade muffin? We have blueberry or banana?"

"Not now, um, thank you, though."

Riley couldn't believe his mood. "Are you okay, Mr. Miller?"

"Yes, I'm perfectly fine," he said sharply.

By this time, Ken was coming down the stairs with Victoria behind him. They both said their hellos to Mr. Miller in passing as they walked into the kitchen. Riley could hear all the introductions being made. She asked Mr. Miller if he would join them, and they walked into the kitchen together.

Ken said, "You're here early, Miller. Care for a muffin and some juice?"

"No, thank you, maybe later. Have you been listening to the news?" Miller asked.

"No, and frankly, I don't care to. Nothing good, I'm sure."

"Well, that fat-mouth president of ours has gone into hiding. There is no government! Not that there ever was one with that little dork of an excuse of a human being! Can you believe they said that loon is hiding in a bunker of some kind, running the country? What country? Everyone is dying. Useless piece of garbage!" Mr. Miller was back.

The universe had realigned itself and was back in order, Riley thought.

"Well, I guess it's time to start getting people up. I'll go get the boys up first. Tony, Keri, and Kelly go get some clean clothes, and I'll show you the bathroom. You all look like you could use a nice, hot shower and some sleep. Unfortunately, sleep will have to wait, but a hot shower should help."

They all got up as Riley requested. Opening the front door for them, Riley discovered they had no car, and what few bags they had were sitting on the porch. She didn't ask them anything, just waited for them to gather their belongings. She showed them the way down to the different rooms with adjoining bathrooms. Once Riley had them settled, she woke the boys up, then the girls.

By 3:30, the house was buzzing with people moving about, collecting last-minute things and getting the car seating figured out. Mr. Miller came with two suitcases, two large coats, some winter boots, and that was it. Ken told Miller he would have to leave his car here and ride with someone. Oddly enough, Mr. Miller agreed. Simon panicked at first, but then Ken said Miller would ride with him and Victoria in the Escalade. Everyone seemed to relax then. Carson was overjoyed when he saw Tony, Keri, and especially his sister. He couldn't hold back the tears. Nor could they. Annie was to drive her grandfather's Jeep with Carolyn and her kids. Riley watched the stress rush out of Carolyn as she told Riley thank you. Sara would ride with Bram, Becca, and the two kids. The three new additions would be split up between the other vehicles.

With everything hitched up to the appropriate vehicles and the seating arrangements taken care of, they were ready to go. Ken told everyone to come and make a circle.

He spoke in a clear and firm voice, "We were twenty-four last night, now we're twenty-eight. This is our new family, and we need to remember that. Marcus and Miller, I know you're not believers, but I'm going to say a quick prayer. No one will hold it against you if you don't join us.

"Father God, please bless this journey, and thank you for these good people you have joined us together with. May our journey be uneventful and safe. Amen."

When Ken was done, everyone headed to their respective vehicle. Ken and the Chef Wagon took the lead with Bram in Becca's truck, hauling the 1000 gallons of gas and the canoe following behind him. Riley with the Polaris Ranger in the trailer pulled out last. The rest fell in line one after another. A total of seven vehicles headed out at exactly 4:00 in the morning.

* * *

Riley spared Mr. Miller and had Goliath ride with her, Landon, Anderson, and Tony. Tony was sharing the nightmare they had endured, trying to get to Park City from Florida. It was an awful trip with them running out of gas, almost getting robbed, running out of food, walking at times, watching people kill one another for things as stupid as a TV, and finally finding some good people that helped them get the rest of the way to Park City.

Anderson was the first to make a comment, "Sorry for your misery, mate. She'll be apples. You needn't worry. The Sheila here and her little joeys have you covered."

Riley laughed, "I think that translates to 'He's sorry you had to go through all that. Everything will be okay now that you're here with us.'" Riley glanced in the rearview mirror at Anderson. "Am I close?"

"Yeah, sure, that's very good," Anderson smiled back at her via the mirror.

"Do you have a wife back home, Anderson?" Tony was curious.

"No, my wife and I split years ago. She was enjoying the company of my best mate, and I'm not very good at sharin'. I've a daughter that's about your age, though," he answered. "I just wish Janie had you lot with her. Last call I got was too short, and she was terrified. Her mum's not much help, I'm afraid. Come to think of it, neither would I have been." He said the last words low, and Riley could tell he was not only in physical pain but in mental anguish too. That kind of pain may never go away.

"I'm sorry, Anderson," was all she could say.

Tony broke the silence, "My parents live in Virginia, close to DC. I called when all this started, and my dad told me not to come home, to go with Kelly. I asked him why, and he said several relatives were sick, and it was only a matter of time before it spread through the whole family. I missed the family reunion because of my trip to Florida. They all went. I got a text from my dad that said, 'Very sick, two uncles dead and your mom, well, I'm sorry, son, she's dead,' and that was it." Tony paused for a moment then peered over at Anderson, "I'm not sure which is worse, knowing for sure or not knowing at all."

"I'm sorry for you, mate, truly. Not knowing leaves one with a bit of hope," he said to Tony.

Landon looked back at them both, "We don't know about my dad. All we know is he's with Bram's mom and sister and some other friends." He glanced over at his mom, "Sorry, Mom, I'm sure he's okay."

"Like Anderson said, there is some hope in not knowing," she said as she reached over and grabbed his hand. Landon accepted it and held it for a little while.

Anderson moved a bit to readjust his body into a better position. He could see Riley was fighting back tears.

"So tell me something, what's with the cranky, ol' codger Miller?"

The mention of Miller brought a smile to her face. "I don't know him well. He's a friend of my dad's. Actually, I think my dad's his only friend. Anyway, his wife died a few years ago, and what kids he has hate him and want nothing to do with him."

Landon jumped in, "And it's no wonder. He's mean, hateful, and doesn't know how to talk to anyone."

Riley turned toward Landon and said, "That's enough, buddy."

"Well, it's true! He's called us every name in the book, and everyone just ignores it," he said in his defense.

"True, but we don't need to bow down to his level, Landon. You don't know what made him the way he is," she replied.

Anderson cut in, "Well, he's a colorful fella, that's for sure. But he likes you, mate, or he wouldn't have come. He needs people, and he doesn't like to have to need them. That's hard for a man when he once was the one needed."

Landon considered what Anderson said, then looked at his mother, "Maybe I can have him help me with some things."

"Might find out what kind of bloke he is, ya know, what he likes to do." Anderson added, "Then maybe he'll be a bit happier about helping you."

Riley just smiled in Landon's direction. Landon gave his head a nod in agreement and leaned back in the seat. He turned his attention to what lay ahead of them when he saw his grandfather's blinker on.

"Mom, Grandpa is pulling over."

All the cars in front of her also pulled over. They had been in the car for three and a half hours, Riley thought, so it must be a restroom break. There was nothing but woods on either side of the road. She pulled in behind the car in front of her. And everyone got out; even Goliath needed to find a tree.

Ken said in a loud voice, "Men, this side, and women, that side."

Carolyn was in the back of the Jeep, getting the toilet paper. She handed it out to the ladies, who took it without hesitation.

Sara walked out away from everyone, complaining how she hated to pee out in the woods, but nonetheless, she kept looking for a good spot. There were too many creepy things in the woods, she thought. She hated snakes most of all and wondered if there were any out here. The ground crunched with every step she took. She felt like she was going too far into the woods, but she needed to get out of sight of the boys. Even though they were on the other side of the street, Sara could still see them. She finally found the perfect bush, if there was such a thing.

She was in a good squatting position and made sure her pants were out of the way. Readjusting her footing, something rustled behind her. Sara jerked around, falling on one knee, as something flew up out of the leaves at her. She let out a bloodcurdling scream and fell forward, trying to get up. Her jeans still around her ankles, she was only able to take two steps and fell again. There was movement under the leaves once more, which caused her to scream again. She spun around onto her bare bottom and was kicking her feet vigorously, trying to get her jeans up while her bare bottom was dragging on the leaves, sticks, and rocks. Her brother was there within seconds, helping her up and looking frantically around for the reason for his sister's scream. Landon moved over to where she said something jumped out at her, being careful with each step he took. His foot came down as the leaves popped up. Landon pushed his foot down again, and the leaves popped up again. Landon turned with a huge grin, telling Sara it was a stick, and laughed at her. She was furious. With her fist curled up tight, she screamed at Landon, calling him a *jerk*. Then she marched off to the car. Her grandfather was halfway to her when he saw the fury in her eyes, causing him to step aside as she passed.

Riley walked over to her, and Sara's only remark to her mother, through clenched teeth, was, "I need to change, and I have leaves stuck to my butt!"

Riley looked in the direction of Landon, who was still laughing as he explained to his grandfather what happened. She could see the smile grow on her father's face. This wasn't good; Riley knew she would never hear the end of it from Sara. Riley was sympathetic to Sara's feelings and was grateful that Annie was there to help her. Riley sighed as she hiked over to Sara and the explosion that awaited her.

* * *

Arriving at the junction where they were to turn off, there was a car parked on the side of the road with a man clearly agitated. He was kicking the tire of his car as if that would fix his problem. He looked up once he saw them and was totally taken off guard by their sudden appearance. Once again, their convoy stopped. This time, Ken and only a couple of people exited from their vehicles to see if they could help. The man was completely surprised to see them. He was out of gas, and the gas container that he thought was full was empty. Riley told Landon to fill him up, which he did happily. The man was very grateful but didn't have much to say about himself or where he was going. However, he was curious about them, which worried Ken. When the man asked where they were going, Marcus jumped in and practically gave the man directions. He told him how far up the road they were going and about the cabins. Riley could tell her father was frustrated with Marcus. There was a look of guile in the man's eyes for the briefest of moments. Riley saw it, as did Ken. The man got into his car and sped off as if he was in a hurry.

Ken turned to Marcus and said sternly, "Next time, don't give out our location. Helping him is one thing, giving him our location is another." Then he ordered, "Everyone, back into your vehicles, and let's go."

It took almost two hours to get to the cabins from the turnoff. The loads they were hauling slowed them down terribly. Once there, Riley was astounded. The place was amazing, she thought, as she let Goliath out. It was a well-thought-out place with plenty of room. Even Mr. Miller seemed pleased when he got out of Riley's parents car. There were five cabins total. Four of them were set back further away from the lake. Of those four, the first two were very large, and the other two were somewhat smaller, but not by much. The fifth cabin, which was huge, was set away from the others and was much closer to the lake. All the cabins were nicely spaced apart from one another and facing the lake. The lake was a bit of a hike, but the view was beautiful. The two smaller cabins, possibly the newer of the four, were set back a short distance from the road coming in and couldn't be seen right away. Each of the cabins had big windows in the front and also on the side. They had very large shutters, which were closed. Riley guessed they were shut when they closed up for the season and hadn't been opened again since this mess with the virus started. She noticed each cabin had a skylight, which was a nice surprise because most cabins didn't have them. She assumed it was because there was no electricity and the skylight brought in more natural light in the evening.

There was another large cabin built mostly with stone, and like the others, it had a tin roof. It was facing the lake but was a bit closer to it. The windows were covered with thick, heavy shutters that were sunk into the wall. It had a huge wooden door that she could tell was thick and heavy. There was a nice, big clearing just in front of it. Riley moved toward that building and found that it also had a huge stone chimney. There was another weird door that resembled an old cellar door, but this door was made out of metal. All the precautions that were taken here must be because of the bear population that lived in the area. She heard someone coming up behind her, and when she turned around, she saw her father with Goliath trotting up beside him and Anderson.

"Ken, this is great, truly great!" Anderson was clearly pleased as he rubbed Goliath on his big head.

"I couldn't have said it better, Dad. This is not at all what I thought it was going to be." Riley looked at her father and said, "How do we open her up?"

"Well, the cabins don't really have locks, but with this one, we'll get in through this cellar door. The front door has a drop bar for security on the inside. The windows have pull bars on them that, once released, the bars drop and are put in holes, which hold the shutters up. We'll have to open the windows from the inside to release the bars. Bears are quite clever, and once they're in, they'll destroy everything inside. So they had to outsmart the bears to keep them from getting inside the place, that's why the owners built this building like a fort."

He walked over, lifted the latch up, slid it sideways, and then pulled up on the handle. It was hard to pull open, so Anderson gave him a hand. The two of them managed to open it with a heave.

"We'll have to grease the hinges," Ken informed them.

Goliath bounded down the steps first without any invitation. The root cellar was deep and musty but also very cool, almost too cool for Riley. It was huge, which Riley knew her mother would love. There was a lot of room to store the food with plenty of shelves and tables. The walls were stone and cool to the touch. Riley couldn't believe how much work the owners put into this place. Goliath was already at the top of the stairs, done with his search of the cellar and wanted into whatever was behind the door. They all followed the dog up the stairs. The door opened into a very spacious room. It was packed with neatly stacked tables and chairs, which they would move outside while it was still nice enough to eat outside. There was plenty of cabinet space and a beautiful, old cast-iron wood burning stove. It even had two large sinks with buckets under them. They would wash dishes outside until winter, but it was really nice how the kitchen was built with winter in mind. There was a large center island that really wasn't in the center of anything. But it was big and had plenty of space for the preparation of daily meals. Sara and her mother were going to love this place. The fireplace was multipurpose. It could be used as a barbeque grill with a movable frame, or a place for cooking with extra-large pots, or simply a fire to keep the room warm during the winter months. Riley loved it! It had a large alcove for firewood. It was empty and would need to be filled, if not tonight, definitely tomorrow. A good job for the kids, Riley thought

"We need to get the food put up before nightfall and work out the cabin arrangements," Ken said as he lifted the bar over the door and pushed the door wide open. Anderson was doing the same to the window to the right of the door. Riley took the one on the left.

"I've already figured out the sleeping arrangements." Riley was satisfied as she surveyed the room. "I guess we better get people organized."

The three of them walked out with Goliath not far behind. Everyone was still wandering around, inspecting the cabins and the grounds. Ken asked them to come in close.

"We have a lot to do before nightfall. First, we need all the food put away. All of you kids can give Victoria a hand with that. Landon and Bram, I'm going to leave you two in charge of getting the showers and toilets up and running. Riley said she had the sleeping arrangements, so I'll turn it over to her."

"I know Landon and Bram want to camp outside, but we'll make the last cabin for the men. Mom, Dad, Norman, Agnes, my girls and I will sleep in this first cabin. Simon and his family will be in the next one. Becca, Carolyn, and the combined kids in the next one over. Kelly and Keri, you will stay with Becca and Carolyn. Does that work for everyone?" She waited, but there were no complaints.

Mr. Miller, who had been very quiet the whole time, strolled over to the men's cabin. He came out, looking very pleased. He made his way over to Landon and, to Landon's surprise, asked him what he wanted him to do.

Landon said, "Um, sure, Mr. Miller, let's go unload the trailer with the Polaris on it."

They walked together to the trailer where they met Bram, Carson, and Tony.

Everyone worked hard to get food, cots, air mattresses, and personal items in place. The larger cabins had a worn leather sofa and two leather chairs in them with some well-crafted end tables. Everything was facing a small potbelly stove used for heating the cabin. There were two rooms with a big loft above them that had a ladder going up to it. Each bedroom had something that resembled a closet but without doors. Inside the closet was a long rod that went from both sides and could be used for hanging things. A large wooden dresser completed the room. The smaller cabins were the same as far as rooms and the loft. The real difference was the furnishings inside, which consisted of some worn-out leather chairs with a round wooden table that had four chairs stationed around it, but no sofa.

Riley went over to the Crawfords' cabin to see if they needed anything and was surprised to see some of the things that Alice and Simon brought with them. When she entered their cabin, there were family pictures, knickknacks, a small throw rug, even some decorative pillows. It actually felt very homey.

"Wow, Alice, I like what you've done with the place," Riley complimented her.

Alice took a look around the place at what she had done and smiled. "Thank you, I know it's not camping material, but you're right, it does make it less drab. These cabins had to be used for more than just hunting. They're rustic, but I can see someone staying here for quite some time."

"My dad said the family that originally built the place used them all summer long but had moved back East and didn't come here much anymore. There's another set of cabins just around the bend of the lake that can't be seen from here. My dad, the boys, and a good friend, Sam, came up here all the time with some other friends to hunt or fish. The owners continued to let them all come up as long as they promised to take care of the upkeep." Riley explained but then asked, "I was just wondering if you needed anything to make it a little easier on you?"

"Marcus wanted to know if we could have one of the toilets for the kids at night? They're too young to go out at night alone."

"I already have the boys putting one in for the women's cabins. They were supposed to bring one and put it in here too. Mind you, it's just a tent and a bucket, so there really isn't much privacy. But they'll have to do."

"Thanks, Riley, thanks for everything, especially for not leaving us. Sometimes I don't know what we would have done without your mom and dad over the years. Their friendship has been a godsend," Alice said sincerely.

"I thought you didn't believe in God?"

Alice leaned in close, speaking in a whisper, "I never said I didn't."

Riley was pleasantly surprised. "Good for you, Alice. I'm glad to hear it."

"Now we need to work on the rest of my family," she said, still in a low whisper.

Riley was about to say something to Alice when Marcus and his wife, Julie, came out of one of the rooms.

Alice turned and asked, "Did you get those bunk cots put together okay? Oh, and Riley already asked the boys to bring a toilet in for us just in case the kids needed it during the night."

Riley smiled, "Yes, they're putting one in the women's cabin now."

"Great! Yeah, I got the bunks up and both air mattresses pumped up ready for your attention. I'll go and give the boys a hand," Marcus answered as he was walking to the door.

Riley followed him out then remembered something and turned back to the two women standing behind her, "When you're done, would you mind giving my mom and Agnes some help organizing the kitchen and the root cellar? There's still a lot to be done. I'm going to take the kids to help with the firewood, if you don't mind."

"Oh my word, yes, we'll go now. Everything here can wait," Alice said in a rushed voice.

They all left together. Riley went in the opposite direction to find the children. Once she found them, she was pleased at how quickly they agreed to help her with the firewood. Riley liked that. These kids were good kids and pleasant to be around. Of course, all that might change in the weeks ahead, but for now, she enjoyed being around them. They followed Riley into the woods until she stopped them. She then explained what she wanted them to do.

"Okay, everyone, we are looking for wood for the stove, fire-places, and for a campfire. You guys think you can help me?"

They all looked around. Marcus's son was full of enthusiasm. Running to something, he picked it up and held it high, "Like this?"

Riley smiled at him and said, "Absolutely, just like that, Carter!"

Carter was the youngest of Marcus' and Julie's three kids. He was seven and had the curliest sandy-blond hair Riley had seen on a boy. He was cute too, and Riley didn't think he would complain much about being here, even after the excitement of this place wore off. She was sure he would enjoy it the most. His two sisters were a different story, however. Claire (who was twelve going on twenty) and Christie (who was ten and growing fast into being like her sister) didn't care much for the outdoors. It was quite evident with just this little outing. They were worried bugs might be on the wood they gathered. Both had already voiced that with an, "Ew, I'm not picking that up, there's something on it!"

Riley knew this personality well as she had lived with it for the last fifteen years with Sara. Surviving the next six months with three "Saras" was going to try her patience. She sighed and prayed for a composed, gentle, and tolerant spirit toward these little ones. Then she realized, Sara would be the perfect person to take these two under her wing. She smiled deviously and began to work with the boys.

It was a lot of work for the kids. Walking back and forth to the kitchen with small armloads was tiring for them, but they all did it, even though a few complained. They had enough wood for dinner tonight as well as a good pile for the campfire. Sara gave the kids three cookies each as payment for their hard work. They all found a seat at one of the tables that had been placed outside the kitchen. When Riley walked into the kitchen, she was totally amazed at how great it looked. All the tin plates, cups, and bowls were placed in the cabinets. Even all the mixing bowls, pots, and pans had been taken out of the Chef Wagon and neatly stored. The utensils were placed in a small basket and put next to the plates. All the other supplies—like toilet paper, shampoo, toothpaste, etc.—were neatly stacked in the back corner. She saw that her father had the fire in the large fireplace going and had a large pot of water over it boiling. There were two very large water jugs on the counter that were ready for the water when it was done. The women had already started to get dinner ready, which tonight would be nothing more than sandwiches. Riley walked down the stairs to inspect the cache of food they had. The flour was arranged from small 5-pound bags to large 25-pound bags. Corn meal, sugar, and rice were the same—some, in bulk, and some, not. Her mother's canned items, as well as store-bought jars and cans of food, lined the shelves, along with large sacks of potatoes and other raw vegetables. All the water and other drinks they brought from Norman's gas station were nicely stacked in the corner. For that matter, everything they had taken from Norman's station was down there, still in the boxes. Riley smiled; her mother hated processed food, but she knew it would get eaten despite her mother. She was confident they had more than enough to get them through the next six months, especially with all the hunting and fishing the boys planned to do. Riley was pleased as she made her way back upstairs to join the others. She was surprised to see Carolyn at ease, working in the kitchen and laughing. She had been worried about her but now thought she might be okay. Carolyn was a beautiful young woman of about thirty-four or so, who managed to take care of herself along with her family. Riley suddenly thought that she would be the one hunting firewood daily as it would be great exercise. Then Riley felt ashamed that she was even worrying about such things; she should feel blessed just to be alive with her family when others weren't so lucky.

She saw her father outside and headed toward him. "Hey, Pop, have you seen the boys?"

"Hey, Riley, yeah, I think they're working on the campfire. I told them to make it a bit closer to the lake."

"Oh, okay. Hey, you boys want to come with me to find the big boys? I think they're getting the campfire area ready," she asked the young boys at the table.

"*Yeah!*" they yelled in unison.

Yep, Sara can handle the girls just fine, Riley thought as she followed the boys down to the lake.

The boys had been busy. They had some rather large logs in a semicircle with a large, wide hole dug in front of them where the campfire would go.

Matt, Carolyn's oldest, asked, pointing to the large hole, "Is this where the campfire is going to be?"

Anderson grinned, "No, mate, this is where the bush telly is going."

All the young boys looked at him and, at the same time but in different volumes, asked him, "What's a bush telly?"

He told them it was the Australian way of saying campfire. He said, "Campfire sounds a little boring, don't you think?" and of course, the kids agreed.

It was now a "bush telly," not a campfire. Riley smiled as he peered over at her. His face was still swollen but seemed much better with the swollen tongue nothing but a memory.

"I thought you said you had never been camping before." Riley recalled their earlier conversation.

"Well, I haven't. But everyone in Australia knows what a bush telly is," he smiled. "I thought I better take some lessons from the experts so I don't get shot in the hindquarters for whining."

Bram glanced over at her and said, "Expert or not, I don't think you have to worry about him whining, he's a natural at this."

"He's agreed to go hunting with us," Landon chimed in.

"You've got a Buckley's chance of that happenin', mate!" Anderson declared. "Now, fishing, I'll do, no worries there."

"'A Buckley's chance?' We're going to need an Aussie dictionary if we're going to be around you for the next six months," Bram chuckled.

"Not a chance," Anderson informed him. "Not a chance!"

"More meat for us then," Landon said.

"Never said I wouldn't eat it, mate. Just not sure I can kill it," Anderson informed them.

"No, worries, mate, gotcha covered!" Bram mimicked Anderson.

Anderson smiled with that and then said, "Right, mates, all done. Just need the wood, and we're ready to go."

All the young boys chimed in, "We'll help find the wood, we're good at that!"

Everyone pitched in to find the wood. Riley went up to retrieve the pile they left up by the kitchen for the campfire. It took about fifteen minutes before the pit was full and they had a large pile on standby. They heard a bell being rung, and they all looked toward the kitchen.

Bram yelled, "Food!" and someone yelled, "Last one, there is poo on a shoe!" and before Riley knew it, all the kids were running back up to the kitchen—even all the big boys.

Landon grabbed Carter and practically threw him on his back, passing everyone along the way. It caused such a frenzy with the other boys trying to beat Landon to the kitchen. Riley and Anderson took their time and walked. Hearing the children's laughter made Riley smile. It was a nice day, and it felt good to be out in it; however, Riley was tired, and she was positive everyone else was too. Riley wasn't sure what time it was, but she figured it had to be close to four or five. She never wore a watch because she always had her cell phone with her. She glanced at Anderson's wrist; he was wearing a watch. She didn't ask him the time, though, because at this point, she felt it was irrelevant. She was hungry and tired and knew she wouldn't be up much longer no matter what time it was. She smiled when she realized that for the next six months, time would have little relevance other than getting up at sunrise, going to bed at sunset, and a lot of work in between.

Anderson saw the smile and commented, "I think this is the first time I've seen you really smile."

Riley's smile grew bigger. "Just a stupid thought about time. Before all this, I was constantly running around with never enough time to do everything. Now it seems I have nothing but time. Owning a watch seems a bit useless now, like a lot of things I was once worried about."

"And what kind of things does Riley Cooper worry about?"

"Me? Well, first and foremost, my kids, and obviously, that hasn't changed. But bills, money, the usual stuff. None of that matters anymore—not time, not any of it. Only the children, of course."

"Just the kids," he said in a low voice. "Yeah, the kids," he repeated.

"I'm sorry, Anderson, I forget you have loved ones back home, and now you're stuck here with us."

"No worries, Riley, no worries. It is what it is. I can't change it and can't worry about it. It's the here and now that I have to work with," he said, more trying to convince himself of that than Riley. "And God has me here for a reason, I'm just not sure what it is yet, ya know?"

Riley understood. "My husband, Jackson, is out there somewhere, along with Bram's mom, Ursula, and his sister, Inge. I feel guilty in a way because I know we're safe. I know I'm right where Jackson wants me to be. But it doesn't make it any easier."

Anderson nodded his head in agreement, "I'm pretty sure my ex wishes I was in hell, not here in the lush mountains, camping out with a bunch of beautiful women."

Riley laughed at that. Anderson liked her smile and her laugh even more. It was good to see her do both. When they arrived at the kitchen, everyone was eating, and Anderson was suddenly hungry. Victoria was waiting for them when they entered the kitchen.

"You two hungry?" she asked

"Starved!" Riley announced.

"Heaps!" Anderson added.

Victoria smiled and handed them each a plate with a sandwich, sliced apples, and some chips—for which they both thanked her. Riley found some water bottles and handed one to Anderson as she followed him out to one of the tables. They found two empty seats next to Becca and Kelly. The women were chatting about Kelly's trip from Florida. At first, it was about the fun things they did, then to the horrors that ensued—which she and her friends had witnessed. Kelly told them about the mob of people out in the streets looting. They had even watched someone get beaten to death. She, Keri, and Tony couldn't get out of there fast enough. But being on the road wasn't much better, and at one point when they had pulled over to get some gas, someone tried to steal their car. It took both Tony and the gas station manager to stop them. Then they ran out of gas in Oklahoma and couldn't find any, so they ended up on foot, walking toward Park City. A truck driver had sympathy for them and gave them a ride to Fort Collins, Colorado, where another truck driver picked them up and then dropped them off close to Park City. From there they had to walk the rest of the way. Kelly wished she had made it sooner so she could have been there with her parents. Riley thought about that and the problems her brother had getting to Park City.

"Kelly, this might not help, but your timing was perfect," Riley told her. "I'm sure your mom and dad were glad you weren't there with them. Your brother too. God may have put those obstacles in your path to slow you down and keep you from making it to your mom and dad's. Carson said your dad told him he was sick and for him not to come into the house just in case it was the virus. Your dad saved your brother's life by telling him that. In turn, Carson saved your life too. I believe God works in weird ways sometimes. Carson said your dad asked you to head to Park City right away, but you didn't, did you?"

"No, I didn't. I was having fun, and I thought my dad was worrying too much. The news made it sound like the CDC had it under control in China. We waited primarily because we were enjoying the beach and the night life, and we weren't going to let a virus in China mess with that. When we finally realized our mistake, we left. Keri asked if we could go to her house to get a few things, which we were about to do, but then things got really crazy. When we finally started to make our way toward Park City, two weeks had gone by. Then it took us another two weeks to make it to Park City," Kelly confessed.

Riley smiled at her and said, "I can only say I think it was God's intervention. For whatever reason, he wanted you here with us."

Kelly was serious now, "I have no idea why. I have nothing to offer you, or anyone, for that matter. I'm not good at anything."

"Well, we're all about to find out what we're all made of. We'll need to be open to what God puts in our path. It's imperative we stay focused on Him and pray for His guidance." Riley paused for a moment and then continued, "My dad quotes the Bible all the time—well, mostly summarizes it—but the one I like the most, the one that gives me a great deal of comfort knowing is, 'Where two or more are gathered in His name, Jesus is right there with them.' He's here with us and is going to use us. How, I don't know. But I can tell you that it won't be easy, whatever it is. Some of the worst of it has already passed us now, with dead or missing family members. And though we might think it can't get any worse, there is a good chance it will. But the blessing is, we have God and each other. I, for one, am glad all of you are here with my family."

"I'm not sure if I should be scared or thankful," Kelly confessed.

"If it gets any worse, I'm glad I'm here with all of you. I don't know what would have happened if you and your family hadn't shown up, Riley. I take it back. I do know what would have happened," Becca said, with chills going down her back.

Anderson interjected, "I have to agree with Becca. I'm grateful to be here with your family too, Riley."

Riley laughed out of embarrassment, "Thank you, but my point is, we were brought together for a reason, and I'm very happy that it's with all of you. We're family now, and that's a good thing."

Carolyn came over to their table with her boys. "Do you mind showing me how the shower works, Riley? I would like to get the day off of me and my boys."

Riley smiled up at Carolyn. "Sure, Becca and Kelly, you might want to come too so I can show all of you how it works."

Becca got up with Riley. "Absolutely, a shower sounds nice. What about you, Anderson? Do you need a lesson?"

"No, I'm good. I helped put them together," he said, smiling at her.

Riley and the other women walked toward the shower with Carolyn's boys. The showers were behind the kitchen but set back in the trees a bit to help protect them from the wind. The frame for the shower was nice and sturdy. It could hold two 5-gallon shower bags at a time easily. Landon and Bram found the pallets that her father said were to be used for the floor of the showers. Riley thought they were an excellent way to keep the feet clean. They put a wooden pallet down inside the showers and two side by side in front of the showers. The pallets in front had a nice non-see-through shower curtain on wire that completely enclosed the front of each shower. It made a nice place to dry off and get changed. They even thought to put a chair inside for putting on shoes. The shower bags, ten of them, were all hanging in the sun on a metal bar just outside the kitchen. Riley showed them the bags and explained that they hung them there because they were solar bags, which helped them to warm up. Riley told them to take two bags for their family, that two would be more than enough for the three of them, then hang them on the hook in the center of the shower tent. The shower water had to be brought up from the lake, and it was their job to refill the bags they used and hang them back up so the sun could warm them. The ladies were okay so far with everything Riley had explained to them. Then she told them the best way to shower was to get the body all wet, then shut the valve off, put on the soap and shampoo, then rinse off. Riley advised them not to use too much shampoo because it would take too much water to rinse it out. And last, Riley told them not to leave any soap or shampoo bottles out there due to the wild animals. They should take them back to the kitchen to store them. That was it. Riley was pleased with the way Landon and the other men had assembled the showers.

"Oh, one last thing, even though the water is in solar bags, the water isn't hot. You'll be lucky to get one that's warm. I'll have them brought in each night, but just be prepared for a chilly shower."

"Uh, okay," was all Carolyn said. She didn't like it but refused to complain. She looked at her boys and said, "Okay, boys, let's see how this works. Matt, would you please go get the bags, and we'll try out this shower. I'll go get everything else. Thanks, Riley."

"Let me know how it goes. I'll get my kids in there next," Becca told Carolyn.

Riley said to Becca, "You can use the other shower. They're unisex. My boys will bathe in the lake most of the summer and only use the showers on rare occasions."

"Rare occasions?" Becca was curious.

"Yes, when I tell them they're stinky," Riley laughed.

Carolyn shivered and turned to her boys, informing them that they wouldn't be doing that. Both boys fussed but then went to get what their mother asked them to.

Riley left them to it and was ready to go lie down. She said her good nights to everyone. She would shower in the morning, knowing the cold water would wake her up and help get her ready for the day ahead.

CHAPTER 4

Riley rose early, before the sun was even up. She and both of her girls slept in the loft, giving her mother and father, as well as Agnes and Norman, the rooms. Each of them had their own cot with a mattress on top. Both of the girls had twin cots and mattresses. Riley was a bit more spoiled and had two twin cots together and a full-size mattress with a foam topper on them. Riley hated sleeping on air mattresses, so she made hers as comfortable as she could.

Riley picked out some clothes for the day, grabbed one of the towels, and headed out the door to the kitchen. Once in the kitchen, she got the fire started in the stove, filled the large kettle with water, and placed it on the stove to heat the water. She grabbed what she needed for the shower and headed out. The shower water was freezing as Riley expected, and as expected, it did its job waking her up. She was showered, dressed, and back in the kitchen in less than ten minutes. She found the coffee, sugar, and a cup; made the coffee; and drank it, standing by the stove where it was warm. When the kitchen door opened, it startled her. It was her mother and father.

"Good morning, baby girl!" Her father was cheerful this morning. "What are you doing up so early?"

"My mind was done with sleep, so I thought it would be a good time to get up, shower, and have a cup of coffee before the masses got up."

"Hope we're not intruding? I just wanted to get breakfast started," her mother said. "Can you give me a hand?"

"Sure. I thought the boys were going hunting this morning? I haven't seen Goliath either." Riley glanced over at her dad for confirmation.

"Yeah, they should have left already. Goliath slept in the tent with the boys and went hunting with them. I'm sure they're gone. Did you check their tent?"

"No, I didn't. It's okay, I just thought Annie was going with them."

"No, Annie is going to set some of the young boys up with bows today—girls too, if they're so inclined—and show them how to shoot them," he told her as he started the fire in the fireplace.

Riley laughed at that. *The girls*, she thought, *would not be inclined*. "That's a great idea. She's definitely the one for that."

* * *

The morning went smoothly. Some of the men took the canoe and went down to the lake to try their hand at fishing. The women were busy doing chores and helping in the kitchen with whatever Victoria asked of them. Annie had Rachel and all the boys with her, teaching them the art of shooting a bow. Sara and the Crawford girls were busy with different things but were enjoying their time together. Everyone seemed to be cheerful this morning as if it was just another day—momentarily forgetting the world, the virus, the unknown whereabouts of loved ones, and even the dead.

Riley was walking over to the cabins when she saw Sara and the Crawford girls coming out of their cabin. She was about to say something to them when a small pickup blasted up their road toward the cabins. It slid in the dirt and came to a stop right in front of Riley. She was waving the dust out of her face when a group of men with guns jumped out of the back end. The men in the cab got out, very pleased with their entrance. Riley and the girls froze for a moment. Then Riley motioned for Sara to take the girls back into the cabin. A man in a black T-shirt yelled at her to "Stop!" Sara didn't listen and went into the cabin, slamming the door behind her.

"Kevin, go get them!" the man ordered. And one of the men took off, running toward the cabin.

"Well, well, what do we have here," the man wasn't asking a question.

Riley figured the man in the black T-shirt was in charge.

"Can I help you?" she said sharply.

"The fat one wants to know if she can help me!" he laughed, as did a few of his men. Then he continued, "Boys, I'm thinking this camp is going to work nicely. It looks like it has everything we need to get us through the winter and then some!"

He walked right up to Riley and put a gun to her forehead. Riley didn't move, even though her body started trembling.

How she did it, she didn't know, but she spoke in a very calm voice, "You don't need to do this. If there's something you need, you only need to ask."

The man laughed and repeated what she said, "If there is something we need, boys, we just need to ask!" Then with the gun, he pushed it harder up against her forehead, leaned his face closer to hers, and said, "This is me asking. We are taking your camp and everything that's in it, you fat pig!" His breath was foul from alcohol and stale cigarettes.

The cabin door flew open with Sara screaming. The man named Kevin had Sara by the hair, dragging her out of the cabin.

"Lookie what I found! I'm gonna have me some good lovin' tonight, Bruce. What do you think? I might even share her with you when I'm done!" He was laughing as he held Sara's hair and whipped her around to show the man standing in front of Riley his catch.

Riley was going crazy with rage now as she watched the man with her daughter. Sara continued to scream. Riley's eyes were seeping tears now, and she could feel the blood in her face, but she didn't move. Both of her hands were in fists, and her mind was racing.

Bruce told the rest of Riley's group, "Stay put, or the pig here gets it in the head."

No one moved. The other men had their guns aimed at no one in particular.

One of the men to Riley's left caught sight of Carolyn, grabbed his crotch, and said, "Well, you're not the only one that's gonna get some tonight, Kevin! And I ain't sharing." His voice was pure evil, and he started walking right for Carolyn, laughing with every step.

Bruce lightened his grip on the gun that he had pointed at Riley while laughing.

Riley, forgetting the position she was in, yelled at Kevin, who was holding her daughter, "You have about two seconds to let her go! She's fifteen, you *idiot*!"

The men roared with laughter, and Kevin said, "Woohoo! I got myself a virgin!"

The laughter continued.

Bruce could barely contain himself and, through his laughter, asked, "*Or what?*"

Riley noticed his grip was still loose on the gun when she recalled something Jackson had shown her and the girls in a self-defense class he gave. She closed her eyes for a split second then opened them; at the same time, her left hand went up for the barrel of the gun, and her right hand opened, hitting his wrist in the opposite direction. The gun was out of his hand and in Riley's within seconds and before Bruce could comprehend what happened. Sheer shock went across his face when it finally registered what she had done, and he lunged at her. The blast hit him with such force he flew backward and landed on the ground dead. The other men were stunned, and before they could come to their senses, Riley had turned the gun onto the man to her right; again the blast knocked the man off his feet. An eerie calm filled Riley. It was a feeling of some kind of euphoria she had never felt before. In a smooth motion, she turned to aim the gun at the man to her left. Before she could shoot, an arrow plowed into the man that had been walking toward Carolyn hitting him square in the chest. Then there was a loud *boom*. All the screaming and laughing stopped. Everything went very still. Riley looked around in a daze, her eyes red and wet; the color in her face had gone pale. Her breathing was mysteriously smooth and slow, but her body didn't move. She heard someone call her name. It was a familiar voice talking to her…asking her for something. She looked around and saw Anderson standing there, reaching for the gun. She let it go without any resistance. Her father was standing over Kevin, who no longer had Sara. The *boom* was a warning shot from Ken's shotgun. Kevin got the message and let go of Sara. He was now begging for mercy from Ken, who had the shotgun aimed at his chest. Riley took a deep breath and let it out slow. Another man somewhere was saying how sorry he was, that this wasn't his idea, that he had a wife and kids. Riley could sense everyone staring at her. Carolyn was on the ground, cradling her nine-year-old Mark, and both were crying. Becca was standing next to her niece. The Crawford girls ran to be with their mother. All the men that were at the lake were now there focused on Riley. She put her hand up to her forehead, where the gun had once been.

The fog began to clear, and the world around her came back into focus. She turned to the man crying and pleading for his life even though there was no one threatening him.

"You have a wife…kids…and you came here to do this to us! To our children? What's the matter with you?"

"I'm sorry…I didn't…didn't want to do it…but Nate there said you had…had tons of supplies and…well…we needed them," he choked through his tears.

Riley glared at the man on the ground holding his wrist. She had shot him in the hand, which knocked the gun out of his grip and put him on the ground. He went down in excruciating pain. She recognized him. He was the man they met stranded on the side of the road and had given him some gas. She moved closer to him.

"This is all your fault. This is all on you, do you understand?"

He didn't speak, only moaned in pain. The other two men were brought over and were made to sit in the dirt with the others. Riley looked back to the other man and asked his name.

"I'm Lyle. I told these guys not to do this, to just ask you for help, but they wouldn't listen. There's no talking to Bruce. He's a hothead and drinks too much."

"He was," Riley corrected him.

Lyle glanced over at the lifeless body. "Was," he mumbled.

Riley turned and told Norman, "Take this gentleman over to the Chef Wagon and see if my mom and Agnes can patch him up please."

Norman was apprehensive at first but then did as Riley asked.

She turned back to the man with a bullet hole in his hand, then back to Lyle, "What did you say his name was?"

Lyle looked at the man and answered, "Nate."

"Okay, Nate, this man is going to help you up," she explained.

She saw Mr. Miller standing close by, and she asked very politely, "Mr. Miller, would you mind getting some cable ties and tie these men up please?"

Mr. Miller didn't say a word, just walked to the Chef Wagon to get what he needed.

Riley saw Annie, still holding her bow, looking at the man with the arrow in his chest. Riley walked over to her and pulled her into her arms, giving her a big hug.

Annie started to cry, "Mom, he was going to shoot you. I didn't want to lose you. I just let the arrow go. Mom, I'm so sorry!"

"It's okay, baby, it's okay. It's not your fault. None of this is anyone's fault except theirs," Riley consoled her.

Sara then ran over to both of them and was pulled into the hug too. Anderson took over and asked Carson and Tony to give him a hand to put the two bodies in the back of the truck that had invaded their camp. Both of them were leery at first but did as they were asked. Mr. Miller had the other three men tied up and left them in the dirt. Ken made his way over to his girls and with his long arms embraced all three. After a moment, Riley pulled away, her mind much clearer. She was moving on to her next move. Riley moved away from her girls and her father as she asked if Bram and Landon had returned. Her father replied no. Riley was mindful of the members of her camp and shared with them what she intended to do.

"I'm going to take these men back to their camp."

"I'm going with you, Riley," her father said.

"I'll go too," Tony offered.

Riley gave that some consideration then said, "Thanks, but Landon and Bram will come with me, neither of you need to go."

"I wasn't asking for your permission, Riley!" her father said sharply.

"Dad, nothing's going to happen, and I actually need you to do something else for me."

"What's that, Riley?" His voice was still sharp.

"You said there was a smaller camp not far from here. I asked you where that road led to, remember? You said that was where the other camp was. Not as nice, but it has four cabins and is close to the lake."

"Yes, why? What are you thinking?" This time, he spoke in a calm voice but was a bit puzzled.

Riley walked back over to Lyle. "How many children are in your camp?"

"We have six small kids, eleven and under. Then there are Allen's two teenage girls," he answered.

"How many women in your group?"

"Five," he answered again.

"How many men in your group including these?" Riley continued quizzing him.

"Two other men. My dad and an older man, a friend of my dad's."

"So, Pop, do you think the camp will hold nineteen people?"

"Yeah, sure," he answered. "You planning to move them in over there?"

"If it was just these men, I would let them all rot! But because of the children, I can't do that. If they need better shelter and provisions, we need them close so we can help them."

Lyle was totally surprised and was quick to inform her, "We're living in tents. I mean, we just left in a hurry. Everyone around us was dying, and we just grabbed what we could and left. We didn't know the area here and only found a small campground for tents, no cabins. I'm sorry for all this. We don't deserve this, I know, but I would be forever in your debt for any help you can give us." Lyle paused for a moment then continued, "I'll make sure these guys behave, you'll have no more trouble from us, I promise."

"We are about to give you sanctuary, so there had better be no more problems!" Riley snapped. Turning to Tony and in a more relaxed tone, she asked, "Tony, will you help the man up and cut his ties, please. Only his, though."

Lyle was relieved when Tony helped him up. "Thank you. What do you want me to do?"

"I want you to go with me back to your camp. But first we need to know everything. How many cars you have, supplies, gas, and what your people can do, etc. Give that info to my dad. That will give him some idea of what he needs to take with him to the other camp," Riley explained.

Just then they heard the Polaris coming in with Landon and Bram excited about their kill. Goliath was bounding down behind them. There was a large buck on the back of it. They pulled up to the kitchen and got out.

"Hey, Mom, look what Bram shot!" Landon was ecstatic.

Everyone looked, but there were no "Atta boys," and both Landon's and Bram's excitement was deflated. Sara ran up to him and gave him a big hug. Landon was surprised and pulled Sara back.

"What's going on?"

Sara glanced up at him, her crystal blue eyes red and filled with tears. "Mom and Annie killed two men!"

Landon was shocked, "*What?*"

"It was the man you gave gas to. He came with some other men, and one had a gun to Mom's head, and another one was going to rape me!" Sara started to cry again, and this time Landon held her tight.

Bram couldn't believe what he was hearing. Landon pulled Sara away from him, telling her in a loving voice that she was okay now, and he needed to go to Mom. She let go of Landon, allowing him to walk over to his mother with Bram following.

"Mom?" he approached her with caution.

When she turned to look at him, he slowed his approach. Her eyes were blazing with a fury that he had never seen, and yet she was speaking in a calm voice. She was very focused, very much in charge, and no one there was challenging her.

"Mom?" he said again. She was looking at Landon, but he didn't think she was seeing him. "Mom, are you okay?" He knew that was a dumb thing to ask, but he was lost as to what to do. "Mom, are you okay? Is there something I can do to help?"

At that, she blinked and then told him as if it were just any other day, "I need you and Bram to come with me to take these men back to their camp. Put the rifles up, and bring your holster with a sidearm. I don't think anything is going to happen, but just in case."

"What about the elk? The hide needs to be taken off, and it needs to be butchered," Bram informed Riley.

Norman spoke up, "I can do it, don't worry about that."

Riley thanked him. The boys ran to put their rifles away as fast as they could. Riley noticed her shirt was covered in blood. She stood, looking at it for a moment, then realized it needed to be changed. She spun around to head for her cabin when she found Marcus standing behind her. His eyes went wide. He tried to say something but couldn't speak the words that he knew he needed to say. Riley saw the fear but didn't care and kept walking. Once inside her cabin, she leaned against the door for a moment to catch her breath. If she stopped, she knew she would crumble. She took another deep breath.

"Not now," she told herself.

She climbed the ladder, found the shirt she wanted, and put it on. Then leaving the cabin, she headed for the kitchen. Once inside, she went over to the fireplace, threw the bloodstained shirt into the fire, and walked out. She washed her face and hands over at the small water jug they had sitting outside that was to be used especially for that purpose. When she was done, she headed over to her father. Her father and Lyle were standing in front of the pickup, waiting for her. They had loaded all the men in the bed of the truck. Bram and Landon came up behind her, ready to go.

"Dad, did you get everything you needed from Lyle?" Riley inquired.

Watching Riley, Ken saw what Landon had seen. Because of his concern for her, he spoke to her in a very calm voice, "Yes, baby girl,

I did. I'll go to the other camp to open it up for them." Ken looked over to Bram, "Would you go get the Jeep, put some gas containers in it, five should do. They won't have enough gas to get them to the camp. Fill the Jeep up along with this truck before you go too."

"Hey, Bram, toss in a couple of shovels too, please," Riley added.

Bram did as they asked him. Riley ordered Lyle to drive their truck back to his camp with Landon. She would ride with Bram in the Jeep because she didn't want Landon asking her a million questions that she wasn't ready to answer. He could ask Lyle everything if he wanted; she didn't care. With her mind racing, she hoped the long drive ahead of them would give her time to think.

* * *

When everything was ready, they set out for Lyle's campsite. Instead of going back the way they had originally come into camp, they went the other direction. Lyle said it would cut their trip in half. It was a pretty drive, and any other day, Riley would have enjoyed it, but the day had gone dark for her. The replay of the day was plaguing her mind, and she couldn't shake it. She needed to be doing something, but there was nothing to do but sit. Bram didn't even look at her; he kept his eyes straight ahead. She leaned her head back, closed her eyes, and in no way did she attempt to control the flow of her mind. She knew it would go wherever it wanted anyway. Instant replay for an hour or more, she thought. *Yay for me.*

When they drove into Lyle's camp, people moved out in the open to watch the vehicles pull in. Lyle pulled the truck in first, swinging it around so the back end could be seen by everyone standing in the clearing of the small camp. They were confused when they saw that the men's hands were tied. Lyle and Landon got out, moved to the back of the truck, and then opened the tailgate to reveal all. One of the women cried out at the sight of the two dead men. Lyle waved everyone back as they tried to come closer to the truck. Riley was out of the Jeep and standing in front of the group. No one said a word. All eyes were locked onto the woman standing before them.

"I'm Riley Cooper, and these are my boys." She paused for a moment to gather her thoughts. "These men came into our camp, put a gun to my head, and threatened to rape my daughter and another woman in our group. I killed Bruce. I shot Nate in the hand, and the other man, AJ, my daughter killed." Riley let all that sink in as she continuously surveyed the group.

A woman amongst the group of people gasped but put her hand over her mouth to stay silent.

Riley continued, "All any of you had to do was ask, and we would have been happy to help you. As it is, you have two dead and one injured. Now, if any of you have a problem with this, your problem lies with me. Despite what these men did, we are going to help you. All of you need to gather up all your belongings. There is a camp with four cabins next to a lake where you will have shelter and plenty of fresh water. Our camp is a short distance from there, and we'll make sure you survive the winter. We leave in an hour or less, so I suggest you get moving."

Everyone in the group looked to Lyle, and he repeated what Riley had said, "Get moving, people, we have a lot of work to do, not only here but at the cabins."

Riley turned her attention to the men in the truck, "Get down. Lyle, cut their restraints please."

He did as he was asked.

Riley told them in a very clear but stern voice, "All of you will dig the hole to bury these men. Dig it deep. And understand me when I tell you, the things that happened today are your fault. The kindness that you are being shown today, none of you deserve. This is a second chance, and I hope you will take advantage of it by putting it to good use." Then, as if it was a last thought, she told them, "None of you men will ever set foot in our camp again, however, the others in your group are welcome. A second chance is just that, there will not be a third."

Allen and Kevin agreed. Nate was still in too much pain but managed to nod his head in agreement while standing there, holding his arm.

Due to the ground being hard, digging the hole was tedious work for the men, but the hole was dug; and once the bodies were dumped in, they were quickly covered up with dirt. The men flipped a picnic table over the top of the grave in the hopes that no wild animal would find them. Riley thought again, *Too much kindness shown to these men even in death.* When they were done, they helped to load the last of their belongings into the vehicles for the new camp. Bram suggested to Lyle that they should take the other picnic table as there might not be one at the cabins. Taking the table meant they would have to off-load everything in the truck then reload it once the table was in, which they did. Riley looked around to see if anything of use was left, and once she was satisfied, she told everyone it was time to go. The two teenagers, both girls, rode with Riley, Landon, and Bram in the Jeep. Their father, Allen, was ashamed of what he had done. He had told his girls as much. Allen explained to Riley that he felt overpowered by Bruce and AJ, but that was no excuse and that he was shocked when Kevin grabbed her daughter. He knew his words were weak, but they needed to be said. Riley said nothing to him. She simply walked away.

* * *

Riley's father was waiting at the turnoff that led to the other camp. He showed them the way, which took them about ten minutes. When they drove up, Carson and Tony were nailing some boards together to make a small outhouse for them. It was almost done. One of the commodes they had brought from Utah Outdoors was just outside the house along with a large bag of toilet paper. Next to it was another structure that had been there for a while, which Riley thought had to be the shower. The pallets were set in front along with the tarp to give privacy. This was something they were going to have to make at their camp for the winter months; the shower tents wouldn't do. Just outside the shower were some shower bags warming in the sun. Riley liked what she saw. The shower and outhouse were much better than at their camp. They were much more durable, she thought. She turned to the group; all of whom, she noticed, were waiting on her.

Riley thought these cabins were in good shape, just not as big as the ones they were staying in. Even though there wasn't a separate kitchen, she felt they could turn one of the cabins into one. That might make it tight for the sleeping arrangements, but it should work. The cabins had two rooms like theirs but with smaller lofts. They did have some old wooden furniture in each. Lyle's group had some chairs, tables, and plenty of air mattresses. Riley's camp had a few spare cots that Ken brought over for them to use as they didn't have any. Riley also noticed they had quite a lot in the way of cooking utensils, pots, pans, and so forth. There was a large outside grill made of brick for cooking. Considering what they had before, Riley was confident this was going to work.

Riley shared her thoughts with Lyle, "Personally, I would make one of these cabins your kitchen and use the other cabins for sleeping quarters. It has two rooms, one to store things in and the other room, someone can sleep in. It looks like you have a working toilet and shower, thanks to Carson and Tony. These two gentlemen will teach you everything you need to know on how to care for them." She looked at Carson, and he smiled in agreement. "My boys came home today with an elk. You can send someone over to our camp to pick some of it up for your group. Whatever we prepare for our people, we'll prepare for yours. We have a root cellar to keep the food fresh, and I promise you won't go without. Dad, did we have any spare poles for fishing?"

"Only two, and they're here with the other items we brought with us." He looked to Lyle and said, "I hope someone here can fish?"

Lyle's father stepped forward, "I can. Thank you."

Looking in the man's direction, Ken said, "You're welcome. If any of you have any problems, feel free to come by our camp, and we'll see if we can help you out. Between the two camps, we should have enough to get us through for a few more months. Carson and Tony will stay here to help you get the camp in good running order."

Riley studied the group before she made one final announcement, "I'm leaving Lyle in charge of this camp. There's no vote." Then directing her attention to Kevin, she said with clarity, "If I ever find you anywhere near my daughter," she paused for a second then said, "for that matter, around any of these young girls, you will wish you had never met me. Do I make myself clear?"

Be it the anger in her voice or the fury still raging in her eyes, he cleared his throat and said, "Yes, ma'am." There was no doubt in Riley's mind that he meant it.

Riley turned her attention to the rest of the group, "We may be two camps, but we are one. If we survive this virus and the rest of the world is dead, it will be left up to us to give our children a fighting chance, to not only survive, but to find a way to live again. They won't have a chance if we don't work together. My family and I are all Christians, and now that you are a part of our group, even if you are not people of faith, you will be treated with respect by us as equal partners. This is your camp, make it your home. We are planning to stay at least six months, then we'll see what the world is like. I would ask that no one leave the camp to go into any towns. If there is a need for that, we'll arrange it, allowing people from both groups to go. But I hope that isn't for quite some time."

Ken stepped in, "Speaking of faith, I will be doing a Wednesday-night Bible study and a Sunday-morning service if any of you care to join us. We need healing after today, and it will be a good time for that, plus it will allow us to get to know one another."

Lyle watched the others in his group for a moment. They all stood in silence. He took the lead, telling Ken and Riley, "Thank you both. I know my family will be there. And, Riley, we won't make a move without letting you know first."

Riley had said all she needed to say then asked her father if he was ready to go. He nodded yes, and as they were making their way to the Jeep, one of the women in the group walked up to Riley. Riley could tell she was nervous, and she felt bad that she made her feel that way.

"Hello, I'm Lisa, I just wanted to say thank you. I know it doesn't mean much, but I am sorry for what happened today. Bruce and AJ were evil in every aspect of the word. We didn't invite them into our lives, they just pushed their way in. My husband, Allen, asked them to leave and got beat up for his efforts." She turned around to look at her two girls and then back to Riley, "Thank you for them too. I think you of all people understand what I mean by that."

Riley glanced over at the girls then back to Lisa. She did understand.

"Kevin is the man that went after my daughter. If you ever feel your girls aren't safe, please feel free to tell me." Both women looked over at Kevin. "And feel free to come to our camp anytime for a visit."

With that, Riley continued to the Jeep. Bram, Landon, and her father were waiting for her.

* * *

Once back at their camp, life had gone back to some normality. The bloodstains where the two men died were gone. Sara was in the kitchen, trying to bake some brownies with her grandmother by her side. Agnes, Keri, Kelly, and Norman had part of the kitchen turned into a butcher shop. The elk was being made into ground meat, steaks, sausage, stew meat, and whatever else they could think of. Anderson was building a smokehouse for the meat with the help of Carolyn and Becca. The kids were playing board games at the tables. Annie was working on a bow with Goliath at her feet. Riley couldn't believe what she was seeing. An uncontrollable desire swept over her. She needed to be anyplace other than where she was at this very moment. She quickly made her escape to the lake.

She started off walking then broke into a run. She ran to the water's edge and collapsed with her knees hitting the water. Her face was in her hands when she began to cry uncontrollably. She and Annie both had killed someone today.

Thou shalt not kill, she repeated over and over in her head. *Thou shalt not kill*. Well, she *had* done that! She wondered how many other commandments she had broken. That one was horrible enough, and now she didn't know what to do. She loved Jesus; she believed in Him. How could she break all His teaching in one fit of anger? And she had been angry—anger mixed with a strange euphoria that she had never felt before. *Be slow to anger*; she had not been slow to anger. *Love thy enemy*; she did not love them. *Thou shalt not kill*, and she did! She couldn't slow her thought process down. She had killed a man, and there was no way she could forgive herself, let alone think God could. Poor Annie, that shouldn't have been her burden to bear. Riley was keenly aware that when she saw the man with an arrow in his chest, she didn't care that he was dead by the hand of her daughter. What kind of mother was she that she didn't care that her daughter had killed someone! She put her hands in the water and splashed her face with it. The water was so cold, but it felt good. She was still sobbing and wasn't sure if she would ever stop.

"Are you done with your pity party?" a voice from behind her said.

Riley spun around, landing her bottom in the water. "Geez, you scared the bajeebees out of me, Mr. Miller!"

"Well, here I was minding my own business when you planted your butt in the middle of it!"

"I'm sorry, I didn't know you were there," she spoke quickly, defending herself to him. She was still crying.

"Well, how would you, with all your wailing. You're acting like you killed someone. Oh, wait, you did!" he said with a devilish grin and without a care for her feelings.

"Mr. Mill—" Riley tried to speak, but he cut her off.

"Excuse me, but I think you've mistaken me for someone who gives a flip! There's not many people I like in this world, and not many people like me back. Mainly because I speak my mind to let them know what dopes they are. Those idiots today deserved what they got! By the way, that was a beautiful move. Did Jackson teach you that? Well, never mind, I was impressed," he spoke without stopping, as if trying to keep her from answering him.

It worked. Riley sat there without uttering a word.

"And as far as all those people at our camp are concerned, they are safer because of you. They know you're a leader that will protect them. They won't be following you because you killed a moron today, they'll follow you because you didn't hesitate. Could they have done it? Maybe, maybe not. But what will keep them loyal to you isn't that you didn't hesitate to kill a man. It will be what you did afterward. And that's what separates you from them."

Riley wasn't following him at all. Miller knew it and continued, "If you would quit using your butt as earmuffs, Riley!"

Now she had a baffled expression on her face.

"Get your head out of your butt! I would have shot all of them and been done with it, but not you! You and your lamebrain ideas, bringing them all over to the camp right next door to us. Why would you do something so *stupid*!" He paused for a moment, and his voice became calmer, "Because you are a good leader, that's why!"

Leader? What was he saying? *Leader?* She knew she was bossy, but a leader, she was not. Leave it to Miller to make my life more confusing and stressful, she thought. She was starting to get cold.

"Well, how long are you going sit there, cooling off that tail end of yours?"

Riley glanced down and noticed she was now sitting in the lake water, which was making her cold. She pulled herself up out of the water and was drenched from the waist down. Ugh. Her life was not her own—even out here in the wilderness where she should be free to cry, scream, or fart without someone telling her otherwise. She got up and found a place in the dirt in front of Miller. He had more to say, and he wouldn't let her go until he was done. So wet, cold, and with puffy eyes, she sat before him in silence.

"Good, I have your attention now. Now tell me, isn't one of the things this God of yours likes to do is 'forgive'? Don't answer, I know it is, your father won't shut up about it. I don't know if He wanted you to kill that guy, but I'm sure He didn't want him to kill you. Otherwise, it would have been your face planted in the dirt! So don't go do something stupid and act like God isn't going to forgive you. Apparently, that's all He does all day long! Boring, if you ask me. I've had to listen to you and your father talk about your God's blessings and grace all day long. So you killed an idiot that was evil, and all of a sudden, God's blessings and grace are gone? If that's the case, I want nothing to do with Him. If I wanted to hang out with someone uncaring and unforgiving, I would plant my butt in front of a mirror all day long! I don't know, but when Jesus was hanging on the cross, He wasn't hurling vile words out at anyone or cussing at His Father, was He? Not if your father is telling Jesus's story correctly. Personally, I would have condemned them all to hell and been done with it. If your God doesn't forgive you, then I don't want to hear you mention

His name ever again to me, not *ever*!" He paused for a moment, waiting for Riley to speak. "Well?"

She couldn't believe her ears—Miller giving her a pep talk on God and His forgiveness!

"I'm…I'm speechless."

"Seriously, this is all I had to do to get you to shut up?"

"Okay, so what, I get to kill a man and then be forgiven? I'm sure it doesn't work that way."

"Did you fall in stupid juice this morning or something? No, dipstick, it doesn't! Did you wake up today saying, 'I'm gonna kill me some moron today! I'll even let that moron stick a gun to my head before I do it!' Didn't think so. God placed that man in front of you today for whatever reason. He's dead, and you're not. Even your daughter had to plug one of them."

"Mr. Miller that's…"

He didn't let her finish. "Why did God place her there? She and the boys were well into the woods, practicing with the bows, yet she was there to ward off the attack that was being aimed at you. I'm not saying that this is the way God wanted this to happen. But this non-believer is looking at it this way, your God might have allowed this to happen, and I don't think He has to ask your pea-brain permission when He does so!"

Miller was finished. He got up and headed for the camp.

Riley just sat there completely dumbfounded. Where did all this come from? And who stole the other Miller? She looked around.

Well, they can keep him, she thought. Her crying had finally stopped. Riley couldn't believe she thought this, but she was glad Mr. Miller was there. However, she would never confess that to anyone. He would be a thorn forever in her side, but she could handle it. She got up and waddled back up to camp in her very wet jeans.

As she walked through camp, she was met with looks of curiosity. With Mr. Miller making it to camp first and her coming in behind him, wet, she could only imagine what they were thinking. She walked past everyone without a word and went straight into her cabin to change. When she came out, Landon was waiting for her. She sighed and went over to him. He pulled her in to him, giving her a long, tight hug. She let him, and it felt good to have his strong arms around her. More importantly, she needed it. Tears began to swell up in her eyes again, but she fought to keep them at bay. She pulled back and wiped her eyes on his shirt. He didn't care. He loved his mom, and although he wasn't his dad, he was the next best thing.

"I'm sorry, Landon, I know we need to talk, but can we do it later? I need to talk to everyone right now," she said as she glanced up at him.

"Sure, Mom, we'll go for a walk later tonight." Landon smiled down at her. "Mom, I love you."

She gave him another quick squeeze and said, "I love you too."

They both walked toward the rest of the group. Everyone stopped what they were doing as they approached the tables. Someone ran into the kitchen to get those that were inside. Riley took a moment to consider those around her. Mr. Miller found a seat at the table with Annie. They in turn were watching her, waiting for her to say something. What would she say? What profound words could she use to tell them how sorry she was for today. She just went for it and said what was on her mind.

"I'm sorry that this happened today…"

"Riley, it wasn't your fault…"

She heard her father start to say but put her hand up for him to stop.

"I know I didn't ask for this to happen. I don't even know if it could have been handled differently. And at this point, it doesn't matter because it happened the way it did. There is no changing that." She looked at Annie now. "I'm sorry you had to take a life today. I can only hope and pray you will never have to do it again."

Annie looked like she was about to cry, but Landon was standing next to her, and he put his arm tightly around her. She fell into his embrace, wrapping both her arms around him while fighting back the tears.

"I love you," she mouthed to her mother.

Riley smiled at her.

"This world of ours isn't ever going to be the same, and at some point, we are going to have to go back into it. I want us all to be prepared, even the children. As I mentioned before we left Park City, the kids are going to need to know how to fish, hunt, and clean their food, how to start a fire, make drinkable water, smoke and cook meat, and anything else they'll need to survive. It needs to come as natural to them as breathing." She paused a moment, then she continued. "Our new neighbors have children that need to be included in this education. For that matter, everyone in that camp needs to be trained." Riley's thoughts strayed to the conversation she had with Mr. Miller. "I didn't wake up this morning with murder on my mind, as someone was kind enough to remind me. I have my own demons now to deal with. Even though God is merciful and forgiving, I am not. And this is the hard part. I need you all to find forgiveness in your hearts for the men that came here today, just as I have to. This is as hard for me to do as it is for you. The anger is still fresh in me, and I hate them as much as myself for what happened today. But in order for this to work, we have to forgive them."

There was grumbling coming from the group.

Anderson spoke up, "The Sheila's right as rain. I like the numbers with them more than without them. Apparently, the two instigators are dead, and there's nothing more that can be done about it. As for forgiving you, Riley, there's nothing to forgive. However, those men over there need it from us so we can move on."

Marcus stood up and looked around at everyone. "If anything, Riley, I owe you an apology. I was the one who told them where to find us. I'm to blame."

"No one is to blame but the men that came in here today. Riley's correct, though, we need to forgive them, all of them." Ken turned to look at his granddaughter Sara, "Honey, I know it's going to be hard for you, but you need to find a way to forgive and forget. There is no one here that thinks what Kevin did to you was right. We most definitely will keep an eye on him. Sara, you don't have to be around any of them when they are here. But with that said, they have children that can learn from us, and keeping him away when everyone is here might cause us more problems than we know."

Sara glanced over at her sister for a moment before she spoke, "If Annie can do it, I can too."

Her heart ached for her sister. She was scared when the man grabbed her, but nothing happened other than her getting her hair pulled. Annie, however, would have a harder time as she lost more than a few strands of hair this morning. She would help her sister as much as she could.

"I'm not afraid of Kevin. Not now." She meant it too.

Annie gave Sara a weak smile but a smile nonetheless.

"Anderson, would you mind going over to the other camp with me to invite them all to dinner?" Riley asked.

"No worries, Riley, I'm there with you."

"Dad, how long do you think it will take to walk over there?"

Ken thought for a moment. "Well, it should only take you about fifteen to twenty minutes. There's a trail along the lake that will take you right to them. It's actually shorter on foot than by car. It will be a good time to show them how to get here. Do you mind if I join the two of you?"

"Absolutely. So is everyone in agreement then?" Riley asked the group. Everyone nodded their heads yes. "Okay then, off we go to our new neighbors."

Riley, Anderson, and Ken set off on foot to the new camp. Riley actually began to enjoy the walk. It was a beautiful day, cool and crisp, with the birds singing and other animals scurrying about without a worry. This is what she loved about camping, the serenity of it all. The walk, along with the conversation that Ken and Anderson were having with their deep voices, put her at ease. This kind of day should not have been interrupted with the nightmare of a scene like the one that took place this morning. Riley said a silent prayer that God would, indeed, forgive her and her daughter, especially Annie. She had lost a great deal today that she would never get back. Part of her innocence was stripped away from her; Riley could see it in her eyes. If Jackson was here, he would know the right words to say to Annie. For that matter, he would know what to say to her. Instead, she got preached to by none other than Mr. Miller. She replayed what he said to her over in her mind, and he was—she hated to admit it—right. She told Kelly that her not making it home in time to be with her parents before they died could very well have been divine intervention. Today's events could have been too. There is always a bigger picture that she was not privy to. That was always the hard part of Christianity, following God and not always knowing where He was leading you. That's faith for you, trusting God in all things, even in dark days like today.

She realized that she hadn't said a word the whole way over to the camp. The laughter of the children invaded her thoughts and brought her back to reality. The cabins were right in front of her when she finally looked up. One of the younger kids ran to tell his parents they were coming. The place looked more habitable than it did a few hours ago. Lyle was the first to greet them.

"Hi. I didn't think we would see any of you today. I was about to find my way over to you," Lyle said as he reached out to shake hands with Anderson.

Anderson hesitated but then reached for his hand. Ken accepted it without hesitation. Lyle looked at Riley and wasn't sure what he should do, so he just waved. Riley smiled at him, which made him feel more at ease.

"Come on in. Carson and Tony really got us and this place organized. We're really happy to have the extra picnic table too. We took your advice and made this cabin our kitchen." Lyle was pointing to the cabin that was closest to them.

Riley finally spoke, "I'm glad you're all moved in. Listen, do you mind if I speak to everyone again?"

"No, sure, I'll get everyone together for you."

Lyle called everyone around.

Riley regarded those standing in front of her, as she was about to say something, but then stopped before she did. Once she was clear on what to say, she spoke with lucidity, "I owe all of you an apology, especially you men." The men seemed confused. "I told you I'm a Christian. However, I let my anger get in the way of the most important part of my faith, and that's forgiveness. I need forgiveness from God, and I don't know how I can seek that from Him when I can't forgive you."

Nate's facial expression was that of pure shock and disbelief. Lyle and Allen both looked at each other; then they all directed their eyes at Kevin.

Nate, who hadn't said anything to anyone since the nightmare he caused, spoke up, "Riley, thanks, but you don't owe anyone an apology. Not now, not ever. I'm so sorry for everything. When Bruce and AJ were here, they brought out the worst in all of us." He looked around and corrected himself, "They brought the worst out in me.

If my hand is the worst of my punishment for what I did, then I got off easy."

"I know you said to stay away from your daughter," Kevin piped in, "but I would like to someday apologize to her. I know this will be hard to believe, but I've never acted that way in my life, not ever."

"Well, that's why we're here. We would like everyone to follow us over to our camp to have dinner with us tonight. We have lots of games for all ages, even some for the adults. It would be a good time to get to know one another. The invitation is for all of you, the men too."

The men glanced at one another; however, it was Kevin that asked the question that was on everyone's mind, "Are you sure? What about your girls?"

"We had a meeting, and everyone agreed," she glared at Anderson, who was staring at Kevin, "everyone is to come!"

Anderson spoke for the first time, "I'm not saying it's going to be an easy first sit-down, mate. But we're willing to give it a burl despite the runnin's of this mornin'. What'd ya say?"

Lyle said with a laugh, "I'm not sure what he said, but we'll come."

Riley grabbed Anderson's arm and laughed. The rest began to laugh too.

Anderson smiled and said, "What, you Yanks don't understand English?"

"I think it's the Aussie part of your English that gets lost in translation," Riley said with a smile.

There it was, Riley's smile. Anderson thought it was a beautiful smile. He was glad it was back. Anderson knew Riley would be fine. It would take some time for all of them to heal, but Riley would grow from this. He wondered if Riley even understood the ramifications that what happened today put her in charge. He knew from the moment he met her that he liked her. And after today, he would follow her lead wherever that lead would take him. He missed his family and his home, but he was here. He would make every effort to make the best of it with this group of people. If at the end of six months, they found the world whole and Australia's borders were open, he would go back home. But if the world was indeed dead, he would never look back. He would do whatever he could do to help Riley and her family.

They gave everyone the time they needed to get ready. The little girls had to brush their hair, and the boys put on clean shirts. While they were getting ready, Riley took the time to walk around the camp. She liked what she saw. The last place these people were living wasn't kept up very well, but she knew how hard it was to live out of tents. It looked like they would keep this place up with Lyle in charge. Of course, the two people that made life harder for them were gone now. Riley tried not to think of it, but she couldn't help it. This is a fresh start for everyone. The other place was temporary; this was home now, and they would make it so. Riley felt good about her decision to bring them here.

She glanced up and saw Lyle and a woman coming toward her. She smiled, "Hi, is everyone ready to go?"

"Almost, a few are still working on getting ready," Lyle said. "Riley, I would like you to meet my wife, Dina."

"Hi. I wish we could have met under difference circumstances." Dina was quite embarrassed. "But I'm glad we met you, and thank you for this. All of this. I feel like we have a real chance now. Thank you."

Riley's smile brought comfort to both of them, "You're welcome. To be honest, we're glad to have you here too. There is safety and comfort in numbers. It's a shame your friends Bruce and AJ couldn't see it that way."

"Believe me, they weren't our friends. We offered them a place to stay, but had we known what kind of men they were, we wouldn't have offered them a thing. Allen tried to get them to leave and had the ever-living tar beaten out of him. We thought they had killed him. That was almost a month ago." Dina looked to her husband, and he in turn put his head down. "The last few weeks were the worst weeks ever for us. We thought, if only one of us could've just gone in at night when they were drunk and killed them both, but none of us had the courage."

Riley understood and felt sorry for them. Killing someone brought no joy—that was for certain, no matter how vile they were.

"I'm sorry, I know that couldn't have been easy, but that's all in the past. You needn't worry about them ever again. However, I hope we can all find a way to be friends."

Some children came running up and fell into Dina's arm. "These are our two little monsters, Steve who's seven and Kayla's nine."

They both looked at Riley and said hi at the same time. They were cute kids. Both were missing a few teeth, which was normal for their age, Riley thought. They were too young to have to be going through this but she thought perhaps because of their young age, they might do better than the adults. Ken came up to Riley and said everyone was ready. Riley saw the rest of the group coming their way. Anderson and Kevin were having a deep conversation as they walked, which concerned Riley, but it seemed civil. She stayed with her father, Lyle, Dina, and their two young ones but, again, only listened to them without interjecting anything into the conversation. There was a sense of peace in walking and listening to those around her. Taking in the sights once again brought a sense of tranquility. Everything in the world at this very moment is the way it should be. It felt normal. It was as if this morning had never happened, but Riley reminded herself it, indeed, had.

Meeting the men again, even under a more civilized manner, was still a little strained. Sara was standoffish, as was Annie. Landon and Bram stayed close to the girls in the hope of making them feel safe. It wasn't until after dinner that Kevin approached Sara to make his apologies. Landon never left her side, and Kevin understood.

When he was done and was about to turn to walk away, Sara told him, "I forgive you."

Those three simple words stopped him dead in his tracks as well as Riley. She had heard Sara say she was sorry for things she had done but never heard her actually forgive someone. It was, "Yeah, whatever," or "Sure, you are," and a few times, she even slammed her bedroom door in their face. But today was a monumental "I forgive you." Annie and Landon were both surprised by it too. Riley was so proud of her daughter for uttering those words. She was conscious of the fact that everyone, from both camps, was watching. Sara felt slightly embarrassed once she realized it too.

Miller couldn't stand it. "Well, that's sweet. Now, everyone feeling better? I know I will after I puke!" He got up and walked off.

Riley just sighed, shaking her head. No one from the other camp had met Miller, and this was their introduction to him. Let them find out now. There was no defending him. He was too old and set in his ways. Nonetheless, Riley went over to Sara, gave her a hug, and told Kevin thank you. There would be peace between the two camps, and trust would come. Now they just needed to get through the next six months.

CHAPTER 5

During the eight weeks that followed, the two camps were busy getting the hothouse up and the plants that her mother brought from Park City in it. It wasn't as big as the one she left behind, but it was temporary and would do for now. They used a heavy-duty clear plastic as a roof. No one was sure how well it would work, but they needed to try. They now had more of an outhouse for the toilets that Anderson called the Dunny, which all the kids loved. Showers were also built that would withstand the weather, which brought a great deal of joy to all the women. They moved the gas trailer and containers away from the cabins in a clearing. The brush was cleared out away from them just in case they went up in flames.

The kids loved learning about camp life, seeing the wild animals, fishing, hiking, and most of all, loved the fact that they all had their own bows—at least the ones that wanted them. It was nice to see the interaction of the children with each other. Even though there were no electronic devices, everyone managed to survive nicely without them. The solar panels were up, and phones were charged just in case, but nothing else. They never saw anyone other than those in the two camps. Lyle had given the camps names, which was actually a good idea. The main camp was now Calumet, which he said meant "Pipe of Peace," from one of the Native American languages.

He felt Riley's camp deserved that name after welcoming them into their camp despite what they had done. The other camp was simply named Mercy, for the obvious reason they had been granted mercy by those in Calumet. The names were well received, but no one ever spoke of the day of their first meeting. However, Riley thought about that morning often—always by way of prayer, lifting up those that lived in Mercy, then Annie, and lastly, herself. That day, she was sure, would haunt her for the rest of her life.

Allen's two girls—Tina, who was fifteen, and Kate, who was seventeen—seemed to get along very well with Riley's kids, and she was grateful for that. There were enough of the younger kids to go around to keep them happy. Riley's teenagers enjoyed having someone new and close to their ages in their lives. Tina and Kate fit in so well with her two girls that they even had a few sleepovers with them. They were great kids, and more importantly, they were eager to learn. Kate even went on a hunt one time with the boys and Annie. Although they came home empty-handed that day, she had fun nonetheless. Not one of them seemed to miss the outside world.

The two camps had managed to survive two nasty rainstorms, which was a true testament to Anderson's carpenter skills. The Dunnies and showers didn't blow away, nor did the smokehouse he built. Of course, he said that if they did, "it would've been because of Tony and Carson's workmanship," never his! Tony and Carson didn't mind the jab; this was all new to them and they found they enjoyed doing the work.

By way of playing cards, chess, and dominos, Norman and Mr. Miller found common ground and enjoyed each other's company. He got along with Mr. Miller as well as her father did, which wasn't saying much, but they played games every evening after dinner and seemed to enjoy it. Riley could swear she even heard a laugh come out of Miller. But it came and went so fast she wasn't sure if she actually heard it at all.

Riley found a little piece of heaven all to herself late one after-noon while she was down by the lake. Goliath had followed her and was lying down, watching and listening to something—but what, Riley didn't know. This was Riley's time to be alone, to think about her husband and her friends that weren't with them. Some days, she just wanted to read a book, even though she only had one set of books with her. It was a trilogy that she had read twice already. All three books were worn out and frayed at the corners, but the pages were still intact. Today she sat alone in one of the camp chairs, thinking about the last eight weeks. She had lost weight, and it was showing in the waist of her jeans. She thought at some point, she was going to need some new clothes. Then she remembered she couldn't just pop down to the local mall anymore. Defeated by knowing she was going to have to make do with what she had, she pushed the thought of her clothes out of her head. It was early October, and the day was gorgeous. The cool breeze filtered in all around Riley, but it didn't bother her. It was peaceful, and for the first time since all this started, she truly felt relaxed. It occurred to her that she would need a heavier coat soon because the evenings were getting chilly.

Her thoughts were interrupted by footsteps coming toward her from the direction of the camp. They were heavy footsteps, so it had to be one of the men. She never turned around to see who it was. Goliath had his ears turned in the direction of the steps, but he didn't move either. Riley waited for whomever it was to come around in front of her. It was Anderson. Looking up at him, she gave him a very soft-spoken, "Hi."

"Hey, Riley, sorry to be messin' with your solitude, but I've a quick question for ya, and then I'll be out of your hair."

Riley loved listening to Anderson's voice. His Australian accent wasn't thick, except when he was goofing around with the kids. It was deep but sweet. They had become close friends and trusted each other immensely. She was convinced Jackson would like him immediately. She knew he wasn't a replacement for Jackson, but it was good to have him around. Goliath got up, stretched, and meandered over to Anderson. Anderson did his part by giving him a good scratch on his head.

"You're not bothering me at all. What do you need?"

"Norman was lookin' around in the Chef Wagon for something and found a radio. He wanted to know if we could use it to find out anything of what's been goin' on? See if there is any news? Wasn't sure if I should ask your Dad."

Riley had forgotten about the radio. Her father always brought it on camping trips just in case someone got injured so they could call for help. They never camped close to anything, so it was just there as a safety precaution.

"You know, I forgot about having it. It's always in the wagon, but we've never used it. We'll have to use the generator to get it to work, but yeah, it should be okay."

"Right then, we'll get her up and running," he said as he slapped his hands and rubbed them together. "Shall we?"

Riley was up before he got the "Shall we?" out.

She needed a belt, she thought, as she pulled her pants up while walking back to camp. She wanted to find her father—not that he would mind, but she wanted to include him. They found him at one of tables talking to Landon and Annie. Ken looked up as they approached the table.

"Hey, baby girl, you look like you're on a mission." It wasn't a question. Her father was merely stating a fact.

"Hi, Dad, um, you know that radio of yours in the wagon? Have you ever used it?"

"Wow! Dagnamit! I totally forgot about that thing!"

Ken headed for the Chef Wagon, and Anderson followed.

Riley asked, "Landon, would you go to Mercy and tell everyone about the radio, they might want to come over just in case there is some news so they can hear it firsthand. Tell Lyle, he'll take care of getting everyone over here but stay just in case he needs you to help find people. Okay?"

Landon agreed and took off running to Mercy. She then asked where Carson and Tony were.

Riley's mother answered, "They were over by the cabins, helping Carolyn with something just a few minutes ago."

"Thanks, Mom, I'll go get them."

She found them with Carolyn nailing a wooden rack up on the wall by the door. Carson and Tony had been commissioned by Carolyn to build something to help with the mess of jackets that were piling up. The rack was long and had fifteen pegs on it, giving plenty of room for jackets to hang on. Riley thought it was an excellent idea, one that would benefit all the cabins.

"Hi, guys, sorry to bother you, but I need your help. We have a radio that we forgot about. In order to use it, we need the generator. Would you mind helping me get it over to the kitchen? It's heavy and will take a few of us to move it."

Carson and Tony both stopped what they were doing. She could see they were surprised to hear about the radio.

Tony turned to Carolyn, saying, "I promise we'll get this up tonight, but this is great news. Do you mind?"

Carolyn said, "Oh my goodness, not at all, go!"

When they came out of the cabin together, Becca was walking toward them and fell in beside them asking, "What's going on? Everyone in the camp is moving around like something bad is coming our way."

Carolyn spoke first, "They have some kind of radio that they think we can get some news from."

"You're kidding?" Becca was surprised.

Riley added, "We totally forgot we had it. I'm not even sure my dad has used it before. Hopefully, it's in good shape. My dad bought it off of a friend some years ago. I'm not sure if it was ever used by its previous owner, but we are about to find out."

Riley, Carson, and Tony broke away from the women and headed for the generator. Anderson had Bram with him when they came up alongside Riley. The generator was one of the big ones they put at the front of the wagon, and it was heavy. They would have to lift it up and over the trailer's rails then carry it over to the kitchen. With its weight and bulk, it would be hard for the men to get it over to the kitchen. The trailer was detached from her parents' Escalade and stored with the other vehicles to give more room around the camp area. They considered hitching it back up to drive it over to the kitchen but then decided against it. Riley remembered Jackson had put brackets on so it could be carried with poles that slipped into loops. It made the load much easier for two or more people to carry. Riley rummaged around the wagon for the poles. Once they were found, she stepped aside to let the men take over.

"Guys, I'm going to go get the gas. I'll meet you over at the kitchen," Riley yelled as she ran the other way to grab a gas container.

She saw Kevin and Nate on the path from Mercy heading toward her. They both waved as they walked up.

"That was fast." Riley was surprised to see anyone from Mercy as Landon had only been gone a few minutes.

Nate told her, "We were on our way here when Landon came running by on his way to Mercy. He told us about the radio."

Nate was still holding the hand that Riley shot on the first day they met. Out of habit, Riley thought. It had healed quiet nicely, thanks to the mothering he got from Agnes and her mother. Riley figured it must still be tender by the way he held it up to his chest or sometimes held it with his good hand.

"Yes, Norman found it in the Chef Wagon. It's always been there, we just never used it, so it was forgotten."

"Wow, I'm glad he found it. Is there something we can do to help?" Nate inquired.

"Sure, I was going to grab one of the gas containers for the generator."

"I'll get it for you, Riley," Kevin said as he turned and walked over to where all the gas containers were stored.

"Thanks, Kevin."

"I'll walk back with you." Nate had his hand up to his chest as they turned to walk back to the kitchen.

"You said you were coming to our camp. Was there something you needed, or was it just a social visit?" Riley questioned.

"Yeah, we ran out of the two-ply for the ladies. I needed some exercise, so I offered to pick some up for them."

"Sure." Riley knew they needed to go into a town soon to find toilet paper because they were running out. What a stupid thing to leave camp for. They would all find out soon what was going on once the radio was up and running. "Just help yourself."

"Thanks."

Nate was a single man. He had divorced a long time ago. He had no children, but he was still young. Riley guessed in his midthirties. He was a nice guy despite the part he played on that horrible day when he and the other men came to their camp. Riley honestly liked him.

At the kitchen, her father had the radio out from its box and the large antenna up. Norman was reading the instructions. Bram, Carson, Tony, and Anderson were coming up with the generator. It took them only a few minutes once the generator was there to get the radio fired up. Norman worked the radios on Navy ships. Even though it was years ago, he said it should be like riding a bike again. Once the generator was running and the radio plugged in, Norman began the job of working the knobs and adjusting the antenna. The static was clear, and that was all any of them could hear at first.

Then he changed the settings again, and this time, a voice came on. Everyone was stunned for a moment and then relieved to hear a voice. It was faint at first, but Norman kept adjusting the antenna and the knobs until it came in clear. By this time, some of the Mercy people were trickling in and found a spot to sit and listen. Landon ran the whole way so as not to miss anything.

"Not sure about that. Just heard green zone was contaminated. They said not to go. Not safe. Over."

"I don't know what we are going to do? The stupid governor said to stay put, and now the city isn't safe. Not sure how we are going to get out. Over."

"Wish we could help you, brother, but every place is bad. How's the food holding out? Over."

"Few cans, few things of dried food, I don't know maybe a week. Over."

"I would say to stay until violence calms down. Half of those dimwits aren't immune, and they're running around like they are. The virus will get them soon enough. But it doesn't sound like you can wait due to food shortage. Over."

"Even if we get out, don't have a clue where to go. Over."

"Copy that, over."

Riley touched Norman on the shoulder as if not to interrupt the two people speaking, "Can we talk to them?"

"Oh, sure, the mic is hooked up. Go ahead."

Riley grabbed the mic, put it to her mouth, and squeezed the button. "Hello, excuse me, sorry, my first time on one of these. Are you still there? Uh, over."

"Yeah. Go ahead, still here. You're doing fine. Over"

"Thanks, my name is Riley. What state are you in? Over."

"Hi, Riley, Benjie here. Out of Georgia. You? Over."

Riley held down the button again, "Wyoming. We've been in the dark for about eight weeks. Can you fill us in on what's been going on? Over."

"Sure. Nothing good, though, just chaos. They had a safe zone in Nebraska, someone sick got in, and everyone ended up sick. Was told everyone died. Whether it's true, I'm not sure. Went out on the radio. I do know no major city is safe. No military or police to help, gangs and others taking over cities. Some reports are brutal. Over."

Riley's chin was leaning on her hand that held the mic. This was terrible. She and the others were placing hope in a cure.

"Not what we were hoping to hear. Then the CDC came up empty?" Riley paused for a second then asked, "The person you were talking to before, where is he? Over." Riley was uncomfortable talking on the radio, but she wanted some answers.

"No cure, CDC did send their best down to the Antarctica to work. But there's been no word. Mitch, you there? Over."

"Yep, here Benjie. Hi, Riley. It sounds like you and I are neighbors. Northern Colorado. Benjie's right about the cities. My son went for supplies and was chased for five blocks. Lost everything he had. We need to get out but not sure how to or where to go. I have a wife, two young girls and my boy. Rapes are just part of the day here. I have to keep wife and girls inside, it's just too risky. We hear lots of screams and gunshots throughout the day and most of the night. Fires too throughout the city. Over."

Riley's heart went out to Mitch. This was a parents' worst nightmare. She was grateful they left when they did.

"Geez, I'm sorry to hear that. Can you stand by for a minute, Mitch? Over."

"Roger that. Over."

The radio fell silent. Riley glanced over at her father then to Anderson. Her father didn't even need to ask her what she was thinking; he knew and didn't like it.

"Riley, I don't think it's a good idea. We don't know if any of us are immune. And we are definitely not an army."

"They need help, and we need supplies. With Calumet and Mercy combined now, we are running low on a lot of things." Riley saw some of the Mercy members and said, "And I'm happy to have all of you, but more people means more supplies used. If they can meet us halfway, we can get to them. I'll take Landon and Bram. They are the best shots in the group."

"Wait a minute, Riley!" her father interrupted. "There is no way you are going with the boys!"

Allen jumped in, "I'll go with her! I'm not as good as them, but Landon said I'm a natural." He looked to Landon for confirmation.

Landon agreed, "He's actually very good, Grandpa. We can do this."

"You can kill someone, Landon? Seriously!" His grandfather was angry.

"I can," Riley said. "Apparently, I'm pretty good at it."

The group went dead silent, and all eyes fell on Riley. Ken couldn't speak. The look on his face was that of pure shock. It was the first time Riley had spoken a word of that day to anyone since she killed Bruce. He was absolutely stunned and had no reply for that. No one did. Even Mr. Miller was speechless.

Riley knew the impact her statement had on everyone, but she was beyond being afraid anymore. But with that thought, she also wasn't going to be careless.

"If we don't have a good plan, we don't go. Okay, Dad? We need a store of some kind that has food and clothes so we don't have to make another trip out."

Ken wasn't happy, but he knew she was correct. Colorado's state line was about four hours away from them at the law-given speed. Without a speed limit, they could make it there faster, so at the most, it would be one night out there for the team going. The worst part of this was, he knew he couldn't go because he would slow them down. Most importantly, Landon and Bram could shoot like no other. They could hit a soda can at 250 yards easily.

"With a plan, Riley! A good plan! Landon, go get the maps out of the Chef Wagon for me. They're in the drawer just inside the side door. I think the third drawer down."

"On it." Landon was off again at full speed.

Riley got back on the radio. "Mitch, do you think you could get your family out of there to meet us? Over."

There was silence for a minute, then, *"I'm not sure, we're around Fort Collins, and it's bad. Let me think for a minute. Over."*

"We're looking over maps, and I'll let you know what we find. Do you have a map of the Western United States? Over."

"We should have something around here. Over." Mitch didn't sound hopeful.

"Mitch, give us an hour to review things here, and we'll get back to you. But someone will be here by the radio at all times if you think of something or need to talk. Over."

"Riley, thank you. The offer alone to help us, well, you have no idea how much it means to us. Over."

Riley smiled, "We haven't done anything yet, but you're welcome anyway. Over and out."

Riley set the mic down just as Landon returned with a stack of worn-out maps. Allen, Anderson, Ken, and Riley followed Landon to a table. He tossed them on the table and started looking for a map of the Western United States. When he found the one he wanted, he pushed the others aside and opened that one.

With it flat on the table, everyone could see it. Ken found Fort Collins and marked it with a highlighter that Landon brought with the maps. Then he marked where they were.

"You can stay on unpaved back roads for a good chunk of the way. But I don't see any way around Kemmerer, and you would be on state One Eighty-Nine for a long time. Then you get off again here on the less-traveled road and smaller towns. I think your best bet is Vernal." Ken paused. "Mitch and his family can take the same type of roads out of Fort Collins, but he'll have to stay on the Forty for the greater part of their journey. I have no idea how easy or dangerous it will be for them. If they don't make it by the time we tell them to meet you, will you be able to leave without them and not look back?"

Anderson's attention was on Riley now, and she could feel his stare. She glanced at him and then at her father.

"I won't risk my kids any more than I have to, Dad, I can promise you that."

She thought back to the time when her kids' safety was first and foremost. Now she was taking two out into the unknown to help people she didn't know. They could easily get supplies much closer, but something was pushing her to help these people. She hoped someone would do the same for them if needed.

"Anderson, I know you want to go, but please don't fight me on this, and stay here. If anything happens to us, these people will need you. You're the only one I trust to care for my girls and my parents. I can't let my boys go without me."

Anderson saw that all eyes were watching them. He could see the fear in all of them. He agreed, but he had a stipulation.

"You're no wuss, Riley, I'll give you that. Make a promise. If it's not safe to go at any point, you'll turn around and come back." His eyes locked on hers, "Like your dad said, if Mitch doesn't come at the time we have set for him, will you leave and head back?"

"I will," she promised.

Kevin cleared his throat to speak, "I would like to go. Allen has a family, he should stay."

Allen drew in a deep breath and let it out slowly, "Thanks, but I'm going. Anderson, I hope you'll extend the same courtesy to my family."

"I'm a bodgy replacement, mate, but yeah, no worries. You bring the bossy Sheila back, right?" Anderson then said in a stern voice to Riley, "No heroics."

Riley was smiling at him, "Bodgy?"

Anderson smiled back, "Poor or inferior quality."

Allen laughed, "As long as I come back and they still speak English."

"Reckon you will, mate." Anderson glanced over to Kevin and then to Allen, "Kevin goes too. You'll need to find a truck of some kind to haul back everything. Don't know what kind of shape Mitch and his family will be in either when you meet up with them."

Kevin stood straight and nodded his head.

"Okay then, what's in Vernal that would be a good landmark to meet them without going too far into the town? Don't they have a purple dinosaur somewhere at the town's entrance?" Riley asked.

Annie laughed at her mom. "No, there's a pink one. Purple is Barney, Mom. And I'm going with you."

Ken and Riley simultaneously said, "*No!*"

"Well, you aren't the only one who can kill someone. I didn't flinch then, and I know I won't if there is a next time. I'm better with a bow than any of you, and they are far quieter. I'm going!"

"I'm not taking my whole family with me, Annie!" Riley couldn't believe Annie wanted to do this.

"Well, you don't have to worry about me coming, Mom, I'm staying right here," Sara calmly stated.

Riley spun around to face Sara and smiled in relief. She was grateful for Sara. She knew Sara would be fine with her grandparents and Anderson. However, Annie coming was a different story. She turned back to face Annie. She knew there was nothing she could do or say to stop her from coming.

"Ugh! Okay, that's it! We'll take my SUV, it's comfy, one vehicle out, and however many we need coming back in. Bring backpacks, load them only with the necessities, nothing more. I'll leave you boys and your grandpa to get guns and ammo." Riley looked to her daughter Annie, "Are you sure you want to do this? You don't need to go."

"I'm sure. I'll get our bows and arrows. And, Mom, I'm only bringing the broadheads this time."

Annie ran to get everything she and her mom were going to need.

"God, help the poor soul who crosses her line of fire. For that matter, God, help us all on this trip please. Let each step we take be the one you would have us take and not one taken on impulse. Please, Father God," Riley prayed.

All around her were "Amens" from everyone. It startled her, not realizing she had said it aloud.

"Okay, so now we relay the plan to Mitch."

Ken passed on the message to Mitch. Mitch had found a map and informed Ken that the best time for them to leave would be early in the morning around four. Most of the crazies were sleeping then. Mitch felt they could get out of town within an hour. It would just depend on if any roads were being blocked. Ken told them only to bring what they absolutely couldn't live without and then cut that in half. Mitch understood, and he knew the pink dinosaur in question. Mitch felt the time Ken gave him to meet Riley was plenty of time for them to get there. The route Riley's group would be taking would take them anywhere from four to six hours. Precaution was everything. It would take them longer, but it was the safest way for now. Ken knew that once they were on the road, things could change at any time and that all the planning in the world could never prepare someone for that. But he knew Riley was smart, that she could manage things on the fly and had done so many times.

Agnes and Victoria went to the kitchen to prepare some food for their trip. They would feed them a good meal now and then sandwiches for tomorrow and anything else that would keep on a road trip like this. Without ice, it would be hard to keep any food fresh for too long. Victoria would give them some canned items out of her homemade selection. They would be okay eating snacks for meals over the next two or three days, she thought. She needed to have enough for their return, in case Mitch and his family didn't have much - better to be overly prepared than not. Victoria was worried about Riley and the kids. She wished Riley wouldn't go, but she understood. Riley would never ask someone else to do something that was her idea and dangerous. They would be leaving at seven tonight, so there wasn't much time. Victoria prayed this wouldn't be the last time she saw her daughter or her grandkids. Agnes came up behind her and put a hand on her arm.

"They'll be fine, Victoria, they'll be fine."

"From your mouth to God's ears," Victoria patted Agnes's hand.

Between the two of them, they put together the best meal plan they could for the travelers.

CHAPTER 6

Riley and the rest of the group left at seven sharp. They were losing daylight because of the time of year, but there was still a bit of light left to see them out. Kevin was driving, and Allen sat up front with him to help navigate. They were all glad to have what little sun there was while heading down the winding road out from their camp. It didn't take as long to get down the mountain as it did going up it. Kevin drove fast when he could, taking advantage of the fact there were no police on the road. At times it was bumpy, and he had to slow down. They slowed almost to a stop when they got close to Kemmerer-Diamondville.

Allen turned around in the front seat to peer back at Riley, who was in the seat behind Bram, "What do you wanna do? It looks dark. We could go slow and see what's there."

"Kevin, do you think you could go in with no lights? Roll all the windows down, and go very slow."

"Sure. Here we go," Kevin moved the SUV at a tortoise-like pace.

Kemmerer was the home of the first JC Penney store, which was still there to this day. The Cooper family had shopped there once, even went to visit James Cash Penney's house, which was just down the road from the store. The store was dark now as they drove casually past it, along with the rest of the town. Thinking back to that trip, Riley remembered they had originally been there for a fossil dig, which they all had enjoyed. Now as the vehicle crept along, that seemed like a lifetime ago. Kemmerer and Diamondville were meshed together, and the road cutting through them seemed long and never-ending. With the windows down, Riley hoped that if there were any noises, they would be able to hear them. The only sound that could be heard was the tires on the SUV rolling slowly along. It was eerie, like some scary movie. Riley couldn't prove it, but it felt like they were being watched. They were all relieved when both towns were behind them. Kevin picked up speed once again, which helped everyone to relax a bit more.

"I can only hope that every town between here and Vernal is as uneventful," Allen voiced what everyone was thinking. "Kevin, we are looking for Four Twelve to Carter, then on to Interstate Eighty."

"Okay, Four Twelve it is." Kevin pressed on the accelerator.

Every town they drove through was the same. They didn't slow down or shut the lights off; however, they didn't blast through them either. The towns were dark and eerie, which led them all to believe that the electricity was off across the state. Either people were afraid to venture out, or they were dead. No place was safe from the deadly virus. Even the smallest of towns were at risk due to the delivery trucks from all over or travelers cutting through the towns on their way to someplace else. Riley's group had to make sure their contact with the outside world was minimal. She hoped Mitch and his family would do the same. Although, Riley was sure he was scared and wouldn't do anything to put his family in harm's way.

* * *

It was still dark when they pulled over just outside of Vernal. The pink dinosaur was in view, but something else was in view too. There was a controlled fire in the middle of the main road going into town. It was big and bright. Someone was alive and wasn't afraid to be out. That bothered Riley. They all got out of the car and pulled out their choice of weapon. They huddled together to discuss what they were going to do. They could hear a faint scream, and then there was laughter and whistling. There were quite a few people outside, but Riley thought they sounded intoxicated.

"I thought Utah was a dry state?" Allen's question was more to himself then to anyone in the group. "They sound drunk, like they're having some street party."

"Someone needs to go down there to see what's going on," Kevin said.

"Landon and I will go," Riley spoke in a soft voice.

Allen and Kevin didn't try to argue. Landon was a good hunter. He knew how to go in quiet, and his mother wasn't about to let him go without her.

"We won't be long. We need to see if we can go around them so we can find what we are looking for."

Riley looked at Landon as he turned and led his mother toward the noise. Landon draped his rifle over his shoulder, checked his nine-millimeter, and holstered it again. Riley followed behind him soundlessly. After a few minutes, they were close enough to hear the people clearly. The building they stood behind had a ladder attached, leading up to the roof. Landon motioned for his mother to climb up while he kept watch. Riley put her arm through her bow, freeing up both hands, allowing her to move up the ladder quickly. When it was Landon's turn, he moved swiftly but quietly, with no effort at all. He was on the roof before his mother had time to turn around to look down at him. They moved silently to the short wall at the front of the building. They could hear everything now with clarity. What they were hearing wasn't good. However, what they saw was a thousand times worse.

There were two men with their hands tied together. A rope ran from their wrists, up to a sign over their heads. Their backs were facing Riley, which didn't allow her to see either of the men's faces. Looking at their backs, however, was enough to make Riley want to puke. One had been burnt badly. His legs were buckled under him, leaving the rope to take all of his body weight. His head was hanging down, not moving. Riley couldn't tell if he was even alive. The other one was moving and moaning as the rope held all of his body weight too. They both watched the young man's head bob up then drop. His back was bloodied from being tortured by some sharp object as well as being burned. Riley dropped her bow, spun around with her back against the wall, slid down on her bottom, and covered her face with both hands. She was beyond crying. The anger she experienced with the men at Utah Outdoors and then again with the men that stormed into her camp was back. The heart of man was truly evil! Riley and her kids had seen the worst of it in the last few months.

"I can't do this," she whispered.

Landon was kneeling in front of her, "Mom, it's okay, we'll just go back to the others and leave."

"Honey, we can't. We can't leave these people."

There was another scream and more laughter coming from some inebriated men.

Riley knew they were raping a woman. She could also tell that they were beyond drunk.

"We can't leave them. What kind of people would that make us? To walk away when we could have helped them." She thought of all the people in their group. "If this is our world, we can't stick our heads in the sand, we have to help. Or there is no hope. And, Landon, there is hope. God's hope for these people just happens to be us. Why did we pick this place to meet Mitch? We drove through countless towns, and there was nothing. We come here, to this place, and we find the most vile and evil of humans. Yeah, we're going back to the others, and then we are all coming back here to free these people. Then we take what we came for, then we go home!"

The screaming continued, but Riley didn't look. Instead, they made their way over to the ladder to leave. They didn't even try to be quiet on their way back. The others were waiting and were glad to see them. Riley relayed everything of what they saw and heard to the others. She also explained her idea of how they were going to go in and help those people.

"They're drunk. In about an hour, we can go in and take over. I want you to drive the car right smack in the middle of the town," Riley instructed Kevin. "We'll have you covered before you drive in. I'm hoping you'll draw anyone out that's coherent. We'll take care of them if they do."

"Not a problem, I'll do it," Kevin agreed.

"The rest of us will go into town behind the buildings. Landon and Bram will go up on the roofs on opposite sides of the street. If any of them are life-threatening, you'll have to shoot them. Can you do that?" Riley looked at both boys.

They both understood and said yes.

"Allen, you and Annie will go on the same side with Bram. I'll go with Landon." Riley was more focused now. "We saw four men outside, and I have no idea how many are in the building we were next to, but it won't matter if they're intoxicated. They'll be no match for us. Allen and Annie, you'll have a better view of them coming out. I'll be where you can see me. If no one comes out, we all go in the front door. If they come out, I'll go in the back door, if I can, to see if there is anyone being held against their will. I think one of the screams came from inside."

Allen asked, "Any questions, or is everyone good?"

Everyone was good.

Riley and the others waited until the noise completely died down. No one was screaming; there was no laughter; no one was talking. It was quiet and time for them to make their move. Riley shed her bow. She would trust Landon, Annie, and Bram to cover her. She was sure Allen could do his part, but she had no doubt about her kids.

Kevin gave everyone time to get to their places then drove right in front of the building where the two men hung. Bram and Landon were in their places and ready. Kevin put the car in park, got out of the car, and slammed the door shut. Nothing.

Riley yelled up to Landon, "Come down! Kevin, grab the cable ties. Start with those two over there. Oh, and take their pants, shoes, and shirts off. They can keep their boxers or briefs as the case may be."

The four men Riley had seen were sleeping, or more likely, passed out on the ground outside.

Kevin looked puzzled but didn't question her motives about the clothes. He moved to the back of the car, opened the back end, and grabbed a large bag. Riley walked over to the two lifeless bodies still hanging by their ropes. The anger was welling up inside of her again. She was sick to her stomach at the sight before her. Landon and Bram were standing next to Riley when she heard Bram gasp.

"Cut them down please, and be careful. Don't let them drop."

Landon gave Bram the knife to cut them down while he held on to them.

"Careful, don't lay them on their backs. Try to lay them more on their sides," Riley instructed.

She checked both of them to see if they were alive. To her surprise, both were breathing, but barely. They were a mess and needed care now, but she knew a few more minutes wouldn't hurt. Riley held their hands while Bram gently cut the ropes off of their wrists. Riley's touch was light while dealing with each of the young men. She leaned in, whispered in their ear that they were safe and that she would return.

Riley rose and saw a pickup parked on the sidewalk, as if someone drunk had parked it. She knew one of the morons had to have the keys.

"Look for some keys. We're going to take that truck."

Kevin saw the truck she was talking about, "You got it!"

Allen was helping Kevin with the men passed out outside. Annie took their clothes and tossed them into the fire. As soon as everything was secured outside, they moved into the building. It turned out to be a restaurant of some kind. Men and women were passed out in the booths with bottles of alcohol scattered everywhere. The smell was awful. It stunk of stale beer, cigarettes, sweat, and urine. It made them all gag.

Riley told Bram and Landon, "Start taking them out one by one. Strip them, and tie them up." Remembering what Annie had done, she added, "Toss their clothes in the fire."

Allen was moving slowly around the room. Riley could tell he was listening for something.

"Allen, what is it?"

"I hear whimpering."

Everyone stood still for a moment. Sure enough, it was coming from the back room. Allen, Riley, and Annie walked carefully through the restaurant to the back. On the floor were two young women. Annie's heart jumped as she moved quickly to them. They were in their early twenties, Annie thought. Both were naked and horribly beaten up. Annie gazed up at her mother, and Riley saw tears glistening in her eyes.

Riley asked Allen in a low voice, "Will you bring me two shirts off of two of those pigs out there, please?"

Allen didn't say anything; he just did as she asked.

Annie spoke softly to the women, "My name is Annie, and this is my mom, Riley. We're here to help you. Please don't be afraid."

Annie gently put her hand on the woman's shoulder closest to her. She jerked, but Annie's voice was soothing as she continued to reassure her that there was nothing to be afraid of. The young woman's eyes were bloodshot from crying and swollen from being beaten.

Allen was back in a few minutes with two clean shirts. Riley and Annie looked up at him puzzled.

"I couldn't have them wear a shirt from one of the men that had violated them. I got these from Landon. He said he wouldn't miss them."

"Thank you." Annie reached up, taking them from Allen.

She worked the shirt around the woman's head then took her hand and put it through the sleeve. The woman managed to help do the same with the other hand and pulled the shirt down over herself. She mouthed thank you to Annie.

"This is our friend, Allen, he's going to help my mom get you outside. He's a father of two teenage girls, so he isn't going to hurt you. They're going to help you up."

Riley was on one side and Allen on her other. Annie went through the same routine with the other girl. She wasn't as badly beaten and was able to put the shirt on by herself. Riley and Allen returned to help her up, since she was too weak to move on her own. Once they were settled outside and out of earshot, Annie spoke to her mother privately.

"I don't know if those two young women will ever be able to recover from this. All those men should be shot for what they did to them and to those men!"

Riley agreed with Annie but kept it to herself. Instead, she told her, "Let God deal with them. We are going to leave them here tied up, and they can rot for all I care, but we won't be killing anyone today."

There was a total of twelve men and four women in the group. The boys tied them up good and tight.

"Okay, their restraints are tight," Bram said, "and I mean tight enough to cut off circulation.

Riley thanked Bram, then she took a moment to speak to the woman that was more alert to see if she could answer a few questions.

"I know my daughter Annie conveyed this to you, but I just want to reiterate that you have nothing to fear from us. You can stay with us, and I promise this will never happen to you again."

The woman swallowed back the tears and barely managed to get her thank you out.

Riley asked, "Is this all of them? There aren't any in a house somewhere sleeping this off, are there?"

She shook her head no. Her voice was barely audible when she spoke, "The big guy there is in charge. When we came into town, they were nice, and we thought we were safe because of the women. Then they got drunk and raped Sheryl and me." She began to cry, "Kota and Jesse did everything they could to protect us, but there were… well, there were just too many of them!" Her crying was becoming uncontrollable. "They made them watch while they raped…raped us, and then we had to watch…watch while they tortured them."

Kevin walked away in shame. Riley knew he was thinking about what he had done to Sara. She let him go. Riley was angry, but she couldn't change what happened and fought it down.

"What's your name?"

"Jena."

"Jena, I promise you, nothing like that will happen to you while you are with us," Riley told her. "These are my boys, Landon and Bram. You know Annie, and these two men are friends. Allen has a family waiting for him back at our camp. I know you tried to trust strangers before, but we really are here to help."

Jena simply nodded her head, while she continued to cry.

Daylight was creeping in, and they still had a few hours left before Mitch and his family arrived.

"Jena, do you know if there is a moving rental place around here as well as a store where we can get some clothes and toilet paper?"

She sniffled and wiped her nose with the back of her hand. Her eyes were puffy from crying.

"Um, yes, I think there is a large western warehouse down the street. It's almost like a Miley's back home, it's a grocery store, with clothes and shoes, anything, really. These guys drove a car into it so they could get stuff they needed."

"Thanks, what about a rental place?" Riley inquired.

Jena shook her head back and forth no.

"Okay, we have a couple of hours to go before Mitch gets here. I need to take care of Kota and Jesse. Kevin, did you find the keys to the truck?"

"Yeah, I did, I've got them here," Kevin held up the keys.

"Great. Let's get them in the bed of the truck and go to the store Jena was talking about. Bram and Allen, I'm going to leave it to the two of you to find a truck of some kind so we can get the supplies back home with us."

"Sure, no problem," Bram said.

"I love your optimism, Bram. I'm not sure where to start, but we'll look around and hopefully find something," Allen said.

"Thanks," Riley was grateful to have Allen with her. He hadn't disappointed her at all on this trip.

"Uh, Jena, where are the rest of the people that live here?"

Jena looked up and started to cry again. "I'm not sure, but don't go into the houses. Some of them have dead people in them. I know because we looked when we first got here. We never went inside. We could see them through the windows."

Riley was afraid of that. "Do you know if any of these fools went into any of the houses?"

Jena shook her head no and then explained, "That's why they stayed here, they were afraid."

"Well, they weren't complete idiots then. Okay, let's get to work."

* * *

The store was more like Wal-Mart and Target leaning heavily in an outdoor sporting department. However, the clothes had more of a Western style to them. It also had a grocery store attached to it with a small café. Riley's first priority was to find blankets, towels, and pillows or whatever she could find to make Kota and Jesse more comfortable. Once she found what she needed, she took an armload to the pickup. Landon had taken off his holster with the gun still inside and wrapped the belt around it, making a nice bundle. Landon then climbed into the back of the truck followed by Kevin. They worked together to move the men so Riley could get a soft pallet underneath them for the long drive home. Riley asked Landon and Kevin to take the clothes off both men as they had urinated all over themselves. Riley was glad she thought to put a tarp underneath the top layer of the pallet, so it would be easier to change if either of them had an accident on it. Annie brought all the blankets, sheets, and towels she could find, stacking them on the tailgate. She also found a first aid kit that was similar to the ones they found in Salt Lake. It wasn't enough for what these two men needed, but it would have to do. Riley cleaned them up as best she could. She knew they both needed a hospital, but that was out of the question. *They must have a pharmacy somewhere around here*, she thought. She stood up and looked in both directions down the street. She saw a sign with "Jensen's Pharmacy" on it. That would be her next stop. For now, both of the men were comfortable. Jena and Sheryl were sitting on the tailgate; however, Sheryl was more sleeping than sitting. She was using the pile that Annie left as a pillow. Riley suggested to Jena that she go inside to find some clothes for herself and Sheryl. She agreed and, with some effort, got off the tailgate and followed Riley inside. Annie, Landon, and Kevin moved into the store and were busy inside making piles of items to go. Riley needed to find some jeans that fit her better and some better boots.

Riley thought a lot about the men and women that were tied up down the street. She also wondered about the locals. Vernal was a nice-size town, and she knew they couldn't all be dead. It had been several months, and if they were locked inside, they would have surely come out for any number of reasons by now. Of course, the only reason she was here was to meet Mitch and replenish supplies; otherwise, she was quite happy staying put. Jena said that the men and women they met here were kind at first. What made the men snap and the women be okay with it? Fear is what drove Allen and Kevin to do what they did. The fear of Bruce and AJ, fear of running out of food, or a combination of both. She knew alcohol and fear was a terrible mix at any time and worried that if there were survivors here, they too could fall victim to these horrible people. They would eventually get free, more than likely be angry and possibly take it out on the first poor soul that came across their path. Riley knew there was no way to help everyone, nor did they have time to go down each street in the hope of finding survivors. Jena said the houses she did go to, she could see the dead through the windows. Carson said the same thing about his parents. Going into any home right now could be signing their death warrant. Until the virus had run its course, survivors would have to join together and find a way to make life livable again. She was confident her group was getting organized and was sure they could manage more people. She was quite aware of the fact that they couldn't stay at the camp forever, and they would have to move to allow growth in the group. She also knew right now, everyone in her group was like-minded, but the more people that joined them could change that unity. She remembered something she read that Robert Winthrop wrote, from the days of the Founding Fathers, which said,

Men, in a word, must necessarily be controlled either by a power within them or a power without them, either by the Word of God or by the strong arm of man, either by the Bible or by the bayonet. [1]

Most of her group was driven by the Word of God, but not everyone crossing their path would share the same faith. The bayonet could be their choice of power. Riley had already encountered that mind-set, and she struck back with a vengeance. Her faith would always come first, but God help anyone if they mistook her Christianity as a sign of weakness. The men that raped Jena and Sheryl should be punished, but she didn't know how to do that without the law, and she wasn't ready to become judge and jury; however, they needed to be reminded that what they did was wrong. She would talk to Allen and see what he thought. She had a pile of jeans she liked in her hands when she heard gunfire.

Boom!

Boom! Boom!

Riley dropped the jeans and took off running.

Boom! Boom!

Landon cut her off and was out the door before she knew it. Annie was right behind her but slowed down for Jena. Kevin blew past Riley and was right on Landon's heels. Both Landon and Kevin slowed to look in the back of the truck. Landon noticed his holster on the ground and the gun gone; so was Sheryl.

"Oh, please, God, no!" Landon pleaded as he took off in the direction of the gunfire—that direction being where they left the men and women tied up.

---

[1]   Robert Winthrop, *Addresses and Speeches on Various Occasions* (Boston: Little, Brown and Co., 1852 p.172, "An Address Delivered at the Annual Meeting of the Massachusetts Bible Society in Boston, May 28, 1849.

As they got closer, they could hear one of the men begging Sheryl to spare him. One woman was yelling and crying; while the rest, still groggy and not sure what was happening, bobbed around on the ground still tied up. Riley saw Sheryl standing over one of her victims.

She called out to her, "Sheryl. Please. You don't need to do this. Please let me help you." As Riley spoke, she moved closer to Sheryl. "Please, Sheryl, it's okay, we'll help you."

Sheryl looked in Riley's direction. Her face puffy and swollen from the beating she had gotten earlier. Fear rose in Riley when she saw the vacant stare in Sheryl's eyes. Riley couldn't move fast enough. Everything seemed to move in slow motion. As Riley moved toward Sheryl, Sheryl, in one fluid motion, put the gun up to her head and pulled the trigger. Human debris came out the other side of her head as her body crumbled to the ground. Riley slid to a stop and fell hard on her tail end. Dazed, she couldn't move. No one did.

Jena hobbled up with Annie. She couldn't believe what she was seeing. She collapsed into a heap with her face in her hands and just sobbed. Annie looked down at her for a minute before it registered, and she bent down, wrapping her arms around Jena. Annie looked over at her mother, who was being helped up by Kevin. The people lying on the ground were stunned as well. All the grumbling, yelling, and crying stopped.

"I...I can't believe this," Riley whispered.

"Mom, I'm sorry! I know better than to leave a gun lying around!" Landon was devastated and almost in tears. "I took it off to help with Kota and Jesse. Sheryl was asleep, and I just forgot about it."

Riley moved toward Landon. He was pale and frozen where he stood. Riley pulled him into her arms and held him tight. He fell into them, and it was all Riley could do to hold him up. Kevin was by her side and grabbed on to both of them so they wouldn't fall.

With care, he helped them down on their knees. Riley spoke gently to Landon and stroked his head as she did.

"Landon, it's okay, it's not your fault. She was brutally raped and beaten. I don't think she was aware of anything or anyone except those that did this to her."

Landon was looking at his mother, eyes red, fighting back the tears.

"I saw the gun on the tailgate and didn't think anything about it," Kevin said to them. "There's nothing any of us can do for her now. The men she killed were dealt the hand they deserved."

Annie was standing next to them with Jena. "They needed to be punished for what they did, but not Sheryl. I hope God will forgive her."

"She was hurting more than her body showed, and God knew that. I can't imagine the pain she felt mentally. I can only hope she's at peace now," Riley said, fighting back the tears.

Riley pulled herself up with the help of Kevin. She walked over to the half-naked bodies on the ground, thought a moment about what she was going to say to them, and then said, "Those of you that didn't die by Sheryl's hand, today count yourselves lucky. Normally, I would say 'blessed,' but knowing what you did to these young people or allowed to happen to them, there's no blessing for you. All of you have a black hole in your heart. I was going to have a conversation with my friends as to what kind of punishment should be bestowed upon you when Sheryl took it upon herself to take care of it for us. The problem is, her death shouldn't have been a part of that punishment. You live by the sword, you will die by the sword. We're going to finish up here, and then we're gone. When we leave here, none of us will ever think of you again. You are worse than the virus that is viciously murdering the human race. None of you are worth saving!"

With that, Riley was done, spun around on her heels, and went back to the store. Their time was running out, and they needed to get a move on. The rest followed her in silence. There was some pleading, more crying, and yelling—which fell on deaf ears. No one looked back. They all knew they needed to get what they came for and go.

The piles they made in the store were moved outside. They found clothes in all sizes for the kids and also for the men and women. Riley wasn't the only one who had lost weight; some of the men and women in the camp had too. They found flour, sugar, and other spices as well as syrup for pancakes, which would make a lot of the children happy. This time, because they were running out of vegetables, they took some of the canned vegetables, even knowing Riley's mother wouldn't like it. They even found sprinkles for Sara's famous sugar cookies. Toilet paper was not forgotten and would take up most of the room in whatever Allen and Bram found to haul everything home in.

As they brought out the last of the stuff, a large truck hauling a huge tank behind it pulled up. Behind it was a very large moving van with "U on the Move Rentals" stenciled on its side.

Bram bounced out of the rental and Allen out of the other truck. Riley couldn't believe her eyes.

"What's in it?"

Allen patted the side of the tanker and, with a very big grin, declared, "Gas! And the best part, it's rim full."

"What? You're kidding?" Kevin couldn't believe what he was hearing.

"Yeah, it was parked in the back of the rental place. We almost missed it. Then it took us forever to find the keys for both trucks. And better yet, both have a full tank of gas."

Riley was happy that they weren't going to have to deal with the gas station. "Well, we should get busy and load everything up. Do we need to fill up the smaller gas containers?"

"Nope. It has a nozzle. There's even a counter on it that shows how much gas you're putting into the vehicle. Pretty cool. They must have used it to refill their trucks as there wasn't a gas station close by," Allen was still smiling, very proud of their find.

"Okay, let's get moving, everyone. Bram, would you fill up all the vehicles for us, please. Allen, would you come with me. I need to go to the pharmacy down the street." She pointed over to Jensen's Pharmacy.

"Sure. What are we looking for?" Allen asked.

"I know our camp has everything, but we need to get these boys on some antibiotics and clean their wounds better. Possibly find something for dehydration, something more than water."

They were walking in the direction of the pharmacy while Riley spoke.

In a more subdued voice, Riley said, "Sheryl's dead."

Allen came to a complete stop. "What! What happened?"

She reported every detail to him, "Sheryl got ahold of Landon's gun and shot five of the men then killed herself. She took her life right in front of us. There was nothing any of us could have done to prevent it. Landon is devastated. He took his gun off to help me with the young men and forgot about it."

"Geez, poor kid. He has to know it's not his fault."

"I told him as much, but a lot of good it did. I can tell he still blames himself. There is no more protecting our children from the violence of this new world. We now have to prepare them for it. It was the most horrible thing I've ever seen. Even the death of Bruce and AJ doesn't compare," Riley said soberly.

Allen didn't know what to say, so they walked the rest of the way in silence. When they arrived and were standing in front of the door, Allen pushed on it, and to his surprise, it swung open. Allen glanced at Riley then turned his attention to the inside of the store. He walked in first calling out, "Anyone here? If there is, we mean you no harm. We just need some medicine for some badly injured friends. Hello?"

No one was there. They stood still for a minute to listen. No sounds. Allen shrugged his shoulders and walked in. Riley stopped him from going any further by grabbing hold of his arm. Her eyes strayed over to his left. There was a bare foot sticking out from behind the shelf. Allen got a glimpse of it just before it disappeared. It was a small foot, Riley thought; it has to belong to a child.

Riley began talking in a soft voice, "I wonder if there is any good candy left in here? I know our kids would love some."

Allen followed her lead, "Well, I know I would love a little candy." He laughed. "And some bubble gum too."

The small child hiding behind the shelves moved a little.

Riley came around the corner and asked, "Hi there, do you know where we can find some candy or bubble gum?"

It was a small boy. He was surprised when she came around the corner, speaking to him. He jumped up to run the other way when Allen caught him. As Allen picked him up, the young boy squirmed, trying to free himself.

"Hey, hey, it's okay, we're not going to hurt you. It's okay," Allen spoke in a gentle tone.

The boy fought for a moment more and then stopped. Riley thought he was maybe seven or eight. He only had one shoe on and was filthy. His hair was in knots, and he smelled terrible. Riley fell into her motherly role once she was able to get past how he looked and smelled.

"Hi, I'm Riley, and this is my friend, Allen. What's your name?" She could tell he was scared, but she continued to press him into talking, "Are you here alone?" Then she pretended to gasp with a horrible thought. "You're not with that group of bad people, are you?"

With that, he quickly shook his head no.

Progress, Riley thought.

"Are you sure? We had to tie them up because they were hurting some girls and boys."

Again, he shook his head harder then said, "No, ma'am, uh-uh, they're very bad people."

Riley smiled, "Good. Now what's your name?"

"Levi," he whispered.

"Levi, where's your mom and dad?" Allen joined in the questioning.

He looked at him and then to Riley, "They're sleeping."

Allen looked at Riley and then asked, "How long have they been sleeping?"

Levi's eyes started to water, and he spoke in a whisper so low they could barely hear him, "A long time, I tried to wake them, but they wouldn't wake up."

"Levi, it's okay, honey, look at me, it's okay." Riley grabbed him gently under the chin, trying her best to comfort him. "I bet you're hungry, aren't you? We have food, and there are kids your age at our camp, so you will have someone to play with. One of my daughters loves to bake brownies and pancakes. Would you like to come with us?"

Levi nodded his head yes.

"Good. We have to find some medicine for our friends, okay? And do you mind if I help you get cleaned up some?" Riley asked.

"My head itches. It itches a lot."

Allen jerked his head back away from Levi's head, making Riley laugh.

"Okay, buddy, let's get the itching to stop. Allen bring him over here to the counter."

Riley found some scissors and told him what she was going to do. He sat there and let her cut his hair short. Allen went to find something and came back with a package of batteries, some shears, and a couple of large bottles of water.

"This is going to tickle your head, okay, buddy? Try not to laugh." Allen told Levi, which made him grin.

"I got this, Riley, if you want to, get the meds and maybe some liquids with electrolytes."

"Thanks, Allen."

Levi turned to see Riley walking to the back of the pharmacy. "She'll be right back, buddy, I promise."

With that, Levi turned his head back so Allen could shave the rest of his hair off. Then Allen took Levi off the counter and stripped him down to nothing. He poured one of the large water bottles of all over Levi, making him giggle. Allen took some soap and scrubbed him thoroughly then rinsed him off with more water. He dried Levi as best he could then put a T-shirt on him that he had found along with some socks. Allen wondered if they found underwear in the other store. If not, the kid was going to have to go commando. At least, the shirt was long enough that it would do.

Allen looked down at Levi and told him, "You look a lot better. How do you feel, buddy? Better?"

Levi ran his tiny hand over the top of his head and looked up at Allen. "Yes, thank you."

"Levi, can you tell me, were either of your parents sick? Did they have a cold or a cough? Do you remember?"

"They both had a cough and runny nose. So did my sisters. They all fell asleep and wouldn't wake up," he replied in a quiet voice.

"Do you remember what kind of work your dad or mom did?"

"Yes, they took people on tours. Dinosaur tours!" Levi said with pride.

"I bet they were good at it too. Thanks, buddy."

Riley came around the counter with a box full of bottles and small boxes. When she saw Levi, she overly exaggerated her amazement, "Oh my word, what happened to Levi? Where did you put him?" She was looking around as if she was searching for him.

Levi giggled, "I'm here, silly!"

Riley smiled as she knelt down next to him and put the box on the floor. "What a handsome young man. You ready to go meet my kids?"

Allen picked up the box as Levi took Riley's hand. Riley mouthed thank you to Allen and rose. They were just about to walk out the door when Levi let go of Riley's hand, running back to get something. When he came back, he had a bag of unopened candy.

Holding it up, he said, "Will your kids like this?"

"They'll love it. Come on, let's go see if they're done."

Annie was the first to see them coming and was surprised to see a little boy with them, bald and in a long T-shirt but nonetheless very cute. She smiled as they came up.

"Well, who's this?"

"Annie, I would like you to meet Levi. Levi this is my oldest child, Annie."

The others came around to meet him, and Levi was genuinely happy to meet them. Riley could tell every time someone said his name, he just beamed. After all the introductions were made, Riley hopped into the back of the truck to check on Kota and Jesse. She took her time cleaning both their backs and managed to get a pill into Kota with some fluids. Jesse wasn't working with her at all, but he was breathing better, which gave her hope. She honestly didn't know what she was doing and prayed a silent prayer for healing despite her ignorance. When she was done, she climbed down. The truck was loaded, and all the cars were filled up and ready to go. It was time for them to go meet Mitch.

Allen suggested that he drive the gas truck and Bram drive the moving van. Kevin volunteered to drive the pickup. There was no argument from Riley. Annie and Riley would drive the SUV with Jena and Levi. Landon had his choice of whom he wanted to ride with, so he rode with Bram. Annie asked if she could drive first, which was fine with Riley. They all got into their vehicles and slowly drove by the bodies of the dead and the living that were still tied up. The living screamed at them as they passed by.

Levi looked out at them then quickly turned to Jena, "I saw them do bad things to you. I wished I could've helped, but I was scared."

Jena fought back tears, "I'm sorry you had to see that." She thought for a moment then spoke softly, "Thanks, but there was nothing you could've done to help."

Levi gave a sorrowful smile. He looked once more at the people left in the street then sat back in his seat. He was happy to be with people again. *Nice people*, he thought. He was about to ask something when Riley spoke.

"So now to the purple dinosaur."

Annie sighed, and Levi giggled.

"What are you giggling about?" Riley turned so she could see Levi.

"It's a pink dinosaur, not purple!" Levi almost shouted through his laughter.

"Are you sure? I swore it was purple. Okay, Levi, then off to the pink dinosaur."

"Levi, you're going to have to help me keep my mom in line. She's getting old and can't remember anything."

"Hey, be nice!"

"She's not old. She's pretty!" Levi said in defense of Riley.

"Why, thank you, young man." Riley glanced over at Annie, "I guess I have someone to help me keep you in line, missy."

Annie just smiled.

Jena quit crying and started to relax with the conversation her three companions were having. Listening to Levi's voice was more comforting to her than she had realized. She gave a brief smile when she glanced over at him and thought that he was too young to be left alone in this world—for that matter, she was too. She was so grateful to these people, that they came when they did. She thought about Sheryl, and the tears started to well up in her eyes again, but she fought to push them back. She had to forget this place and all that happened to her. Levi's chatty little voice broke through her thoughts, for which she was grateful.

"Why are we going to this dinosaur? We have them everywhere." He was curious.

"We came here to meet someone that needed to get away from where they were living. There are a lot of bad people where they live too. We thought when we arrived here we would just get a few things then leave. That's when we came upon Jena and the two men," Riley explained. "Mitch and his family should be here soon if they aren't already."

When they arrived at the meeting place, there was a large Dodge pickup with a travel trailer hooked up to it. Their setup was very nice, and Riley was relieved because even though she knew they would be able to accommodate all these people in the cabins, it was going to be tight. Annie pulled up alongside the truck, and Riley rolled down her window.

The window of the truck came down too.

"Riley?" a big man in the driver's seat asked.

Riley smiled, "Yes, I take it you're Mitch? Nice to finally meet you."

He looked at all the vehicles behind her, "You don't travel light, do you?"

Once Riley was out of the SUV, Annie moved it to the other side of the street. Riley waved Allen to come up with the gas truck so Mitch could fill his truck up.

She then explained, "Yeah, I guess not, they found a small tanker filled with gas. It will help us get home. He'll fill you up if you need it."

Mitch hopped out. "Thanks, I wasn't sure what we were going to do. We're about out of gas, and the gas jugs are all empty. With the travel trailer hooked up, this thing guzzles gas."

Allen handed the nozzle over the back end of the truck to Mitch. He took it with a "thank you." Mitch introduced his family once he got the gas nozzle situated.

"This is my wife, Angela, and my kids, Trisha, Marsha, and Greyson."

Allen said hello and introduced himself. Kevin and the others came up and did the same. Riley looked back at the truck Kevin drove and then at him. He let her know his cargo was okay.

"I thought you didn't have the means to get out of Fort Collins? This is a very nice setup. Why didn't you leave earlier to one of the campgrounds?" Riley questioned as she looked at the huge travel trailer.

"It's not mine. It's my neighbors'. I thought about taking it a million times, but it would have been stealing, and it didn't feel right. Then by the time I realized he probably wouldn't mind, our area had gotten so bad I didn't dare try to get my family out." He paused for a moment then said, "Talking to you on the radio gave me some hope, and I figured it was now or never."

"Did you have any trouble?" Kevin inquired.

"No, not really. Gas was the hardest part, but we just siphoned it out from other vehicles. I thought at one point we were being followed, but we weren't."

That perked Riley up, and she turned to Landon, "Honey, would you please get the binoculars, then crawl up on the cab of the truck, and have a look around?"

"Sure, no problem."

He was on it right away. Bram went with him. Riley turned back to Mitch and told him of the trouble they had in town. All of it. Angela was horrified by what she heard. She looked over to the car Riley came in but couldn't see inside because the tinted windows were up. Mitch was saddened by what he heard.

"I can't believe how people are acting. People that never did a wrong thing their entire life are now becoming their own worst nightmare." Riley could hear the disgust in Mitch's voice.

"That's twenty-two gallons. That should do, Mitch," Allen informed him.

"Yeah. Right. Here you go." Mitch took the nozzle out and handed it back to Allen.

"Because of our passengers in the back of Kevin's truck, we need to go a different way, preferably less bumpy," Riley advised them.

Allen thought for a minute. "You're right, and we need to cover them up somehow to protect them from the weather."

"Oh, boy, you're right, the sun will only add to their discomfort," Riley agreed.

"We have a few extra tarps we can fold in half and tie down. That way, they'll still get some air," Allen said as he walked over to the truck with Riley.

They took care of the tarp to shade Kota and Jesse from the sun. Riley thought it would do nicely and asked for a map so they could find a better way home. Allen and Kevin believed the best route was for them to go back the way they came, all the way through to Kemmerer. From there, however, they would take the One Eighty-Nine all the way up just past Daniel and then cut over. It would be faster than the way they came except they would have to cut through more towns which could present a problem if people were around. Hopefully, every place would be quiet. Landon asked if they could have a word of prayer, so everyone joined in—even Levi and Jena. It was close to 8:00 in the morning, and everyone was tired, but there was no more time to waste. It would take them five to six hours to get home as it was, maybe longer. They moved out one by one. Allen went first, then Mitch, and the rest followed.

CHAPTER 7

They were making good time, only stopping once for a restroom break and to check on Kota and Jesse. Jesse was awake long enough to get some fluids and a pill down him. Kota woke up and spoke incoherently, took a drink, and then fell back to sleep. Passing ranches along the way, they saw quite a few dead animals. Riley guessed they died from starvation or lack of water. Other animals grazed in fields with no concern, their water troughs were probably full with the help of windmills, or perhaps there was a natural spring close by. Riley wished they could do something for them too, but they kept driving. They were four hours into their trip when Riley saw smoke off in the distance. It was coming from a ranch, but the house couldn't be seen from the road. The dirt road went almost in a straight line up over a small hill. Riley pulled over into the fast lane and passed everyone to take the lead. She slowed when she got closer to the entrance and saw an iron archway with the name Sagebrush Trail Ranch. She turned on her blinker, slowly maneuvering the SUV up the long dirt road. Remembering the boys in the bed of Kevin's truck, she drove slow. As they approached the top of the hill, Riley stopped the car and got out. The dust they were kicking up would more than likely let the occupants, if there were any, know someone was coming, but Riley wanted to be cautious.

Allen was by her side within seconds. "What's up?"

"Smoke. People maybe. Chicken and eggs maybe," Riley was talking more to herself than to Allen.

"Yum, eggs sound good."

Mitch came up, "Why are we here?"

"Eggs," was all Allen said.

Mitch looked confused but said nothing.

"I'm sure we kicked up enough dirt driving up here that whoever's there knows we're here. But just to play it safe, you and I should go in first," Riley told Allen. "The rest will stay here."

They went back to explain what they were planning to do to the rest of their group. Jena, Levi, and Annie got out of the car and stayed with the others as Riley and Allen drove down to the huge ranch house. Allen parked the car on the side of the house under a huge shade tree. They both sat there for a moment, looking around but saw no one. Satisfied, they both got out of the vehicle at the same time. Staying vigilant, they only saw a fire with three large pots over it with a wonderful smell coming from them. Allen and Riley both were hopeful and walked cautiously toward the house. They could hear chickens in the background along with the neighing of a horse or horses. Riley was all smiles as she listened to all the chatter from the livestock. A small Mexican woman came out of the house, holding a big bowl. Seeing Riley and Allen standing in front of the house, she set the bowl down and ran back inside. A few seconds later, a man came out. He was Mexican as well and about the same age as the woman. Riley went on the assumption they were husband and wife or brother and sister. She went with husband and wife because of the way the woman stood behind the man.

Riley took a few steps forward to introduce herself, "Hi, I'm Riley, and this is my friend, Allen. We're not here to hurt you, and more importantly, we're not sick. We left the rest of our friends just over the hill. They won't come down if you don't want them to."

The man moved down the steps and walked right up to Riley with his hand out. Riley shook it and then he offered it to Allen.

"I'm Alejandro. This my wife, Guadalupe. We are happy to meet you. Please come. Your friends too. We have lunch, come."

"I'll go get the others," Allen offered.

"Sure, sure, we have lots of food. I kill a goat. We have goat milk too, no cold. Sorry, no luz," Alejandro explained cheerfully.

Riley smiled, "Thank you, Alejandro, you're very kind. May I help?"

"No, no. Come, we have table inside. How many with you?"

"Fifteen," she answered.

Alejandro's eyes went wide. "You kidding? Fifteen? We no see anybody in months, and today we see fifteen! *Ay Dios mio*! Come, come, this is good news, come."

Alejandro showed Riley the way inside the house, which was very nice and clean. It was weird being in a house again after living in the cabins for so long. Riley loved the feeling of being in a real home and hoped that this could be life once again for all of them. To live in houses once more, going to restaurants again, going to church with a real pastor, having kids back in school, simply to have life be what it once was. She wondered if it could be possible. Movement outside caught her attention. It was Allen bringing everyone in. Thinking of all those children and young adults, life would have to come back to some resemblance of what it once was—if for no other reason than for those kids. She would try to make it happen. She walked to the door to open it for everyone. Kevin came in and had a quiet word with her. She left with him, making their way over to the truck with Kota and Jesse still in the back. He pulled back the tarp, revealing the two men that lay there. They didn't look good. The combination of the long drive and the lack of food and liquids definitely didn't help.

"Would you mind pulling the truck under the tree over there?" Riley asked as she pointed in the direction of a big tree. "I'll see if Guadalupe has any hot water boiled."

Kevin did as she instructed while Riley went in to speak with Guadalupe. When she entered the house, she found everyone with a look of awe on their faces. She knew they were thinking the same thing she did when she first walked in. She didn't say anything to anyone, just went straight to the kitchen where she found both Alejandro and Guadalupe.

"I'm sorry, we have two badly injured men in our group. You wouldn't happen to have any hot water, would you?"

Alejandro said. "Sure, on fire outside. I help you. Come. I get some clean towels."

Alejandro opened a cabinet and took some towels then led Riley outside. Off to the side of the fire was a larger silver pot. It had been scorched by the flames and was full of hot water. He took the towels and used them to grab the handles.

"They're over here in the back of the truck. I need to warn you, they're hurt badly. But not by us. We saved them from the ones who did this to them," Riley explained.

Alejandro said nothing, but she could see the worry on his face. When they came up to the back of the truck, Kevin was sitting on the backend. He got off to help put the pot of water on the tailgate.

Alejandro's eyes went wide with horror when he saw the backs of the two men.

"*Ay Dios mio!*" he said as he did the Catholic motion of crossing himself.

Riley climbed up on the bed of the truck, positioning herself over the boys. Kevin was there to give her any assistance he could. She rolled Jesse over first. He stank so bad from the foul smell of urine and body odor it gagged both of them.

"We need to bathe them and change the bedding," Riley informed them.

"I have big bath in barn. Water pump work with windmill. *Es frio.* Have salt too if you want."

"Salt!" Kevin was shocked.

"Good for cuts. We no put much. Just a little." Alejandro showed with his fingers how little. "*Un poco.*"

"They both look terrible, and at this point, anything is better than doing nothing," Riley said with little assurance.

"Okay, I'll move the truck over there," Kevin offered.

Alejandro grabbed the pot of hot water then headed for the barn. Riley rode in the back with the boys. It was a cool day, and Riley was sure the water was going to be freezing. It would take too long to heat enough water for both men, so a cold bath was it for them. Riley was becoming more stressed on how to care for them and wished there was a doctor in the group. All she could offer was a bunch of second guesses. She said a silent prayer for both of the young men and asked for guidance for herself.

Alejandro was inside filling the tub with water when Riley walked in and said, "Wow, Alejandro. The water is so clear."

"Jefe, he put water filter on. Only wants best for horses," he told her.

"Jefe? You work here?"

"*Si.* Wife too, for four years."

"Where is the…your jefe, where is he?" Riley was curious.

"He take family to Europe for vacation. No back yet. No talk to him in months." Alejandro shut off the water and turned to Riley. "Me think he's no coming back. Lupe and I stay just in case to care for animals."

Riley didn't know why she was surprised by that but was glad to know they worked here because that meant he knew the operation of the place.

"Alejandro, do you mind if we stay here for one night? We're tired, and after this big meal you've prepared, we're going to want to rest."

"Sure, sure. You stay as long as you need. It's okay. No problem."

Riley thanked him and then turned to Kevin, "Are you okay with that?"

"Sure. I'm having a hard time keeping my eyes open anyway."

"I know we're only a few hours out from camp, but this will be a good place to rest," Riley said as if she needed to explain her decision.

"What about the others? Back at the camp, I mean? They'll be expecting us," Kevin reminded her.

"You with others?" Alejandro asked, surprised.

"Yeah, we have a camp in the mountains about two to three hours from here," Kevin replied. "Forty-one people plus the fifteen of us."

"Your jefe, he no mind if my Lupe and I come? We work hard for your jefe," Alejandro offered.

Kevin laughed, "Well, she's right there in front of you."

Alejandro looked to Riley. Embarrassed, Riley shook her head and laughed, "I'm bossy, but a jefe I'm not. But of course, you and your wife are welcome. And as far as work goes, we all have to work, Alejandro, we work together. But yes, I would love it if you and Lupe came."

Alejandro was happy with that. He walked over to the truck to assist Kevin with both of the young men. They maneuvered Jesse easily out of the back of the truck then gently set him in the tub. He jerked as his body was submerged in the frigid water. His eyes opened for only a minute; then they closed again. He moaned, rolled his head back and forth for a moment, then he settled down. Riley grabbed the shampoo and a towel to bathe him with. She washed his hair first then rinsed it. His hair was thick, dark, and very long. Thankfully, Riley didn't see any bugs in it like she had in Levi's. Alejandro gave

Riley shears as well as a razor to shave off his thick facial hair. She asked Alejandro for scissors, which he found and gave to her. Riley thanked him and began to cut Jesse's. When she was done, she let him soak for a few minutes before they pulled him out and laid him on the clean blanket that Alejandro placed on the ground for them. After they had Jesse settled, Alejandro drained the water, cleaned the tub with some kind of spray, and then refilled it. Both of the men were about six feet or more, although Jesse wasn't quite as heavy as Kota. Kevin and Alejandro followed the same sequence of moving Kota as they did with Jesse. However, when Kota went into the tub, his eyes flew open and stayed open. His eyes were crystal blue, like Sara's. He fought for a few seconds and mumbled words that none of them could understand. Riley could tell he was fighting himself to stay awake. She searched for bugs in his long, blond curly hair but couldn't find any, which made Riley extremely happy.

"Hi there," Riley spoke in a tender voice, "you're safe now. No one is going to hurt you anymore. I need to clean you up some, though." She looked to Kevin and asked him if he would get the juice and antibiotics for her. She then turned her attention back to Kota, who was still staring at her. "Kota, my name is Riley, and these are my friends. You're going to be okay."

He mouthed something that Riley didn't understand, so she continued to speak to him in a gentle tone, "Your friends, Jena and Jesse, are with us, and they're all okay."

She cringed once she realized she made a rookie mistake by singling out Sheryl. She was sure he didn't notice, but she needed to be careful with her words. He blinked his eyes but kept them on Riley.

"I'm going to put shampoo in your hair and on this rag to get you cleaned up. Hopefully, this will help you feel better. Okay?" She got him lathered up, scrubbed down, and then rinsed him thoroughly.

Kevin came back with the pills and juice. "Here you go."

"Thank you," she said to Kevin. "Kota, I need you to swallow this and drink the juice please."

Riley put the pills in Kota's mouth, then she held the juice for him. He drank it by grabbing a hold of Riley's hand so she wouldn't pull the bottle away. He was thirsty. That was a good sign, she thought. Riley cut his hair and shaved his face the same way she did Jesse's. When she was done, she moved out of the way so the men could get him out. Because Kota was awake when they moved him, the pain jolted through his body, making him scream in agony. Kevin and Alejandro worked as quickly as they could to get him onto the blanket. Riley was there instantly, trying to calm him down once he was on the blanket.

Alejandro left quickly, heading into the barn and brought out a huge can of salve. He handed it to Riley, saying, "We use on animal when hurt. You use on men, it heal them faster."

Riley was apprehensive at first then took it.

"Well, our vet in Bakersfield did tell me once that they don't make special medicine for animals, it's all the same as humans. I'll use it, thanks."

"Put on thick. Cover with this. I make more, no problem," Alejandro told her.

Riley put the salve all over Kota's back, his skin quivered, but he didn't move. She then lay a large piece of cheesecloth over it when she was done. She did the same to Jesse; he didn't move at all. She rolled them both on their sides to give their necks a rest from being turned to one side for too long. Kevin brought some towels over to keep them propped up. Riley couldn't leave them naked and needed to find some pants or some shorts for them.

"I need to see if I can find some clothes for them and then clean their pallet. Why don't you go up and get something to eat, Kevin? If you would, send one of the other men down here to give a me hand," Riley said as she got up to wash her hands.

"I'll stay, Riley. Annie thought about the clothes when we took off their old ones. I'll go get them."

Riley smiled as he ran back to the truck. She walked back into the barn to wash her hands in the sink that she found inside. While she was drying her hands, she walked over to the horses. They had four of them, and they were absolutely beautiful. Riley knew nothing about horses, but she did love them.

Alejandro was standing by her. "What about the horses, Alejandro? What will you do with them?"

"Maybe take them. Mountains have lots of room. We have trailer for them. I come maybe make two trips. No problem. And the chickens too," he said.

"Bring them and your chickens?"

"Sure, chickens, goats, and horses. We take all?" Alejandro didn't seem worried at all about bringing the animals to the mountains.

"Sure, if you promise to teach me how to ride. You do know how to ride the horses?" she asked.

"Sure, no problem. I teach you. These are the best, good to ride," he assured her. "But jefe's pride outside, you come look."

She followed him out another door. Kevin came up beside her.

"The boys have some sweats on them now. Where are you going?"

"Thanks, Kevin, Alejandro said there is an amazing horse out here that he wants me to see."

They walked out back, and standing in the field was a massive Clydesdale.

"Oh my word, he's beautiful. How old is he?"

"Jefe bought him last year. Maybe two, yes two," Alejandro thought.

"Yeah, they can come, and we'll help you get them up to the camp. I don't know how we'll do it, but we'll think of something. Now, I haven't ever had goat meat before, and I'm starved. I need to take care of the pallet in the truck then go eat. Thanks for your help, Kevin and Alejandro." Riley was grateful.

She reluctantly left the corral and headed for the truck. She decided she would come back to visit the horses after dinner as they had a calming presence over her. Riley noticed that Kevin wasn't leaving her side. He told her when she was done, he would be done. Alejandro stayed as well. He took the soiled blankets, sheets, and towels at Riley's request and threw them away. They wouldn't need them as they had plenty. They washed down the tarp and then put the clean sheets and blankets on the pallet, which took them less than five minutes. When they were done, they all headed for the house to eat. Riley decided she would eat her meal while she sat with Kota and Jesse. She wanted to stay close to them in case they woke. She figured if they did, she would do her best to get them to eat and drink something.

* * *

The goat wasn't as bad as Riley thought, but the best part of the meal was the tortillas. Mexican food was her favorite and in her book; there was nothing better than homemade tortillas. She would have to ask Lupe how to make them so she could have them whenever she wanted. She was standing by the fence, looking out at the Clydesdale, thinking how magnificent he was. He had come over to her several times, allowing her the privilege of petting him. She climbed on the top of the fence railing, waiting for him to come back. The fence moved, startling Riley, making her grab hold of the railing. She turned to see what was causing the movement and saw Annie, Landon, and Bram.

"Hey, Mom, how's it going? Wow, he's pretty!" Annie said in awe of the horse.

"I think you mean handsome, and yes, he is," her mother corrected.

"Are we seriously taking the horses? That's so cool. Can we take them hunting?" Landon asked.

"I'm not sure you even know how to ride one of these guys, let alone take them hunting. But with that said, I asked Alejandro if he would teach us, which he's agreed to do."

"Yes!" Landon couldn't wait.

Riley smiled at him. She realized the events of the last twenty-four hours were forgotten momentarily, and she was glad for it. This place was heaven on earth, and she hated the fact they had to leave. People were counting on them, and she wouldn't let them down. They would return to Calumet tomorrow. Riley couldn't wait to see the look on all their faces when they arrived home with a mountain instead of a hill. More people, eggs – she smiled when she thought about the eggs. She almost busted into a huge grin, thinking of the horses, when all of a sudden, she had a huge head in her lap that almost knocked her off the fence. She hung on to the ears of the monstrous head of the Clydesdale, the very thing that threatened to knock her off, with everything she had. All three of the teenagers couldn't help but laugh.

"Whoa there, big guy!" Riley was leaning back with her feet locked in the rail just below her. Bram was behind her and helped push her forward.

"I think he likes you, Mom," Annie offered, still laughing.

"Well, I 'love' him. He's a beauty, that's for sure. I don't know how we are going to do it, but we are taking him with us," she assured them.

"Anderson is handy with tools and wood. He'll make some kind of enclosure for them. We're going to help Alejandro load his flatbed truck up with hay and food for all the critters. Enough to get them through the winter," Bram informed her.

"Have any of you gotten any rest today?" Riley was concerned for all of them.

"You mean like a nap? *No!* We're not two. We'll sleep well enough tonight, no doubt. Anyway, just looking at this guy is relaxing enough." Landon reached over to pet the big head of the Clydesdale. "What's his name?"

"Duke. Apparently, the owner was a huge John Wayne fan. All the horses are named after movies that he did. Even the ranch is named after a movie," she told him.

"John Wayne? Who's that?" Bram asked.

"Okay, you have led a sheltered life if you don't know who John Wayne is," Riley was still loving on Duke.

Annie laughed, "Um, Mom, I don't know who he his."

Riley sighed. She looked at Duke, saying, "I failed my children, Duke. They have gone through life not knowing who the Duke is."

All three of the kids laughed. They heard voices coming from behind them. When they turned to see who it was, they saw Allen, Mitch, and Kevin coming their way.

"Wow, he's a beauty!" Mitch was astounded at the size of Duke.

"Yes, he is," Riley agreed.

"Alejandro wants to go to a ranch just down the road and get his female," Kevin said as he looked at Duke.

"He has a female somewhere? You mean like a girlfriend?" Annie was pleasantly surprised.

"Yeah, apparently, they were meant to be bred. Alejandro said the neighbor bought his because these people had Duke. He has been caring for the animals there and doesn't want to leave them where they'll starve. Alejandro needs help and asked if some of us would go with him while the rest of us start loading the flatbed, horse trailer, and trucks," Kevin told Riley.

"Okay," Riley gave the huge head in her lap a big squeeze and then pushed it away so she could climb down, "Allen, you and Landon go with him. The rest of us will start loading. If that works for everyone? Oh, and take guns just in case."

Everyone agreed to the arrangements and headed back to the house. Riley stopped for a moment to check on Kota and Jesse. They both were doing much better. Lupe gave Riley some broth for the two boys, and she managed to get most of it down them. Jesse also took his antibiotics with the juice that had the electrolytes in it. They were on the mend, and that was a relief for Riley. Jena sat with Riley while she fed them. She was so happy to see them eat. Kevin helped Kota walk to the side of the barn so he could use the restroom, which Riley thought was a very good sign. Once she was satisfied, she continued on with the rest of the group. When they got to the house, Alejandro was waiting. Allen and Landon grabbed their guns on the way to the house and told Alejandro that they were ready to go.

"Don't you need the trailer?" Riley asked Alejandro.

"No, we take trailer from Harper's place. It's good one. We take it so we have plenty room for animals," he explained to Riley.

"Oh, okay. Guys, I know I don't need to tell you this, but please be careful," Riley said. Alejandro didn't say what happened to the Harpers, but she hoped they weren't home dead.

"No worries, Mom, we'll be careful," Landon reassured his mother.

After the three of them left, the rest went to work on loading the hay and the other food for the animals. The chickens were put four to a cage. There was a fair amount of spare lumber that they took to be used to house the chickens and goats. What they were going to do with the horses, Riley didn't know. They came here with five vehicles but would be leaving with eight. This meant Mitch's son, Greyson, would be driving as well as Landon. They would be pulling two horse trailers and one very large flatbed and would need to stay on the main roads to make it more comfortable for the animals. She figured it would take them two, perhaps three, hours to get to the camp with this load. Riley was ready. She missed her daughter Sara and her parents. She knew they would be worried about them and didn't want that worry to linger. She would have everyone ready to go early in the morning so they could get back to the camp long before noon tomorrow.

It took them until well after dark to get everything loaded. Lupe was a canner too and had a lot of food that needed to be packed up to go with them. Lupe wanted them to take the large filtering unit in the hopes they could find a way to use it, and Riley was happy to oblige her. Lupe also packed more towels, blankets, and sheets. They decided to take two sofas, a love seat, and two recliners for camp Mercy. Mercy didn't have much in the way of furniture and could use them. Doing that meant they had to reload the rental truck so everything would fit.

Riley noticed that Allen, Landon, and Alejandro hadn't come back yet, and that worried her. She would give them another hour and then go find them. Her worry was for nothing as they showed up thirty minutes into her hour deadline. They arrived back with another truck and a trailer that was beyond massive. Alejandro was driving it and headed for the barn. Allen and Landon were in the truck behind him. Riley was totally amazed at the sight. She walked over to have a look at the trailer and the new addition to their flock.

"Can I give you a hand?" she asked Alejandro as he got out of the truck.

Landon and Allen came over and were standing next to her.

"Sure, she very pretty, this one. Very sweet," Alejandro said as he pulled out what Riley thought was the walk board or plank for the horse, then he opened one of the side doors and went into the trailer.

"This is really nice, isn't it?" Allen remarked to Riley.

"Yes. I know nothing about horses or their trailers, but this one looks like a luxury liner of all trailers." She was amazed at its size. "And this big lady is a beauty. What's her name?"

"Jefe called her Maureen, sometimes Senora O'Hara," Alejandro informed her.

Riley got a big laugh out of that. "Well, the name fits her with that beautiful red coat. And with the man's obvious love of all things John Wayne, it doesn't surprise me. I love it, and I love her! She is something. Have they bred yet?"

Alejandro smiled and said, "Yes, she's pregnant. Couldn't leave her. We freed others, so they no starve. Winter coming, hopefully, they be okay."

Riley remembered the scene of some of the ranches along the road. Some dead, some doing well.

"If they survive, we'll come back for them. We'll be moving after winter to a more permanent place. So we'll make sure they are in the planning when we move."

Allen was surprised but happy to hear it. "You have something in mind?"

"Yes. Jackson," she said it as if it was common knowledge.

"You mean the town of Jackson and not your husband?" he asked, surprised.

Riley thought a moment about her husband but then answered Allen, "Yes, the town. It's big, and we need a place to grow. If there are survivors, we'll ask them to let us in, and if there aren't, we'll take it, making it ours. And then hopefully, we'll find more people that want to live again and not just survive. It's for our kids. They need a home, a place with security. We also need room because our little shanty town can't hold much more. And I don't know about you, but I would like some normality back in my life."

"I'm all for it! I know my wife and girls will be happy to hear the news," he said with relief in his voice, then smiling, "I mean, we would have stayed as long as you wanted to, but I was hoping there was going to be an end to our sleeping on an air mattress."

Riley laughed, "You're not kidding!"

Alejandro had Maureen out of the trailer and handed the reins to Riley. She was happy to lead the beautiful mom to be into the barn. Alejandro had an empty stall waiting for her. Once she was out and the trailer doors closed, Alejandro had Allen back the other truck up to another very large horse trailer so that it could be hitched up. With that done, everything would be ready for the animals in the morning. It was late, and morning would arrive early for everyone. Riley was tired, and she knew everyone else had to be too. Bram and Greyson had already moved Kota and Jesse in the house hours ago. Once back at the house, Lupe told them there were six bedrooms and showed them where they were. Mitch and his family chose to sleep in the travel trailer they brought with them. This left the bedrooms to be split up by the rest. The teenage boys slept on the floor downstairs so they could keep an eye on Kota and Jesse. Riley and Levi slept in a room with twin beds. Annie and Jena shared a room with bunks. Kevin and Allen each graciously accepted one of the spare rooms. Riley couldn't believe there was one room not in use. She relished the thought of having one night to remember what it felt like to sleep in a regular bed. When Riley's head hit the pillow, she was out cold.

CHAPTER 8

Landon gently shook his mother, "Hey, Mom, it's time to get up. The animals are almost loaded."

"What? What do you mean?" Riley was confused, and it took a moment for her to realize where she was. Rubbing her eyes, she noticed something was in bed with her. She couldn't focus at first. Once her vision cleared, she saw a small form lying next to her. It was Levi. She cleared her thoughts.

"Why didn't you wake me earlier?"

"Allen and Kevin said to let you sleep a little longer. Oh, Kota and Jesse are awake."

"What? That's great news!" She moved as quickly as she could out of bed, trying not to wake Levi. "Well, I haven't had that in a while." She smiled, looking down at Levi tangled up in the covers.

Landon chuckled, "No, I guess not. I guess I have a new little brother, huh?"

"He's definitely a keeper. Um, you want to grab him for me please?"

"Sure, no problem." Landon moved the covers and picked the little guy up.

Riley kissed his little bald head before she headed out of the bedroom. Annie and Jena both came out of their room at the same time. Jena looked a thousand times better. Riley had both of the girls, along with herself, take a bath in the tub at the barn. It felt good to soak in the tub even with the freezing water. She thought how odd it was that bathing could have such an effect on a person. Walking down the stairs with the girls, she prayed this would be a really good day and they would make it home safely. When she stepped outside, it was still dark. She could see the silhouettes of bodies moving all around, finishing the last of the packing. Lupe came up to her and handed her a stuffed burrito, which was still warm.

"Thank you so much, Lupe. What's in it?" Riley's mouth started to water.

"*Huevos con queso*," Lupe said.

"*Queso?*" Riley asked.

"*Si, queso de cabra*," she smiled.

"Wow, goat cheese. Yummy. Thank you, Lupe, thank you very much!" Riley was very happy to have an egg and cheese burrito of any kind. "Did you make the goat cheese?"

Lupe was happy Riley liked it. "*Si*, I make. Goats good for much things."

"This taste so good, Lupe." Riley took another bite.

Allen and Mitch came over as she was biting into her breakfast. "You're in for a treat there, Riley. Those burritos are wonderful."

The spices mixed in with the eggs and goat cheese were a flavor sensation that burst in her mouth. She closed her eyes for a moment to enjoy it. Both of the men laughed, as did Lupe. She didn't care how silly she looked eating it; it was delicious.

"I have no regrets stopping here and meeting Lupe and Alejandro. None at all!" She took another bite, and both men laughed again.

She walked and ate while Allen and Mitch talked. They told her what had been done, that they were almost ready to go, and Allen gave her an update on Kota and Jesse. Lupe was able to get them to take some more broth this morning, but once Kota saw the burritos, he wanted one. He could only eat half of one and Jesse had the other half. Allen said their backs weren't as inflamed as they were yesterday, that he thought the salve was working. Riley was very happy to hear that.

Once she swallowed the last bite, she asked, "Do they want to ride in the back of the truck or ride inside one of the vehicles?"

Mitch said, "I offered them a ride in the travel trailer, and they said no, that they would stay in the back of the truck. Both of them felt that their backs couldn't take leaning up against anything now."

"Yeah, and, Riley, they're asking about Sheryl," Allen added.

"Oh, boy, they're alert now and probably won't stop asking. I'm afraid, if someone doesn't tell them, Jena will, and she shouldn't have to relive that. Not now. She looks so much better." Riley looked around. "Where are they?"

"Already in the back of the truck," Allen informed her.

"Thanks, I'll handle it." She said walking toward the truck.

She saw both of the young men sitting on the tailgate. She knew there was no good way to tell them what happened, and she wouldn't lie to them or sugarcoat it. She would tell them everything. When she approached them, the first thing she asked was if they remembered her, and both replied yes. Then she proceeded to tell them the horrible story of what happened to their good friend Sheryl. When she was done, both cried and repeatedly said how sorry they were. They had tried to help both her and Jena but had failed. Riley did her best to convince them that it wasn't their fault, that the fault lay squarely on the shoulders of the men who had done this to them. She let them know that Jena was okay and had been down to sit with them while they slept and that she held no ill feeling toward either of them. Why Jena did better than Sheryl, she said she didn't know. But if there was any comfort in her death at all, it was that she punished the men who raped her by taking their lives first. She expressed to them that if Jena could move forward from this, as hard as it would be for them, that they needed to as well.

Riley concluded, "A lot of people have died because of the virus and many more because of people like the ones in Vernal. I killed a man a few months back, and that was something I never thought I would do in my life. This world of ours is nothing like it once was. Right now, all we're trying to do is survive. My prayer is that we can get out of survival mode and get back to living once again. I hope that once you're well, you will stay with us. There are forty-one people waiting for us back in our two camps. I want us to grow. We're stronger in numbers. So I hope you'll consider that and stay with us."

Kota and Jesse didn't have to think about it. They both said they would stay. Riley couldn't express how happy she was to hear that. She said she would give them a hug, but she didn't want to hurt them. They both gave a half smile and said they would take that hug another day. She smiled at them briefly then left them as there was nothing more to say. It would take time for them to heal physically and mentally. The scarring on their backs would be a constant reminder that would last them a lifetime.

They got on the road around five. Allen said he would drive the first horse trailer out followed by Alejandro. Landon took over driving the gas tanker, and Greyson drove the truck, hauling the flatbed, carrying everything that couldn't fit in the horse trailers or trucks. Every vehicle was packed in tight. Riley was impressed with how well they managed to squeeze everything in. She knew everyone was ready to get back to camp to see family and friends. And heading home with everything they had was an extra added bonus.

Mitch's wife rode with Riley. She told her husband she wanted to get to know Riley, and felt this was the best time to do so. Riley liked the company, as Jena and Levi's conversations were spotty at best. Riley let Angela do most of the talking, and Angela was happy to divulge her life's story. She was originally from Denver but moved to Fort Collins a few years ago. Mitch was from South Beach, Florida, and wanted to get away from the beach, so he moved to the mountains. That was how they met. Greyson was going to the University of Colorado in Boulder when the outbreak got so bad that his dad asked him to come home. Because Colorado was a huge tourist state, the virus made its way there very quickly. Close friends called to say that their entire family was sick. Then Angela said they didn't hear from anyone anymore. Mitch managed to get enough supplies for the first month, but then things got worse. People started killing one another and raping women who were just out looking for food for their children. It was horrible for her and the girls. She said she felt trapped or in prison because they couldn't leave their house. It wasn't until Mitch started to get on the radio that they realized it wasn't just happening in Fort Collins, but it was happening everywhere.

Riley cringed at that. Remembering they had forgotten about their radio, she was now glad that they did. Had they heard this news any earlier, they wouldn't have left the camp for anything. Leaves would have been the toilet paper of choice. She thought about their group totals now. Fifty-eight people. It was a nice mix of women and men, young kids and teenagers, single and married. This was a start, but the unknown left them with no guarantees, and she didn't like that. She guessed there was one guarantee: that nothing was ever going to be the same.

* * *

The dust cloud was huge, announcing to everyone from both camps that someone was coming. At the sight of the dust, Anderson and Ken ran to get their guns. They ran over to the entrance to the camp to stand their ground. Both men were standing in the middle of the road when they caught sight of a truck hauling a massive horse trailer.

"Riley, what have you brought with you, a rodeo?" Anderson spoke his thoughts out loud.

"There's no telling with that girl of mine," Ken replied.

Both men stepped out of the way, waving as one vehicle after another pulled into Calumet. Ken and Anderson were stunned. There were two enormous horse trailers with horses in them, a flatbed stacked high, a large rental, a tanker, and a travel trailer along with Riley's SUV and another truck. They couldn't believe their eyes. People from both camps marveled at the sight of the caravan pulling in. When the vehicles stopped, everyone happily greeted the journeymen and women, as the case may be, back home.

Sara and Riley's parents greeted her as soon as she stepped out of the SUV. Riley gave Sara a big hug then one to each of her parents. It was so good to see them. Annie, Landon, and Bram came over, joining in the reunion.

Anderson met Riley with a hug too and said, "You know how to make an entrance, Riley, I'll give you that."

She smiled at him while latching on to his arm directing him over to Kevin's truck. Kevin was already in the back, helping Kota up. Anderson saw his back, stopped, then took off running to the back end of the truck.

"Here, I'll give ya a hand, Kevin. What happened, mate? Oh... geez, there's two of them! What happened to them?"

Anderson was completely unprepared for the sight that was before him. He quickly took control of his emotions while he helped Kevin get the two men down. They carefully walked them over to one of the chairs by the kitchen. Victoria and Agnes took over their care immediately and began to tend to them.

With the sight of Kota and Jesse, everyone fell silent. Some gasped when they saw their backs. Riley thought it was probably a good idea to get people moving and asked everyone to come around.

That got the attention off of the two young men as they gathered around Riley.

"I'm going to delegate some jobs, and those jobs will have team leaders. If you think you would be a better fit with one group over another, then please feel free to work in that group." Riley paused for a moment. "Anderson is very handy with a hammer, so anyone that can help him, we need pens built for the livestock. My mother and Agnes will head up the food group. Becca, Dina, Carolyn, and Lisa, I'll let you take care of the clothes. Also, ladies, we have some furniture that will be going to Mercy. Alejandro, you are in charge of the animals. Landon and Bram, you'll help him. The rest of you, pick a group, and let's get started. We can rest when we're done."

Riley went over to help Alejandro. "Looking at what we have, where do you want to put the animals and supplies?"

"Is very nice here. The hay over here maybe, between trees. It's okay." He looked at Riley as if he had asked her a question.

"That works. Boys, let's put the hay over there." Then Riley thought, *This is going to be one long backbreaking day.*

It was several hours before they got everything done. Victoria and Agnes welcomed Lupe with open arms. With their large kitchen staff of young girls, they had a wonderful meal prepared for everyone. It felt good to be back with family and friends. Their little community was growing, and that felt good. Riley was standing off from the group, leaning against a tree close to the horse corral, watching all the people interact with one another. It was relaxing, listening to all the chatter from people talking and laughing. She could hear Duke behind her and then felt his breath in her hair tickling her. She reached back for his nose when he brought it over her shoulder and around to the side of her face. He was gentle with Riley and rubbed his muzzle against her cheek.

"Hey there, big fella." She spun around to pet him and gave him a big kiss on the nose.

"He like you very much," Alejandro said. "Horses, like people, find friends and friends for life. You his friend, Jefe, Duke like you very much."

Jefe didn't pass by Riley, but she didn't know how to handle that right now so she let it go.

"Well, I'm in love with him, Alejandro." She gave Duke another kiss on the nose.

"Jefe, *mi esposa* wants to know if you okay, we sleep in horse trailer," he asked.

"Horse trailer?" She was shocked at the request. "Alejandro, you're not servants, and I get that everyone here is white, but you'll sleep in a cabin in your own room. Becca and her kids are moving in with us. Carolyn, her two boys, and the other young women in the cabin are happy to have you," she reassured him.

"We no want to be a problem. It's okay." He looked concerned.

"No, you and Lupe are not a problem. Becca and her kids have moved out already. Please come. I'd love to show you." She gave one last squeeze to Duke, then they walked together to the third cabin and entered.

Kelly was there with Jena, trying to get her settled too. They both said hi, and once introductions were made, Riley took him into the back and showed him his and Lupe's room.

"I'm sorry, it's not much, especially after living in the house you were living in, but it will have to do for now," Riley told him.

"No, it's very good. We no need much, just a place to rest our heads." Riley could see Alejandro was truly grateful.

"There are girls sleeping in the loft above you, and Carolyn and her boys are sleeping in this room next door. We all eat together and sleep together, unfortunately, but it'll only be through the winter, I promise, then we'll find a more permanent place to live," Riley sounded hopeful.

"Okay, Jefe, you the boss, we stay here. *Gracias,*" he said with gratitude.

"Not a problem. Oh, Alejandro, you have a lot of kids that want to help you with the animals. I think it would be good for them to help you and learn everything they can about them. Would you mind teaching them?" Riley thought for a moment. "For that matter, would you teach all of us how to care for the animals?"

"Sure, sure, no problem. I teach you. No problem," Alejandro reassured her.

"Good, now go get your wife so the two of you can get moved in." Riley smiled at her own bossiness.

CHAPTER 9

Breakfast was amazing. Lupe made soup with the leftover goat and more of her now-famous egg and goat cheese burritos. Riley could only get half the soup down her and one burrito. She thought if she wasn't careful, Lupe's cooking would put all the weight that she lost back on her. Then she thought about all the work she did yesterday and felt a little indulgence was okay. She put the last of the dishes up from breakfast and thought a walk would be nice. She wondered if it would be okay to take Duke with her. Riley found Alejandro and asked him if she could walk Duke down to the lake. He said that it was a good idea to take the horse out every day if possible. He showed her how to get him ready for his daily dose of exercise. Riley walked the massive beast down the path to the lake, letting him eat and drink at his leisure. She could tell he was happy to be out of the small horse corral. A few times, he even got playful, head butting her in the back, making Riley laugh. Even though it was cold this morning, she loved being outside. The beauty of the day with the crisp air felt good, and to be sharing it with Duke made it even more beautiful. Seeing him stand with the lake and mountains in the background took her breath away. Riley's serenity was interrupted by Goliath as he bounded down the path with Allen, Anderson, Lyle, and her father following. She knew they were coming for her.

"Hi, guys, what's up?"

Allen took the lead. "Hey, Riley, I didn't tell you this when I found out, but now we're home, I think it's important you know. I thought they should hear it too."

He had Riley's attention. "What is it, Allen?"

"While we were in Vernal and I was cleaning Levi up, I asked him some questions about his family. You remember when he said he tried to wake his family but he couldn't?" Riley nodded her head. "Well, I think he's not only a survivor, but I think he's immune to the virus." He let that sink in for a minute. "I'm concerned for his safety, not that I think anyone here would do anything to him. However, I think we should probably keep this quiet."

Why she hadn't thought about that, she didn't know. This was paramount, and yes, they definitely needed to keep this quiet. For the sake of Levi's safety.

"You're right, Allen, this can't be shared right now. When the time is right and only if we need it to be known, then we'll say something. No one in our group is showing signs of being sick. I mean, he's been sleeping with me, and I feel fine. So he's not contagious, this means no one needs to know about this right now."

"Yeah, everyone seems fine. I'm sure we'll run into more people that are immune, but Levi is just a kid, and I, for one, want him protected." Allen's fatherly concern came out for the young boy.

Duke and Goliath were getting to know one another. Riley looked in their direction, and it brought a smile to her face. All the men looked in the same direction to see what she was smiling at. When they saw the sight of dog and horse, they all smiled too.

Riley brought the conversation back, "No one leaves the camp until the first of spring. We have more than enough to get us through the next several months. We took a big risk going out so soon. For now, the radio is only to be listened to by one of us or Norman. If people are in trouble, we stay put but can give verbal assistance, and that's it. I'll have patrols going out to make sure no one is too close to us, especially now that we have the horses. Once people get trained on them, we can use them for extended patrols." Riley remembered something that she was thinking about on the way home yesterday and needed to share it with the men. "Also, the five of us are the council for these two camps. Sorry, our camp outnumbers Mercy on the council, Lyle and Allen."

They looked at her, then smiled, as did Ken and Anderson.

"What?" she asked.

"Nothing, it's even. The four of us, and one leader," Ken said, pointing at Riley, "one bossy leader."

"Ha-ha, you're funny, Dad."

All the men laughed. Riley was embarrassed and changed the subject.

"What does the council think about finding a more permanent place to live once spring is here?"

Allen was the only one that knew of her plan, and it showed on their faces.

Allen jumped in, "Riley mentioned it while we were coming back from Vernal. I think it's a great idea. We need more room, especially if we're going to move out of survival mode back to living. We need to find a safe place to live. Riley thought of one place already, but since she's throwing it out there, this will give all of us some time to think of other places. Then we can start a conversation about what we want to do."

"What place did you have in mind, Riley?" her father was curious.

"Jackson."

"The town of Jackson? That's a big place to start with, don't you think?" her father continued with his questioning.

"It is, but we can clean out the city of any bodies, or if there are survivors, we can ask to join them. But knowing that it's a tourist town, I don't think there will be a lot of people left. Vernal was wiped out due to the traffic of people going to see the dinosaur fossils. And knowing that it only takes one person to bring the virus in, I'm sure Jackson was hit hard."

"But the springtime? Don't you think that's a bit early?" Lyle inquired.

"Actually, when the Bubonic Plague hit Europe, it was around for years. But in some of the coldest places, the plague came and went. Rodents and mosquitos died out, which helped end the plague in those areas. Of course, in the day, there was no proof, but many believe that the cold is what killed the plague." She paused. "And when I say clean the city out, I mean the rodents as well. Rats and mice, anyway," Riley finished, leaving the men to think about what she said for a minute.

"Look," she continued, "it's going to be a disgusting job, and not everyone is going to be able to do it. That means it's going to be a slow process. Four or five houses at first. We'll clean them out completely, burn everything, scrub everything down with bleach, or rip the walls out. I don't care. Then the rest, we can take our time with. We'll have plenty of time for it."

All the men thought about what she said.

Anderson spoke up, "It's good oil, mates, it doesn't matter where we go, cleaning out houses is what we have ta do. We might get lucky and find some that no one was living in at the time of the outbreak. Building from the ground up would be a heap of work. I know I don't have to ask, but I'm askin', who would go in to check things out? Most everyone here is scared and won't want to go."

Anderson and Ken both knew what Riley was going to say before she said it.

"I will and any volunteers. I'm sure Jackson has a funeral home with a crematorium in it, and if not, we'll dig a deep hole, throw the bodies in, burn them, then bury them. Maybe put a monument up in honor of the townspeople or something."

"You're going to cremate nine thousand plus people?" her father asked.

"Uh, not all at once. But yes. If that's how many we find, then that's how many we'll cremate," she said as a matter of fact.

Anderson shook his head. "Okay, count me in, Riley, and no, this time you can't ask me to stay. I volunteer now so there is no confusion later." Anderson was adamant, and Riley knew she wouldn't be able to talk him out of it.

"Well, we have a few months before we go. Now let's just make this place secure. We also have Thanksgiving and Christmas coming, and I would like to have those days of celebrations part of our lives here. We've missed a few birthdays due to everything that has been going on. Let's not forget anymore. Okay?"

She knew birthdays were a trivial thing, but it was a day of recognition, especially for the children. It was important that they bring some of the old life back in to their lives now. As far as Thanksgiving, they had a lot to be thankful for, and Christmas was a must. The birth of Jesus was always going to be celebrated. With all of the secular stuff gone now, it would be a day of worship and celebration. Gifts were going to be a thing of the past as there were no stores for shopping. Knowing her mother, she would find a way to make it special for all the families. She looked at the men, and they seemed to be in agreement.

Lyle had one more thing to say before their meeting was over. "In the same line of thinking, my wife wanted to know if she could organize a dance or a social of some kind?"

Riley was surprised but thought it would be a great idea. "Sure, I don't know why not. I think it's a great idea!"

Duke came over to Riley and butted her in the back. She laughed, telling everyone, "I guess the meeting is adjourned, gentlemen."

Riley turned and tried to give him a hug but couldn't wrap her arms around any part of him. He put his head down, and she hugged it. Allen came up and patted Duke on the side, just as Goliath came up, demanding his attention. He obliged him.

"I'm glad we brought the animals, they've been therapeutic for everyone," Allen said as he looked at Duke. "I would like to be part of the patrol, if that's okay with you."

"Sure, and if someone else from Mercy wants to do it too, just let me know. We've already started a foot patrol today. Annie, Tony, Landon, and Bram have already gone out to have a good look around," Riley said.

Lyle thought a moment and then said, "I'll ask around and see if anyone wants to pitch in. Like Allen, I would like to join in on the patrols too."

* * *

Lisa and Dina, along with a few ladies from Calumet, managed to get a dance organized before it got too cold. The ladies thought the clearing by the lake was a wonderful place to have it. With the solar lights, along with the four small fires Landon and Bram made around the dance area, it was pretty well lit up. Chairs were set out along with tables that were filled with food and drinks. Alice Crawford brought some of her decorations from her cabin to decorate the tables. The kids made handmade decorations that were added around the dance area. Ken had Sara charge her MP3 player and speakers so they would have music. With what little they had, the women managed to make everything beautiful. The night sky was clear, and though in jackets, everyone was happy and ready for a night on the town.

Riley walked around on the outside edge to watch as everyone enjoyed themselves. She thought about Jackson and how he would love this. She said a silent prayer for his and Ursula's safety and also thanked God for keeping all these people safe. She heard someone walk up next to her, which brought her thoughts back to her surroundings. It was Kevin.

"Hi, Riley, why aren't you joining in with the festivities?"

"Hey, Kevin, I'm enjoying myself just watching. Why aren't you out there dancing?"

"Well, I thought I would ask you to dance," he said.

"Ah," she laughed, "I'm not very good at dancing," she explained.

"Don't worry, I'm good at leading." He held out his hand.

Riley was hesitant and then accepted it. "Sure, thanks, Kevin."

They walked out to the dance floor, joining those already dancing. Riley hadn't danced since her wedding, but she quickly found her footing. She began to loosen up and started to enjoy herself. It felt good to let the worries of the world go for a few moments. Those worries would still be waiting for her when she was done. When the song was over, she thanked Kevin. But before her words were completely out, Anderson had her around her waist, pulling her back to the dance floor. Kevin was surprised how rudely Anderson cut in but let it pass. Riley was on the floor, dancing for the rest of the night. Kevin tried to get another dance with her, but everyone wanted to dance with Riley, so he stood back and watched. The cold air was forgotten, and half the people had taken their coats off. Everyone was having so much fun that the party went on well into the night.

When Riley finally slowed down, she noticed Levi had fallen asleep in a chair. He had his fill of dancing and eating, Riley thought. She looked for Landon but instead found Kevin next to her.

"Would you like to dance again?" he asked.

Riley smiled at him. "Thank you, but no, I have a kid over there that I need to get to bed. I was looking for Landon to see if he would give me a hand getting him to the cabin."

"Here, let me. I'll be happy to take him for you."

"Thanks, Kevin. I would really appreciate that."

He walked over to pick Levi up. Riley saw Becca rounding up her kids too. She was walking toward Riley when Kevin came up with Levi. They walked over to the cabin together, leaving all the noise behind them. Ahead of them were Alice and Simon, taking their grandchildren home.

"That was fun, wasn't it?" Becca asked no one in particular.

"It was fun. I'm not sure who had more fun, the kids or the adults." Riley thought about Levi and knew he had had a blast. She had too.

Kevin was quiet on the walk up to the cabin. Riley thought it was strange as he seemed to always have something to say.

The silence was broken by Timothy, "I had fun, but I'm tired. Can we sleep in tomorrow, Aunt Becca? Please Aunt Becca?"

Becca laughed, "Sure, buddy, but those animals will miss you feeding them. I'll feed them for you just this once."

"Um, never mind, Aunt Becca, I'll get up to feed them. They are the best part of my day. Ms. Riley, will you get me up when you get up please?" Timothy was now facing Riley, pleading with her.

Riley reached over and messed up his hair. "Sure, but I get up early."

"That's okay. I like to play with the goats," he said happily.

When they all made it to the cabins, Riley reached over to take Levi. Kevin said he had him, and he walked into the cabin with them. Riley went up to the loft after Becca got her lot up there and had Kevin hand Levi up to her. She got him changed and put him into bed. When she was done, she went back down to walk Kevin out. Jesse was in his bed on the floor. Kevin didn't realize he was even there until Riley walked over to check on him. Jesse mumbled something to Riley as she stroked his hair and bent down to kiss the top of his head. Kevin was amazed at the affection Riley had for not only Levi but Kota and Jesse too.

Once they were outside, Riley shut the door and turned to walk back to the dance when, out of nowhere, Kevin kissed her. Riley pulled back, hitting her head on the door. She grabbed her head and said, "Ouch." Riley's other hand went up to Kevin's chest, pushing him off of her.

"Kevin, please!" she whispered in shock.

"Why? You have to know how I feel about you," his voice was rising.

"Uh, no, I don't! How would I know that?" she said, still whispering and stepping further away from him.

"I go to Vernal with you, stick to you like glue. I work with you daily! We talk, we confide in one another! You have to know," he said with his voice raised.

Riley was angry now and looked at him square in the eyes. "I'm married, Kevin! My husband is out there somewhere. You know that!"

"It's not that! It's because of what I did to your daughter, isn't it? Or Anderson? It's him, isn't it? You're in love with Anderson!" Kevin was fuming now.

"Wow! Where is this coming from, Kevin? I work side by side with a lot of people, and I'm pretty sure I'm not in love with any of them or them with me." Riley was talking in a loud whisper now. "And I am not in love with Anderson nor him with me. We're just good friends, which I thought you and I were. And where have you been? Is my faith not out there for you to see? Do you think I'm going to shame my faith by having an affair? You're calling me a hypocrite! I haven't done anything to make you think I had feelings for you, I know I haven't! Lastly, I forgave you for your part on that horrible day with Bruce and AJ. Just as my daughter has!"

Riley knew Kevin's reasoning was way off. He just stood there and looked at her with anger flaring from his eyes.

"I've watched you with Anderson. I see the way you talk in whispers to each other. How you quit talking when I walk up. It's obvious! And I'm pretty sure your husband is dead anyway!"

After those last words came out of his mouth, he realized his mistake. He had taken it too far, and if there was any way to recover from this, he had just nailed it shut with those final words. He said nothing more. The look on Riley's face said it all. Her tears were flowing, and the hurt was beyond anything he had seen. Riley was in love with her husband, and he could see it now. What was he thinking? He just destroyed a friendship in a few short seconds.

"I'm sorry, Riley. I was way out of line. I'm so sorry. You're a beautiful woman, and I just thought, I don't know what I was thinking. I'm sorry, I'm…I'm going." Kevin turned and walked quickly away.

Riley leaned against the wall of the cabin and slid down to the ground. She was shocked, angry, and very sad all at once. She just sat and cried. Becca cracked opened the door.

"Did he leave?"

Riley didn't look at her. Wiping her eyes on the inside of her coat she whispered, "Yes."

Becca came out of the cabin, slid down next to her, and draped her arm around Riley. Riley let herself fall into Becca's embrace.

"Riley, I know this isn't going to help, but I still have hope about my sister and brother-in-law. I can't believe they're dead. I won't believe it! So don't give up hope because of something Kevin said. I've seen the same things that Kevin has seen with you and Anderson, but never once did I think there was something romantic going on. You're our leaders, and there are things to be discussed that don't involve anyone else right now. There isn't a soul in either of these camps that doesn't trust you. And as far as your faith, I never knew what a true Christian was until I met you. Anderson says your 'fair dinkum,' he said that means you're the real deal, genuine, and I have to agree." She paused for a moment then finished with, "I think Kevin is lonely, that's all."

Riley pulled away from Becca, sniffling, and thought about what she said.

"Thanks, Becca. It does matter that you are holding out hope for your sister and her husband. I miss my husband, and I know that if anyone can survive this, he can. That's if he got out of Bakersfield. But you know one thing I'm not? I'm not lonely. With my kids and the new additions to my family with Levi, Kota, Jesse, Jena, and the rest of you, I'm okay. Having someone to love me in any way other than that of a mom or a friend hasn't even crossed my mind. I get that people are lonely here. I really get it. Some people have lost their entire families. You can't replace that. Nate and Carolyn have hit it off pretty well, and I thought that was a good thing. But I'm afraid if Jackson doesn't come soon, I will die of old age waiting for him. I hope that doesn't make me a fool?"

"I don't think it does. I think you're in love with your husband and are hoping for the best. I don't think that makes you a fool. It makes you human," Becca explained.

"Do me a favor, Becca?"

"Sure, anything."

"Please don't tell anyone what happened tonight. There's no reason to embarrass Kevin any more than he is."

Riley got up and put her hand out for Becca. Becca took it, and Riley pulled her up. "I was going to head back to the party, but I think I'll go see Duke. Will you keep an eye on Levi?"

"Absolutely, don't worry one minute about him."

* * *

The weather had gone from cold to flat freezing in the weeks that followed. It seemed every morning lately, Riley woke up with a small fist in her face. Levi was in her bed again. She smiled and remembered the time she and Jackson tried to break Sara from coming into their bed. Nothing they did worked. Sara was going to sleep where she wanted, and no one was going to tell her otherwise. Levi had a bed, which he started off in every night; however, every morning he was in bed with Riley. The loft was crowded now that Becca and her kids were up there. If they moved Levi's mattress, they would have more room. She should just take it out and let him sleep with her. She would worry about that later; right now she needed to get up and go start the fire in the kitchen.

She dressed and climbed down the ladder. Riley moved quietly as Kota and Jesse were both asleep on the floor. They were doing much better and would be moving soon. Riley wanted them close in case they needed something but now that they were almost healed, they could be moved into the men's cabin. She felt sad about that. She had fallen in love with both boys as well as Jena. She loved them as she loved her own children. She stood looking at both of them for a moment before she grabbed her coat off the new coat rack Carson and Tony had put in a few days before. She opened the door to find it was snowing. The snow was big heavy flakes, which were absolutely beautiful. She shivered as she stepped outside and shut the door. It was dark, and she wished she had remembered the lantern since the solar lights had long since gone out. Zipping up her coat, she slowly made her way over to the kitchen. Once she found the door, she slid the latch open, stepped inside, then closed the door behind her. That simple action of shutting the door behind her brought back the memory of the unwanted kiss that took place a few weeks earlier. She and Kevin hadn't spoken to each other very much since that night, and that was fine with her. Riley sighed, thinking to herself that it was just one more thing to forgive and forget, but as in all things unwanted, it seemed to linger. She shook her head, as if shaking the thought of the kiss out of it. The kitchen was very cold and dark, which brought her back to the task at hand. She started the big fire first, in the hopes of warming up the place, then the stove. Once both fires were going, she put the water on, then grabbed one of the lanterns from the kitchen and went out to check the animals. Riley saw a streak of light bouncing around, coming toward her and then heard Alejandro and Lupe speaking softly in Spanish.

"Good morning. You two are up early," Riley was cheerful.

"*Buenos dias, Jefe*. No more sleep. Come to check animals and start fire," Alejandro told her.

"Fires are started, and water is on. I was just heading over to the animals," Riley told them.

Alejandro said something to Lupe that Riley didn't understand. He handed his wife the flashlight, then she walked over to the kitchen. He turned to Riley, "I go with you, Jefe."

They walked over to the animal's small barn, which only housed the chickens and the goats. The two horse trailers had become two sides of the horse's housing. Anderson had done a wonderful job on the structures. The animals were safe at night from any wild animals that might come by. Together they worked to clean out the stalls, put out fresh water, then feed them. Once they were done with the chickens and goats they moved over to the horses. It took a little longer with the horses because Duke wanted attention. When they were done, Alejandro went into one of the horse trailers only to return a few minutes later with a large saddle which he set on the fence.

"Jefe, this for you."

"For me?" Riley was surprised.

"Duke, too big for other saddle. I take from Harper's place for Duke. Other saddles no fit Duke. I fix this one to fit you." Alejandro was pleased with his gift to Riley.

Riley couldn't believe it. "Wow! Thank you, Alejandro. Thank you very much. So can I ride him today?"

"Sure, you ride every day. No problem," he told her.

Riley couldn't wait for the sun to come up so she could go for a ride. She felt like a kid getting to go to Disneyland for the first time.

After breakfast, Alejandro showed her how to put the saddle on Duke and how to mount him. She had to use some steps to get on him, which Riley found funny. She knew she would never be able to get off of him as she would have no means to get back up on him. And what if she fell off? She laughed at herself, knowing full well if she fell off Duke, it would probably kill her. So getting back on wouldn't matter much anyway.

"Again, Alejandro, thank you so much. I was content just walking him everywhere. I never imagined this," Riley said with a huge smile. She leaned over Dukes neck and whispered into his ear, "It's just you and me, Duke, the rest of the world is officially on hold."

CHAPTER 10

Annie, Landon, and Bram were saddled up. Quivers were filled and tied onto the saddles for both Riley and Annie. They all had backpacks filled with everything they would need for emergencies, as well as the food Riley's mother had prepared for them. They would be gone most of the day, checking out some of the campgrounds that were quite a distance from them. Bram had smelled smoke a few days back but never found where it came from. Today they were going to look northwest in the direction that Bram thought the smoke had come from. Ken gave them a map of the area and told them to be back before dark, and Riley assured him they would. She was a little apprehensive with this being their first long ride without Alejandro. They had never been too far from him before. He was like a security blanket for Riley when it came to the horses, a security blanket that wouldn't be there for them today. The foot patrol was preparing to leave at the same time but in the opposite direction. Riley was happy so many people were helping on patrols. There had been plenty of wildlife sightings so far but no humans. She hoped today would be the same. Everyone bid their farewells and headed out. The early-morning sky was overcast and the air crisp. She loved riding Duke on any day but hoped it wouldn't rain today. He was gentle with Riley like he knew his limits with her, but no matter how gentle he was with her, no horse liked thunder or lightning. She felt a kindred spirit with Duke, which she knew was more one-sided, as he calmed her more than she calmed him. She hoped today's ride would be calming for both of them. Riding him gave her a false sense of incredible human strength. She could feel his power radiate under her which made her feel safe.

They had ridden for several hours when Bram asked everyone to hold up.

"It looks like we are about an hour or so away from a campsite. The smoke I smelled awhile back couldn't have come from this far, could it?"

"Who knows?" Riley doubted it but wasn't sure. "If the wind was right, but honestly, I don't think so. A campfire would dissipate long before it got to us."

Landon looked around but saw nothing. "I think we should still go see the campground that's on the map, at least from a distance."

"Sure," Riley said, "but only from a distance."

Bram got down off his horse. "I'm going to walk for a while. My tail end isn't used to riding, and I'm sure this horse could stand a break from me."

That sounded like a great idea to Riley as she slid off Duke. "Oh, boy, that feels good. One of you will have to give me a lift back up when the time comes. Unless there is a large rock somewhere."

Landon laughed. "I'll give you a boost up."

They walked for about forty-five minutes when they smelled smoke. It was coming from the other side of the ridge. It took them a few minutes to find a good spot that would give them a better view without being seen.

They left the horses tied up to a tree and climbed to the top so they could survey the area. They saw seven motor homes along with several tents. Three motor homes were parked in a horseshoe manner, giving shelter to the tents that were in the center. They had several large tarps tied to either side of the motor homes, giving the tents more protection from the weather. It was thoughtful, Riley thought. They saw a few people mingling around a campfire. Riley saw no food but thought perhaps they cooked inside. None of them looked sick, just cold.

"I'm going to make contact with them. I'll stay on this side so you'll always be able to see me. If something does happen, please don't kill anyone, just aim for the kneecap or something non-life-threatening," she said, waving her arms around as if a shot to the knee was no big deal. "That will let them know I'm not alone and stop them from doing anything else stupid."

Bram went to the horses to retrieve both rifles. He was back within a minute and handed Landon his. They both found an excellent spot to lie and wait. Once both were settled, Riley started to make her move down the slope on what looked like an animal trail of some kind. Annie stayed close to the boys as she watched her mother walk down the trail.

Riley was halfway down when someone from the camp saw her coming. They yelled, sending an alarm throughout the camp. Riley stopped just at the bottom, waiting a few seconds to let the people of the camp get a good look at her. She hoped someone would come out to speak with her. She started to move closer when she finally got her wish. An older gentleman walked toward her but stopped, keeping some distance between them.

"Um, who are you and where did you come from?" he asked.

"I'm Riley. I'm not here to harm you, nor am I sick," Riley told him.

He looked her over, then up the ridge where she came from. "I'm Philip. I'm sorry none of us has seen anyone from the outside world in five months."

Riley was happy to hear that. She quickly reasoned if no one had left the camp, they couldn't be sick either. "I'm actually glad to hear that. The outside world is a scary place right now. If you have been here this long, how are you holding up on food?"

Philip didn't like that question and looked back at his group. "We have enough."

Riley didn't believe him but understood the mistrust. What they did have, they needed. Because she was a stranger, he wasn't going to divulge everything to her on the off chance she was there to rob them.

"I thought if you needed anything like meat, we could help you out. But if you don't need anything, we'll move on."

Philip hesitated a moment and then said, "We could use the help. We're running out of everything, and no one wants to go into town to get anything." He wanted to say more but then stopped. He just stared at Riley for a moment; then the floodgates opened. "Some of our people left, and they never came back. We presume they're dead, either killed or they got sick and wouldn't come back. Most of us here were on our annual camping trip. We usually stay all summer, so for the most part, we had plenty of food, but we weren't prepared to live out the winter here. Some of these people have to live in tents, and I'm not sure if they are going to survive the winter in those flimsy things."

Riley thought about everything he said. "Look, we can help. How many are in your group?"

Philip had to think a moment. "Twenty-six, I think, yes, twenty-six."

"How much gas do you have?"

"We're about out. With the weather turning cold, we've been burning it more, trying to keep warm," he answered.

Riley waved up to where her teenagers were. Philip looked startled.

"Don't worry, they're my kids."

A few minutes later, Annie, Landon, and Bram along with the horses came down to Riley.

"Well, you did say *we*, I should have known there were more of you," Philip said.

Riley smiled at him and then turned to Bram. "Bram, can I have the map please?"

Bram handed her the map. She then walked past Philip right into the camp. Riley could see the fear but said nothing until Philip and her kids were close.

"Hi, I'm Riley, and these are my kids. We're going to see if we can help you." She asked Bram and Landon, "Would you two go see if you can find them some fresh meat? Don't be long. An hour tops. If you can't find anything, we'll think of something else."

"Sure, we'll be back," Landon said. The boys got on their horses and headed back the way they came. Annie was left holding her horse and Duke.

"We are staying in some cabins a few miles away from here, and we have gas but not for heating. And I'm guessing you didn't pack for winter?"

Almost everyone shook their heads no. Riley looked around and then to the tents. "Is there any reason why the people in the tents can't sleep in the motor homes with those of you that own them?"

This time, heads went down in shame, and Riley knew that the young people in the tents were not in the original group that came up with the motor homes. The motor home group thought they were helping by making a wall around the tents and putting the tarps over their heads.

"We can get the gas to you that you need to drive your motor homes over to our camp. But until then, you'll have to let these young people sleep in the motor homes with you, or they'll freeze. Looking at them, they don't even look like they came prepared for winter either. Do you think you can do that?"

Philip looked around the group. He realized that the reason why they never invited them inside was because they were strangers; however, they hadn't been strangers for quite some time.

"Sure, we can, and I'm sorry it's taken someone from the outside to tell us to do so. We should've done that awhile back. I'm truly sorry."

"It will be cold at our camp this winter too, just like here, but we have lots of blankets, winter clothes, and more than enough food to get everyone through the winter. It will take up to a day or so to get it organized and get the truck here with the gas." Riley turned her attention to the young people in the group. "Did you come in cars?"

A young man stepped forward and stuck out his hand, which Riley took. "Hi, I'm Jasper. And yeah, we did, but the people who went into town took both of them, and now we don't have any."

Riley looked at Jasper and then back at Annie. "Where is the town they went to?"

"Mom, Grandpa said to be back before nightfall. If we go looking for the town, we won't make it back in time," Annie was leaning toward her mother when she spoke.

"I know, baby, but we need to look. We won't go in," Riley explained.

"Mom, you said that about this camp, and look where we're standing," Annie said with a smile.

Riley smiled at that and sighed, "Well, we'll have to be flexible then. Now where is that town?"

Everyone in the group looked at one another when Jasper informed Riley, "The town is about thirty to forty-five minutes from here. I can show you on your map." Jasper reached for the map in Riley's hand. "There's a gas station there, and I'm sure we can get one of the motor homes there, get some gas, and then bring some back here for the rest of them." Jasper glanced at everyone in his group, "I don't know about you, but I'm sick of this place. The wolves or coyotes, whichever they were, coming into the camp last night were scary, and it's only going to get worse now that they know we're here."

Riley thought about her boys out there with the dogs. She knew they could handle them, but the horses might freak out and throw them if they caught wind of them first. Riley pushed the thought out of her head.

"Okay, so who's willing to drive their motor home into town?"

No one was willing to do it. Riley knew they were all too scared, and no stranger was going to change that.

Jasper again offered, "I'll do it if someone will let me drive one of them." No one said anything. Jasper was exasperated with them. "Seriously! We have a chance to get out of here, and you're all acting like babies!"

Riley put her hands up in the hopes of calming down Jasper. "It's okay, Jasper. I need to tell all of you something. My group can help you, but once winter gets here, you're on your own. The pass we came over will be covered in snow, making it unpassable. The roads will be the same. No one will come to clear them. This campground was never intended for winter camping, so getting out of here then will be a moot point. So it's now or never. I'm not bringing gas for you to burn through for heat. We need it for our vehicles because come the first of spring, we are looking for a more permanent place to live. You're welcome to come and be a part of that, or you can stay here and die of starvation or freeze to death. Your choice."

She had everyone's attention now. Jasper was relieved along with the other young men and women. They were the ones roughing it the most, and Riley could understand their frustration. These older people did the bare minimum to help these young adults.

Philip shook his head, "We're scared, and we don't know you. You could be leading us to the slaughter."

"Yes, I could, but you will die if you don't trust me," Riley was blunt.

Annie tried to plead with them, "I know this won't help you much, but we're Christians. We have no desire to harm you, or anyone, for that matter. My brothers have gone out to find you food apparently with wolves or coyotes out there with them. Once they smell the fresh kill, they will follow. Would someone do that for people they were going to kill? No, I don't think so. Please, let us help you help yourselves by coming with us. You will survive the winter, and come spring, we'll find a new place to live where you'll never have to worry about sleeping in the cold again."

"Philip, I'm going. I'm not staying here. Riley and her daughter are right. There is nothing but death for us here if we stay. Even if they find food for us, it won't last, and then what?" The man looked around at everyone. "We eat each other?"

That got people to grumbling. Philip was still being stubborn. "You go if you want, but we're staying here." He glanced at his wife. "We have plenty, leaving here is just plain dumb! It's safe here. We know that. Going with her, there's no telling what will happen. Just because they said they're Christians means nothing to me. I never met one I could trust. They're all hypocrites, and I won't be a part of them, not before this and definitely not now!"

"Stay if you want to, but we're going. And I would advise the rest of you to do the same," the man concluded.

After almost an hour of trying to convince the group to go, four of the motor home owners decided to stay while everyone else was leaving. Those who were leaving started to pack up their stuff. Even though their gas tanks weren't full and they might not make it to the gas station, Riley wasn't worried. They had the horses and would get the gas to them one way or another. Landon and Bram came back empty-handed. Riley was disappointed, but she knew it was a hit or a miss this high up in the mountains this close to winter.

"I'll send someone this way with some supplies tomorrow," Riley promised Philip.

"Don't bother, we'll manage just fine!" he replied in a callous tone. Riley didn't know what Christians had done to him in the past that made him act this way. Maybe she would send Mr. Miller over here tomorrow. He might be able to talk some sense into him. She would have to find a way to get through to him, or this would be a death sentence for all those who stayed. She asked those leaving with her to leave all their food and water for those remaining. She could tell they didn't want to at first. But Jasper reminded them they needed to trust Riley. They agreed and emptied everything from their storage and cabinets. Riley looked at the pile and thought they might have enough with just this to get them through to spring if they managed their food correctly.

Jasper walked over to Riley to tell her they were ready to go. Riley took a moment to look at those who refused to leave and shook her head in defeat. She made her way over to Landon, who was waiting next to Duke, so he could give her a boost up. Annie and Bram were already on their horses, and Landon got on his with ease. Bram moved his horse closer to Duke and advised Riley that they should take a shortcut through the woods since the horses were going to be slower. The shortcut might offset the slow pace of the horses somewhat. Riley updated Jasper on what direction they would be going and why, to which he in turn gave her a thumbs-up. The three motor homes took off down the road while the horses with their riders took off through the rough mountain terrain.

No one said anything for the first half of the ride, then Annie's thoughts got the best of her, and she had to say something. She rode up alongside her mother.

"What's the matter with those people? They know they aren't going to make it through the winter, and yet they stayed!"

Landon didn't have to think too much about it. "They have no faith at all in other people and certainly none in God. They're relying on self-sufficiency, which will get them killed. But, Sissy, we tried, and that's all we can do. At least God opened some of their hearts, and they won't all die."

"It still stinks. Did you see his wife? I swear, she wanted to come, but she wouldn't leave her husband!" Annie was frustrated.

Riley had seen his wife and felt badly for her, but she made her choice, which she would now have to live with. No one could force them to leave. She would have a long talk with her father when she got back to camp about them. For now, they needed to stay focused on what lay ahead of them. Once again, they were risking their lives by going into the unknown. She hoped there would be no trouble awaiting them.

Riley pulled back on Duke's reins to stop him then turned to face her kids, "We need to pray."

The teenagers fell in as Riley prayed for safe passage for everyone. She prayed that their trip would be uneventful and that they would find what they needed. She ended the prayer with thanks for the blessings they had received and for the guidance that God had given them. They all said "Amen," and even the horses seemed to know when the prayer was over and snorted. They resumed their trek through the rough terrain. Their path finally brought them back to the road, and they could see the motor homes some distance behind them. Bram had been right, and Riley was grateful for his amazing sense of direction. They had the horses in a gallop now that they were on the open road, and within a few minutes, they could see the town from where they were. The horses could take a shortcut straight down from the side of the road into town. When the motor homes caught up to them, only a couple of people got out to have a look. The town was quiet. No fires and no noise. They saw the gas station that Jasper spoke of, and the road they were on led right to it. But what else it led them straight to, Riley couldn't imagine. Landon had his binoculars out, looking around. It was quiet. He handed them to his mother so she could have a look.

He said almost in a whisper, "I don't see anything. It's creepy in the daylight, not like when we drove through all those towns at night where we couldn't see anything."

Riley had a look around then handed the binoculars to Jasper. "I have to agree with you, Landon. People are asleep at night, but during the day, we should see people driving or walking around, but when they're not, calling it creepy is putting it mildly."

Riley had a bad feeling about this. Her skin felt like it was crawling, and she rubbed her arm up and down to try to brush off the feeling.

Jasper had a good long look and then directed his attention to Riley, "What do you think?"

"I think we go in slow and easy. Landon, get on the roof of the lead motor home with your rifle. Bram and I will cut in through the town this way. Annie, take your brother's horse, and stay out of sight. But be ready. Again, if there is someone threatening, please don't kill them. Just aim for the knee. Okay?"

Jasper was taken aback by the casual comment.

"Don't worry, it was the same order she gave when we arrived at your camp," Bram said with a smile.

Jasper smiled back at him. "Makes me feel like a wimp. I thought I had my best threatening look on when your mom showed up."

Bram smiled, "You did. It was your knee I was aiming at!"

Jasper's face went white. Bram turned the horse in the direction Riley wanted to go, while the rest got back into the motor homes and moved slowly down the road as Riley had requested. Jasper unconsciously rubbed his knees going into town. Landon was on the roof, and Jasper wondered how good of a shot he actually was. He hoped he wouldn't find out today. He wanted to get in and out of this town as quickly as possible. As it was, it would take them some time to get the motor homes filled up. They moved at a snail's pace, Jasper thought, but it was just his nerves. When they came around the corner, the gas station was right in front of them, as was Jasper's car. Jasper swallowed hard. They pulled into the gas station and nestled up to the pumps.

Landon got down from the motor home, and Annie handed him the reins to his horse. He took hold of Annie's horse so she could climb down.

"No electricity. We need to find a generator," Landon told his sister handing her back the reins.

Landon slung his rifle over his shoulder and went to the front door of the station's store. He pushed on it, and it swung open. He looked around and found another door leading into the mechanic shop. He took it and browsed around inside until he found what he was looking for. The generator was stacked in a corner behind some other equipment. Landon opened the gas tank and was grateful it was full.

He walked over to the big bay doors and opening one of them, yelled out, "Jasper, can you give me a hand?"

Jasper ran rather than walked. "Sure, what do you need?"

"I found the generator. We need to hook it up to the power box so we can get the pumps running." Landon told him.

"Yeah, okay, I take it you've done this before?" Jasper asked.

Landon smiled. "No, first time. But a friend of ours told us how to do it, so it should be easy."

It took everything they both had to get the generator over to the box. Once it was plugged in, they started up the generator, flipping a switch in the box to change the power source to the generator. All the pumps lit up. Then Landon found the lever for the manual override and pushed it up. Cheers came from the group outside, and with the nozzles already in the motor home's gas tank, they started pumping gas. Once that was done, Annie and Landon got on their horses to go find their mother. They rode down the street where she and Bram would have come into town. They found the horses outside several buildings that obviously had been on fire. Landon looked at his sister with concern. They got off their horses and tied them to the same post as Duke. Annie engaged her arrow as she started to go in through what once was the front door of one of the buildings. Landon had his rifle ready too. But before either of them could enter, Bram ran out past them, gagging as if he was about to puke. Landon and Annie were next to him immediately.

"What's up man, what is it?" Landon asked uneasily.

Bram couldn't speak; he just looked at them with horror in his eyes. Landon didn't wait; he ran into the building, calling for his mother.

"Mom, Mom, where are yo—"

He stopped dead in his tracks and couldn't believe his eyes. There were charred bodies of what looked to be adults and children everywhere. Riley grabbed him from behind, and he screamed.

"Mom!" He put his hand to his mouth as if to stop the contents of his stomach from spewing out. Then he whispered, "Mom, what happened?"

"Come on, son, let's get out of here," Riley was calm and spoke softly to Landon as they both exited the building.

Annie took one look at Landon and knew that whatever was inside, she didn't need to see it.

Bram spoke up now that he had regained control of his stomach. "There had to be fifty people in there. I swear I saw a baby." He choked again. "They didn't even seem like they ran from the fire. It's as if they just let it consume them." His eyes were watering now.

"Just when we thought we had seen the worst of this nightmare we're living in, we walk into this." Riley shook her head. "I'm sure the smoke you smelled was this. These buildings in flames would have been more than enough for you to smell, especially with the help of the wind."

"What do you think happened, Mom?" Annie was curious.

"I don't know, but look across the street. It looks like there was some kind of shoot-out here. The windows have been shot out, and there are bullet holes everywhere." Riley directed their gaze to the buildings on the other side of the road.

"But the place looks deserted," Bram said, looking at the war zone.

"Yeah, well, I'm ready to desert this place too," Annie was nervous and wanted to leave.

"Let's go back to the station," Landon said as he walked over to Duke with his mother so he could help her back up on the Clydesdale.

Bram and Annie were on their horses, already making their way down the street; none of them had to be asked twice.

Walking the horses down the middle of the road, they looked into each of the buildings as they passed them. Many of them had been part of the of the shoot-out or fire, while other buildings looked as though they were just closed for the day. The town was very quiet except the clicking of the horse's hooves. A few times, Bram turned around to look behind him, but nothing was there. By the time they got back to the gas station, one motor home was filled up. The third one had moved into its place and was now pumping gas. Jasper walked over as they rode up and taking one look at them; he knew something was horribly wrong.

"What is it?" He had a worried look on his face.

"I'm not sure, but it's not good. We need to get a move on and get as far away from here as possible," Riley said.

Jasper was alarmed more by the sight of Riley than from what she said. "Sure, but um, that car over there is mine. There's no sign of the guys that drove it or the other car they used to come here for supplies in. The doors were wide open. I don't know what could've happened to them," Jasper explained to Riley.

Annie, Landon, and Bram looked at Riley, which made Jasper look at her too.

"There was either a mass murder or a mass suicide. Your friends could have gotten caught up in it." Duke shook his big head, and Riley patted the side of his neck. "I'm sorry, but we aren't going any further into this place to look for anyone. I honestly don't believe anyone is alive here… only the dead."

Jasper swallowed hard. "I knew it was bad, but honestly, I thought when we finally came out from hiding, we would find life was normal. You know, like this was nothing but a bad dream or something."

"No dream, pal, the world is dying," Landon rephrased his comment. "The world is dead, and for whatever reason, people are helping it along by killing one another or taking their own lives."

The second motor home was filled now and pulled out. Riley guided Duke over to the man that led them into town.

"You have the map; are you comfortable to go on your own?" The man replied that he was, and Riley continued, "We're going to have to take the scenic route if we're going to get home by dark. We'll be close to you for a little while then we won't. But with the three motor homes, there is no reason why you should have problems. If one breaks down, you all get in the other ones and keep moving. Don't waste time trying to fix it. You need to be in camp before nightfall." Then it dawned on Riley that she didn't even know the man's name. "I'm sorry, I don't know your name."

"Zane Rourke, and thank you, Riley," he told her

Zane assured her they would be okay. He and the others knew what to do. They would keep moving, he promised. Riley told everyone standing around outside to get ready to go, that as soon as the last tank was filled, they would be leaving. Everyone obeyed and ran to the motor home they had come in. They had to wait another five minutes for the last tank to be filled. Once the nozzle was replaced on the pump, they left quite a bit faster than they had come in. As a matter a fact, the motor homes were moving so fast that the horses were left behind in their dust. Bram rode ahead, leading the way back to Calumet. Riley became conscious of the fact that they were always following Bram. He had a great sense of direction and always got them where they were going. As Riley pulled in behind him, it started to sprinkle, and they all pulled out their slickers. Riley had hoped that it would just snow, but the last couple of days had warmed up, and she knew any dark clouds would mean rain. She didn't mind because they had prepared for the worst, and it came. Thunder and lightning blasted through the air with a strobe light effect dancing through the dark skies. The horses didn't care for the thunder or lightning, nor did Riley. It would have been more beautiful, Riley thought, had she been inside watching it from one of the cabins. The rain came down harder now, and the horses didn't care much for that either, but they kept trudging along. In defiance of the rain, they managed to get home faster than they had left. Riley thought it was because they knew exactly where they were going this time, or at least Bram did. Riley was happy when she saw the smoke coming from the camp. The rain had completely stopped by the time they arrived; however, it was freezing. Being wet and cold felt horrible, and the only thing on their minds was getting home. Making their way back into camp, they saw all three of the motor homes parked in amongst the tree line, side by side. Levi came running up to Riley, asking if he could ride in with her. She pulled him up and got him settled in front of her giving him the reins so he could lead Duke in. Alejandro was waiting for them by the corral, ready to help both Levi and Riley down. Her legs were sore from the long ride home, and it felt good to be walking on solid ground again. Her father and Anderson walked over to welcome her home.

"Well, I guess you found where the smoke came from," her dad said as he gave her a hug.

Riley was exhausted. Her only thought was to take a cold shower and get into her flannel PJs, dry socks, and boots.

"Several buildings in a town a few hours from here had been on fire."

She left out what they found inside of those buildings; however, she would tell the council about it later. Now she just moved toward her cabin to get her things. Levi stayed behind with Alejandro to help feed and water the horses, then do his favorite part, brushing them down.

Anderson could tell she wasn't telling them everything but left it alone. She would tell him soon enough. She looked tired, and he knew she needed something to eat.

"The food is still hot, why don't you go grab a bite?"

"I will, I just need to shower first then get into some warm clothes," she answered.

Bram, Landon, and Annie were all tired and wet. The only thing any of them could think of was getting into some dry clothes. By the time Riley was done with her shower and dressed, Annie was finished too. The kitchen now housed all the tables from outside since the climate became colder. Annie and Riley walked over to the kitchen together, and once inside, Riley was amazed at how well everything fit in the kitchen. She was very surprised at how many people could fit inside the place at one time. Riley's mother told them to find some place to sit and she would bring them their food. After thanking her, they went to the table that was closest to the warm fire. Bram and Landon came in a few minutes later and sat with them. Once their food arrived, they were so grateful to be home with a hot meal and a warm fire. Riley relaxed as she began to eat.

"Mom, what do you think we'll find in the spring? I mean, there is nothing out there that resembles the life we once knew," Landon's words were soft-spoken.

Riley looked into her son's emerald eyes and saw nothing but sorrow. Then she glanced over at Bram and Annie, who were also staring at her.

"I don't know, but we have a large group of people with us that have a long life ahead of them, all of you included, so whatever we find, we deal with it. That's all we can do. What we found today, we can only speculate, which normally doesn't do any good. But we have to realize that in every scenario we think of, there could be some truth to it as to what happened there. But the fact remains that we'll never know. But here's what I do know:

"Mark 7:21–23 says, 'For from within, out of the heart of men, proceed the evil thoughts, fornications, thefts, murders, adulteries, deeds of coveting and wickedness, as well as deceit, sensuality, envy, slander, pride and foolishness. All these evil things proceed from within and defile the man.'

"We have seen the vilest of men and women in the past few months, and I can only foresee it getting worse. You young adults need to keep Christ very close to you. That's what will set you apart from the rest." Riley thought of something else. "Our Founding Fathers believed that the war they were fighting to gain their freedom was worth going broke for, even worth dying for. How much greater is our fight? We're fighting for our right to live. We have been stripped of everything except our lives and, most importantly, our God. I don't believe God has forsaken us. I believe He's here, and I believe more than anything, we're here for a reason."

As Riley spoke to her kids, the rest of the people around them began to listen to their conversation. When Riley realized they were, it made her uncomfortable, and she squirmed in her chair for a second. Anderson was sitting in a chair off to the side of her. She never even saw him come in. Riley knew she must really be tired. Her mother and father were there along with just about everyone from the camp. Riley stood up, even knowing how ridiculous she must seem in her PJs, so everyone could see and hear her.

"Today we found where the smoke came from. It wasn't a pretty sight. Inside the building we found human remains, adults and children. I don't know what happened, be it murder or suicide. There were signs of some kind of gunfight across the street from the charred buildings. We also found Jasper's car but not his friends. We were told they had gone there for supplies, and we're not sure if they got caught up in the mess we saw in the burnt buildings or something else. You all need to understand something, I have one goal in mind, and that is finding a safe place to live. The key word there is *live*. We have a large number of young people, and they have to make a life for themselves. I feel it's up to the older adults to help them make that happen. I cannot fail my children, and therefore, I won't fail yours either. I know I've talked about this to the council, but now you are going to hear it from me. We have close to a hundred people between our two camps. My goal is to have a thousand one day, even if I have to go out and find them myself. The more people we have, the greater chance we have for success. That success is going to have to involve us moving to someplace safe, someplace already built. That means we are going to have to go into whatever town and clean out the bodies. We'll have to burn all the furniture from homes and scrub the houses down. It's my opinion that the cold weather will kill off the virus. You may be asking how I came to that assumption? In the 1400s, the Bubonic Plague seemed to disappear in the winter but came back in the spring and summer months. I plan on going in before spring is here and doing my very best to clean out as many houses as I can. Only volunteers will go with me, and only a few at first to test out my theory. Those of us that go will stay for two weeks. That will be more than enough time to see if we are going to get sick."

Riley couldn't think of anything else to say so she just let everything sink in. She noticed the shocked looks on most of their faces.

Becca came through once again when she spoke up, "I have two young teenagers, and I want to see them grow into adults. I have nothing to leave them as way of an inheritance, except this. I need to know they have a chance. I never knew God before I met Riley and her family. They don't preach a lot about God, but they do live Him every day. I, for one, think actions are stronger than words. That evil she was talking about, I met it firsthand, as did Anderson, my niece and nephew, along with Kota, Jesse, and Jena. If we don't find a way to live again, if we give up hope, then each breath we take is for nothing. I'll volunteer to go with the first group." Her gaze went to Riley. "As long as you don't mind me up chucking a few times right at first?" Becca said seriously.

Kota stood up, "Riley, you have treated both me and Jesse like sons and Jena like a daughter. You'll never know how much we appreciate that. This inheritance Becca was speaking of is also for me, so you can count me in. I should be strong enough by the time you're ready to go. As one of your kids, you can count on me for everything."

Riley smiled at him, "You remember you owe me a hug." Kota walked over and gave her a big hug and kissed her on the cheek. "Thank you, Kota, and I do love you."

Kota smiled back, "I know."

Lyle was standing next to the sink and spoke, "Are you still thinking of the town of Jackson here in Wyoming?"

"Yes. It's big but not too big. Some of those homes are lived in all year long, and then some are just vacation homes. I'm sure we can find quite a few that weren't being lived in at the time of the outbreak. Also, we'll have a continuous food supply with the lakes close by as well as Yellowstone and the Grand Tetons National Parks," she explained. "I know there are plenty of ideal places, but I chose this place because of the abundance of food all year long. Hunting in Yellowstone isn't allowed, but when we become the new keepers of that area, it will be used the way we need it to be used. The rest, we'll grow, or when we travel, we'll bring back what we find. We have been thrust back into the seventeenth and eighteenth centuries with the exception of twenty-first century technology, most of which we can't use anymore. Meaning, it won't be easy. Everyone is going to have to work, much like we do now. Our community has thrived because no one has complained, you've all just done the work that has been asked of you. Because you've done your part, look around you, we've been blessed. We have more people, plenty of food, livestock, and a roof over our heads. We have applied the old ways in with the new, and it has worked for us. I know Jackson will thrive with us, especially knowing how well we've done here in a very short amount of time. I'm willing to take other places into consideration, and I promise I will listen to you, but I need to know why you chose those places. So until someplace better is chosen, we'll prepare for Jackson."

Everyone nodded their heads in agreement. Mr. Miller cleared his throat to speak, "I normally would say this is a pea-brain idea coming from a dimwit, but I think it's a good one. You have my vote, for what it's worth."

Everyone cheered and applauded, "Yay, Miller!"

When everyone quieted down, Riley said, "That means the world to me, Mr. Miller."

"Well, don't get used to it, I don't plan on agreeing with you very often, if ever again," he said.

That made people laugh, and Riley told him, "I would never presume that, Mr. Miller, and thank you."

Everyone began to talk among themselves, and they all seemed truly happy. They had a plan, one that everyone liked. Thanksgiving was coming up in a few days, and with spirits being high, Riley knew the celebration of Thanksgiving would be for the blessings they had received and the ones to come. Riley and her kids finished their meals about the time Victoria came over with brownies and sat with them.

"I think you've made a lot of people happy today, Riley, especially the parents of small children and these young people."

"Thanks, Mom, but really, it's for the children and the young adults. I don't want anyone in our group to feel they need to take their own life because there's no future. God didn't leave us destitute, and though we may be at the bottom of some imaginary barrel right now, we won't be for long. We have a lot of smart people here. With God's guidance and their intellect, we're going to be fine."

"I'm not sure you are aware of this, but while you were gone today, Lyle and Dina came over and had a long talk with your father. They accepted Christ. Lyle is so ashamed for his part in coming over here, waving their guns around, trying to take possession of this place. He told your father that what we all did for them afterward turned his life around," Victoria said in a gentle voice. Then she remembered something else. "Dina was crying when she talked about her children. She said she knows it's been God's doing, but you have been such a huge blessing. Forgiving all the men the way you did and bringing them here. Not to mention, when you left here to go help Mitch and then what you did for Kota, Jesse, Jena, and Levi. Dina said she can see God in your life, and she wanted that for herself. I think that's the highest compliment a person can give a Christian. I just wanted you to know how proud I am of you for everything you've done."

"Wow! I'm happy for them. That's great news. And thanks, Mom, but I did the only thing I could have done. They had kids. If they hadn't, I don't know what I would've done." Riley smiled at that.

"You joke, Riley, but you would have done the same thing. I think for the first time, people are seeing the true God in action even in the midst of all this horror. Before the virus, there were so many interpretations of God no one could see him clearly. Now I believe they can. And he is working through you."

"That's crazy, Mom, I'm not holier than thou. It's just me! Have you forgotten I killed someone and really didn't care that I did at the time?" Riley reminded her mother.

"Do you feel the same now?" her mother asked.

"Well, of course not. I know we're fighting a war out there, but killing people isn't high on my agenda." Riley paused for a second then continued with a smile, "We're now aiming for the knees!"

Her mother almost broke into a laugh but managed to stifle it. "Well, I'm glad to hear that. I guess Agnes and I better become educated on knee surgeries."

Riley laughed. "Ugh. Because of my bossiness, I've put myself in a position that I really don't care for. All because I have my kids to think of," Riley lowered her voice and leaned in so only her mother could hear, "I'm going to continue to be bossy and not let someone else make those decisions for me. If anyone else chooses to join me, then so be it!"

Victoria smiled at her daughter and leaned in to kiss her. "That's my girl. Just remember who is really in charge, missy. I think I heard you tell the kids to keep Jesus close to them, you remember to do the same."

Riley smiled at her mother and promised her, "I will."

Riley leaned back in her chair and enjoyed the brownie. Everyone was in deep conversation about the news they had just received. Even the kids had joined in and were laughing about something. Riley didn't miss the old life, where people pulled into their garages, walked into their houses without so much as a hello to their neighbors. Here they were forced to talk to one another on a daily basis, and Riley liked that. Wherever they moved to, they would still have a community kitchen. They couldn't be wasteful with anything when it came to the food. She realized that money had no value now. Neither did gold, jewels, oil paintings, cars, or anything else people once held as valuable. They're all worthless now. Food and water were the new coin, and very soon the food left in stores would rot, leaving people in the cities to starve. The virus might be gone, but then there would be a food shortage for those that did survive. From there it would be "Bullies Rule". The strongest would kill and take what they wanted. It would be the whole *Mad Max* story coming to reality. Riley thought they would need to be well established by then and have a strong system in place so no one could come in and take it from them. They would eventually need an army. Right now, there were plenty of people already in the group that would fight to defend this place without a second thought. The larger the community grew, the more problems would arise. They would have to deal with them when it happened. For now, it would be baby steps, and she would make sure they did it right the first time. She had made a decision, and that was, she would be leaving in February with the first group to Jackson. There would still be snow, which meant it would still be cold enough that she would feel safe to go in. The CDC sent their scientists down to Antarctica to work on a cure. The cold may be why they were there. She would continue to pray about it and unless she felt 100 percent sure about going, she wouldn't go.

Keeping Jesus close, she thought.

CHAPTER 11

Riley was warm all night and didn't want to leave the comfort or warmth of her bed to battle the cold. She felt the warm body of Levi next to her, which brought a smile to her face. He was her little heater and a good snuggle bunny that kept her warm all night, which she absolutely loved. She missed having a young one and was convinced he was filling a void she didn't know she had. She cuddled up to him, and he pushed himself closer into her so that her whole body engulfed him. She lay there for quite some time, holding him and listening to the world all around her. It was very quiet, and she wondered if everyone was having the same thought of staying in bed as she was. She heard some rustling around downstairs. It sounded as if someone was trying to start the fire in the potbelly stove. Riley felt that thing did very little heating. It did, however, take the bite out of the chill but never quite got rid of the cold. Riley kissed Levi on the top of his head and slowly slid out of bed. She tucked the covers in tight around him before she climbed down the ladder. She was right; Kota was starting the fire. He looked up at her as he shut the door to the stove.

"It's beautiful outside, but it's freezing."

Riley gazed out the window and saw the snow. It was coming down in large flakes, and was beyond beautiful.

"Well, that explains why I had to get up last night to put on my sweatshirt."

Kota laughed, "Well, that's how I've been sleeping for the last few weeks. I'm not used to the cold."

Riley walked over to the sofa and sat down. Jesse was still bundled up so much that Riley couldn't even see his head.

"You know something, Kota, I don't even know where you're from. We've talked so much about so many things but not that, not about your family."

Kota grabbed the blankets from his mattress and gave one to her while he took the other then sat down beside her.

"Okay, what do you want to know?"

"Everything, of course," Riley smiled.

Kota felt so comfortable around Riley. She had spent endless nights staying up with both him and Jesse, caring for their backs. Some nights she would sit on the floor and let him lay his head in her lap while she rubbed it. He knew she loved him and Jesse as her own because of how she loved her own kids. They were two and the same. He felt at home with Riley and didn't feel the need to keep anything from her.

"Well, I told you that my mom named me Dakota because she was from South Dakota. She met my dad, and they moved to Arizona, where I was born, Tucson, to be exact. I'm twenty-seven, and I have a sister"—he swallowed and corrected himself—"had a sister, Cheyenne. She was twenty-four. My mom and dad had gone on a cruise someplace in Mexico right before the outbreak. Cheyenne talked to them both when they returned, and they seemed fine. A few days later, they were sick. Cheyenne was going to see them the following week but decided to go early to help them out while they weren't feeling well. I told her I would come as soon as I finished helping Jesse move. Jena and Sheryl were also helping him move, so that's why we were all together. The last time I spoke to my sister, she said Dad had died and Mom was very close to it. She told me that she had caught whatever it was they had, and she was pretty sure what they had was the virus. She felt they must have caught it while on the cruise. I cried because there was absolutely nothing I could do."

"Kota, I'm sorry to hear that. Some families weren't hit at all by the virus, and then other families have no one left." Riley truly felt his pain, and he knew it.

"I have you and your family now, if that's okay with you," Kota's eyes watered.

Riley pulled back the blanket and leaned over to give him a big hug. "I wouldn't have it any other way."

Kota continued, "Thanks, Riley, that means the world to me. Um, Jesse had a really good job in Houston but never got to work a day at it. We watched people drop dead in the street, which caused us to totally freak out. We left everything we had worked so hard to get organized for Jesse and just took off. Like you, we were heading for the mountains to get away from everyone. We got as far as Vernal, met some people that seemed all right, and then something happened. The men just snapped. There were too many of them when the craziness started. Jesse and I couldn't do anything about it. It was terrible! They made us watch them as they…" he was choking back the tears now…"they made us watch them rape Jena and Sheryl. The other women just watched and laughed. Afterward, they made Jena and Sheryl watch as they tortured us. I passed out, missing most of it."

Riley had tears in her eyes, and she wiped them away with the sleeve of her sweatshirt. Then she gathered his hand into hers, "As long as this body draws breath, that will never happen again to anyone in our group. You—I mean, all of us are going to learn to fight back, to protect ourselves and our loved ones."

"I know. Jesse and I are going to do our part, I promise. We've been working out with Landon and Bram. Landon said today we're going to learn to shoot. Your dad said he would help us after breakfast. I think he said we're also going to learn to make our own bullets. That should be interesting." Kota thought about that for a moment and smiled. "I've never even shot a gun before, and now I'm going to learn how to make my own bullets."

"Well, I'm sure you'll be a natural at both, and it's important to know how to do both. My dad taught everyone in my family. He's very patient with people," Riley thought of her father's relationship with Mr. Miller, and she changed her wording, "extremely patient. You'll do fine, I'm sure. I'll come out and watch you shoot."

He smiled, "Thanks, Riley, for everything. You…"

She put her fingers to his lips to make him stop. He took it and kissed it.

"I'm going to be busy today, trying to keep the trail clear of snow so we can get to Mercy and they can get to us," Riley said as she glanced past Kota out to the window once again.

"How do you plan on doing that?" he asked her.

"The old-fashioned way, with a shovel," she laughed.

He got up off the couch and extended his muscular arm to her and helped her up. "Let's get a move on then. Breakfast or shovels first?"

"Um, shovels, I guess, that way I won't feel guilty eating two of Lupe's burritos," Riley surmised.

At that, Jesse was up shaking off his sleep. "Okay, let me get dressed, and I'm with you."

Riley laughed, "You're with me and the shovels, or me and the burritos?"

"Oh, man, yeah, shovels first but then food!" Jesse grabbed his jeans.

Riley climbed up the stairs, found her clothes, and went behind the little curtain they had set up for changing and got dressed. She found her socks and her good winter boots that she brought back from Vernal. Once she was dressed, she looked under the covers and found Levi still out cold. She looked across the room at the rest of her loft mates, and they were still sound asleep. Once down the ladder, she found both Jesse and Kota ready to go. She had her little travel bag and noticed they did too. Bathroom first then brush her teeth. The shoveling can wait at least that long.

* * *

It had snowed all night and well into the morning. There was some wind, but it wasn't too bad. Riley thought about something that Mr. Miller had said to her and her father when they went by his house the first time to check on him. He said they were "acting like a bunch of doomsday preppers." She thought about those that had been preparing for this kind of thing for a long time. Those people were stuck underground, hiding, having nothing to look at but the walls around them and the few people that were with them. She was happy that she had the snow to deal with and even happier to have all these people with her. She knew she would go crazy being stuck underground. A person could get lost in the mountains forever and never worry about bumping into someone. She chuckled at that thought. She had bumped into a lot of people while up here, but she felt they had all been a blessing, and she was grateful for crossing paths with all of them. Leaving Park City with twenty-eight people, she thought, was a lot; now they had roughly seventy people here. Not quite a hundred but getting there. She didn't like leaving Phillip and the others behind at their camp. But America was a free country still, and if they didn't want to come, she couldn't have made them. The fact that it snowed meant they might not be able to get the supplies to them now. If the snow didn't stick, then she would leave as promised and take things over to them. The Christians they had met in the past had given Christianity a bad name, so she was going to have to fix that. She couldn't let them down, but Phillip wasn't making it easy for her.

Kota was next to Riley, digging out the snow. It wasn't terrible, and the path could be seen again. She knew with every day that it snowed, the path would have to be dug out again. But it would help having people use it each day, and they would use it. Riley's thoughts were interrupted by Landon running toward her. She stopped what she was doing as Landon came up to her out of breath. He bent over, placing both hands on his knees, trying to catch his breath.

"Is everything okay, honey?" Riley put her hand on Landon's back, waiting for him to speak.

"No, you need...you need to come back to Calumet. You need to come now!" he stressed the urgency through each breath he took.

She dropped the shovel and took off running as fast as she could back to Calumet. She didn't want to speculate, so she just kept running. When she arrived, she saw that the patrol had come back. They had come back with a body draped over the back end of one of the horses. A dead body. She looked at everyone, but no one spoke.

"Okay, is somebody going to tell me who this is and what happened?" Riley's voice was almost to commanding.

Tony spoke up, "Yeah, Boss, we found him lying facedown in the snow about five miles east of here."

He stopped and looked from one person to another, as if seeking help from one of them. His eyes went back to Riley.

"The guy's been shot."

With that, everyone standing around gasped. Riley went over to look at the body. She asked the men to take him down from the horse so she could get a better look. Riley's father came up and stood next to her. Once they got the man down, she and her father were able to examine the body more closely. He had been shot in the back, but Ken felt the wound wouldn't have killed the man—at least, not right away. Riley didn't ask her father how he knew that but just accepted what he said to be true.

"Did anyone hear any gunshots or sounds that were out of the norm?" Riley's question was answered with heads shaking no.

"Okay, I know it's not going to be easy with the ground near frozen, but will someone bury the poor man? Tony and Carson, you need to show me where you found him. Landon and Bram, you're coming too. Grab your gear and rifles. We'll meet at the corral in five minutes," Riley ordered.

Taking one look at Carson, Annie could tell he wasn't doing very well. He looked like he was going to vomit.

"It's okay, Carson, I'll go. You've seen enough."

Riley was about to object until she got a good look at Carson. Annie was correct; he looked like he was going to be sick.

"Carson, go on, it's okay. You both did the right thing bringing him here. Tony, are you going to be okay?"

"Yeah, Boss, sure."

There it was again. Riley thought she misheard him the first time, but he did call her "Boss."

"Annie, you don't have to go. What we find might not be something you want to see."

Riley was concerned about the boys too. What they saw in the last town they traveled to was enough to make her stomach churn. Charred bodies were the worst, but it only seemed to get worse with every outing, and she didn't know what lay ahead of them, but she was sure it was going to make her sick.

"I'll go," came a voice from behind them. One that almost made her cringe.

It was Kevin. Kevin hadn't come over to Calumet much since he kissed her, but here he stood and was offering to take Annie's place. She was going to have to suck it up and work with him.

"Thanks, Kevin, that would be great. Get your gear and meet at the corral in five minutes."

"Right, Boss."

And before Riley could say anything about the "Boss" comments, everyone was going in all different directions.

She looked at her father, and he just held his hands up as if he surrendered. Then he laughed a good, hearty laugh. Riley was not amused.

"It's not funny, Dad!"

"Well, I'm sure it's because Alejandro calls you Jefe. There has been a hierarchy put into place here, whether any of us wanted it or not, and you're at the top of it. Maybe calling you Mrs. Cooper is to formal and calling you Riley is too informal. Boss falls somewhere in between," Ken smiled at his own logic.

"You still find this funny, don't you?" She glared at her father.

Again his hands went up as if defending himself, then he reminded her, "Aren't you supposed to be somewhere…Boss?"

"Ugh! Fine! I already have a Mr. Miller, Dad. There is no need for you to act like him." Riley spun around, stomping off.

"Uh, Riley, that's not very *presidential* of you," her father yelled at her as she stomped her way over to the corral.

That stopped Riley dead in her tracks. She flung herself around to give him a piece of her mind but found he was walking off, laughing with Simon Crawford. She took a deep breath and told herself that she needed to find out what happened to the poor soul that had been shot. She turned, fuming, and headed for the corral. Alejandro was waiting for her with Duke. She sighed at the sight of the massive Clydesdale standing in front of her. Walking over to him, Riley managed to calm down considerably. She walked to the steps and climbed to the top so she could get on. Annie showed up with Riley's bow.

"I put plenty water for you in bag, Jefe. No worry 'bout Duke he eat and drink plenty," Alejandro explained to her.

Riley looked at Alejandro; she knew that his calling her jefe was out of total respect for her, and she couldn't be mad about that. In all honesty, it could be worse, she thought. Her frustration left her as she took the reins.

Looking down at Alejandro, she said, "Thank you so much, Alejandro. You are far too kind to me. Thanks."

"No, no. Jefe, you very good to me and my Lupe," he said with a smile.

"You'll never know how much you and Lupe mean to me. We'll be back soon."

She pulled on the reins, leading Duke away from the corral.

The others were already on their horses, ready to go. Tony took the lead and headed back the way he and Carson had come. Kevin pulled in beside Riley; however, they rode in silence for quite some time before Riley decided to say something.

"I haven't seen you around much the last few weeks," she told him.

"Ah, well, I didn't think you wanted to see me," he confessed.

Riley looked at him with a smile and said, "I didn't want you to kiss me. Seeing you was never the problem."

Kevin laughed at that. "No, I guess that's true. Is there any chance we can be friends again?"

"Yeah, sure. But just some friendly advice, the next time you find a woman that you're interested in, it wouldn't hurt to ask her if it's okay to kiss her. If you don't, you might find your crown jewels somewhere around your throat." Riley smiled at him.

"Ah, yeah, manners are always a plus in dealing with women. You would think I would've learned that at some point in my life. And thanks, Boss, for keeping it between us," Kevin said.

Riley was laughing now. "What's with the 'Boss' bit? Tony, now you? Where did this come from?"

Now he had a big smile on his face. "You came back to camp the other night from town, giving that big speech about moving us all to Jackson, and how everything you do is for us to have a civilized life once again. Well, at that moment, everyone knew you were our leader. Not that I think anyone thought anything differently before, but that kind of sealed the deal, I think, in a lot of people's minds. Some of us were sitting around afterward, discussing it. You know, talking about what your title should be? *Mayor*, *Governor*, or even *President* maybe. Honestly, none of them suit you, that's when someone said that Alejandro always calls you Jefe and that *Boss* would fit you fine. So *Boss* it is. Sorry, you don't have a say in it. But know it's said out of total respect for you."

Riley thought about it and grinned. "Honestly, I thought it was because of my bossy personality."

Kevin laughed, "If you're bossy, then that would make the rest of us tyrants. You work harder than anyone in the camp. I mean, when everyone was looking for you this morning, where did they find you? Out shoveling snow. You're the first to volunteer for anything when the rest of us are afraid of our own shadows right now. When you're gone, everyone keeps busy out of shame or loyalty because they know where you are, they don't want to be."

"Except you. And I want you to know how much I appreciate it," Riley conveyed to him.

"Well, I want you to know you can count on me for this kind of stuff. I'm not heroic, mind you, but this I can do. After Vernal, I didn't want to go around not knowing what was out there. I need to know," Kevin said with confidence.

"Well, if it's any consolation, I'm just as afraid, but like you, I need to know. I also don't have the patience to wait for someone to come back and tell me what's going on," Riley confessed.

"What do you think we'll find today?" he asked in a concerned voice.

"Whatever lies ahead of us, I don't think we're going to like it much. If my dad is correct, that wound on the dead man wouldn't have killed him right away, which probably means he was running from whomever and died away from where the shooting took place. We'll have to follow his tracks back to where he came from. That's if we can," Riley answered.

They rode the rest of the way in silence. Riley was happy to have Kevin there and was even happier that the awkwardness was over between them. She honestly enjoyed his company and considered him a good friend as she did Anderson. She could trust him. Then she smiled, as long as he kept his lips to himself. Tony came to a stop then pointed to where the body was found.

"We found him there."

Riley saw the blood, and there were tracks. They were heading east.

Riley looked at her son, who was riding behind her, "Landon, is our camp too far away to hear gunfire from here?"

"Um, yeah, there's no way to hear it from here. Unless our camp was inside the valley but we're on the other side of it. Depending on how the guy came, I'm positive we wouldn't have heard anything."

"On any of the patrols has there been any smell of smoke or signs of smoke coming from anywhere around here?" Riley continued with her questions.

Tony looked at the tracks, then back to Riley. "Boss, I know I haven't gone this way before. If anyone else has, I'm not aware of it."

Landon looked to Bram, who in turn, said, "I know I haven't been this way either."

"What made you come this way today, Tony?" Riley asked him.

"I don't know. Carson asked if I would mind going in this direction because he hadn't been over here before either. I told him I didn't care, so we just went."

"Landon, would you look at the map Grandpa gave you of the area. Let's see what's around here, if there is a campground or a cabin or whatever," Riley instructed.

Landon took the map out so he and Kevin could look at it. Kevin shook his head no; there was nothing to indicate any cabins or campgrounds anywhere around here. The map might not show private cabins, Riley thought. She told them to follow the tracks to wherever they might lead. She asked Tony to let Bram lead, and he was happy to fall to the back. They went down into the valley and around the side of the mountain for about an hour. Riley couldn't believe how far the man had gone. Bram finally stopped and got off his horse and instructed everyone else to do the same. Once everyone was down, he pointed to the camp just below them. They couldn't see the fires, but their smell was still lingering. There were three tents that they could see. Riley had the binoculars and saw nothing but the tents, no life. She handed them to Kevin who looked but couldn't see anything either. Riley told Bram and Landon to go higher with their rifles and try to get somewhere where they would have a good view of the camp. She gave them a few minutes to get situated, then asked Tony to stay with the horses while she and Kevin went down to check everything out. Tony was relieved. He had seen enough dead people for one day, and from what they were seeing now, he didn't think they would find anyone alive.

When they saw Landon wave to them, Riley and Kevin crept into the camp. They couldn't see Bram at all, which was good because it meant no one else could. They took it slow, both keeping their eyes on the camp in front of them. They found nothing except a little blood, but no bodies. They went into all the tents, which were empty of people—however, not their stuff. It was a little eerie; whoever had been here left in a hurry. Riley realized they wouldn't find any answers here. There was a whistle from above, making her and Kevin look up at the same time. Landon was moving further over away from the campsite. Riley and Kevin did the same and found a small path that they took for a short time before she heard someone.

"Do you hear someone crying?" she whispered to Kevin.

He answered in a low voice, "Yeah."

They moved in closer and heard a man's voice consoling someone. There were other muffled voices. The crying was uncontrollable, and someone was now yelling. Riley looked at Kevin; it was now or never.

Riley walked out around the bush into the open. Kevin followed. "Hello, is everything okay?"

A big black man jumped up, holding a knife, and pointed it at Riley, yelling at her, "*Stay away! Get outta here! I'll kill you if you don't! Get back!*"

"Whoa! Hold on, we're here to help. Put the knife down," Riley pleaded with man.

"*Hell, no! Get outta here!*" the man kept yelling.

"Please, mister, we're here to help. My name is Riley, and this is my friend, Kevin. We have a camp on the other side of the mountain. I have a first aid kit in my backpack, please let me help," Riley was speaking fast to get everything out before the big man did anything stupid.

"Martin, please…put the knife down…it's not helping!" the woman said through her sobbing. "I want…I want my…my baby back…Martin!" she was crying again.

"Your baby? What do you mean?" Riley asked.

"Oh, sure you're here to help! Two white guys from your camp come in here and shoot up our place, taking my daughter, and you come waltzing in here to save the day! So take your help and *get out!*" Martin yelled the last of his words.

Riley was about to tell him the men didn't come from their camp when someone behind Martin asked for help. Riley pushed past the big man to see what she could do. Kevin just stood there, not sure if he was willing to risk Martin and his knife like Riley did. Riley called for Landon and Bram to come down, which made Martin angrier. Landon and Bram made it down faster than Riley had expected and she could see Tony approaching slowly with the horses. This caused Martin even more distress as his yelling started up again, which wasn't helping anyone. Riley was trying to help another couple when she thought Martin was actually going to kill someone. That someone being her son Landon. Riley got up and kicked Martin as hard as she could in the back of his knee. His knee buckled under him, and the big man went down hard. Kevin jumped in, grabbed the knife from Martin and threw it off into a bush.

"I'm not going to tell you again, we're here to help!" Riley took a deep breath to calm down then proceeded to speak in a more controlled voice, "Thank you, Kevin. Now we're here to help, and we can't do that with you threatening us. Now, that's my son you were about to go all crazy on, and I can't have that. Now please, calm down, and would someone please tell me what happened?"

The crying woman started to speak in between breathing and crying, "This is…my husband, Martin…and I'm Shauna…Some white men," she started to catch her breath and was able to speak better, "found our…camp and robbed us…then something happened with one of…one of them just shot the other one. The guy with the gun…he took what he could carry and took…he took my daughter! He shot at us, and we scattered. But he has my baby!" Now Shauna was crying again.

"Martin, were the men on foot? How did they get up here? There's no road."

Martin was sitting on the ground with his big hands rubbing his leg. "They were on foot!"

"Okay, why didn't you go after him?" Riley was curious.

"I couldn't, okay? He had a gun to my little girl's head." Now Martin was crying, but he managed to finish what he had to say, "He said he would kill her if we did!"

"Kevin, help these people. Tony, you stay here to help him. Make sure they pack everything they need. All of you have a long hike home." Riley took quick inventory of all the adults and kids. She then looked at her boys, "I'm so sorry, but you both are going to have to come with me. If he's threatening their little girl with a gun, I need someone that has perfect aim."

Landon and Bram knew what she meant. Martin just looked at them. "I'm going with you! She's my daughter," Martin yelled at them.

"I'm sorry, I know you want to go, but we can move faster with the horses. You would only slow us down." Riley understood his wanting to go, but they needed the horses, and she needed the boys with their rifles. "I promise we won't come back without her." Riley hoped she could keep that promise.

"Which way did he go?" Bram asked.

Shauna spoke as she stood up and pointed across the stream. "That way, he took my baby up that side, heading in that direction. He left about an hour ago!"

Bram gave Riley a boost up on Duke. He got on his horse with ease, and the three of them road off as fast as the terrain would allow them. Once they were on the other side, there was a deer trail, nice and worn. Even through the snow, it could be seen. They found the tracks with no effort. The snow from the night before was a tremendous help, and having a person with him that didn't want to go was even a bigger help. There were drag marks; he had to set something down that left an impression in the snow. There were fresh breaks in the bushes they were climbing through. The man was leaving a road map for them. Bram slowed the horses and then came to a complete stop where they all listened. There it was, the faint sound of crying and a man's voice. They had the horses walk until the voices got louder. Bram motioned them all to get off the horses. Riley grabbed her bow and engaged an arrow. Landon motioned for Riley to go ahead and that he and Bram would go to either side. Riley nodded her head in agreement; the boys moved off quietly. Riley walked slowly until she saw the man; his fist was up ready to plow it into the young teenager's face.

Riley pulled back on the bow. "Hit her, and this arrow will go right through your heart!"

The man jerked around, pulling the teenager right in front of him so fast it surprised Riley. "Go ahead, and I'll slit her throat!" Riley knew he would do it.

Riley didn't put the arrow down. She knew one of the boys would have him in their line of sight soon, and this would all be over with.

"Look, just let the girl go. You can keep the stuff. We'll leave, and you'll never see us again."

"No way! She's mine!" He was adamant. "I found her, she stays!"

"You found her? What does that mean? You stole her from her parents, and they want her back!" Riley was flabbergasted at his reasoning. "And why did you kill your partner? That was a little extreme, wasn't it?"

He laughed and said, "Yeah, well, that psycho didn't want me to take what was mine! And I always get what I want!"

"Landon or Bram, if you have a shot, take it now!" Riley yelled.

The man looked off to the right. As he did, he moved the young woman just enough to the left with the knife still to her throat, leaving himself open—a mistake Riley took advantage of. She released the arrow just as he began to press the knife deeper into the young woman's neck. When the arrow hit him, he had a look of fear on his face as he crumbled to the ground. The girl went with him. Riley ran as fast as she could, but the knife had already penetrated into her neck. She quickly took her backpack off, taking out the first aid kit. Bram and Landon were there in seconds. Riley took out some gauze and pressed it up to the young girl's neck. Riley held it tight. The teenager's eyes went wide, and Riley could see the fear in them.

"Hold on, baby, hold on!" Riley worked fast.

Landon handed her the bag of powder that would help stop the bleeding. Riley took it, pulled the gauze back, and saw that it wasn't a deep cut.

"Thank you, Lord, thank you!"

She poured the powder on the wound, took some clean gauze, covered it, and then loosely wrapped a roll of gauze all the way around her neck. She tucked it in so that it wouldn't come loose while she found the tape. Finally placing the tape on the gauze to hold it, Riley sat down for a minute to catch her breath.

"I'm sorry, I didn't even ask your parents your name," Riley spoke softly.

"I'm Tamera." She was fighting back tears while holding her throat.

"So, Tamera, how much trouble am I in for letting this nut cut you? Your dad is one big fella."

Tamera swallowed, making sure she still could. "He's an old softy, really. It's my mom you have to worry about." Her crying had stopped.

Riley smiled as she recalled kicking Tamera's dad in the back of his knee because he was threatening Landon. "Never underestimate a mother when her children are threatened."

Landon laughed at that. He had seen it firsthand a number of times. Then he looked over to the man on the ground. "Sorry, Mom, I didn't have a clear shot."

Bram confessed, "I didn't either. I was afraid I was going to hit Tamera." He looked at Tamera then.

"It's okay. Killing someone isn't an easy thing to get over. I was actually aiming for the shoulder. Clearly, I missed, it went into his chest. I'm just grateful I didn't hit Tamera. Again here I sit, looking at someone I just killed, not caring he's dead. What kind of person does that make me? I don't know what's gotten into people attacking each other these days, but I'm about sick of it!" she said as she glanced at the lifeless body on the ground.

"Mom, he was going to kill her – you had to shoot. Seriously, the fact that you even hit him was a miracle." Landon cracked a smile at his mother.

Riley knew he was right, even the part about hitting him. She really didn't like any kind of weapons, but her husband, Jackson, loved to go to the gun or archery range. She did it for him. This was the second life she had taken. She hoped there was room for God's forgiveness once again. She would never get used to killing and had a newfound respect for the armed forces. She knew they would all have to fight one day just for the simple right to live. She had hoped it wouldn't happen again for some time, though. All of a sudden, she felt sick to her stomach. Riley stood up with her hand extended to Tamera. Tamera was slow to take it but then gave in, letting Riley pull her up. Bram had her by the elbow, helping her to balance, then informed Riley that Tamera could ride with him. Landon smiled at his mother, who in turn smiled at Bram. Bram turned bright red, making all three of them laugh. Even Tamera managed a smile. Landon gave his mother a boost back on Duke and then helped Tamera on the back of Bram's horse. The moment Tamera was on Bram's horse, she closed her eyes. Without any thought, she put her arms around Bram's waist then lay her head on his back. Riley knew Tamera was drained. She hoped she could hang on for just a few more hours. Bram took the lead as they headed back the way they had come.

They rode back at a slow-moving pace to where they first encountered Tamera's parents. It took them quite some time to arrive back to the small camp. No one was there when they led the horses through the camp. Riley knew that Kevin and Tony had started the long trek back to Calumet with the new additions to their community. She was positive they would soon catch up to the group. There were eleven, Riley thought. Yes, she had counted eleven. This brought their total up to eighty-seven people. It would be extremely tight now. They were going to have do some finagling to make room for everyone in this group, but they could manage it. The horse trailers might have to be used now as living quarters for some people. Maybe some of the young men wouldn't mind moving into one since it would only be used for sleeping anyway. Alejandro offered to move into one of them for that very thing. She was sure the young men wouldn't mind giving up their rooms. Landon and Bram could sleep on her cabin floor with Kota and Jesse. She actually liked the idea of having her whole family under one roof again.

It took them another hour to catch up with the others. When they came up to the top of the ridge, they found the group resting from their long hike up. Shauna was kneeling down next to one of the other men when she saw Bram's horse with her daughter on it. She was on her feet and next to her daughter within seconds. Martin was only a step behind his wife. With no effort at all, Tamera's father had her in his arms, holding her. Shauna was crying and kissing her daughter all over. Martin, through wet eyes, mouthed thank you to Riley. Seeing a big man like Martin crying almost made her cry too. She ushered Duke to move ahead.

Kevin took hold of Duke's reins. "We have a problem."

Riley gazed in the direction he was looking. She slid down off Duke then proceeded to move in that direction.

"What happened?" Riley asked as she knelt down in front of one of the men.

"I'm positive he has a broken leg. His sister was just about to check it when you rode up."

"Hi, I'm Riley. What's your name?" She glanced at his leg as she questioned him.

"Joseph, um, Joseph Price."

"Joseph, I need to look at your leg. Okay?"

"Are you a doctor?" he asked.

"No, but I'm the best we have until I can get you to camp."

Riley wasn't going to touch him until he said it was okay.

"If you don't mind, I would rather my sister take a look at it," he said through gritted teeth.

About that time, Shauna was kneeling down beside Riley.

"Joseph, there's no need to be rude. I'm only a family practitioner. I don't know anything about broken bones other than the fact that yours is broken."

Riley was happily surprised. "You're a doctor?"

"Family medicine, that's all," she explained.

"Ha, well, that is better than what we have, which is my mother and Agnes. Don't get me wrong, they do an excellent job, but having you around is a saving grace." Riley was overjoyed.

"Well, I don't know about that. But I'll do everything I can." Then looking at her brother she said, "Starting with you, I guess."

"Tony and Kevin, see if you can find a tree that is small enough to make into poles so we can make a stretcher. Oh, and get the rope from my saddle please," Riley instructed them.

"Right away, Boss," Tony said as he made his way over to her horse to get what he needed. Kevin followed.

"Landon, we need some wood for a splint. Would you see if you could find some please?"

Riley had a small knife that she pulled out of its sheath and started to cut through the fabric on Joseph's pants.

Shauna saw the concentration on Riley's face and informed her brother that he seemed to be in capable hands. Riley smiled but didn't look up from what she was doing. When she was done, she pulled the material back and was aghast to see the bone sticking out. Riley turned her head so as not to vomit. Shauna thankfully took over from Riley at that point.

"Joseph, you have a compound fracture. It's going to hurt, and I mean, the excruciating kind of hurt. I have nothing for the pain and nothing for an infection," Shauna was almost in tears while giving her brother the bad news.

"Shauna, we have meds at our camp, antibiotics too. Can this wait until we get him home? It's about three miles or so. We can put him on the stretcher and carry him."

"Yes, it's going to be uncomfortable for him, but that would be best. Are you okay with that, brother?"

Shauna had her hand on her brother's shoulder. He laced his fingers into hers and gave a nod in agreement. Landon was the first to get back and handed his mother the sticks along with the first aid bag. He gagged when he saw the bone protruding out of the man's leg. Riley took the ace bandage out and slowly worked with Shauna to get the sticks in place, then together the women wrapped the bandage around his leg. He cried out a few times, but for the most part, he gritted his teeth, bearing the pain. When they were done, Tony and Kevin were standing next to them with two very nice wooden poles. Landon took them, tied the rope in a fancy knot his father had shown him around one end of the pole and did the same on the other. Then he went over and under, wrapping the rope several times around each pole so it wouldn't slip. When he got to the end, he tied the rope again in the same knots his father taught him. When he was finished, he pulled hard on the poles. Once he was satisfied, he laid them down on the ground. Riley asked Martin and another man, Troy, if they would mind moving Joseph onto the stretcher. As they did, Joseph let out a bloodcurdling scream. He was in agony, which made it difficult for the men as they lay him on the stretcher.

Riley turned to Kevin, "What happened anyway?"

"We were climbing up the last bit of the steep incline when he slipped in the snow. His foot must have gotten caught between some rocks because his body kept going but not his foot. I heard the snap when his leg broke. It was all we could do to get him up here." Kevin looked back at Joseph.

"Oh, boy, poor guy." Chills went down Riley's spine, hearing how it happened. "So do you think everyone has had a long-enough break? We really need to get moving if we're going to get back to camp before nightfall. It's going to be slow having to carry him," Riley expressed her concerns.

"Yeah, we're ready to go." Kevin was looking toward the sky. "The weather isn't going to hold out much longer either."

Riley agreed. She instructed everyone that they needed to get moving. She had some of the younger kids ride on Duke while she walked him. The kids were apprehensive at first, but once on, they enjoyed the ride. Riley wasn't sure how old they were. Perhaps seven and nine, maybe older. Whatever their age, they were cute and well mannered. Martin and Troy, another member of Martin's group, carried Joseph first, then they swapped out with Landon and Bram, and finally, Tony and Kevin. The rotation worked out beautifully as it kept them moving. Every now and then, the terrain would dictate that four men were needed to carry him. Whatever the case was, the men worked together as a team to keep moving.

Riley had the rest of the party double up on horses while she walked them. It took them an hour and a half before they saw the smoke from their camp. Riley asked Bram for a boost up on Duke, which he was happy to do. Riley sat behind the saddle, cradling the two children in front of her. The kids started to laugh when Riley had Duke in a gallop heading for the camp. Some of the people in Calumet who saw her coming in from a distance could tell something was up when they noticed the two young black children riding in with her. Her father and Anderson ran forward, catching hold of

Duke's reins as she came closer to them. Both of them helped her with the children.

"There are others coming, and we have a badly injured man. We need someplace we can work on him."

Anderson took off running, nabbing Nate and Allen along the way.

Matt and Mark, Carolyn's two boys, took care of the two children once they were on the ground, showing them the way into the kitchen. Victoria, Agnes, and Lupe were preparing the evening meal when the children walked in. All three women were surprised by the sight of the two black children standing there. Victoria told the boys to take the children over to one of the tables, that she would bring some juice and cookies over for them. The two children perked up at the sound of cookies and happily followed Matt and Mark over to a table.

The men made a triage of sorts, using one of the big tents since there was no other place to work on Joseph's leg. Allen brought in the huge metal table they used for butchering the large game after a hunt. Riley ran into the storeroom, looking for the bleach and a few towels. She then ran back to the tent and poured the bleach all over the table and then wiped it down. Agnes was carrying a box of what looked to be medical supplies and bottles of medicine. Riley knew what they needed was an IV, surgeon, and anesthesiologist but they had what they had, and it was going to have to be enough. Shauna, being a doctor of any kind, was their good fortune, Riley thought. Walking outside to wait for the others' arrival, Riley thanked the men for their ingenuity. The horses and their riders came in first, followed by those carrying the stretcher. Alejandro and Lyle took the horses back to the corral once they got everyone off. Victoria directed people to the kitchen so they could get a bite to eat. Shauna followed Riley into the tent, as did the men carrying the stretcher. Anderson and Allen helped the others move Joseph onto the table. Agnes brought in a large pot of hot water followed by Becca carrying some bowls and towels. Allen found another small table and placed it next to Shauna so she would have whatever she needed within arm's reach.

Shauna asked Anderson, Martin, and Allen to stay to hold Joseph down. She took the splint off then used the hot water and hydrogen peroxide to clean the wound as best she could. Once it was clean, Shauna was ready to do what she needed to do. She took a moment to think about what exactly that was. She had sharp knives but no medical ones. This made Shauna nervous at first, but then she realized this was it, and she would have to work with what she had. She was grateful Anderson gave Joseph some leather to bite on. She took a deep breath, picked up the knife, and began to cut into her brother's flesh. Joseph screamed while the three men held him down. Shauna worked as fast as she could. She had Riley pull on the leg as she pushed the bone back in. The thought of doing that made Riley sick to her stomach, but she did as she was asked. Joseph screamed again then passed out. Shauna took advantage of that and stuck her fingers into her brother's leg, moving the bone back into the right place. Once she was done with that, she cleaned the area again, took the needle and what looked to be very fine fishing line, and stitched the leg up. Then she put thick gauze over the wound and wrapped his leg. Anderson moved in to cut the rest of Joseph's pants off. With the help of Martin, they managed to put sweats on him along with some clean socks that Becca had given them. Once they had her brother's filthy shirt off, Shauna gave him a sponge bath. After a good cleaning, Martin and Anderson put a T-shirt on him then a sweatshirt. Ken brought in a better splint for Shauna to use, which she was happy to have. Now the only thing left was for Riley to think of a place to put him.

Zane was outside the tent, waiting for Riley when she stepped outside. She was surprised to see him standing there.

"Oh, hey, is everything okay?"

"Yes, sure, sure, everything's fine. We were talking," he cleared his throat, "my wife, Jasper, and the others feel that with this man's injury and them not having a place to stay, well, we thought we would give up our place. We'll move in with the Kellers. Jasper and his friends have already moved into the large horse trailer. Alejandro said they would be fine because it's insulated. We would like for these people to have our motor home. There will be plenty of room for the kids, and their parents, as well as the injured man."

Riley didn't know what to say to this amazing act of kindness. "Are you sure, Zane? I mean, that would be incredible! Really, you have no idea."

"Yes, I'm very sure. We've only been here a day and are extremely happy to be here. We want to contribute, and I think this is the best way for us to do that."

"Thank you, Zane, I really appreciate it. I'll send someone over to help you get whatever you need out of there."

"We have plenty of help, and anyway, we're almost done," he told her.

"Zane, hold on," Riley went back into the tent only to come out a few seconds later with Martin and Shauna. "Zane, I would like you to meet our doctor, Shauna, and her husband, Martin."

"Hi, how are you?" Shauna asked. Martin reached around to offer his hand, and Zane took it.

"Zane and his wife have offered you and your family his motor home. They have it almost cleared out. The best part is, your brother will be able to stay with you."

They were both overwhelmed and thanked him. With their placement resolved, Riley said she needed to figure something out for the others. Overhearing the conversation, Allen told them he would make room for them over at Mercy. Both Shauna and Martin looked confused, so Riley promptly explained to them about the other camp and cabins. Shauna and Martin seemed relieved. Riley thanked Allen for his help, then showed Shauna and Martin to the kitchen. The look on their faces was priceless. They were amazed at how incredible it was inside. The smell of the food made their stomachs growl, as it did Riley's. She realized then that she had missed those wonderful burritos this morning for breakfast. Lupe must have been reading her mind, though, because she had a burrito with a small cup of stew waiting for her. She thanked Lupe then offered a table to Shauna and Martin. They took the table next to the one their daughters and son were sitting at with Bram, Landon, and Annie. Sara brought two bowls of stew with corn bread over to Shauna and Martin. Martin's eyes went big.

"Food, real food!" He looked at Riley then again at the bowl. "It smells fantastic!"

Riley grinned at him and pushed her shoulder into his big arm, saying, "It tastes wonderful too. Dig in."

That was all Riley had to say. Martin was in his chair, savoring ever bite as if it were his last.

"Heaven at last," he said and then asked, "Are there seconds?"

CHAPTER 12

It was Thanksgiving morning, and for whatever reason, everyone was excited for today. Instead of having turkey, though, it would be trout, chicken, and elk. Alejandro, Kota, and Landon were in charge of killing the chickens they would need for the feast. Agnes thought five would do as they had forty trout, which were caught the day before. The chickens would be stuffed and then baked. The fish were to be cooked with a savory lemon sauce from Victoria's homemade stash. Pies were made the day before along with cookies and brownies. Against Victoria's wishes, they used canned yams and marshmallows to make the candied yams. Sara made her famous green bean casserole, although it had to be altered since she didn't have all the ingredients. The smell of homemade bread filled the air and was making everyone hungry.

The tent used for a triage was cleaned out, and they put tables and chairs in it from Mercy. The young men stacked some hay around the tent to help insulate it from the wind. This made the tent door the only part visible besides the roof. Sara gave her MP3 player up again so there would be music. With the help from the kid's decorations, they had the tent looking very festive. They used pine cones and other amazing things found in the forest as centerpieces. Riley was impressed with everything and thought it looked perfect. She wanted to go see how Joseph was before she got too caught up in her day. She left the tent and headed for the motor homes. As people passed her, they greeted her with, "Hey, Boss," "Good morning, Boss," "Beautiful morning, Boss," or "How's it goin', Boss?" Riley could only smile and wave. She couldn't do a thing about it. "Boss" had stuck with everyone. She knew her husband would get a tremendous laugh out of it. For that matter, Jackson would never let her live it down. Thinking about him today didn't make her feel sad. Instead, the thought of him made her smile. By the time she made it to the doc's place, her smile was huge. Martin was outside and saw her coming.

"Are those clean thoughts you're having there, Riley?"

Riley laughed, "Thinking about something my husband would've said, and thank you for calling me Riley."

"What, you have another name people call you around here?"

"Don't ask. You'll find out soon enough. How's Joe doing today?"

"Better. The pain is still bad, but the drink, whatever it was, that Lupe gave him last night helped a lot. Shauna didn't even want to know what was in it."

"No telling. Alejandro had a salve that he makes that did wonders on a few men here." Riley surveyed the area for a moment then asked, "Where is everyone?"

"Well, Tamera and Trent went with Bram, and your daughter, Sara, came over and invited Shyla over to help out in the kitchen. She was thrilled that there was anything around here called 'the kitchen,'" Martin said with a smile. "For that matter, so am I."

"Yes, this place is a wonder. How about your wife?"

"Yeah, that's another funny wonder about this place. Now that there's a doctor on the premises, she is making some house calls. She walked over to Mercy to see someone."

"Thank you, I'll walk over there."

Riley was in a great mood and loving the atmosphere that today's festivity brought. She was on the path that led to Mercy when she heard footsteps coming fast behind her. She cringed at the thought it might be bad news. She stopped and turn around to see who it was. It was Anderson. She waited for him to catch up with her.

"G'morning, Riley."

She was very happy that he had declined calling her Boss.

"It is a good morning as long as you aren't bringing me bad news."

"Ah, no bad news. Just wonderin' if our fearless leader had given much thought about what she might say to her loyal subjects today at the feast?"

Riley laughed and shook her finger at him. "You're enjoying this far too much, aren't you?"

"Actually, I am," he said, picking up his pace to keep up with her.

"I think I said everything that needed to be said a few days ago. What else needs to be said?"

"Riley, listen." He seized her arm and pulled her in front of him. "I know you aren't keen on this 'Boss' thing, but it is what it is. Right? You didn't ask for this, but I hate to tell you there is nothing you can do about it. You're the commander in chief, so to speak, for this lot. You can't have one foot in and one foot out anymore. Everyone trusts you - geez, Riley, half of us owe you our lives! I know you're uncomfortable with the title, but you've earned it. We have new people here that don't know what your future plans are for the community, and they need to hear it firsthand from their leader, which means you! It will also be the first time we've had everyone from Mercy here at the same time in a while." He started walking again but continued looking at her. "After you gave that impromptu speech, in your jammies, I might add, this place was filled with excitement of a newfound hope. It was doom and gloom for so long, and then you opened the door with all kinds of possibilities. You did that, Riley, and people need to hear it again from you."

Riley put her hands in her coat pockets as she continued her trek to Mercy. "Okay, okay, you win. I'll think of something." She glanced at him. "I've decided when the first team will leave for Jackson."

"Really?"

"Yes, the first of February."

He thought about that for a minute. "Won't there still be snow?"

"Yes, that's the idea. If the virus goes dormant or even dies due to the cold, then it's the perfect time to go."

"Um, if you don't mind me askin', how are we going to get there?"

"Well, that's the million-dollar question, isn't it?" she said with little concern.

"Okay, so you've an idea. What is it?"

"We have snow chains for my SUV, and it's a four-wheel drive. We have another set, but they're for my folks' Escalade, although I don't want to take that vehicle. I want to take Becca's truck. Allen was a mechanic, actually, I guess he still is. Anyway, he grabbed a lot more than the rental truck in Vernal, and he said he had a surprise for me. It's one of the reasons for my trip over to Mercy, that and to find the doc."

Anderson's interest was piqued. "Does he then? Well, now, you've got a Buckley's chance at stopping me from tagging along, Boss."

"Seriously, Anderson, you are not allowed to call me that!" Riley said playfully.

He laughed, and they walked in silence the rest of the way to Mercy. Riley didn't go over to Mercy very often except on the rare days that the person she was looking for wasn't at Calumet. Everyone from Mercy began to come over to Calumet to eat every meal quite some time ago. The fourth cabin went back to being living quarters, which was a huge help now that they had added eleven new members to their community. Riley did enjoy the walk over when she did go to Mercy. Riley's mind was going over the things she needed to speak to

Shauna about when Nate and Carolyn greeted them as they entered Mercy. Riley had noticed they had been spending a great deal of time together. She was happy for them. Life had some normality to it up here away from the rest of the world.

"Hey, you two. You wouldn't happen to know where the doc is, would you?"

Nate pointed over to the first cabin. "Yeah, she went in to see Lyle and Dina."

"Thank you," Riley said and started to turn to walk away.

Nate stopped her. "Eh, Boss, I have a quick question. Um, it's a personal one. One that Carolyn and I would like to talk to you about if you have a second."

Riley glanced at Anderson, who in turned held his hands up and backed away, saying, "No, worries, mate, I'll go find Allen. See you shortly, bo—eh, Riley."

Riley smiled at him as he walked away. Then she gave her undivided attention to Nate and Carolyn. "Okay, I'm all yours. What can I do for you?"

Carolyn was acting a bit coy and didn't say anything. Nate cleared his throat and began to speak, "Well, I'm sure you're aware that Carolyn and I have been seeing one another." He looked at Carolyn then cleared his throat again as he looked back to Riley. "And well, we've fallen in love, and we would like to get married."

Riley was surprised at this, and it must have shown because Carolyn finally spoke up, "I know is seems quick, but it really hasn't been. It's been five months, and we've had nothing but time up here to get to know one another."

Laughing, Riley put her hands up, as if defeated. "Okay, look, it's fine. The only problem is, you're married, Carolyn."

"Well, that's why we're talking to you now about it," Nate declared.

"Me? What can I do about it?"

"Give Carolyn a divorce."

"A divorce? I don't have the power to do that, and the Bible's very clear about divorce. I just can't write you a 'get out of marriage free' card."

"But Adam abandoned not just Carolyn but his boys too. There has to be something you can do."

"Look, I'll talk to my dad. This is way over my head, but you're right, Adam abandoned his family. Carolyn and the boys shouldn't be punished because of him."

"Please, I'm in love with her, and I love those boys. There has to be a way."

Riley thought about it a minute. Whether she liked it or not, she was thrust into a leadership role. Anderson was correct; she couldn't have one foot in and one foot out anymore. They came to her as their leader to make something right for them, and she needed to try and help.

"Okay. I'll talk to my dad, and we'll see if there is something we can do. Come find me tomorrow, and hopefully, I'll have something for you. I take it you want to get married soon?"

They both said yes at the same time. Riley gave Carolyn a hug and shook hands with Nate. They parted from Riley extremely happy, leaving her feeling somewhat giddy for them too. She inhaled the fresh mountain air and let it out slowly.

Yes, Riley thought, this was an amazing start for the community to get part of their lives back. Riley was happy as she continued on to Lyle's cabin.

She knocked on the door of the cabin and was greeted by Lyle. "Hi, Boss, what brings you over here?"

"I need to speak to the doc. If she's still busy, I can come back."

"Oh, no, I'm sorry, come in. Please come in."

Riley stepped into the cabin and noticed one of the sofas they brought back from the Vernal trip. She saw Shauna and Dina sitting on it, talking. They both looked up at her when she came in.

Riley smiled, "I don't want to interrupt anything, I can come back."

Dina was crying but wiped away her tears and smiled at Riley. "No, you're never a bother." She looked at her husband and then back to Riley. "I'm pregnant."

That took Riley's breath away. "Wow! Congratulations! I'm truly happy for you. How far along are you?"

"The doctor thinks five months," Dina said.

"Without proper equipment, I can't be sure. But the baby is there, and my best guess is four more months and the baby will be here," Shauna advised.

"It could be risky, but if you need something, there's a town a few hours from here. I don't mind going back there to get what you need," Riley offered.

Lyle stepped in then, "Boss, I can't ask you to do that. It's too risky, and with the snow, it will be near impossible to get there."

"Doc, make me a list of what you need, and I'll be happy to collect everything on it."

"Well, it might be better if I go with you." Shauna knew what she needed better than anyone.

"Sorry, Doc, you'll have to stay here. Make the list, and hopefully, the weather will cooperate so we can leave in the next day or two. Besides, I promised some supplies to some people who are at another campsite."

Lyle looked at his wife. "Baby, I need to go with her. It's for us, and I can't let her go without me. It'll be okay. She always seems to bring everyone back and then some."

"Lyle, you don't have to go, I…" Riley was about to object when he stopped her.

"Yes, I do. We're going to need a lot more than just what's on the doc's list."

Riley laughed, "Yes, you are!"

Riley gave Dina a big hug, then turned to Lyle, and told him he should probably come with her. She also told Shauna that she still needed to speak with her and asked if she would find her before she went back to Calumet. She agreed. Lyle and Riley went to find Anderson and Allen.

What they found was the trailer that they brought from her father's house in pieces and a plow—a snowplow to be exact.

"Wow, you've been busy. How did you do this?"

"They had tools, a sheet of steel, and a welding machine at the rental place. I figured we were going to need all of it more than the rental place was, so Bram and I packed it all up and brought it with us."

"Allen, this is terrific!" Riley was truly amazed.

"What truck are you going to attach it to?" she asked.

"I thought we would use the one we brought the boys back in from Vernal. It's a good tough truck and should do fine."

"Excellent! We'll have our first test run in the next day or so," Riley announced.

"What do you mean 'test run,' Boss?" Allen inquired.

"We have to go back into town." She looked at Lyle. "Um, Lyle, do you mind telling them?"

"Sure, yeah, it's okay. Dina's five months pregnant," he said.

"Because of that the doc is in need of a few things, so we have to go. This time, we really don't have a choice," Riley added.

Anderson and Allen were stunned. Anderson walked over and shook Lyle's hand. "Congratulations, mate! Truly, congratulations."

Allen did the same. They all stood, looking at the thing that they hoped would cut through the snow.

Allen spoke the thoughts going through his head, "I need to go with you. I can fix anything if one of the vehicles breaks down or something goes wrong with this."

"Okay, Anderson, you'll have to hold the fort down for us. And this is me with both feet in," Riley said seriously.

The other two men were puzzled by her comment. "Okay, but I'm going with you when you leave for Jackson in February. One of these two can stay behind."

"That will be me. I won't be leaving my wife after Christmas. We're guessing four months, it could be less."

"Okay, then it's settled. This is really terrific work, Allen. Thank you."

"You're welcome. While back in town, I would like to search for a few items if that's okay?" Allen asked Riley.

"Sure, we'll make a day of it," Riley said, still admiring his work.

"Hi, Riley, you wanted to speak with me?"

Riley and the others turned to see the doc behind them. Riley couldn't help but notice how tall she was. She and her husband were a perfect match. Riley always liked her height but was a little envious of taller women. Shauna was a beautiful woman. She had her hair in long tiny braids that went past her shoulders. Her skin was lighter than her husband's, more of a light brown. Riley could definitely see the resemblance between Shauna and her girls; they even had their mother's sweet disposition. Trent definitely took after his dad in height and looks. He even had his dad's wicked smile.

"Oh, yes, thanks, Doc. Gentlemen, this will require all your attention too, so is there someplace where we can talk?" Riley said as she was looking around for a place.

"Yeah, it'll be a bit cold, but there's privacy over by the lake," Lyle offered.

"That will do. Would you mind walking over there with us, Doc?" Riley asked.

"Sure."

Lyle showed them the way to the lake, and like Calumet, they had tree trunks laid out in a circle with a pit in the middle containing burnt wood. The snow had melted off the logs, allowing them a place to sit. Riley gazed out over the lake. Calumet couldn't be seen from here because there was a bend in the lake on this side and Calumet was around that bend. It was a beautiful day, but it was cold. The sun felt good on Riley's face, and she closed her eyes enjoying the warmth, taking a moment before she spoke. When she opened her eyes, everyone was staring at her waiting.

"Sorry, the sun feels so good." Riley knew she needed to get this conversation started, but she also knew none of them would like what they might hear. "Doc, I'm not sure if you've met everyone. This is Anderson, he's our resident Aussie who got stranded here in the United States. This gentleman is Allen, who's our mechanical guru, and of course, you know Lyle. My dad, whom you met, can't be with us this morning. This makes up our council. I'm afraid you've just been thrust onto it as well."

"Oh, I'm not sure why you would want me on your council."

"You're now the doctor of this little community of ours, so you will have a lot to contribute. For instance, right now we need some information about this virus that seems to be lurking about, devouring the human race. Would you mind telling us what you know about it?" Riley asked.

"Well, I really don't know much. Although, I can share with you what a friend of mine said. He worked at the hospital in Boston where the first case is said to have been."

Riley perked up when she said that. "The hospital Mr. Blakely was in?"

"Who's Mr. Blakely?" Allen asked.

"Yes, he was one of the doctors that tended to him."

"Okay, can someone catch me up? I don't know who this Blakely guy is?" Allen was persistent now.

Shauna took the lead by telling him, "The officials believe Craig Blakely was patient zero for the United States. For whatever reason, he was in China. On his way home, he flew into San Francisco with a layover and then flew on to Boston, his hometown. His roommate found him in his room nonresponsive and called 911. It was all downhill from then on. My friend was working the day Blakely was admitted and was handed his case. He said that whatever this virus is, it attacks the immune system rapidly. It comes on like a cold, but then within a few hours, the symptoms change to a nasty stomach virus, and from there, it gets into the intestines. It then attacks everything in the body, which by that time has nothing to fight it off with. Nothing they did could save him or his roommate. The symptoms are high fever, very sore throat, diarrhea, and vomiting. I was told that when they did the autopsy, the lining of the throat, esophagus, and stomach were covered in little ulcers; some were filled with a pus-like substance. Oh, one other thing, my friend said the eyes hemorrhage, and at death, there's a white substance coming from the mouth. The white substance could easily be due to the ulcers they found."

Riley was surprised at first, not able to say anything for a few minutes. The men could only manage to look at one another.

Riley regained control of her thoughts and explained, "I have a theory that I would like to run by you. I'm a history nut, so my theory comes from the past, which might seem a bit far-fetched. But I believe – let me rephrase that – it is my opinion – and one I hope will be fact—that the frigid temperatures might kill the virus or put it in some state of dormancy, allowing us to go in and possibly clear out a town of its bodies, which in turn would allow us to find a more permanent place to live. Don't get me wrong, I love our tight-knit community, but with a child on the way and another couple getting married, we need room to grow. We can't grow here. My children, your children, along with all the other families with children need to have a future. We need to give them that. We can't do that here."

Shauna gave some careful thought about what Riley said.

"I think you might be onto something. But I still would take some precautions. Use gloves, a full-face mask, and some disposable suits. But, Riley, everything inside a house would have to be burned. We couldn't use any of it. You have to remember some things thrive in the cold and/or heat. None of the medicine they had could fight against this disease."

Anderson added, "Riley thought that we might have to burn everything. The thing is, she wants us to go into Jackson, a town of eight to nine thousand people. What happens if we don't get it all cleared out before winter is over?"

"That's a good question and one I don't know the answer to. What I can tell you is, most viruses are carried by something—what that is in this case, I don't know. But the cold will kill out fleas, mosquitos, and possibly rodents. You would need to burn bodies, clothes, and linen of the dead as well as furniture. If there are survivors, that would help. We could see what's in their blood that's not in the rest of ours," she explained.

Riley diverted her eyes, as did the others.

Shauna caught it. "You have someone here that's immune?"

"Yes, but it wouldn't do any good anyway, there is no one here that can do the research," Riley confessed.

Shauna knew what Riley was saying was true. She was a family practitioner and was already being used in areas that she had no business going into.

"Then I suppose we're going to have to clear the town of its people before spring comes into full bloom."

Anderson stood up and walked around in a circle then went back to sit again. He put both hands through his long hair then looked up at the group.

"We need to go in January then, not February. And the team going in needs to be larger than a few people, Riley. We have eighty-seven people, half of which are young adults or kids. I don't want to exclude women, but the men need to go."

"Yes, I've thought of that. Bram, Landon, and Annie will go as well as Kota and Jesse. Sara and Jena can't do it, they'll stay here to take care of Levi. I'll only take volunteers with me."

"Riley, you're sacrificing too much. You could lose your entire family!" Allen was sick at the thought of losing her, let alone any of her children.

Riley knew that too. She had spoken with both of her parents about it along with her children, which now included Levi, Kota, Jesse, and Jena. They all understood the risk involved. They knew that in order to get on with living, sacrifices were going to have to be made. What kind of leader would she be to order people to go and then be too afraid to go herself? She would put all her trust in God. She felt this is what they needed to do if they were going to get back to living again. What Shauna said did nothing to deter her from this. She would take all the necessary precautions, especially because most of her children were going. January would be arriving very soon, which meant they would need to prepare for it now. A whole month earlier, she thought. Well, as Anderson said, "It is what it is," and it has to be done.

"I want you to know that I would have done it with just my family. Maybe not clean out a whole town, but nonetheless, I would have gone someplace and done it," Riley said.

"Riley, you don't need to go. Let us go! You for once can stay here. You're already going out again in the next couple of days. Let someone else do this," Allen continued pleading with her.

"Thank you, but my part has been decided. Now it's up to the rest of you to make that decision for yourselves. While in this other town, we'll grab what we need for our Jackson trip. I'm comfortable going into this town, but I should warn you, it's creepy. However, I do recall seeing a sign for a clinic there. Sorry, Doc, I didn't see one for a hospital. Hope the clinic will have what you need."

"Yes, it should do. May I ask, how many times have you gone out? You never explained how you even found us."

"Our patrol found a dead body, and his trail led us to you. The rest, you know."

"You also never said what happened when you found my daughter, which by the way, my family appreciates immensely. However, Tamera won't say anything about it yet. How did you manage to get her away from that crazy lunatic?"

All the men's eyes rested on Riley. Riley had hoped to forget about it. Killing this guy didn't put her in the spiral of guilt that she had with the killing of Bruce. What did that say about her? What did God think about that?

She looked directly into Shauna's eyes and said, "I killed him. One arrow in the chest. He was in the process of slitting Tamera's throat, so I took the shot. He made the mistake of pushing Tamera to one side. I was aiming for the shoulder and hit him in the chest."

Riley's eyes were burning with anger. She stood up and walked around for a moment. She guessed she did have some emotions about it after all. She looked out at the lake, feeling the warmth of the sun again, which calmed her down some. She spun back around to the group, who were all staring at her again.

"I'm sorry you had to do that, Riley," Allen said, "but you had no choice. Tamera did nothing to deserve what happened to her. As far as I'm concerned, I'm glad you were there. If he had lived, who's to say he wouldn't do the same to some other poor soul?"

"Thank you, Allen. I'm okay, really."

Anderson knew what this was doing to Riley. They had long, quiet conversations about the death of Bruce and AJ, of her worries for the kids and their innocence that was being lost in this new world. This time, Riley looked lost on her feeling about the death of this man. He was going to have to make sure he had a talk with her about it. Riley would not, or could not, let any harm come to anyone in this camp. Knowing this about Riley was what drove the men here and made the people in both camps want to follow her. She took on a role that no one else wanted. Though he joked with her earlier about her status within the two camps, he knew she took it seriously. He had no doubt that she would find a way for everyone to get back to living, even if she had to kill a hundred more insane people in the process. He hoped and prayed it wouldn't come to that.

"Then it's settled. We leave for Jackson in January. When do you plan to make the announcement?" Anderson was curious.

"I honestly don't want to do it tonight, but I think I can do it in a way that won't ruin the festivities. Everyone will be at Calumet, which will give them a chance to talk about it afterward. It will give them plenty of time to decide whether or not they want to volunteer. I'm confident that our people can handle the news and enjoy the festivities at the same time," Riley reassured them.

* * *

"Good afternoon, everyone."

Riley stood before all the people of Calumet and Mercy on a small wooden box Anderson made for her just for these impromptu speeches. Since Riley loved history, primarily the Founding Fathers, she loved using their principles and managed to apply them to current times. The Founders were mindful of God's presence in all things. George Washington even made it personal by acknowledging, *"I have only been an instrument in the hands of Providence,"*[2] and for Riley, that gave her something to stand on for herself too. She was

---

[2]   *Washington, The Writing of George Washington*, p. 120, to Lucretia van Winter on March 30, 1785.

merely a tool to be used by His Most High Grace, God Himself. The Founding Fathers had incredible insight that was valuable then, and Riley felt it was still of great value now. As she looked out at these wonderful men, women, and children, she wondered if they understood how much their road and the road of the Founding Fathers were the same. They were fighting for their freedom—maybe not against the overly oppressive British, but nevertheless it was for a freedom of equal importance: the freedom to live and to live free. She knew what to say. It was a letter written to George Washington from a friend and a Founding Father, Thomas Paine. General Washington had the letter read to his troops. That short letter, note, or whatever they called it back then had as much to do with today as it did back then. This would be her opening.

"On December 25, 1776, a man by the name of Thomas Paine wrote a letter that George Washington read to his troops before they made that historic crossing of the Delaware River to fight the Hessians. You're probably wondering why a letter from so long ago could be so significant for us today. Well, today we celebrate a day of Thanksgiving, but tomorrow we move forward to take our future, to fight for it and then to sustain it. What Thomas Paine wrote back then is every bit as important to us as it was to them back then. He wrote,

> *These are the times that try men's souls. The summer soldier and the sunshine patriot will, in this crisis, shrink from the service of his country; but he that stands it now deserves the love and thanks of the men and women. Tyranny, like hell, is not easily conquered; yet more glorious the triumph. What we obtain too cheap, we esteem too lightly: it is dearness only that gives everything its value. Heaven knows how to put a proper price on its goods; and it would*

be strange indeed if so celestial an article as freedom
should not be highly rated. [3]

Riley continued, "These are trying times for us, but I promise I will not shrink back. I'm not heroic. I'm simply a mother. I understand that neither the tyranny he wrote of nor hell itself is easily conquered. Neither will the road that lies ahead of us, be it the virus or humans that want to stop us. One wants to stop us from living, and the other wants to own our freedom. I know that neither will be easily conquered, but both must be fought. God set the price for our lives when he sent Jesus, and he paid the ultimate price for each of us. No one can take that away from us as long as we have faith. It's also said that Washington knew that if he didn't do something soon, he would lose his army. Dr. Benjamin Rush said that he saw Washington write on a piece of paper, '*Victory or Death.*' [4] It will be the same for us. If we don't move forward, we will lose some of our people. At some point, one, if not all, will tire of this place and move on. In order for us to stay together and get back to living again, we have to move forward. I prefer victory over death. I know all of you do too. We have a fighting chance together and a really good chance to have that victory. After speaking with our doctor, the council decided to move our Jackson date up to January."

That got people's attention, and Riley heard the whispers of concerns, but she continued.

"The freezing cold weather may possibly be our ally. I know it's soon, and no one wants to risk the trip in weather that we can't predict anymore, nor face a virus that we have no understanding of.

---

[3]   William B. Cairns, *Selections from Early American Writers, 1607–1800* (New York: The Macmillan Company, 1909), pp. 347–352.

[4]   Richard Ketchum, *The Winter Soldiers: The Battle for Triton and Princeton* (New York: Holt Paperbacks, 1999), p. 236

The doctor thinks this might be the best time, better than spring or summer, and I agree with her. Folks, we have a lot to be thankful for, and I believe more blessings await us. We've had tremendous growth in just the few short months that we have been here. We started off with twenty-eight people and now we have eighty-seven. I wasn't kidding when I said I hope that we grow to a thousand by the end of next year. This will be our victory! This will be our children's future. My dad told me before we arrived here that 'the world is not how I want to leave it for you and my grandkids.' Well, when my body goes into the ground, I can only hope and pray that I did my part to make this world someplace where my kids and grandkids can live and have a future. A future where they can live as free men and women and not hide from the world around them. Our children give this value, and I trust God will guide us in every step we take. I've prayed for this and said I would not go to Jackson if I wasn't 100 percent sure. Well, I feel 110 percent sure about this. So much so that my children, Landon, Annie, Bram, Kota, and Jesse will be going with me when I leave. I will only take volunteers. No one will think any less of you if you stay. As a matter of fact, we need some to stay to protect this place, so at some point, I will say we have enough. Anderson, along with Allen, have already volunteered. The doctor, my father, and Lyle will be staying here along with my daughters Sara, Jena, and son Levi. Today we give thanks and tomorrow we plan for our move forward. May God bless us and protect us all!"

With that, Riley stepped off her podium. The applause was strange to hear, but as she moved through family and friends, they shook her hand or patted her on the shoulder.

Simon Crawford was one of the first to shake her hand and thank her. "I know I can't go, but I promise to have this place waiting for you when you return for us."

"Thank you, Simon. That means more to me than you'll ever know."

Martin pulled his wife in for a side hug. "You knew about this? Does she even know what's out there, Shauna?"

"She does on a small scale. She's been out there a few times since they've been here and has seen some horrible stuff." Shauna turned, looking up at her husband's face. "But something more importantly you should know is that she killed the man that took Tamera."

"What?"

"The cut on Tamera's neck didn't happen before she got to her. It happened when she got there. She killed him without a second thought to save our daughter. Apparently, it's not the first time either."

"What do you mean not the first time?"

"Apparently, some of the men that live here came here to take over the camp. Allen said they came blasting in with guns. He also said one of the men had a gun crammed up to Riley's head. He said she took the gun away from the man so fast that the rest were stunned and couldn't move. She shot the man point-blank then shot another one in the hand."

"You mean, some of the men in this camp?"

"Yes. Allen was one of them. So was Lyle, Kevin, and a guy named Nate."

"Wow! You've got to be kidding," Martin was in shock.

"That's not all. Annie, Riley's oldest daughter, killed one of the men that day too. A man named AJ was about to shoot her mother, and she shot him with an arrow."

"Wow! Wow! That has to be hard," he said.

"They're leaving in a day or so to make a run into a town a couple of hours from here for medical supplies. They're going to try and find some other items that the team will need for their trip to Jackson."

"Um, babe, would you mind if I went with them on the first trip?" Martin was now standing right in front of her, with his big hands on both of her shoulders.

"Well, I was hoping you would offer. I told them you were in pharmaceuticals before all this. That seemed to make all of them very happy."

"Good. I'll go find Riley and let her know."

Ken asked everyone to quiet down for a moment of prayer. He looked around, and once it was all quiet, he prayed, giving thanks first for the many blessings already received and for all the people that were there, and then he asked the Lord to bless all their future endeavors. He also prayed for their leaders, that God would guide them. When he was done, everyone said, "Amen!"

The food was abundant, and jubilation filled the air. Mr. Miller came over and sat with Riley and Anderson. He said nothing right away, but Riley knew something was on his mind.

"Mr. Miller, if you have something you need to say or ask, please don't keep me in suspense."

Anderson watched Mr. Miller look first at Riley then at him. "If this is a private conversation, I can go," Anderson informed Mr. Miller.

"Anderson, you twit, can't a man gather his thoughts before he speaks?"

Riley smiled but was biting the inside of her mouth so as not to start laughing. Anderson smiled and made his apologies to Mr. Miller.

"I know you all take me for some fool, but actually, I have some skills that might be useful to you. As you know, one doesn't get to own a house in Park City without having money. I made mine in construction back east. I build things, or did, and made a gob of money doing it. I had the largest construction company in the state of New York," Miller said with pride.

Riley saw Anderson from the corner of her eye. This was wonderful news to hear, but she knew something was coming.

"Do you both have minds of simpletons? I mean, I hate to think that two of our most prominent leaders are half-wit lamebrains!"

Mr. Miller is a piece of work, Riley thought. "Are you, in your own little weird way, asking us to let you join our trip to Jackson?"

Anderson slapped his hand a little too hard on the table, which made Riley jump, and he laughed, "Miller, if you want to come, mate, I, for one, would love for you to. If for nothing else, you'll keep me in stitches!"

Mr. Miller wasn't put off by Anderson's outburst. "If ignorance is bliss, Anderson, you must be the happiest person on the planet!" Turning to Riley, he said, "Don't let this dork persuade your thinking. I may be old, but at least my brain still functions on full capacity, unlike this dope you're sitting with!"

Anderson could normally handle Miller's attacks, but he was getting agitated, and Riley could see it.

"Okay, boys, enough! Yes, you can come, but you do understand it's going to be a lot of work. Are you really up for that?"

"Yes," Miller took a moment then finished, "Landon and Bram have made me feel useful again, and that's something that I haven't felt in a long time. I guess I'm being selfish, as this is as much for me as it is for anyone else. And well, isn't this still a free country? I should have the right to go!"

Riley leaned in close to Miller, "Mr. Miller, what part of 'Yes you can' did you not understand?" Riley smiled at him.

Miller was puzzled at first, then he got up smiling. He began to walk away when he suddenly spun back around. "Thank you, Riley," he said, then turned around, and left.

"Our list of people is growing for both trips. You know, Martin wants to come on this first trip as well as Marcus. I would have never thought Marcus would have volunteered for any of them," Anderson told her.

"I think he wants to get his feet wet with this first trip. Little does he know, this one isn't going to be much fun."

Anderson stared at her. "The fire? You're still bothered by it?"

"Yes. I don't know what happened, and that bothers me. I don't think anyone is there, not alive anyway. And if someone is there, what state of mind will they be in? Did you ever see any of those *Twilight Zone* shows?"

"One or two."

"The town is like one of those shows where something is lurking, watching, but you can't see it, but you know it's there," Riley's voice was low, and it sent chills down Anderson's back.

"That's a beauty, Riley! Enough of the rubbish creep stories. I get it, it's creepy, and the beauty here is that zombies aren't real! I think every town we go into is going to be somewhat creepy. Even Jackson."

"Zombies aren't real, but crazy is, and that to me is more terrifying than any zombies could ever be."

"Look," Anderson spun Riley's chair around to where she was facing him, "if you can't do this, then stay here. Don't go. I'll go in your place."

She never thought of not going, but remembering the charred bodies and all the death she was standing in that day was overwhelming.

"No, I'm fine. I'll have plenty of people around me, and no one will go anywhere alone."

With that, she got up, placed both hands on his face, kissed his forehead, and left. Anderson sat there. He knew, in that simpleton mind of his, he was going to have to figure a way to get on this first trip. He needed to talk to Ken.

CHAPTER 13

The sun was rising, and the sky was clear. The temperature was holding at a nice twenty degrees, which made the earth crunch with every step Riley took. They were taking two trucks. Sometime last night, Allen made the decision as to which vehicles were going. The back end of one of the trucks was filled with gas containers and a large amount of the elk they were storing in the cellar. Shauna still felt she should go, but Riley was adamant about her staying. Besides herself, Bram, Landon, Allen, Lyle, and Martin were going. Marcus found Riley earlier in the morning and told her he wasn't ready yet. She assured him no one would hold it against him, and she understood that not everyone was cut out for these outings. She saw Annie coming her way, carrying her backpack and bow with a quiver of arrows. Anderson, who had a holster on with her father's 9-millimeter Berretta, was walking beside Annie. Riley knew she couldn't stop either of them from coming, so she didn't even try.

She turned to the rest and said, "It's time, let's get moving."

Their first stop would be the camp where they left Philip and then on to the town. She realized she didn't even know the name of the town that they were heading to. She rode with Allen, Annie, and Anderson in the truck with the snowplow attached to it. The others followed in Becca's truck.

It had snowed a few more times during the week, and though the snow wasn't deep everywhere, the plow was handy the few times it was. It took them almost two full hours just to get to the road that led up to Philip's camp. The road leading into the camp was bumpy, and at times the forest seemed impenetrable on either side. Once they were clear of the thick trees, they could see the four motor homes. There was a large fire going between two of them, but no one was outside. Allen honked the horn several times as they drove in. The door opened to one of the homes, and a man came out. Behind him, another man and a woman followed. It was Philip, his wife, and another man whose name Riley couldn't recall. Allen found a good place to park. Philip was surprised to see everyone exit the trucks.

"Hello, Philip." Philip took Riley's hand when she extended it to him. "These are some of my friends, Allen, Lyle, Martin, Anderson, and you remember my kids, Annie, Landon, and Bram."

He shook all their hands, even the teenagers. "I'm surprised you came back!"

"I told you we would, and we come bearing gifts."

The boys were already taking the gas containers and meat from the back end of the truck. The rest of Philip's group was outside now, and a couple of the men went over to help the boys with their task.

Philip's stunned expression said everything. He told Riley, "I thought you weren't going to give us any gas?"

"Well, I wouldn't have, except we're heading back into town where we'll get more. How are all of you holding up?"

"We're doing okay – better now with the meat and gas. Thank you so much for not forgetting us." He paused and glanced at his wife then back to Riley. "I may have been extremely rude to you the last time you were here, and I want you to know how sorry I am for that."

"One day, mate, she's going to have to introduce you to Miller," Anderson chimed in.

Everyone in Riley's group laughed. Philip didn't get it but hoped that one day he would have the privilege of meeting Miller.

Philip's wife asked if any of them cared for coffee, to which Lyle and Martin both said yes. They were standing around the campfire, staying warm. Riley explained that Martin's wife was a doctor and their reasons for going into town. Then she moved the conversation to their plans for moving to Jackson, Wyoming, which they all seemed excited about. They asked about their friends, and Riley's group was glad to answer all their questions. Riley could see the sadness in some of their faces. She knew Philip and the others were probably wishing they had taken up the offer to leave the first time it was offered. Riley was sure they would never ask again, but she could open that door once more for them.

"You know, it's still not too late for you to move to one of our camps, Mercy or Calumet. We would love to have you, and I'm sure your friends would be ecstatic to see you all again."

The entire group perked up, then they looked at Philip. One of the men said, "I'm sorry, Philip, you're a good man, and we've done well because of you, but they have a plan. We seriously don't want to stay here forever."

"Philip, he's right, honey," his wife said, gently touching his arm.

"Thank you, Riley, I've been a fool. Not all Christians are bad, I get that now. I judged you on the merits of others that I've known, and I know I was wrong to do so." Philip was near tears, which drove Riley to give him a big hug, one he gladly accepted. When he pulled back, he wiped his eyes.

"You can either come to town with us, or you can go straight to camp. We left bread crumbs, so to speak, for you with the tire tracks and the plow. If you leave now, the tracks will still be there for you to follow," Riley explained.

One man spoke up, "No, thank you, on going into town! We sent people in there once, and they never came back."

Riley remembered what Jasper told her about his car. She understood his fear and thought about whether or not they would have enough gas. "I'm not sure we brought enough gas for all the motor homes to make it to camp. They can't take all of them, can they?"

Allen thought for a moment then shared his idea, "Eh, Riley, I think it would be best to take all of them. Put most of the gas into two of them and then drive the others until they run out. We can get gas for them in town then drive them in ourselves when we head back."

"Okay, does that work with all of you?"

The entire group agreed. Allen took it upon himself to check out all the engines and tires, and put the gas in the ones he felt would make it to camp without any problems. There wasn't much to put up; however, they did take all the food from the two motor homes that Allen gave the least amount of gas to and put it in the other two. Once they were sure they had everything, Allen told everyone it was time to leave and to load up.

The motor homes led the way out. Once on the main road, they went left, and the pickups went right. Riley was very happy the group decided to finally join them at the camp. She knew they would be happier there, and she knew they would be overjoyed when they finally saw their friends again. It would be a wonderful surprise for those at camp too. She wished she could be there to see the looks on everyone's faces, but instead of a joyous occasion awaiting her, she had a scary one.

The weather went from sunny to overcast. Riley knew that if it did anything, it would snow. She wanted to get in and out of town as soon as possible. The drive for the most part was quiet. Annie slept most of the way, and Riley wished she could. Sleep didn't come easy for her anymore. She always went to bed tired and woke up exhausted. So instead of sleep, she thought she would lean her head against the window and rest her eyes. The next thing Riley felt was the gentle touch of Anderson waking her.

"Riley, sorry to be messin' with your sleep, but we're here." She looked up confused. "Riley, you awake?" he was chuckling.

"Yeah, yes, I'm up. Sorry, I can't believe I fell asleep."

Anderson stood back and helped her out of the truck. "Well, if anyone needs it, it's you."

They stopped just outside of town in the same spot they stopped the first time they were there. Nothing had changed except snow now covered the ground and rooftops of the buildings. A flood of memories came back—ones that she wished she could forget. Lyle looked through his binoculars and when he was done handed them to Riley. She declined them.

Lyle studied the town again, looking through them and then asked, "Okay, Boss, it seems clear. You want us to split up? Some go for gas and the others go to the clinic?"

"No! Sorry, I mean, no. No one splits up, we stay together."

"No worries, Riley. It's okay, we'll stay together. Right, everyone, let's hit it." Anderson went back to the truck as did the rest of their group.

They went slow at first, passing the gas station. Allen explained they would come back here last. They drove down main street and came up to the burnt building. Once in front of it, Anderson asked Allen to stop. Riley didn't understand why he wanted to stop, nor did she ask him. They all got out of the truck. Landon came up behind his mother as did Bram. Riley watched Allen, Lyle, Martin, and Anderson go in. She didn't need to nor want to go in again. The blackened bodies of babies and small children were forever scarred into her memory. Anger and sorrow filtered through her body as she stood there waiting, and the torment caused by the two emotions made her knees feel weak. She moved her legs just enough to make sure they were going to hold her. She felt her eyes burning, but she made no effort to wipe them. She just stood very still and waited.

It didn't take long for Riley and the teenagers to see what the effect of going into the building had on the men. The first one to come out was Martin, and the big man came outside spewing. He gagged again and vomited some more. When Lyle came out, he looked like he was going to be sick but managed to keep it at bay with a lot of deep breaths. Then he glanced over to Riley and saw tears in her eyes. Allen and Anderson came out together a few minutes later, neither looking any better than the other two. Allen went over to Martin to see if he was okay.

Anderson, however, stopped right in front of Riley.

"I'm sorry, Riley. I had to know. I had to know what haunted you. I hope you can understand that."

Riley for the first time wiped her eyes but said nothing to him as she walked back to the truck. Once they were on the move again, her nerves began to calm. She saw the sign for the clinic and pointed to it. Allen saw what she was referring to and followed its direction.

Halfway down the road, Anderson yelled, "*Stop!*"

"What is it?" Allen wanted to know.

"I think it's a hardware store. We should be able to find masks, gloves, and whatever else the doc told us to get. I'm not sure what we're going to find at the clinic, but we should be prepared."

All the emotions Riley had felt outside of the buildings were now under control, and she could feel the strength back in her legs as she got out of the truck. Lyle strolled over and asked why they were stopping again. Anderson nodded his head over to the hardware store. He looked in the direction Anderson was talking about and smiled. Everyone remained alert, keeping an eye out in every direction as they walked up to the front door of the store. They tried the door, but it was locked. Allen went to the truck to get a tire iron, and used it to break the window. The noise was so loud everyone spun around, looking up and down the street, making sure he hadn't wakened the dead. Once Allen had the door opened, everyone was surprised that it hadn't been touched and that everything was still on the shelves.

Anderson slapped his hands together and said, "Right, mates, let's get to it!"

Allen had a list of things he needed and went on his own to search for them. The rest wandered around, taking things they thought they might need. Martin, who had wandered off on his own, went back to the front of the store to find Riley. Once he found her, he whispered something into her ear. Without any hesitation, she followed him to the back where the office was located. He opened the door slowly. An old man sat in the chair with his head slung back and a gun in his lap. Blood splattered everywhere. There was a piece of paper on the desk in front of him. Riley stepped in just far enough to get the paper. She was surprised he actually left a note:

> To whomever finds me, which I'm sure will be no one, the town has gone crazy with fear. Some have locked themselves up in their homes and others have done the unthinkable. I sit here in the middle at a loss as to what to do. I feel I am the last man on earth. Ed Tilley.

"Well, at least that explains what happened in town," Martin said it more as a thought than a comment.

Riley spoke in a soft voice, "Close the door, and let him be."

Martin did as she asked and closed the door. He saw something in Riley at that moment and understood why the others had such respect for her. She had a kind heart, he thought, much like his wife. He liked the combination of their strength and tenderness. Even with all that Riley had seen, she hadn't become hardened by it.

He knew it would only get worse—not just for Riley, but for all those that traveled out of the camp. Watching Riley now as she gracefully moved through the store, he wondered how one of the most horrific experiences of his life could have brought him and his family to one of the most amazing group of people. He knew it was God's intervention; it had to be. He didn't know what he had been thinking, dragging his family out into the wilderness. At the time, it seemed like the right thing to do. Now, watching Riley, he was so grateful for all that had happened—even that he chose to take his family where he did. Although he could have done without Tamera getting hurt. Martin gave a silent word of thanks to God for taking care of his family when he could not.

Allen made several trips out to the truck to put things away with Bram and Annie helping him. Anderson and Landon had two large boxes that were filled with masks, white jumpsuits that were possibly used for commercial purposes, and more gloves than they could use. The boxes were found in the back storeroom, and they decided to just take everything. Riley found duct tape, shovels, rubber boots in all sizes with lining in them, more heavy work coats, and a couple of medium-size generators. She would have to tell Anderson and the boys about the generators. On Riley's third trip out to the truck, she saw Annie carrying out three full backpacks and put them in the backseat of the truck.

"What did you find, Annie?"

"Oh, hey, Mom. Just some stuff for the kids for Christmas. Flashlights, those glow sticks, candy, that kind of stuff."

"That was thoughtful of you. We've been so busy thinking of other things that the children's needs have been pushed aside."

"Well, I would like to take the credit for it, but it was Carolyn's idea," Annie confessed. "She asked if we found any balls and board games to please bring them too, if there's room."

Riley smiled at the mention of Carolyn's name. She thought back to Carolyn's first day at Calumet. Riley hadn't thought Carolyn would do well there and was glad she had been wrong. Carolyn was a trooper and never complained about anything. Riley remembered the conversation she had with her father about Carolyn's request for a divorce. Her father simply referred her to 1 Corinthians 7:10–16, which more or less applied to marriage between the believer and non-believer. But the part her father said that would help with Carolyn was 1 Corinthians 7:15. It states, "Yet if the unbelieving one leaves, let him leave; the brother or sister is not under bondage in such cases, but God has called us to peace." Adam was never a believer in anything but himself. However, Carolyn came to Christ over a year ago. In Adam's eyes, he did nothing wrong when he decided to leave his wife and boys behind. He did what he did best, which was to think only of himself. Riley and her father felt 1 Corinthians 7:15 removed any obligation Carolyn had with her marriage to Adam. The last of the verse explains why; put simply, Carolyn and the boys couldn't make Adam stay, and they had found peace despite Adam's abandonment. In light of this, Riley's father said they could grant Carolyn's request—that he would finalize it and the members of the council would sign off on it. She appreciated the fact that Carolyn and Nate truly believed they had a future together. Carolyn deserved to be happy, Riley thought; she had earned it. With their impending wedding and Dina's baby on the way, life was looking good.

"Shoot! We need to find a grocery store. I almost forgot, we need baby supplies." Riley saw nothing on this road but hoped they would find something closer to the clinic.

Anderson came out with his load when Riley got his attention. "Did you see the generators in there?"

"I did. Lyle and your boys are getting them."

"Great. I can't think of anything else that we need. Annie and Allen are done, do you need any help?"

"No, that's it for me too. I'll see if I can give the men a hand with those generators."

Riley walked over to Annie, gave her a hug, then kissed her on top of her head. Annie hugged her mother back. "Thanks, Mom, I needed that."

"Me too, baby girl."

The men came out, carrying the first generator. Riley quickly went to the back of the truck to lay the tailgate down. Landon and Bram jumped in the back of the bed to pull the generator in as the others lifted it. They pulled it all the way back so they had room for the other one. It took them only a few minutes more until they had the second one in the bed of the truck too. Satisfied with what they found, they were ready to leave.

Riley faced the hardware store and said, "Thank you, Ed Tilley."

Martin was the only one that understood what she meant. Once back in the trucks, they headed to the clinic. Riley reminded Allen that they needed to find a grocery store or someplace that would have baby items. Allen said he would see if he could find a phone book once inside the clinic, which made Annie laugh.

"What do you find so funny, young lady?" Allen asked jokingly.

"Phone book? Do they even have those anymore?"

Allen thought about it and laughed too. "Well, we can't look it up on our smartphones anymore. They did business ones, where I lived. Hopefully, they did the same here."

"Where exactly are you from, Allen?" Anderson asked him.

"That would be Lincoln, Nebraska. Population nearly three hundred thousand last census." He choked on the last words. "Probably not anywhere near that now."

"I feel like the population is eighty-seven—no, wait, ninety-five people now, with Philip's group. I know there are pockets of people throughout the United States, but it's like the note said, 'It feels like

I'm the last man on earth.'" Riley's voice was faint when she spoke the last of her words.

Anderson spun around fast, asking, "What d'ya mean, what note?"

Riley answered him in a soft voice. "The owner of the hardware store was in his office. He ended his life and left a note. It said that half the town went crazy, and the other half locked themselves up in their homes. I think he felt he was caught somewhere in between. We were so close to these people, and they killed themselves or let someone else do it for them. Now Mr. Tilley. I can't help but think we could have helped them."

"Riley, you're aware you can't save everyone, correct? It's amazing the number of people you have helped. Once we're settled in Jackson, we can search for more people. If they need our help we'll give it, if not, we'll map them and move on," he reasoned with her.

"I know, but it's just one of those thoughts that cloud my mind. I just want to keep moving. You know, standing around waiting is killing me, but I know we have to be patient and move at the right time. Coming here feels like a start, anyway."

Allen interrupted, "The clinic is just ahead."

It was a two-story red brick building, possibly three stories, if there was a bottom floor or a basement, Riley thought. There were stairs heading up to the front door. On the door was a large sign that stated, "The clinic is closed. There is no help here. You need to go to Driggs Idaho or Jackson Wyoming. God bless you, and we wish you the best."

They all looked at one another. Anderson was the first to say it, "I don't think there's going to be anyone dead inside. Sounds like they just palmed them off to neighboring towns or told them to go home and die."

"Well, I'm sure the door is locked. Allen, do you mind getting your key to the place?" Riley studied the area as she spoke.

Nothing but them. No noise, people, dogs, or cats. That was strange, Riley thought. But then she realized they too must be dead if no one was around to feed them. The silence was deafening to her. No wonder Ed Tilley felt so alone. Allen was back with the tire iron, and they all walked up the stairs together. Allen smashed the window without a second thought. The lock this time was for a key, so everyone had to crawl under the handle bar to get in. The glass crunched under their feet as they moved through the door.

On the main floor, they found the reception office, waiting room, and five examining rooms as well as two offices. Everyone took a room searching through everything. Bags had been handed out by Annie so everyone had something to put the items in. They found tongue depressors, Otoscope (for checking ears and throats), stethoscope, and cotton balls in every examining room. Martin and Allen had located the room where the clinic kept all its medicine. The door had to be kicked in, which Martin did easily. The two men went in while Riley investigated the rest of the floor. She found a supply closet and asked Annie if she would come with her to see what they could find. The small room was filled with everything a clinic could possibly need, including three wheelchairs with the clinic's name stenciled on them. She thought immediately about Joseph and his broken leg. She had Annie help her to load one of the wheelchairs up with blankets, towels, tissues, and the toilet paper. They even found some newborn items and added them to their pile. Toilet paper always took up so much room, but they took all that the clinic had.

Martin said they found everything on Shauna's list and were ready to go. Everyone was out the door, putting the last of the items in the truck, when Riley thought she heard something. The men were talking and laughing about something when Riley slapped her hand over Anderson's mouth to stop him from speaking. The others quickly fell silent too. Landon and Bram readied their rifles while Annie reached into the truck for her bow. She immediately engaged an arrow. There it was again. This time Martin and Lyle both heard it; it was crying. They all drifted toward the sound of a crying child. Riley signaled Bram to go across the street, and Landon to stay on her side. They all moved forward in one fluid motion, quickly and quietly down the street. Anderson went with Bram while Lyle, who had a shotgun, followed Landon. The rest fell in behind them. The crying was hard, then the child would gasp for air, then begin to cry again. Bram ran to the corner and peeked around it. He saw no one and waved everyone over to him. Landon and Lyle ran caddy corner across the intersection where they were once again on opposite sides from Bram and Anderson. The crying was louder now as they continued down the short block to another two-story red brick building. Anderson ran past Bram to the next corner, looking both ways down the street. He glanced back to the others and shook his head with a silent no. Riley walked up to the door but found it was locked. Allen and Martin ran up the stairs to the door, slamming both of their bodies into it. It didn't budge. They both kicked it as hard as they could, but still it didn't budge. Lyle came over with the shotgun and took aim, which made everyone scatter from the door. He shot both barrels into the lock. Martin once again slammed his body into it with all his might. This time, he flew through the door, nearly falling. The crying stopped for a moment and then started up again. Riley took two stairs at a time. Martin and Anderson were on her heels, but she let them pass once she got to the top. This time, Martin got the door open on the first kick. The smell was so rancid it drove them all back gagging. No one went in as they knew the smell was death. The question was what kind of death. In their eagerness to get up to the baby, they forgot about what they might find and didn't bring any of the gloves or face masks with them.

Anderson leaned over the railing and yelled down to Allen, "We need the masks and gloves!"

"Got it!" Allen, Landon, and Bram scrambled for the trucks.

With her nose plugged, Riley looked in through the door and began to speak in a gentle voice to the baby inside. "Hey, baby, it's okay – we're going to help you."

The baby was now whimpering with hiccups, but the crying had stopped. Riley knew the baby was trying to calm down. She continued to talk to the baby.

"Hey, little one, it's okay, we're still here. We're coming, we just need to get our gloves and masks on."

"You think the baby's going to understand that, Riley?" Anderson asked.

"It's not what she's says, it's how she says it. It's all about the tone," Martin informed him.

Anderson heard the trucks pull up outside. Riley continued with her adult conversation in her ever-so-sweet voice with the baby while Allen ran up the stairs with gloves and masks. The smell nearly knocked him to the floor. He handed the gloves and masks to both Riley and Anderson then moved away from the door. Riley managed to get hers on first and swiftly moved inside the apartment before Anderson had time to get his gloves on. Riley was still talking to the baby as she moved quickly through the apartment. Anderson was impressed by Riley's actions and followed her lead. When they came around the corner, they saw what was causing the horrific smell. A woman's body was on the floor of the kitchen, dead and bloated. There was also a body of a small child lying next to the woman. Riley held it together for the sake of the baby still whimpering. She followed the sound of the small child. When the baby saw Riley, the little girl's arms went up in the air and she began to cry once more. Riley went to her. She was filthy, and although her diaper was full, it wasn't overly full, which meant someone had changed it recently. Riley took the little girl's clothes off and asked Anderson if he would find some water for her. She lay the girl on the floor to take off the diaper. Anderson returned with two bottles of water. Riley stood up, searching for something she could use to clean the baby with. She found some clothes along with a box of diapers but no wipes. Riley was relieved when Anderson gave her a towel. With the baby cleaned and clothed, Riley picked her up and held her close. The baby instantly went quiet, resting her head on Riley's shoulder.

Riley told Anderson, "This baby is hungry but not starving. Would you mind checking all the rooms and bodies? I'm going to take her downstairs to Annie."

Anderson went back into the kitchen at Riley's request. Riley fell in behind him but continued to the door where Martin was waiting.

As she was about to step out of the apartment, Anderson yelled, "*Riley!*"

Without any hesitation, she handed the baby to Martin and gave him quick orders to take the baby to Annie. Riley ran back into the kitchen to find Anderson kneeling on the floor next to the other little girl who looked to be five or six.

"She breathing, but it's faint. I don't think this is the virus. No telling how long they've been here, but the Sheila has been dead for a while. I'm not sure what happened to her, but I bet my life it's not the virus," Anderson said with certainty.

Turning the mother's body over, Riley saw nothing of what Shauna described to them about the virus. Riley was of the same mind; this wasn't the virus. She examined the kitchen and didn't see much in the way of food. The place was a mess with empty boxes, food crumbs, and unopened cans strung all over the room. Adding to the mix were dirty diapers and the girl's dead mother. What food was left in the cabinets was up high. The little girl probably couldn't figure out how to get to the food in the cabinets above. Riley had to admit; whatever happened here was of natural causes. The one person that could tell them was out cold from lack of food or something non-virus related.

Riley went back to the girls' room to look for clothes for each of them. She nabbed two pillowcases and crammed what she found into them. Diapers and other necessities she knew the baby would need, Riley took. When she was done, she went back into the kitchen and cleaned the little girl up as best she could then put clean clothes on her and some socks but no shoes. Anderson picked her up, and they all left together. Lyle was at the door and snatched the pillowcases and diapers from Riley. Thanking him, she took her mask off along with her gloves and discarded them. They moved swiftly down the stairs with Anderson in the lead. When they arrived back at the trucks, Annie was giving the baby some juice that she had in her bag along with a little bread from her sandwich. Annie had the baby bundled up in one of the work coats that Riley found at the hardware store to keep her warm. The baby seemed very content. Allen had a thermos and handed it to Riley.

Riley opened the lid and smelled it. "Broth?"

"Call me weird, but I love Lupe's broth. It's good with sandwiches."

Riley smiled. "Today I'm grateful for your weirdness. Annie, do your best to get this down the baby and her sister."

Annie handed Martin the baby only to have her arms refilled with the little girl. "Mom, did you see this on her head? Wow! She has a huge knot right here and another big one on the back of her head."

Riley slid into the backseat. Annie took her mother's hand and placed it where the bumps were. "No, I didn't, but you're right, those are pretty good bumps. Anderson, I bet she got hit on the head with one of those cans. Maybe hitting her head again when she fell?"

"She's quite small, a can would do it, and there were a few on the floor," he agreed.

"Okay, Annie, do your best to wake her up. Sit her up and talk to her. Try to get some water in her as well as the broth."

"Boss?" Lyle was at the door, staring down the street.

"Yes, what is it?"

"I swear I just saw someone."

She stepped out of the truck. "Listen, everyone, I'm not leaving this place until we are sure there are no people here, especially small children that have lost their parents. I get that we can't save everyone, but this is not a big town. We can honk the horn, yell, or something." Riley wasn't going to budge on this, and the men knew it. If there were more kids, they needed to find them.

Landon came up to his mother. "Or maybe use this." He handed his mother a bullhorn.

"Oh my word! Where did you find this?" Riley was stunned.

"In the clinic. They must've had to use it to tell people to go away. I can't think of any other reason why they would have one."

"Thank you, Landon, this will work beautifully. Allen, would you pull the truck into the middle of that intersection and start honking the horn please?"

Allen did as Riley asked, and once in the intersection, he honked the horn multiple times. Riley walked out into the middle of the street with her eyes darting in every direction. She waited a few seconds; then she squeezed the trigger on the bullhorn, making it squawk.

She raised it to her mouth and began to speak, "Hello. If there is anyone here, please don't be afraid, we're not here to harm you. We have a small camp just outside of town with plenty of fresh water and food." She paused for a moment and then continued, "We'll wait for about twenty minutes, then we are going to the gas station at the end of town. Once we are done there, we'll be leaving. We won't be coming back this way again."

She looked over at Allen, signaling him to honk the horn again, which he did. Whatever or whoever Lyle saw didn't show themselves. It was quiet. Riley put the bullhorn up to her mouth to speak once more when a man came around the corner at the far end of the street. He was an older man, bundled in a big coat, hat, denim pants, and boots. Riley put the bullhorn back in the bed of the truck and walked slowly toward the man. As they came closer to one another, Riley could see the lines on his face. He looked tired. Riley stopped as the man came closer.

He stopped about six feet from where she stood. "Hello. I'm Anthony Scully. I'm the pastor at Rocky Mountain Christian Church down around the corner from here."

"I'm Riley Cooper. We mean you no harm. For the most part, everyone in our group is a Christian." She looked over her shoulder to the truck with the two kids. "We came here for medical supplies for our doctor. We found two children in the apartment around the corner from here. Their mother is dead."

"Yeah, one of our men heard the crying but couldn't get the door open. When he came back with help, they saw your people go in."

"Pastor Scully, if you don't mind me asking, what happened here? We found the burnt building with bodies inside. We also found Ed Tilley dead in his office. If there are survivors with you, what happened to those people in the building, and why did Ed leave a note, saying he felt like he was the last man on earth?"

Anderson, Allen, and Lyle walked up while they were talking. Riley introduced them. Scully reached out and shook each of their hands. Riley waited for an answer.

"Ed's dead? I'm sorry to hear that. He was a good man. I don't know what to tell you. There was an old-fashioned shoot-out at first. Then someone managed to talk everyone into drinking something that I don't think killed them but knocked them out long enough for the fire to do the rest. I think whoever torched the building left, because you're the first people we've seen in a long time. As for the town, half of them left because they thought it was what they were supposed to do. Others locked themselves in their homes. I'm sure the virus made it here, but who died from it, I don't know. I haven't left the church since all this started. I wanted the church to be a sanctuary for those that wanted to come and ride this thing out. The church is stockpiled with canned goods and dry foods. We've been making do, but now I have one man with a broken arm and two women that are about to give birth. I was in need of help, and then you drove into town."

Riley smiled. "This is actually our second time here. We were here less than a week ago. We made it as far as the burnt buildings and left. Because of that, I thought everyone was dead. How many are in your group, Pastor?"

"Thirty-three."

"Whoa, Riley, that's a lot," Allen was shocked.

"Yes, it is. You wouldn't happen to know if anyone in your group has a motor home or a travel trailer, do you? Or maybe a bus?" Riley inquired.

Lyle started laughing, which caused some confusion with the pastor as he didn't understand the outburst.

"Sorry, Pastor, it's just, I told my wife, Riley here has a tendency to bring all her people home and then some. And your thirty-three is a lot of 'then some.'"

The pastor smiled at him and then said, "There's a church bus, and two of the families have their motor homes in our parking lot."

Anderson nudged Riley with his shoulder, "I think you got your hundred, Riley."

Scully had another confused expression on his face. Anderson clued him in, "Eh, sorry, mate, we've eighty-seven people between our two camps. We're crammed in, but no one complains. We're all just happy to be alive and have all the company."

"Oh. Praise God! We couldn't imagine ever seeing anyone ever again, let alone a group that size. Please come, the church is this way."

Landon and Bram came up behind the pastor and startled him. "Pastor, these are my two boys. Landon and Bram, Pastor Scully."

"Hey, Pastor," Bram said as he extended his hand to the pastor.

"There's a church down at the end of the road with folks inside. Nothing threatening," Landon informed them.

"I'm sorry, Pastor. We had to make sure we were safe. This town already has too many ghosts. Whoever did all this to it could still be around waiting for their next victims. We can't just walk in somewhere without checking it out first," Riley explained.

"No, I understand. To be perfectly honest with you, I've had the same concerns. Nothing has happened on this side of town, and we don't go anywhere near that end. Now, if you're ready to meet the rest of us, please follow me."

Anderson stayed with Riley while the others went back to the trucks. Riley's legs were cold. It felt good to be moving them again. Because the wind had picked up and the sun was completely blocked out by the impending storm, Riley could feel it getting even colder. It took only a few minutes to walk to the church, but it was enough to warm Riley up. When they arrived at the church, the people inside were surprised by the strangers. The sight of them stopped everyone from doing whatever it was they were doing and caused them to stare. Riley could hear their low inaudible whispers. She immediately noticed all the children that were there.

This time, she was the one with the puzzled look on her face. "Ah, Pastor, you have mostly kids. Where are the rest of the adults?" Riley asked.

"Well, most of the children were at summer camp. Some parents drove up to get their children, and others didn't. These children came from all over and arrived at camp right at the cusp of everything being shut down. Five of the adults here are their actual camp leaders who brought them to the church for safety reasons, and the rest are townspeople that came to help out with them."

"How many kids total?" Landon asked.

"Twenty-two."

"Wow! Why would they send their kids to camp?" Landon was shocked.

"Well, I guess it was a lack of honesty on our government's part. It was happening in China and not here. They led everybody to believe that the CDC had it under control. So there was absolutely no reason for them not to send their children."

Landon just shook his head in disbelief. Then he remembered about leaving for Park City on vacation. They had no clue what the truth was. From the time they went to sleep the night before until they made it to Saint George the next day, total chaos had ensued. He looked at his mother and thanked God she wasn't one to sugar-coat anything. She had been honest with everyone from the beginning. He was positive she had her secrets, but he was sure she would never hide anything as important as a virus. He felt bad for these kids. He watched as some of the adults came over to meet his mother as well as the others in their group. Pastor Scully introduced everyone in the church, and his mother did the same for their group. The best that Landon could tell was the kids seemed healthy. Landon walked around the room and found a couple of kids to talk to.

Riley came up with the same assumption concerning the children. They were healthy and well cared for. She surveyed the large sanctuary and was pleased to see how clean it was, especially with this many children. She saw a man in the corner holding his hand. He had to be the one with the broken arm. Riley made eye contact with him, and he quickly diverted his eyes. As she approached the young man, a small boy grabbed her arm. Riley looked down and saw the sweetest face looking up at her. Riley knelt down to be eye level with him.

"Hi there, young man, what's your name?"

"Gauge."

"Hi, Gauge, I'm Riley. Is there something I can do for you?"

He snorted back tears. "Can you help me find my mommy and daddy? I want to go home."

Riley pulled Gauge into her arms and held him tight. Tears started streaming down her face. She kissed him on the side of his face and then pulled him back, looking him in the eyes. Both of her thumbs wiped away the tears on his cheeks. She kissed him again on the forehead then pulled him in for another hug. This time, the boy hugged her back hard and wouldn't let go.

Riley whispered in his ear, "I will do the best that I can to make that happen." She pulled him back once again, looking him in the eyes, "There are a lot of us that are separated from our families. We all want to go home. When we get settled, I hope we can go and find some of those loved ones, but we have a lot to do before that can happen. So until then can you do me a favor?"

Gauge swallowed hard, nodding his head yes. "Good. I need you to help me get these people ready to go. Can you help me do that?"

Gauge swallowed back his tears and said, "Yes."

Riley got up, still holding Gauge's hand, when she realized she had an audience. She took a moment to study all the faces with all their eyes directed at her. All these poor children separated from their parents was heart-wrenching. The sorrow in the eyes of the adults wasn't any better. They were in God's house, a house that had given them protection from the craziness in town. She could tell, though, even in the house of God, they were worn out with worry. Even the pastor looked drained. She took a look at the cross on the back wall, which gave her a sense of peace. She knew, at that very moment in her life, since all this started, God had been completely in charge and that their coming here today was all Him. The chain of events that had taken place since she left Bakersfield, she was 100 percent positive, was every bit orchestrated by God. Every step that she took, with all her uncertainties, He was there with her. She almost started to cry again but pulled herself together as everyone was still watching her. The thought that God would use her in any capacity was overwhelming. She smiled down at Gauge. Releasing his hand, she put her hand in his hair and messed it up. She walked to the front of the church and stood on one of the steps going up to the stage.

"Back in June, my kids and I were unaware of the severity of this virus and left on vacation to see my parents. Looking back now, the path we took back then and have continued to take that has led us here today wasn't orchestrated by human hands. Thinking back on the chain of events that brought us here, I am convinced that God's hands have been in it from the beginning. Moving us, placing us, and readjusting us so that we have been right where He wanted us to be. We left camp today for medical supplies. We were here less than a week ago with every intention of never returning. And yet here we stand. One of the men with us at the time wanted to come into town to look for his friends, but after seeing the burnt buildings, I said no. A friend told me not too long ago that God has a master plan, one that we are not privy to. I honestly believe that the reason that brought us here is only a partial one. I'm convinced that the other part of that reason is because of you. God works in His own time, and I'm sure at some point you thought He had forsaken you as many of us have. And yet, here we stand, once again in the same town, doing exactly what we had no intention of doing and that is, come back here. To come back here for you. Some might call it dumb luck, but I choose to call it a blessing from a wondrous God."

Riley continued to tell them about the two camps with all the people living there and that God had blessed them with a doctor. She told them the plans to move into Jackson and the hopes of finding others to bring into their already growing community. Some of the women were crying and gave thanks to God. The children were happy to hear of the other children and the prospect of being able to play outside again. Having pizza and hamburgers again made everyone's mouth water. When she was done talking, Allen stepped in and talked about the vehicles needed. There wasn't even a question as to whether or not those at the church were going to leave with Riley's group. Allen told everyone to start packing, which they did without question. He urged them to move quickly as he didn't feel the weather was going to hold out much longer. Immediately, everyone, even the children, were moving at a good pace.

Riley found Gauge and asked if he would mind helping her. They found the man with the broken arm still huddled in the corner.

"Hi, what's your name?"

The man stared at her and first didn't say anything. Riley waited. "Scott."

"Hi, Scott, what happened to your arm?"

"I was doing something stupid. I fell and broke it or something. The pastor told me he thought it was broken."

"Do you mind if I examine it?"

"It hurts."

"I'm only going to look and nothing more, I promise."

Riley helped him pull off his coat. Once his coat was off, Riley did her best not to breathe in too deep as the young man hadn't bathed in a while. She unbuttoned the buttons on the cuff of his shirt. The smell was getting to her, but she proceeded with the process of rolling back the sleeve. His arm was black and blue and very swollen. Gauge's face went white.

"How long ago did this happen?" she asked him.

"About ten days ago."

"Okay, you need to do something for me. I'm going to ask one of these men to give you a hand, but you need to go clean up. I hate to tell you, but you smell awful, and since you're going to be in a car with other people for about three hours, it would be nice for them not to have to smell you. Would you do that for me? I'll put a splint on your arm, then we'll put it in a sling if you'll let me? I'll find you some clean clothes too."

At first he was a little apprehensive but then agreed. Riley asked Gauge to stay with Scott while she went to find someone to help and get her medical bag. Riley found one of the men that knew Scott and asked if he would help him, which he graciously agreed to do. She went out to the truck to get her bag and found Annie still in the truck with the girls.

"How are they?"

"The little one ate and fell asleep immediately. This one is in and out, but I managed to get a little water and broth in her."

"Are you warm enough in here? Do you want to bring them in?"

"Not now. We're pretty warm, and I think we're okay out here. If we're much longer, I might have someone switch out with me just to stretch my legs and maybe use the restroom."

"I'll come out and switch with you. They have running water still. Don't drink it, though, it has a smell to it. There's bottled water inside."

"Okay, thanks, Mom."

Riley took her bag from the floor of the truck and shut the door easy so as not to wake the baby. When she returned to the church, she asked one of the women from there if they had clothes. The woman showed her the way to one of the back rooms where they kept the donated clothes. Riley thanked her and set her bag down so that she had both hands to rummage through the clothes. She found a couple of pairs of jeans she thought were Scott's size as well as quite a few shirts that she knew would fit him. She saw a box labeled "socks and underwear men." She was pleased to find they were new and not used. She grabbed the ones she thought would fit. She scooped up everything into her arms, then she found the man that was helping Scott.

"Hi, I found Scott some clean clothes, would you mind taking them to him?"

"Oh, yeah, thank you. I was just heading to donations to see if I could find him something to wear. Thank you very much."

When Scott and Gauge returned, they were talking about something that made Gauge smile. Gauge looked like he had cleaned up some too. He also had a clean shirt on. Scott was somewhere between twenty-two to twenty-six. He was not a big man, size-wise, but he was tall. He had bad acne and dark-brown hair along with brown eyes. She directed them to one of the pews, where she set down her bag and opened it. After taking care of Kota and Jesse, Riley had a delicate touch when it came to this kind of thing. She knew it was painful and didn't want to hurt it more. When she was done, Scott thanked her. She was about to walk away then she thought to ask him something.

"You wouldn't happen to know a young man by the name of Jasper, would you?"

Scott's face lit up. "Jasper! You've seen Jasper?"

Riley smiled then. "Yes. What happened inside that building, Scott?"

"What building?" He tried to hide it by looking down; however, Riley could tell he knew exactly what she was talking about.

"Your arm hairs have been singed, and your clothes smelled of smoke, and they haven't had a fire around here. So please just tell me what happened. It's okay. I know you and another friend came to town to find supplies. Jasper recognized his car."

"Jasper was here?" tears welled up in his eyes.

"Yes, he's at our camp along with Zane and the rest of your friends."

"I don't know what happened, really, I don't! Chris and I found the gas station, and just as we got out of the cars, this crazy guy starts yelling and shooting up the place. At first, we thought he was shooting at us, but then we realized he hadn't seen us. Chris thought we could get around him, so we went on the other side of the street and hid behind cars. One of the bullets somehow hit Chris. He was dead that fast. I freaked out, and the guy heard me." Scott was crying now. "I froze, and the guy came around the car and caught me. He dragged me into that building with all the people in it. It was horrible. They were all dead, I thought. It was about that time when the nutso crazy guy hit me so hard in the head that I didn't wake up until the place was totally engulfed in flames and smoke. That's when I noticed that the people weren't dead. They must have been drugged or something because they couldn't move. Every time someone tried to get up, they fell. It was all I could do to get myself out of there. I crawled into the bathroom and somehow managed to climb out through the window. I actually just fell through the opening, and I landed on my arm. I couldn't run fast enough from the place. All the screaming and crying. I couldn't help them! I couldn't help any of them!" He broke down and cried uncontrollably. The people working close by stopped and were horrified hearing Scott recall his story. Riley walked up to Scott while he was sitting on the pew and hugged him.

"Scott, please look at me. Scott, honey, look, it's not your fault. Scott, look up here, I need you to look at me. None of this is your fault." Scott looked up at Riley, and she took his face in both hands. "Scott, it's not your fault. The world outside is sick. And the sickness is driving people to do things they would have never done on any other day. You just got caught up in someone else's insanity. Those people died not because of you but because of one man's sick deprived mind. We're going to get you to the camp with your friends, and you are going to heal from this physically and mentally. Okay?"

Scott nodded his head yes and then leaned back in to Riley, hugging her. She thought he would never let go. Anderson was sickened by the story. He was there to tell her that they were about to leave when he stopped to listen to Scott. He would have to make sure everyone stayed alert while in town. The nutcase could still be out there. Anderson had gathered a few men from the church, and they were about to head out to two stores, a grocery store, and a small clothing store for babies and toddlers. Lyle and one of the women were going with them to help find everything they would need, not just for one baby, but for three. Riley saw Anderson, and he motioned to her that they were leaving. She acknowledged him with a nod. She stood there a while longer, holding Scott. When he finally pulled back, he thanked her. She told him that it wasn't a problem as she brushed his hair out of his face then asked him if he would help with the kids while the others were packing up. Scott got up to see where he would be most useful while Gauge stayed with Riley helping her with whatever she needed him to do. She noticed that Gauge was crying too.

Anderson's group returned a little over an hour later. They found two travel trailers and had them hooked up to two trucks. Riley was impressed. The best sight of all was that each travel trailer had been filled to the brim with supplies. One had been filled with everything a baby could possibly need—from baby clothes, formula, diapers of every size, binkies, bottles, wipes still moist, shampoos, and lotions. Riley was sure they took everything that had a baby face on it and was amazed at how much they found. The other was filled with dry foods, water, juice, and of course, the never-ending supply of toilet paper. Riley laughed. They had a lot of vehicles and she wasn't sure with the motor homes what vehicles they would need to take with them.

Riley asked Allen, "Do you think we need the bus?"

"No, I don't think so. We're only going to take three of the trucks. There is a van that the kids came in from camp. We'll use it and then the motor homes. I honestly think that's all we need. We're about to change out one of the trucks with one of the travel trailers."

"Thanks, Allen, for everything you've done. I'm not sure what we would've done without you." Riley gave him a hug. It took him by surprise, but he hugged her back.

Anderson came up to them. "Sorry, mate, to be messin' with your tender moment with the bo—Sheila, but can I have a word with both of you?"

Allen was a little embarrassed, but Riley just smiled at Anderson. "Sure, what's up?"

"The boys found a gun store. Do you mind if we hit it too? We'll be about another hour or so. We struck gold with both stores, finding everything for the babies and enough pasta and rice to last us a very long time. I reckon the extra ammo would be greatly appreciated by your dad."

"Yes, that would be great. Look, grab everything this time. All the shotguns, rifles, handguns, and all the ammo. Leave nothing behind."

"That's gonna to be a lot, Riley. Are ya sure?"

"Yes, Anderson, I am. We have a lot of young people that are going to have to learn how to use them. I'm sorry, Allen, we are going to need one more truck to haul all the gun store items."

"Sure, let's go, Anderson, I'll give you and the boys a hand. We still have to stop at the gas station. Unfortunately, I don't think the weather is going to hold out much longer," Allen said as he turned to leave with Anderson.

There was one more thing Riley was absolutely sure they were going to bring. She went on the hunt to find Pastor Scully. She found him in a back room of the church that had been made into a kitchen. He was helping to pack up all the food items they had to take with them.

"Excuse me, Pastor, can I have minute?"

"Sure, Riley, what can I do for you?"

"Would you mind terribly if we brought some of the Bibles with us? I can get the kids to give me a hand, if it's all right with you?"

"Sure, absolutely! Let me show you where they are. We can take all of them if you would like."

"I wish we could, but we only need about fifty. We're taking a lot with us, and won't have the room. Um, also we have a marriage pending. I hope you are up for the task?"

Scully looked pleasantly surprised. "You're kidding, right?"

Riley grinned, "No, I'm serious. Why not? We have three pregnant women, why not a marriage?"

"Three?"

"Yes, there is an expectant mother at our camp too. Hence, our need for the medical supplies."

"Ah." He shook his head and laughed. "It would be my pleasure to perform the ceremony."

"Great! Now where are those Bibles?"

* * *

It was almost 3:00 when they finally made it to the gas station. Allen found some large square plastic containers to put the gas in. They filled all the vehicles up and anything else they could use to transport the gas back to the camp. Allen was excited with the amount they managed to take back with them. They also found a place for all the oil, filters, and anything else Allen felt they needed to go with them. Allen grabbed an air compressor too. It was right at 4:00 when they pulled out. It was dark, and the snow began to fall again. Allen drove the truck with the plow and led the convoy home, with Lyle driving the last of the vehicles out. They drove almost two hours before they came up to the first motor home of Philip's that had run out of gas. It was parked on the side of the road. Allen promptly pulled up next to it, got out in the now full-on snowstorm, and filled it with gas. Anderson volunteered to drive it into Mercy as Calumet was bursting at the seams with people and vehicles. Allen explained that with the storm, it would be best to take it straight to Calumet; he would clear the road in the morning and take over vehicles then. Anderson agreed, then pulled into the convoy. It was about forty minutes later when they found the second motor home. Allen was pleased they made it as far as they did with what little gas they had in them. Martin offered to drive it once it was filled with gas, and from there, it was a slow drive back to camp. The snow was making it hard to see, and even with the plow, it was still hard for the motor homes to move too fast. They finally found the road leading to Calumet and Mercy. By the time they pulled into Calumet, it was well after eight. The worst of the storm was gone, but it was still snowing. Almost everyone in Calumet came out to greet them. Even a few from Mercy were there, waiting for their return. It was freezing cold, but no one cared. Everyone was extremely happy to see them safely home.

Levi came running up to Riley when he saw her get out of the truck and nearly knocked her over. She gave him a big hug and a kiss. Philip was there with a huge smile on his face when he walked up and gave Riley a hug.

When he pulled away, he looked up to the night sky and said, "I think we just made it. Tomorrow the snow would've had us stuck at the other camp for good. It was perfect timing on your part."

Riley smiled. "You mean God's perfect timing, don't you?"

Philip smiled back. "I deserve that. Yes, God's perfect timing."

Riley saw Shauna with Martin and made her way over to her. "Hi, Doc, we have a little girl with a head injury that needs your attention as well as a young man with a broken arm. I'll find a few people to give you a hand with them."

"Don't worry, Boss, I got this," Martin winked at Riley on his way back to the truck to get the girls, making Riley smile.

Shauna and Riley headed in the same direction together. Martin had the little girl in his arms as the two women walked up. Shauna was clearly concerned at the sight of her.

"How long has she been like this?"

"We found her this way. She has two large bumps on her head," Riley told her.

"Martin, take her to the trailer, but don't lay her flat. Prop her up with some pillows. I'll be in as soon as possible. Ask Shyla to stay with her until I get there, please."

They found Scott surrounded by all of his friends. The girls were crying as were some of the young men. Riley and Shauna pushed their way into the circle of friends, latching on to Scott.

"Sorry, everyone, the doc needs him."

They moved out of the way as Riley and Shauna gently guided him toward the tent. Landon came up with bags of medical supplies for the doctor and followed them into the tent. They had a heater running inside, which made the place cozy. Riley figured it must have come from Philip's group and was used during mealtime. Landon set the bags down and found a chair for Scott to sit on. He moved a table close to Scott then set the bags for the doctor on it. Riley left Scott in the caring hands of the doctor. She asked Landon to stay just in case Shauna needed a hand. As she was walking out of the tent, Martin walked in.

"Perfect timing, Martin, I was just going to find some men to help your wife."

"I have a few coming."

Just as he said that, Carson, Tony, and Norman came in to help. Riley smiled and left them to it.

Some people pitched in and got the children settled in the kitchen, where they had a hot meal waiting for them. The rest were busy outside, trying to get things put up in their proper places. Riley walked into the kitchen after she was sure there was nothing left for her to do. Gauge ran up to her giving her a bear hug. She bent down to pick him up and took him over to the table where Levi, Sara, Annie, and Tamera were.

"Hi, guys, this is Gauge. He's the newest addition to our family."

Jesse and Kota snuck up behind Riley. Kota playfully took Gauge from her arms, holding him out to get a better look at him.

"Let's have a look at you, buddy. Yes, I think you'll do just fine with us. What do you think, Jesse?"

Gauge was a little startled. Jesse reached over and messed up Gauge's hair as Riley patted him on the back.

"Why don't you sit him next to Sara so he can eat," Riley instructed.

Tamera got up to get Gauge some food, while Kota sat him in a chair. About that time, Ken entered the kitchen with some of the people from the church. Riley worked her way over to her father to make the introductions. She was correct about her father's reaction at having a real pastor. He said they were finally complete now that they had a doctor and a pastor. What more could they ask for? Both of her parents sat down with her, Scully, and Allen to eat. The conversation was nonintrusive, which helped Riley relax. All the difficult stuff would be dealt with tomorrow. For now, she just wanted to unwind with her family. Her parents told them about their day, which Riley was pleased it had been such a good one. As far as the day went, over all, it ended with everyone safe. None of them could ask for anything more. She knew they would need to figure out everyone's sleeping arrangements soon. The pregnant women would have to stay in Calumet to be close to the doctor. They both looked like they were ready to give birth any day now. She would have to talk to Philip about the use of their homes until after the babies were born. The kids would be split up throughout the two camps. Allen's camp would have more room for them once the travel trailers were moved over to Mercy. Her mind drifted back to the conversation taking place around her. Scully was telling her parents how surprised they were when Riley and the others showed up. Riley just smiled. Her father took one look at her and knew her mind was spinning.

"What's on your mind, Riley?"

"Sorry, what?"

"What are you thinking about?"

"Oh, the sleeping arrangements."

"That's being taken care of as we speak."

"Oh, really? Uh, good. Then I can go to bed. Pastor, I leave you in good hands. I have two boys I need to clean up and put to bed. Mom, Dad, I love you both and will see you in the morning."

"Good night, Riley. And thank you for everything," Pastor Scully stood up, taking Riley's hand.

She smiled at him and said, "You're welcome. Good night, everyone."

Riley weaved through the tables to get to Levi and Gauge. Both boys looked as if they were about to fall asleep.

"Are you two boys ready to go to bed?"

Both of them slid out of their chairs. Levi took Gauge's hand, and they all headed for the door. Riley took them to the restroom first and then guided them into the cabin. Becca, Timothy, and Rachel were playing cards when they entered.

"Hi, Riley and Levi. Who do we have here?"

Levi scratched his nose and then answered her. "This is Gauge. He's my new brother."

"How cool is that! Gauge, it's nice to meet you. I have a surprise for you, little guy." Becca leaned over to grab something off the table, which she handed to Gauge. "I'm not sure what you were sleeping in, but these are yours, and they're toasty warm."

Gauge took them then rubbed them against his face. He looked up to Riley then back to Becca, "Thank you."

"Okay, Levi. Take Gauge up the ladder, and show him how to wash up before bed. I'll be up in a minute."

Riley watched both boys go up the ladder. They were giggling about something, which warmed Riley's heart.

"Thank you for the PJs, Becca."

"You're welcome, anytime."

Riley started for the ladder then hesitated. "I have a favor to ask of you."

"Sure, anything."

"I would like a census of all the people here. Obviously, get their names but also their age, date of birth, where they're from, and most importantly, their occupation before the virus. That's important because if we have electricians or electronic technicians, those people might be able to get us up and running again into the twenty-first century when we move. Also, list any hobbies. Sometimes hobbies will be better than their actual occupation. Find someone to help you. Make a standardized form and follow it. It will help in keeping up with the numbers and help us place people with jobs that they will be better suited for."

"Absolutely, that's a great idea. I'll ask one of the ladies from Mercy."

"You know, Lisa might be a good one to ask. Thanks again, Becca. That will be a tremendous help."

"It's my pleasure, Riley. I'll talk to Lisa tomorrow."

"Great, um, sorry for interrupting the game. Good night. I'll see you all in the morning."

They all said their good nights to Riley as she headed for the ladder. When she got up to the loft, she saw two heads popping out from under the covers. Both boys were fast asleep in her bed, no less. She went behind the curtain, and with the basin of water, tooth-brush, and a clean cloth, she washed, trying to get the day off of her as best she could. Once in her PJs, she felt much better. She crawled into bed with the boys and fell asleep with no effort at all.

CHAPTER 14

Morning came too fast. Riley lay in bed, listening to the world around her. The two warm bodies were still fast asleep next to her. She could hear the boys downstairs, talking in low whispers. She could tell one of them had kept the fire burning in the stove all night. Although it was cold, it wasn't freezing. Today she thought was going to be a very busy day. For the first time in a long time, she wasn't feeling apprehensive about her day. She wasn't running off anywhere and really didn't have to worry about people she left behind, now that they were finally here. The next month would be easy. They would be leaving for Jackson, and for whatever reason, she wasn't worried about going there. The prolonged wait was harder to deal with. She knew that as the time drew nearer, her inner peace might not be there. For now, she would just lie in bed, keeping warm without a care in the world. She laughed at herself. Riley rolled over on her side and with a tender touch pushed back Gauge's hair. She remembered it was her cares that got her up every morning, and she loved having the two new additions in her life. She wondered what Jackson would think of these two. She smiled at the thought of her husband and prayed he was safe.

Riley's thoughts were interrupted by a soft voice from the bed next to her.

"Mom, are they really going to be our little brothers?"

"Good morning, Sara. Yes, they chose me. I can't have them stay with someone else when all they want to do is be with me. Who does Levi stay with when I'm gone?"

Sara stretched and chuckled. "Me or grandpa."

"Now see, Levi belongs with us. Gauge was the same. The moment I entered the church, he came to me and has stuck to me like glue."

"What's going to happen to all the other kids?"

"We'll watch them and see who they migrate to and go from there. The baby and the little girl we found will stay with Shauna's family. Now that they are taking care of them, Shauna said she would love to have them be a part of her family. I think they'll feel safe with Shauna and her family. Once a child feels safe, there is no need to pull them from that security. They've lost so much already."

"There are five other black children. Don't they want to take them in?"

"The world is no longer black or white, Sara. God may have given us a variety in color, shape, and personality, but in the end, we're all humans. In times like these, there can't be a separate race anymore. Who knows – you may fall in love with Trent and marry him."

"Oh, Mom!" Sara giggled. "Well, he is cute and my age."

Becca chimed in, "Are we planning a wedding then, Sara?"

All three of them laughed.

"No, just wondering about a few things."

"Well, I would say you have time before you have to worry about getting married and settling down," Riley said.

"I like having little brothers. Although I don't know how they are going to handle you being gone for so long when you go to Jackson."

"They'll have you and your grandparents. I couldn't be leaving them in better hands."

"Uh, Sara?"

"Yes, Ms. Becca?"

"Would you mind taking care of my niece and nephew for me while I'm gone. They really like being around you. Come to think of it, you're like the pied piper around here with all the children."

Sara chuckled again. "It's because of all the baking I do. They think their sweet smiles can con me into giving them a cookie or brownie."

"So that's all we had to do to get a cookie?" Becca laughed.

"Ms. Becca, I'll be happy to take care of them while you're gone. Honestly, I can't believe you're going with my mom."

"Thank you, Sara. I can't believe it either, but I need to go. This is a big deal for all of us, and it's going to take a lot of people to get the job done. It's history in the making for us, and I really want to be a part of it. Most importantly, I need to do it for my niece and nephew. What kind of aunt would I be if I didn't carve out a little piece of the future for them?"

"I'm glad I'm not in charge. I would just make everyone stay here. Chop down a few trees and build log cabins," Sara said.

"Believe me, I've thought about that, but it's just not feasible. Really, there is no room for growth, and the hothouse isn't working out very well. Hauling supplies up this mountain would take far more work than it would be worth. No, moving is the best thing to do. If there is a chance we can have electricity and running water again, then I will clean out a city to have it."

"Mmmm, a hot shower or bath. Now that would be wonderful!"

"You're not kidding!" Sara liked the idea of a hot bath.

All three of the women laughed.

"Okay, ladies, the day awaits. Anyone care to join me for a hot cup of coffee?"

"Brrrr, not a chance!" Sara said as she pulled the covers up over her head.

"Maybe we can have a few of those cookies with our coffee," Becca added.

A mumbling noise came out from under Sara's covers, "Stay out of the cookies."

Levi rolled over and said, "Cookies?"

All three of them laughed. Riley and Becca got up, dressed quickly, then climbed down the ladder. There were four young men staring at them.

"What?" Riley inquired.

"You women are awfully noisy," Landon answered.

"Ha, I heard you all talking down here long before any of us were," his mother told him.

"Grandpa said the meat supply is getting low. He asked if we would go out today and see what we could find." His eyes drifted to Kota and Jesse then back to his mother. "They want to go. I think they're ready. We'll take the horses, but we're going to have to go down the mountain some because of the snow."

"You boys feeling up to it?"

"Yes, definitely!"

"Okay. But if you don't find anything by midafternoon, then come back to camp. I don't want any of you out after dark."

Bram jumped in, "No, worries. Right, mates? Let's get moving."

"Okay, Bram, you've been hanging around Anderson far too much," Riley laughed at him. "Becca, how about that coffee?"

The two women left the cabin. As they were heading to the kitchen, they heard chopping sounds, then a snort, and then the weirdest mooing sound.

Riley said, "Uh-oh," while latching on to a fist full of Becca's coat just above the shoulders.

Riley hauled her as fast as she could toward the kitchen, all the while hearing hoofs and snorts coming at them. Riley couldn't get them inside the kitchen fast enough! Once inside, Becca saw Riley's silhouette grab something over the fireplace. It was one of the rifles Ken left inside the kitchen for emergencies. All within a matter of seconds, Riley had it loaded and was at the door again. Becca followed behind her.

"Geez, Riley, you're scaring me," Becca whispered.

"You need to be scared. There's a moose eating the insulation to our tent over there."

"What?"

"It found the livestock food we've been using as an outside wall for the tent. He's not going to move from there while he can eat."

Riley opened the door to listen for a minute; then she stepped outside and walked to the corner of the building when she saw all the boys huddled up outside the women's cabin. One of them had the rifle up, aiming at the huge bull. It was dark, but she could make out the silhouette of the enormous beast. She aimed but waited for one of the boys to take the shot first. There was a loud boom from the rifle when the shot was finally taken. Whoever took the shot hit it, but it didn't go down. Riley took the next shot immediately after, bringing the bull down. By this time, the whole camp was awake. Everyone came out to see what the commotion was. Flashlight beams fluttered everywhere. Riley and Becca found their way over to the moose, as did all the boys.

"Wow! What a monster!" Landon was clearly excited.

"You're not kidding," Becca said.

Riley's father was standing next to them now. "Well, this guy is going to feed us for a while." He bent down to pet the belly of the big moose. "There you go, fella. Thank you for your sacrifice. You're going to keep a lot of people alive. Thank you, God, for the food you provide for us. We have been truly blessed. Amen."

There were "Amens" all around them. Her father stood up, telling the boys to prepare the moose for butchering. All four of them moved quickly. Bram gave the honor of the first cut to Kota, as he was the one that shot first. Bram showed him where to cut the moose so they could take the guts out. Alejandro came over with Norman to give the young men a hand. Alejandro was amazed at the size of the moose. He looked over at the hay that was being used for insulation, and he just shook his head. The moose had eaten his fair share of the hay, but there was still plenty left. He wasn't worried. Lupe came up, carrying two very large pots. Alejandro instructed Kota to put the guts of the moose in the pots. Lupe would use them for cooking. Riley wrinkled her nose up at the sound of that. They usually left the guts for the bears or other wild animals, but she knew they couldn't do that here. The boys did as Alejandro asked. Tony and Carson carried the pots back over to the kitchen for Lupe, who was talking so fast in Spanish that Riley couldn't even pick out one familiar word. But the expression on her face told Riley everything: Lupe was elated to have the guts. Riley wasn't sure she would be eating any stew for a while.

Nate, Allen, and Kevin heard the gunshots and got there as fast as they could.

"Wow!" was all any of them could say. They too stood in awe at the sight of the magnificent beast that lay before them.

"Who shot him?" Nate asked.

"Kota got him first. Where, we don't know yet, but then my mom got the kill shot, which brought him down."

"Nice job. We were running low on meat. This guy couldn't have come at a better time," Nate said.

"Jefe, we cook head too," Alejandro said.

Riley had a furrowed look on her face, which made Alejandro laugh at her. He then explained that some of the best meat is on the head. Riley looked doubtful.

"Please don't tell me what I'm eating until long after I'm done, like maybe a week or a month afterward. You know, so I have some time to enjoy it and can keep it down."

"Jefe, you going to enjoy dinner tonight." Alejandro had his thumb to his fingers, put them to his lips, and kissed them with a loud *smack* and said, "*Delicioso!*"

Riley laughed. "Great, I can't wait!"

Alejandro continued laughing. Some of the other men joined in the laughter too. She wondered if they understood they would be having the same food for dinner that she was. She left the boys to it and headed back to the kitchen for that long-overdue cup of coffee. She found Becca inside with some of the other women, telling them the story of the moose and how Riley dragged her by the collar of her coat into the kitchen.

"I'm sorry about that. My eyes hadn't focused just yet, and I couldn't see him. A full-grown moose in the vicinity is dangerous. They would kill you in a heartbeat. Beautiful to look at, but very mean," Riley said as she put the gun back up.

"No, thank you for taking care of me. The only thought going through my head was, 'When did we get a cow?'"

That made Riley and her mother laugh, which caused the other women to laugh too.

"Where's the coffee?" Riley asked.

"Here you go, Riley." Carolyn handed her a cup of coffee.

Riley put sugar in it with some goat's milk. Riley thought it was funny how much she was loving goat's milk these days. She couldn't even remember what cow's milk tasted like anymore. She meandered over to one of the tables with her cup, taking one of the empty seats. Becca followed Riley, grabbing the seat next to her.

Alice Crawford came into the kitchen bundled in her coat with her arms wrapped around herself. "My, what a lot of excitement this morning. I'm sure we have a few more hours of sleep left, but everyone's up ready for the day to begin. What can I do to help?"

Victoria had her help with the biscuits while she started to prepare the soup by putting the water on to boil. Soup every morning must be something Mexicans did a lot. Lupe said it's full of protein and would help people get started with their workday. It was usually served with sausage or fish. Riley never liked fish soup until she met Lupe. That woman had changed her taste buds forever. No one ever complained about any of the meals, ever. But when they knew Lupe was the head chef for a meal, everyone was happy. It didn't hurt the feelings of the other chefs either because they loved her cooking too. Lupe always made Riley fresh tortillas every morning, which she loved. She and Alejandro spoiled Riley. Although, Riley did her best not to take advantage of. But she would never say no to freshly made tortillas. The aroma from the soup, along with the meat cooking, was making Riley feel hungry. Carolyn asked everyone if they would give her a minute of their time. Riley, for one, was happy for the distraction.

"Thanks. Most of you know that the council was kind enough to grant me a divorce from my worst excuse of a human being husband, Adam. Well, Nate and I would like to be married sometime before Christmas. We aren't expecting a thing from anyone but would love it if all of you would come to the ceremony."

All the women were elated and conveyed their sentiments to her.

Becca said over all the hoopla, "Fat chance of that happening! You'll never get away with not having all the fluff that goes with a wedding!"

"Oh, yes, another excuse for a celebration!" Alice said cheerfully.

The ladies started rattling out ideas for the upcoming wedding. Riley just sat there listening, enjoying all the commotion. Once she was done with her coffee, she got up to give Carolyn a hug. Then she took her cup, washed it, and set it to dry. She left the women to discuss the wedding while they continued to do their work. She passed the men still working on the moose while making her way back to the cabin to check on Levi and Gauge. Annie and Sara were both up. Rachel, Timothy, and the other two boys were still asleep. Annie and Sara said they would stay until the boys woke up. Riley thanked them then explained that she needed to make some rounds, but she would stop back by when she was done.

It had stopped snowing but not until it had left a ton of snow everywhere. Allen said he would keep the snow cleared out of the camp with the plow but would need some daylight before he could get started. Riley forged ahead through the deep snow to the doc's place. She knocked on the door a couple of times before Shauna opened it and invited Riley in.

"You know, it's so nice to hear a knock at the door. Just the fact that I have a door to be knocked on is such a treat."

Riley smiled as she looked around the trailer. Zane and his wife had done a nice job of cleaning the place up. There was a full-wall slide out, which made the place look much larger. The trailer now housed Shauna and Martin's entire family, along with their two new additions to their family. The baby was on the floor, playing with a large plastic spoon.

"How's she doing, Doc?"

"Oh, this one is doing just fine. A little diaper rash, but other than that, she's great. Her sister, however, is another story. That hit on the head caused a concussion, I'm sure, but without the proper equipment, it's hard to tell."

"Will she be okay?"

"That's the million-dollar question. Shyla got her to drink some of the broth last night and again this morning. She comes in and out of consciousness, so I'm sure she'll be fine, it's just hard to know without an MRI. Concussions don't usually leave you unconscious like this, they just give you bad headaches, lack of concentration, and so forth. But I think she hit her head hard when she fell. Anderson said he wasn't sure if she was on the chair or counter when she fell. He did say there were a lot of cans on the floor around her. So the best I can do is watch her carefully. Pastor Scully came by last night to pray for her."

"Good. How's your brother doing?"

"Much better. He wants to get out of the trailer, but he's too big to carry, and he can't walk on that leg of his at all. For that matter, I want it up, so in bed he stays or on the couch out here. Zane and another man came by yesterday and kept him company all day, playing cards and dominos."

"I'm glad to hear that. We did find a wheelchair, but a lot of good it's going to do him with the snow. Allen said he would get the plow out to clear as much of the snow as possible from both camps today. If he's able to get it cleared, maybe we can get him at least to the kitchen for a little while."

"Amen, sister!" Joseph yelled from the back room that had all the bunks in it.

Riley and Shauna laughed. "Do you mind if I pop my head back there to see him and the girl?"

Shauna motioned for Riley to go ahead. Riley went into the room that Joseph and the little girl were in.

"Hi, Joe, how are you?"

"Feeling much better now that I know there is a wheelchair out there with my name on it. The possibility of getting out of this tin can today helps!"

Riley smiled at him. "How's your little roommate doing?"

"She's doing great. Just wish she didn't talk so much."

Riley took it as a joke, but Shauna read more into it.

"What do you mean, talking too much?"

"She kept talking about some girl last night. An Olive or Olivia, something like that.

Shauna walked back into the other room where the baby was playing with her spoon.

"Hi, Olivia. Hi, little one. Olivia?"

The baby looked up at her grinning while pounding the floor with the spoon.

Riley was behind her. "How old do you think she is?"

"Hey, ladies, just because there are two very cute little girls in this place doesn't mean you can shun me!"

"Oh, hush up, you big baby!" Shauna playfully ordered. "I think she's about eighteen months old, give or take a month."

"Doc, give her a birthday. Your choice on the day, but she needs a birthday."

Shauna was surprised at the request but then realized that if she didn't, this poor thing would never know how old she was.

"Sure, I'll do it."

"Also, the kids we brought back with us, I'm sure you were planning to check them all out, however, would you do your best to find them a family that will raise them?"

"Uh, sure, but I'm not sure I'm the best person for that."

"You're the perfect person for it, and I'll ask the pastor to help you."

"Okay, sure. Why not. I'll be happy to do it."

"Um, Sara said something to me this morning about the black children might want to be raised by black families. I told her there wasn't any more room for racial issues. We have to unite as one, as Americans, of course, but we couldn't have a skin color issue, not now and not ever again. I didn't like it before the virus, and I won't tolerate it now. These girls, I assumed, are going to be raised by you. Was I wrong in that assumption?"

Shauna was on the floor now with the baby in her lap. Shauna glanced down at the baby and then back to Riley. She began to laugh. Riley wasn't sure what was funny, but she smiled anyway.

"Oh my, I wasn't going to give them up easily, so yeah, I'm keeping them. And, Riley, none of us or our friends have felt anything but 100 percent a part of this community. And I'm with you,

I didn't like the racial divide either, and I don't ever care to see that kind of hate again. For crying out loud, your son Bram came over and asked Tamera's dad if it was okay to come over to visit Tamera. I wish you could have been here to see both Tamera's and Martin's faces! Tamera was about to pop with joy, and Martin was about to have a major meltdown. But what was he going to say, no? She's nineteen years old. Martin did say he appreciated that Bram had enough respect to ask him first."

Riley laughed at that. "He's a great kid! You'll love his mother, Ursula. She is an amazing woman and fun to be around."

"Wait, what, you're not his mom? But you always introduce him as your son."

Riley smiled. "Yes, it's easier, and I truly love him like a son. He's a good kid with a heart of gold and a hard worker. I would claim him as mine anytime. He and Landon have been best friends for the last eleven years."

"Well, I hope I will have the pleasure of meeting her someday."

Riley looked at her and swallowed back the tears. "I hope to see her again someday too. If she shows up, so will my husband Jackson. The last we heard, they were together, trying to get out of Bakersfield."

"I'm sorry, Riley, truly, I am."

"It's okay, if I know my husband at all, I'm sure they're fine. They're probably held up somewhere, waiting for winter to pass. Anyway, it's the here and now that concerns me, and if you are okay raising these little girls as your own, that will be one less concern."

"Oh, you're going to have to fight me to take them!"

"Great. I'm going to go see if breakfast is ready and then help get the stuff we brought with us yesterday put away. Bye, Joe!"

"Riley, you get on that Allen dude and get that snow outta here so I can get outta this trailer! Tell him I'm beggin' him!"

Shauna just shook her head, and Riley laughed. "I'll let him know right away."

"You do that! Now don't you forget, Riley! Please don't forget!"

The door closed behind Riley as the last of his words faded behind her. She took her time going back to the cabin. The crisp fresh air felt good in her lungs. She noticed Anderson and Allen talking to one another. She waved to them and had every intention of walking past them. However both men had a difference of opinion, practically ran over to her, positioning themselves on either side of her.

"Okay, you two look like you're up to something."

"Well, this is one smart Sheila."

"Is there any other kind of Sheila?"

"Ah, well, now, I'm not going there. That's another day's conversation. But yeah, we're up to something. We were considering what the ultimate wedding gift would be for Carolyn and Nate? Uh, well, you know, for…"

"A little bit of privacy?" Riley said, finishing his sentence.

"Too right! And we have a solution for that, if you would hear us out for a moment."

"Okay, sure." Riley spun around to look at both of them. "I think it would be a great idea. What are you thinking?"

"Well, we've the new travel trailers still full of stuff from our outing yesterday. Would ya mind terribly if we made one a honeymoon suite for the couple?" Anderson was doing all the talking while Allen just stood there, nodding his head in agreement.

What a nice surprise it would be for the newly married couple, Riley thought.

"That would be a terrific gift! Can you put it someplace set back away from the camp so they can truly be alone but not too far that if there's an emergency, we can't get to them or they can't get to us?"

"We actually have a perfect spot picked out. We would love to show you to get your opinion."

"Absolutely, but can we do it after breakfast? I need to gather my boys so I can get them fed."

"Actually, that sounds like a great plan. My stomach's rumbling," Anderson put his hand to his stomach as he spoke.

* * *

It was midafternoon before they were done emptying out all the supplies from all the vehicles. Allen and Lyle, along with all the young adult men, first used the snowplow to move the snow from inside each campground, then they shoveled what they couldn't get with the plow. Finally, they took on the task of moving the snow from the path between the two camps. Motor homes were driven to Mercy once the road was cleared. The women were busy splitting supplies up between Calumet and Mercy, getting the food stored properly, and helping the doc get her medical supplies and medicine stored away. The kids took care of the daily chores of bringing the water up from the lake, feeding the animals, and making sure all cabins were restocked with firewood. By the time everything was done, everyone was exhausted. Alejandro had dug a deep hole in the ground for cooking tonight's meal deep-pit style. Riley had no idea how he dug the hole because the ground was frozen solid. Riley didn't see the head of the moose anywhere, so she was sure it was down in the pit. It took most of the morning and part of the afternoon cutting up the moose, grinding parts of it up, and packaging it. Part of it was turned into sausage and put into the smokehouse. Riley was pleased at how well everything went today, but before she called it quits, she had two stinky boys that were in need of showers. Now that there were motor homes with showers, anyone that wanted to shower in them could. She went back to her cabin and selected some clothes for herself and both boys. They were going to shower at Shauna's, but she had to catch the boys first.

With her arms full of clothes, Riley was headed for Shauna's when Gauge and Levi came running around the corner of the cabin. She managed to catch one of them by the arm.

"Whoa! Slow down, you two. We're going to take a shower."

"Now? We want to play!" Levi argued.

"Sorry, pal. You stink, and I'm not sharing a bed with any stinky boys."

"Can we play after the shower?" Gauge asked.

"Not outside. It's getting dark, and I want you inside before dark from now on. With that moose showing up this morning, I don't want you going behind the cabins without an adult anymore either. There could be coyotes, wolves, or another moose out there, and I might not be able to get to you in time."

"Landon said you killed the moose today," Levi said with pride.

"Yes, I did. But here's the deal, if you had stumbled into the moose by accident, he would have killed you. Wild animals are very dangerous, and you two need to take them seriously. Please remember that, okay?"

"We take Goliath with us," Levi informed Riley.

"That's good, but he wasn't with you just now, was he?"

"No, sorry, Mom," Levi was looking up at Riley.

Her heart skipped a beat as she looked down at him. She fought off her tears. Levi had called her Mom. She knelt down to him so she was eye to eye with him.

"I love you, young man."

Levi gave her a big hug and a kiss. Gauge looked at her and Levi.

"Is it okay if I call you Mom too?"

She smiled at him, dropped her bundle, and pulled him into her arms. She told Gauge that he most certainly could and that she loved him too. Riley picked up her bundle, got up, wiped her eyes, then continued on to Shauna's. Martin opened the door before she had time to knock.

"Oh, Riley, I was just coming to find you. Come in, come in! We have a surprise for you. Come on in, boys."

Riley and the boys took their shoes off as they entered. To Riley's surprise, Shauna was on the couch with Olivia and her sister. The little girl was awake.

"Wow! This is a surprise." Riley knelt down in front of the couch. "Hi, my name is Riley. This is Levi and Gauge. What's your name?"

The little girl was a little shy and put her face into Shauna. Shauna told her it was okay and that Riley was one of the ones that found her and Olivia. The little girl looked up to Shauna and then back to Riley.

"Ava," she said in the sweetest voice ever.

"After we shower, you want to come play?" Levi asked.

Ava nodded her head yes. Shauna laughed and said, "Maybe tomorrow," since she was still weak from the head injury.

"It's still okay to shower?" Riley asked.

"Oh, yeah, we are going to the kitchen to find Joseph and get these two beautiful girls some food," Martin said.

"Thanks. We'll see you shortly," Riley said as she herded the boys into the bathroom.

After their showers, Riley and the boys put their dirty clothes inside their cabin then headed to the kitchen. The place was buzzing. Everyone from Mercy was there too. Both the tent and the kitchen were full of people. The boys ran in to the kitchen, calling for their grandmother, when it dawned on Riley that Levi and Gauge had been calling her mother Grandma from the very beginning, that her entire family had loved them from day one. Even the older boys doted on them.

Riley gave her mother a hug. "Do you mind keeping an eye on them? Anderson and Allen asked me to check on something."

Her mother eyed the two boys. "Do you honestly think they are going anywhere?"

Riley glanced over at them. They were both looking at all the desserts while licking their little lips. She and her mother laughed.

Riley thanked her mother as she left to find Anderson and Allen. Both men were standing by the pit talking to Alejandro.

"Hi, gentlemen, are you ready so show me your handiwork?"

"Right as rain, Riley, let's be off. Alejandro, we'll see you later, mate," Anderson slapped Alejandro on the shoulder as he left to show Riley what they had done.

The three of them walked past the men's cabin into a small row of trees, only to find themselves standing in a clearing. Riley was surprised at the beautiful surroundings and spun around to see the lake. It was breathtaking, and she loved it! Riley told the men so.

"Do you think it would be totally selfish if we just gave them this as their permanent home? I mean, it would only be a couple of months at the most anyway. We should have everyone in Jackson by spring or by early summer at the latest," Riley reasoned.

"I would say no if it was for you or for one of us. But yeah, it's a gift for the newlyweds, something I'm sure the rest of the community won't mind giving them," Allen said thoughtfully.

"Not to mention, it's truly the only gift any of us can give them," Riley said, more relaxed. "Okay, then we only tell the women. We'll have a mutiny on our hands if they don't get to be a part of this." Both of the men were confused. "Decorating! You two surprise me sometimes. Did you think this would be it?" She swung one arm out to the trailer.

"Hey now! We got half of it right. What do we know about decorating? We took care of Nate's half of the gift, you women can take care of Carolyn's half!"

Riley laughed at Allen's comment. He and Anderson were proud of their efforts, and rightly so. Riley expressed her appreciation for all they had done. Sometimes she was surprised by the tender hearts of both of these men. The fact that they thought of this was amazing and, more importantly, that there was anything at all to give the newlyweds was a wonderful surprise. She couldn't wait for Carolyn and

Nate to get married. It was going to be a cold ceremony because there was nowhere big enough to house the entire community. For now, they would have to settle with nature at its coldest. Or so it seemed to Riley, coming from the desert to the mountains. It was somewhat of an adjustment, but she didn't mind as long as she had a nice, warm bed to lie in each night. She realized she was staring out at the lake, lost in her thoughts.

"I love it! I'll be happy to let the women know. It's going to be a chore to keep it a secret from Carolyn, but I think it can be done," Riley announced. "Also, this moose business this morning could have been worse. The children need to stay inside the campgrounds, and no adult leaves without some protection, especially on the path from here to Mercy. The winter is hard on the wildlife, and I know the coyotes as well as any bears that haven't gone into hibernation yet can smell the meat. We just need to be extra careful."

"No, worries. Your dad had the boys cleaning rifles and shotguns. With the heaps of weapons and ammo we hauled back, both camps are stocked. We'll give the parents a heads-up on the confinement for the kids. No one needs to go out anywhere right now anyway," Anderson said.

With everything settled, they headed back to the kitchen. From the look of things, a person might get the impression that there was a party going on. The laughter was nice to hear. Listening to all the different conversations taking place gave the sense of enjoying life once again. When the food was ready, the pastor asked everyone to join him outside for a moment of prayer.

"First, I would like to tell all of you, what a pleasure it has been meeting you. Yesterday seems a lifetime ago, however, it was only yesterday that the people at Rocky Mountain Christian Church were feeling forsaken by God. Riley reminded us that God is a wondrous God, and He does things in His own perfect time. It was the second time the travelers from this camp entered our small town.

The first time, they refused to go any further than the burnt buildings. However, God had another thought in mind when He sent them back. The second time, God had them go all the way through town and with an amplified voice of a small child, that I'm convinced should have never been heard, brought them to us. To be used by God in any capacity is a true gift in and of itself. As I look around at all of you, I see the beauty of that gift's blessings. There is no greater joy than to see God's hand at work, and here in this place, I can see God everywhere. So today we give thanks not only for the food we eat but for our amazing leaders that God has chosen for us and also for this amazing body of Christ that stands before me. Now let's give thanks."

Riley didn't know Pastor Scully very well, but she liked him. She felt he would do well with this group and didn't have to convince anyone when she mentioned adding Scully to the council. Riley's father had done an outstanding job as their spiritual leader, but it was becoming too much, even for him. Saving people's souls was far too important to be left in any of their hands, and comforting those souls would be a chore only a pastor could do. Riley would like to think she had the patience that her father and the pastor had for that kind of work, but she knew she didn't. Even her father was happy to relinquish all spiritual duties to the pastor. There was a reason God gave people spiritual leaders; there were pastors that had a very special role to play in the lives of God's children. Just like moms and dads had their roles, so did pastors. Now that they had one, Riley was happy to join her father in relinquishing all spiritual matters to Pastor Scully. She had one thing to focus on now, and that was their trip to Jackson. Christmas was only a few short weeks away. Between now and then, Riley knew the weeks ahead would be preparing for all of them at once—for the trip, a wedding, and the Christmas celebration. As she looked around at the group of people God had placed in her life, she had no doubt it would all come together perfectly.

Pastor Scully caught on to the order of serving food in the kitchen very quickly – mothers with small children would go first, then kids that could help themselves, then the women, and finally, the men. Riley and the other leaders set another unspoken rule; that was, all the leaders were to go last. She, Lyle, Anderson, Allen and Ken stood together, waiting their turn. Pastor Scully followed their lead. Because Shauna now had the two very young girls living with her, she went first; however, once she got them settled in with Shyla, she fell back and waited until everyone had their food before she got her own. The leaders were the first to volunteer and the last to eat. Pastor Scully liked the order in which these men and women placed themselves in the community. He once again gave thanks for the leadership of this community in a silent prayer.

* * *

The day of the wedding seemed to sneak up on everyone. With Alice Crawford as the self-appointed wedding planner, everything was ready to go. Alice even managed to get the weather to cooperate with its clear blue skies. However, the chill factor could only be dealt with by everyone bundling up. The wedding ceremony was to take place at eleven with the reception following immediately after. To Riley's surprise, Carolyn and Nate were clueless about the gift that awaited them. She wondered what they thought they were going to do for a honeymoon. A tent maybe? Knowing the men, they were probably hounding Nate about it. Riley didn't want to know. The women did a spectacular job on Carolyn's portion of the wedding gift. Alice once again came through with decorative pillows and other odds and ends that she brought from her home. The place looked amazing, and she knew Carolyn would love it. She would have her own shower and toilet, which Riley knew would make her cry. Riley couldn't wait for both of them to see it.

People began to file in, taking their seats. Riley found her mother and directed the boys to the seats next to her. Sara and Annie followed them in, taking the seats in the row directly behind her and the boys. It wasn't long before the place was full of people. The chairs were mismatched, but no one seemed to care. Nate was clean shaven and was sporting a new, short haircut. He was already standing up front along with his best man, Kevin, and the pastor. Jasper, who was a talented guitarist, was playing the guitar to something that wasn't quite the wedding march, but nonetheless, Carolyn took it as her cue to start the procession. Riley's father walked her down the aisle, and he too had his hair cut short. Everyone stood as Ken and Carolyn walked toward the front of their outdoor venue. Ken handed her off to Nate, who was beaming ear to ear. Carolyn looked beautiful. She had actually brought dresses with her and was wearing one for the ceremony. With the snow-covered mountains and the lake as their backdrop, no flowers were needed. It was breathtaking. The ceremony took all of fifteen minutes, which was a relief because of the cold. Riley remembered her wedding day. It was 106 degrees, and she had insisted it be outside under the most amazing tree at the country club. Tree or not, she didn't know what she was thinking. And now it was just the opposite temperature from her wedding, and it wasn't any better, she thought. But nonetheless, it was beautiful, cold and all.

The reception was as festive as Thanksgiving was. The food was only moose meat, but Alejandro and Lupe did a spectacular job with it. Lupe's homemade salsa only added to the savory meat. Riley was sad when she got full and couldn't eat anymore. She was grateful this was lunch and that dinner was only six hours away. She would have her fill again before the day's end, which made her smile.

Martin caught her smiling and leaned over the table asking, "Those clean thoughts you're having there, Riley?"

Riley laughed out loud. "Yes! I was thinking how upset I am that I'm full. This food is beyond tasty, and I can't put another bite in my mouth. However, six hours from now, I'll be able to."

Martin laughed. "I'm stuffed too. You know, like idiots, we went into the mountains with only cans of food. Thinking back now, we would have died of starvation if you all hadn't come along. My first meal here was just as mouthwatering as this. I didn't think I would ever eat a meal like this again. And for a big man like me, that's a scary thought."

"I knew we would be fine even if we didn't find any food, thanks to my mom and her obsessive canning habits. But even as good of a cook as my mom is, she can't come close to this."

Martin waved his hands in front of him, as if backing away from the issue. "Now I'm never going to say anything bad about your mom's cooking. She does a mighty fine job. But yes, Alejandro and Lupe are pretty magnificent when it comes to cooking."

"Riley, sorry to be messin' with your conversation, but you need to give a speech or something to send these two off packin'," Anderson instructed her. "And yes, it needs to be you, so get a move on, Boss."

Anderson was smiling the whole time, and Riley knew he was joking but not about the speech. She hadn't thought about what she was going to say and was totally unprepared. She stood up and headed outside, where she noticed everyone was scattered and wasn't sure how to get everyone's attention. Suddenly, an amplified voice was telling everyone to come outside. Riley chuckled; she had forgotten about the bullhorn.

Riley walked up to Allen who had the bullhorn and asked, "Where are the newlyweds?"

Anderson had her platform box back out, and Riley stepped up on it, waiting for Carolyn and Nate to come forward. Allen offered

Riley the bullhorn, but she declined to take it. Once Carolyn and Nate were there, Riley began.

"Thank you, Allen, for corralling everyone for me. Okay, I'm not going to take too long, but some words need to be said. When we arrived here in July, we had our first encounter with Nate. Mind you, it wasn't a pleasant one. I would have told you then that this union would've never happened. But forgiveness has a strange way of making drastic changes in the hearts of men and women, and because of that forgiveness, powerful friendships have been made. Even a beautiful union between two amazing people was made possible. I'm truly happy for Carolyn and Nate. However, because our lives are not what they once were, we all know that gifts at this time were not feasible. That was until Anderson and Allen put their heads together and came up with a wonderful idea. All the women put the finishing touches to it and made it fantastic. And the rest of us in the community agreed to give it to you for the duration of our stay here. Nate and Carolyn, there is a travel trailer set off a short distance from us, not too far, but far enough away for you to have some privacy."

Carolyn had her hands up to her face, wiping away her joyful tears as Nate held her in his arms. They both looked genuinely surprised.

"Allen and Anderson, if you'll do the honors and lead the newlyweds out. The rest of us make two lines for the couple to walk through as we bid them farewell. Sorry, rice is far too expensive to throw, but the clapping of our hands costs nothing."

Everyone did as she asked. Riley gave Carolyn and Nate a big hug as she wished them both well. Riley started the clapping, signaling everyone to join in, as the couple walked down the middle of the two rows. Becca shouted out to Carolyn that the boys would be in her care. Carolyn was glowing as she mouthed her thanks. Once they faded off into the woods, everyone else started the task of cleaning up.

Riley took on dish duty, with Gauge and Levi having the honor of drying, but now as in all things with the two boys, it became a contest. Riley quickly got them to settle down with a promise of a horseback ride on Duke if they would do their chores in peace. The place was put back together within the hour, and some of the Mercy people went home, while others stayed to chat or play some games.

Riley decided to go to the corral with the boys once she finished cleaning up. She took her time as she made her way over to the animals. Levi and Gauge took off running to see who could get there first. Riley sighed at their never-ending competitiveness. When Duke saw Riley and the boys, he reared his head, which was his way of letting Riley know he was ready for her to take him out. The two boys jumped up on some hay to wait for Riley to get Duke ready. Alejandro came in about the time Riley was struggling with the saddle.

"Jefe, I do. Please let me, I do."

"Thank you, Alejandro, but if I don't start doing it myself, I'm never going to learn. By the way, the food was marvelous!"

"Good. Meat tender. Moose is very good. No have moose before until now."

"Elk, moose, and bison are all yummy. When we get to Jackson, we'll have bison. However, we do need to find some cows. Hopefully, they're not all dead. Plus, we need more chickens."

"Cows, okay, no problem. Chickens, maybe problem. Have gift for you, Jefe."

Riley was confused by the word *gift*. She followed Alejandro over to a large container nestled into hay and blankets, where she noticed one of the smaller generators running to power the heat lamp. Both the boys had their faces inside the container, whispering to each other in awe of the chicks. There were eight little chicks moving about.

"Wow. They're beautiful, Alejandro. I didn't think chicks hatched in the winter."

"No, not much. But these did. Good, no?"

Riley chuckled. "Yes, of course, very good!"

"I make test with few hens and rooster then babies come, it good test work."

"Yes, it is. You're amazing with animals, raising them and cooking them."

Riley gave Alejandro a quick hug then went back to looking at the chicks in awe and laughed. Riley thought she saw a tear in Alejandro's eye but looked away so as not to make him feel uncomfortable. Duke was behind her, resting his enormous head on her shoulder. She pulled his head into hers then turned to give him a kiss.

"Come on, boys, Duke needs to get out of here for a while. Thank you, Alejandro, for everything you and Lupe do. There are no words to express how happy I am that you're both here with all of us."

"*Gracias, Jefe. De nada, con mucho gusto.*"

"Oh, and Alejandro, you have a place on the council. I should have made you part of the council a long time ago. You're in charge of all the animals, and that makes you a valuable member," she said as she got the boys up on Duke. "You're officially part of the decision-making for the community."

This time, with an expression of pure shock on his face, he repeated in a more bewildered tone what he had just said, "*Gracias, Jefe. De nada, con mucho gusto.*"

Riley smiled. "You're welcome, and with much pleasure," was always his response to her. The man was the epitome of kindness in every regard, and Riley loved him and Lupe dearly. Telling him he was on the council because he was in charge of the livestock nearly caused him to break down and cry. She was so grateful that she and the boys were riding out, giving him time to get his composure back. He almost had her crying too. Lupe and Alejandro had taken care of everyone as if they were their own children from the very first day of meeting them. They were the first up and the last to go to bed. Riley managed a few times to beat them up, but that was seldom. And though she did stay up late with them, she soon found that they both would wait for her to go to bed, then they did. Riley finally gave up and went to bed early. Riley thanked God for them daily, and she honestly didn't know how the group would've survived without them.

Riley and the boys rode Duke down to the lake just a little way past Mercy before turning Duke around to make their way back to Calumet. As they approached Calumet, Annie, Sara, Landon, and her father were waiting for them on the other horses. Levi switched horses and got on with Annie, which meant he got to hold the reins on Annie's horse, while Gauge got to take Duke's reins. They rode well past Calumet and up the mountain. The day was still beautiful with the sun still out and the wind quiet. At the top, they could see for miles. The valley below stretched out in what seemed like forever covered in snow with green popping out here and there. It was peaceful.

Riley's father broke the silence, "This is truly God's country. If the human race disappears, there will be no one to admire it."

"The human race won't disappear, and I can't believe we are the last humans alive either. Someone is out there, and we'll find them. If they need our help, we'll give it to them; if not, we'll keep records of them and keep a supply line to them. If this is just another virus to weed out the human race like the Bubonic Plague, just to name one of many that have plagued this world, then I believe it will be over soon. What will be left is going to be worse, I think. People in the cities will be starving or dying because they are eating food that has long outlived its shelf life or killing one another for food. The rats and mice will be having a field day eating the human remains, which in turn will wreak havoc with another deadly disease."

"Okay, that's it! I finally come on a ride with you, and you scare the bajeebees out of me! Mom, seriously, you have Levi and Gauge here!" Sara's frustration and fear were clearly seen by the others.

"I'm not afraid, Mom, really, I'm not!" Levi tried to convince her.

"Me either, Grandpa is teaching us all kinds of things about how to survive. Levi and I will take good care of you, Sara. Promise."

"Well, Mom is right. We can't have our heads stuck in the sand either, Sara. The more informed we are, the safer it will be for all of us," Landon told his sister.

"I know, but the way Mom explains it, it's like a horror story, and even in broad daylight, it's freaking me out! Levi and Gauge are going to have to sleep in my bed, just so I can sleep with Mom."

"Uh-uh, no way!" Gauge argued.

"I'll sleep with you, Sara. I'll keep you safe, I promise," Levi meant it too.

"I'm going to take you up on that if Mom doesn't stop."

"Sara, you better get used to the idea of both of them sleeping with you while I'm gone. You boys will take good care of Sara for me, won't you?"

Both the boys said yes at the same time. Sara asked if Gauge wanted to ride back with her, that he could start that protection now. He jumped at the chance of taking care of his big sister. They all turned the horses around and headed back to camp. The boys had managed to turn Sara's spirits back to being happy as they chatted all the way home. The sky was so clear and the sun so bright that Riley hated to go back. Her mind kept jumping forward to Jackson, wondering what they would find there. Norman told her a week ago that he couldn't get in touch with Benjie anymore on the radio. That bothered her terribly. He had been their eyes and ears, but now he was gone. She knew he was moving out of the city with some people, and her hope was that he just didn't have his radio up and running yet. They had also met others on the radio, giving the same reports.

People were taking Norman's advice, though. Hopefully, they would all find safety in numbers and out of the cities. Riley got on the radio a few times since all the leaders had to rotate radio duty. It was hard to listen at times, but every now and then, there would be a positive report. Once they were settled, they would put the call out for people to head their way. But for now, they had to stay quiet to make sure they didn't all die in Jackson while removing bodies.

Riley shifted her thoughts to Christmas. She was excited about Christmas and was glad for once that Christmas would be celebrated the way she always thought it should be, without secularism. Christians would finally get their holiday back. Carolyn and Annie did put some thought into it for the children, but Riley wanted to keep it simple. The gifts would be handed out the night before. Less like gifts and more like treats, she thought. She knew that once society started back up, Christmas would more than likely go back to the secular ways again, but for now, it would be solely the celebration of Christ's birth, which brought Riley a great deal of joy. She loved Christmas trees, the lights around the eves of the house, and the decorations she and the girls put out. She even loved it when Sara made cookies, fudge, and peanut butter balls. Some of it was fun, but she could live without all the gift-giving and the mailing of cards. Church was closed on Christmas, and Riley thought it should have been open, like at Easter. She knew Catholics had Mass on Christmas day, but her church's doors were always closed. But here, there would be a day of celebration on Christmas Day. That in and of itself was worth everything to her. She hoped the rest of the community would be just as thrilled as she was.

Riley wasn't sure if it was the yelling or the waving of the arms that cut into her thoughts, but whichever it was, she and the others were at full gallop through the snow back into Calumet. Riley pulled up on Duke's reins to listen to Becca explain what was happening.

"The babies," she was out of breath from all her jumping around trying to get their attention, "the babies are coming!"

"The babies? Oh, the babies! Wait, both women are delivering their babies at the same time?" Riley questioned.

"Yes, apparently, one of them is having twins!"

"Oh, boy." Riley turned Duke toward the corral. Alejandro was waiting for her and the others. He held Duke while Riley slid off, and began to run in the direction of all the excitement when she suddenly slid to a halt, nearly falling on her bottom. She knew she wasn't needed. With a sigh of relief, she spun around, slowly making her way back to the corral to help with the horses.

"Mom, what are you doing? I thought you were going over to help with the births?" Sara was shocked to see her back in the corral.

"Uh, no. There is a real doctor now, not to mention your grandmother, Agnes and Lupe. I'm not needed in any capacity for once, and you know, I'm okay with that. Hand me the brush, please. Here you go, big boy."

Riley and Sara brushed the horses down then put them in their stalls. They both helped with the feeding of all the animals. By the time they were done with everything, including locking the animals up for the night, word came of the first baby to be born in the community. It was a boy. Those that went back to Mercy were now back with the news of the impeding births. A wedding and three births in one day—what an exciting day! Becca saw Riley and Sara coming toward her, and she waved, ushering them over to her.

"Okay, I'm so excited about everything that has happened today that I know I won't be able to sleep at all tonight!"

"It seems like everyone is. This is the true definition of a great day. Carolyn is going to be sad she missed this, though," Riley thought out loud.

Becca leaned in to Riley and whispered, "I think she is a little preoccupied right now."

Riley laughed, "Yes, I guess she is."

Alice came out of the travel trailer and announced that the baby boy had a twin sister. Everyone cheered, and the father of the twins was showered with congratulations. Riley took a backseat to everyone as she watched all the jubilation. The pastor found his way over to her and stood next to her.

"You're not getting into all the excitement?"

Riley smiled. "I'll congratulate them tomorrow when it calms down. Today, is for all of them. If I step in, it would feel like I'm taking over, which I don't want. Today it's all about the moms, the dads, and of course, the babies."

"Riley, you are a rare breed, indeed. Most politicians would make it all about them."

"Huh? Did you just mistake me for a politician?" she said with a shocked look on her face and then smiled. "Ha! Now, that's funny. Never cared much for them and awfully glad we don't have any here amongst us."

The pastor was smiling too. "No, we don't have much use for one around here. I'm just glad you don't think like one either. Power does strange things to people."

"Pastor, the only thing I'm driven by is helping to place a future in front of my children. Other than that, I just want to survive, like everyone else does. I've taken it a bit further than most have, I guess."

"What do you mean?"

"You should know I've killed two people since we've been here. The little tidbit about our meeting Nate was the day I killed a man. I'm the one that shot Nate in the hand." She paused to let it sink in. "The second was up in the mountains, rescuing Tamera. That time, I actually wasn't trying to kill him, but the arrow went into his chest and not his shoulder as I had planned."

"I'm sorry, Riley. I had no idea," he said with a surprised look on his face.

"Most of the people in Mercy are from the group that Nate came from. It's funny how those very same people who wanted to do us harm are now the very people I trust with my life. You should know that my daughter Annie killed a man too."

"Riley, I had no idea!"

"Pastor, why don't you come with me so we can have a talk about some of the people in this group, to give you a little more insight on your flock, so to speak."

The pastor and Riley took a walk along the edge of the lake. Riley started at the beginning, taking Scully down the long and, at times, gruesome path that led this group to where they were today. Pastor Scully at times looked as if he was going to cry but held it together as he listened, never once asking a question. Walking the pastor back in time brought back a flood of vivid memories for Riley—all the tragedies and blessings in living color with all the horrifying sounds and repulsive smells. She wondered if the pastor could visualize it the way she did. She knew he couldn't really; one would've had to have been there. She knew his story wasn't going to be any better, but she hoped and prayed that his story would not be as bad, that the church had protected him and the others for the most part. The hardest part was telling him how she felt after she had taken a life or more, the lack of feeling. When she was done, they walked in silence for a while. She could tell he was thinking about what he was going to say. She liked that about him. He was a good listener, and he thought before he spoke. When he did finally speak, Riley just listened.

"Riley, I hope you write this testimony of yours down. This is a testimony like none I've ever heard. What you and the others have gone through these last five and a half months, well, it's remarkable! The Bible is full of men and women doing the work of God. I recognized it immediately when the men came back to the church to inform me about you and the others. I knew God had answered our prayers. And hearing the story of all the people here, I'm convinced even more of God's hand in all this. God is using all of you for His good purpose. As for the killing of those men, there are just as many places in the Bible that would defend your actions as there are condemning them. I believe you didn't have murder in your heart then and definitely not now. At some point, people have to take responsibility for their own actions and the two men, Bruce and AJ, are taking responsibility for their actions now in hell. Exodus 22:2 states, 'If a thief is caught while breaking in at night and is struck so that he dies there will be no bloodguilt on his account.' Why is it okay to kill at night? Why is there no 'bloodguilt'? For only one reason I can think of, and that is that one can't know what the intent of a person is when breaking in at night. Sure, he may just be a thief, but then again, he might be there to murder, rape, or kidnap. In the daytime, one can see better what someone's intent is, and it seems to me that the intent of Bruce and AJ was more than that of thieving. Psalm 82:4 says, 'Rescue the weak and the needy, deliver them from the hand of the wicked.' Then there is Proverbs 24:11, and it states, 'Rescue those who are being led away to death, hold back those who are staggering toward slaughter.' In that Proverb, it goes on to say not to rejoice when your enemy falls. I don't think you rejoiced when those men died, and I know no one else did either. And that was proven by the forgiveness all of you bestowed on the other men that came here with evil in their hearts. Forgiveness, Riley, is a beautiful thing. And because of it, you and the others have reaped the benefits of that forgiveness. Romans 13:3 states, 'For rulers hold no terror for those who do right, but for those who do wrong. Do you want to be free from fear of the one in authority? Then do what is right, and you will be commended. For the one in authority is God's servant for your good.' Leaders aren't and should never be a terror to good people but only to those that are evil. You are these people's leader, and it's your job to protect them, to be fair, and always to be in control when others are not. As long as you continue to put God first, then we will all continue to be blessed."

"I lost control with Bruce."

"Actually, I don't think you did. It may seem that way, but I honestly don't think you did. You didn't kill Nate. He was standing next to you, and you could have, but you didn't. Neither did Annie. She saw the man turn his weapon on you, and she killed him. She didn't kill anyone else. That in my book is control. The other man that kidnapped Tamera, you spoke with him and gave him a choice. His decision gave you no choice, whether you meant to kill him or not, you had to shoot him. He was going to kill Tamera. Remember, it's your job to protect, which is exactly what you did. You have an awesome responsibility being a leader, and no one understands that more than God. Continue to trust Him, Riley, He will never steer you wrong."

"Thanks, Pastor, I needed to hear this. I'm really glad you're here."

"There are no words to express how happy I am to be here. What do you say we go back and see how those babies are doing and then grab us some more of that moose?"

"Yes, please! You must have read my mind."

CHAPTER 15

Christmas morning finally arrived, bringing with it another beautiful day. The boys had Riley and their sisters up early with the excitement of singing Christmas songs during church service. Jasper and Barbra, one of the ladies from Scully's original church, had put a choir of children together for the Christmas service. Gauge and Levi were so elated to be a part of the choir that they sang for anyone who would listen to them. Riley was waiting outside for both of the boys, while Annie put the finishing touches on their hair and clothes. The door of the cabin flew open with the two young boys bursting through it, making Riley spin around startled.

"Geez, you two are going to give me a heart attack!" she laughed, then she playfully took a good look at both boys. "Okay, where are they? What have you done with my two troublemakers?"

Levi giggled, "You know it's us! You're being silly."

"Um, do I? You're too clean to be my boys." Riley bent over and put Levi's little chin in her hand. She turned it to one side than the other. "You have a lot more hair too. Let me have a look in those eyes."

With that, Levi jumped up to give his mom a kiss then took her hand, pulling her toward the kitchen. Gauge held on to the other hand, helping to pull her.

"Whoa, slow down, guys, you're going to yank my arms out of their sockets!"

"Sara's making pancakes this morning. Landon said he was going to eat all of them!" Gauge yelled.

"He better not, or I'm going to hit him in his big belly!" Levi added.

"Okay, you boys better slow down. Landon can't eat all the pancakes. He'll be lucky if he gets one. You know the rules. Little kids get pancakes, not the big kids, not unless there are leftovers."

With that, the boys slowed their pace. Although once they smelled the food, they let go of Riley's hands and took off running full speed. Riley, the last to arrive, found both boys finishing up their morning ritual. First, they gave hugs to family and then the chefs. When they were done, they took their seats and waited for their pancakes. Since the bananas had long been used up, this morning it was chocolate chip pancakes—which just happened to be Levi's and Gauge's favorite. Riley said her "good mornings" to everyone, and finding the coffee, she poured herself a cup. Lupe handed her a plate with a burrito on it. It was moose meat with spicy Mexican seasoning on it. Riley's tummy rumbled as she told Lupe thank you. She found a seat next to the little boys. They were in an argument with Landon about their pancakes.

"Come on, guys, give your favorite brother one bite, that's all I'm asking!" Landon was pleading with Levi and Gauge.

"Nope, you know the rules. Mom said you can't have any," Gauge reminded him.

"Geez, not fair, not fair at all!" Landon griped.

"That's what you get for teasing them this morning, Landon."

"Come on, Mom, just one lousy bite." Landon stretched out his long muscular arms across the table and dropped his head as if he were dying. It made the little ones laugh.

Riley enjoyed the breakfast burrito. Lupe had made some more of her famous goat cheese, which Riley could never get enough of. Just as Riley sank her teeth into her burrito, Nate came over with Carolyn and her boys.

"Hey, Boss, do you mind if we sit with you?"

Riley said, "Wes," her mouth was full of burrito, and that was the best she could get out.

Levi yelled at her not to talk with her mouth full then busted up laughing at her. How she hated to hear her own words thrown back at her, Riley thought.

Carolyn smiled as Nate pulled out the chair for his new wife. "I'll go get our food. Matt, come and give me a hand, please."

"Sure," Matt was up following Nate.

"Thanks, Riley, for everything. The last few days have been heaven. The boys had so much fun last night. I wasn't sure they were ever going to fall asleep."

"I'm glad they had a good time. But really, it was all the teenage girls doing. They had more fun setting everything up for the kids. How was this morning? Were the boys disappointed not having presents when they woke up?"

"Oh, no, they were great! I think they're happy just to have all their friends with them that the presents were forgotten. With that said, they did ask about their father."

"I'm sorry, Carolyn. It has to be hard on them. Gauge asked about his too. Because I don't fully understand his story yet, I didn't know what to say. I just held him."

"I'm sorry for you too. Just looking at the three of you, I thought they had settled in completely with you. In my case, I thought it would be hard, but Nate spoke with our boys, and I'm really glad he did. He told them that Ken went back up to the house right before we left Park City to see if Adam had second thoughts and returned. Of course, the weasel hadn't. Nate told them that when he leaves, he is coming back to us, God willing. That he would do everything in his power to come home."

Some keywords popped up in Riley's mind. First was the fact that Carolyn said the words "our boys," which made Riley very happy. However, the other needed some explanation.

"Okay, Nate using God in any form in a sentence seems odd, and where is Nate going?"

Nate and Matt were back, setting four plates and three cups down on the table in front of Carolyn and Mark.

"That's what I wanted to talk to you about. Let me grab another cup of coffee. Go ahead and have a seat, Matt, and thanks for your help, buddy."

"Thank you, honey," Carolyn said as Nate walked off. She turned back to Riley. "Nate had been speaking with your father about Christ and the gift of salvation. Before we got married, he accepted Jesus as his Lord and Savior. Pastor Scully is talking with Matt and Mark now that they are old enough. Adam was mad when I became a Christian, so I never got baptized. I hope we can all be baptized together as a family in late spring when it warms up some. I don't know how Landon and Bram do it, swimming in that freezing lake water."

Nate was back with his coffee. "Ladies. Man, this smells good!"

"So, Mom, are you done with your burrito?" Landon asked.

Riley handed her plate to Landon, which he took. He took a huge bite that was far too big to chew and had all the kids around him laughing. Even Carolyn and Riley couldn't help but laugh.

Riley brought the conversation back to Nate. "First off, Nate, I want you to know how truly happy I am that you accepted Christ into your life. I know that was a huge decision for you. But, Nate, where are you going?"

"It wasn't that hard after everyone at Calumet forgave us for our stupidity. Ken was kind enough to put up with all my questions

I had. He shared the gospel with me in a way I could understand. Being forgiven by all of you changed my life. When I told your dad about Carolyn and me, he gave me a bunch of scriptures to read. The one that made me kick into high gear was 2 Corinthians 6:14–18. The part that caught my attention was verse 14 that said, 'Do not be yoked together with unbelievers. For what do righteousness and wickedness have in common?' I wanted my marriage to work, and God needed to lead the way. Carolyn was already a Christian, and I needed to put God first in my life." Looking at his new bride, he said, "I've been blessed in ways I never thought possible, and I know I have God to thank for that. And as far as where I'm going, I'm going to Jackson with you."

"Wow! I knew my dad had been counseling you and Carolyn—for that matter, a lot of people here. But I honestly had no idea." Riley was happy her father had taken on the job of people's salvation at camp because she was horrible at it. However, Nate's going to Jackson was too much. "But seriously, Nate, you just got married! Why would you want to go to a town with no certainties when you have a beautiful wife and two boys that need a father? Besides, I'm sure the roster is full."

"It's for them that I'm going, and you could use someone with my skills. Fortunately, there are two slots left, and I'm taking one."

Riley sighed. "It's all volunteers, so I can't make you stay. You said 'your skills'? What kind of skills do you have that would help get rid of..." Riley remembered the children around her, "the not so living?"

"I used to work for the water company in Nebraska. I worked my way from the ground up. There is nothing that I don't know about pumping water into homes. If I can get running water back into the houses, I'll be extremely happy."

The census! Of course. She had forgotten the census that Becca and Lisa had put together for her. Most of the volunteers were young adults that didn't have much to offer in the way of skills. But what they did bring was the ability to be trained in all things and the eagerness to want to learn. Kevin was a large machine operator, which was going to be a tremendous help. Of course, Allen, with his knowledge of all things mechanical, was a no-brainer. Now Nate with his knowledge of the water system. Well, he would have every woman in Calumet and Mercy wrapped around his finger if he manages to bring water into their homes. Mr. Miller and Anderson were builders; both of whom she hoped wouldn't have to build too much. But they did understand structures and the safety therein. She chuckled at herself; her skills were that of being a mother, and that was it! Mothering 101, be forceful and manipulative in a tender and loving way. If that doesn't work, then pull out the nasty bossy card and run with it. Riley was smiling then remembered she was in a conversation with Nate and Carolyn, who both happened to be looking right at her.

"Sorry, just thinking about what you were saying." She realized there wasn't anything funny about what he was saying, and her smile disappeared. "Okay, you can come, but if at any time you feel you can't, or don't want to go, don't hesitate to say so. No one will think less of you."

Nate took hold of Carolyn's hand and gazed into her eyes. "I need to do this, for the boys, for us."

"I know. We'll be here waiting, just remember that," Carolyn said.

"I don't want you to go!" Mark was leaning over now with his arms around Nate.

Nate let go of Carolyn's hand and put his arms around Mark.

"Hey, buddy. Mark, look at me. It's going to be okay. Has Riley ever come home without someone? It's been quite the opposite, she has an uncanny way of bringing more people to us. I'll come home to get you, Matt, and your mom, I promise." Then as if taking all the responsibility back off Riley's shoulders, he added, "God willing."

Directing his attention now at Riley, Mark got up and moved, so he was now standing in front of her. "Ms. Riley, please bring my dad home."

Tears were welling up in his eyes, which was killing Riley. She had no way to know what waited for them in Jackson, and now she had a small boy pleading for his father's life as if she were the one in total control of that outcome.

"Here's the deal I can make you. I'll do everything within my power to bring everyone home, even your dad. But, Mark, I have no idea what's in Jackson. However, there is something you can do for us. Pray for us daily, will you? Remember whatever happens, God's in charge. I know you might not understand this now, but everything your mom, dad, and I do is for you. We can't stay here if we want to live. I understand you may think we can, but we can't. Most importantly, the part I need you to remember is that Nate must love you very much because no one would do this out of self-gratification or pride. He is doing this out of total and complete love for you, Matt, and your mother." Riley was holding his hand, from which he broke loose and fell into her arms.

"Thank you, Ms. Riley," and in a whisper to her ear, he said, "I love you."

Riley, now near to tears herself, pulled him back. "It's Christmas, and we're crying. Let's enjoy the day with no more talk of the trip, okay? And, buddy, I love you too."

Levi and Gauge were staring at them, and Riley could see the tears trailing down their cheeks.

"Okay, you two. You ready to go find Jasper and Barbra? I'm sure they want to have one last practice with you knuckleheads."

With the talk of the trip to Jackson over with and remembering of the upcoming celebration today, Gauge and Levi cleared off their portion of the table. Then they took off running outside, toward the trees where the church service was going to take place today.

Due to the number of people now living in Calumet and Mercy, there was no place but outside to house the church services. Since the arrival of Pastor Scully, the weather had wreaked havoc on the day and time of those services. But as all good citizens of the two camps, they were flexible and met on whichever day or time they could. They used an area close to the trees to help block the wind and tied tarps from one tree to another, which helped considerably. Nevertheless, people usually had blankets with them, which helped even more. Riley found the preacher and most of the children up front. Jasper and Barbra were there; both seemed to be quite happy to be surrounded by the children. Riley knew this was what she was going to miss most—the casualness of life up here. Her father had come up behind her, kissing her on the top of her head. She looked up at him and fell into his embrace.

"You're doing the right thing, Riley. Matt and Mark will understand that someday, as will those two youngsters."

Riley sighed, wiping the tears from her eyes, "I fell hard in love with those two, Dad. Please take good care of them."

"Roger that, baby girl! With your mom, Agnes, Lupe, Sara, Jena…do I need to go on?"

Riley laughed at that. She knew they would be well cared for, just not by her, and that's the part that hurt the most. Even knowing she was leaving with most of her kids didn't help leaving the others. She needed to clear her head and concentrate on the here and now.

People began meandering in finding a place to sit. Matt and Mark joined the other kids in front while their parents found a seat. Riley's father took her hand, walking her to a row of chairs where they each took a seat. The rest of her family fell in next to them or the row behind them. Once the congregation was settled, Pastor Scully took over and began the service. Levi and Gauge sang with such animation that Riley couldn't control her giggles. Everyone joined in singing the carols as if they were caroling to an audience, which today happened to be nature itself.

Pastor Scully took to the podium and began the story of Jesus's birth. As the story unfolded, Riley's mind stopped spinning, being filled only with the words the pastor spoke. For the first time, Riley felt free of all the worries of the past and those to come. Before she knew it, Pastor Scully was done. Riley's heart was overjoyed when Kota and Jesse, along with a few others, went up during the altar call. Seeing these young adults shed their past to begin their future with a fresh start was almost too overwhelming for Riley. She gave a silent prayer of thanks. Then she heard the pastor ask all those going to Jackson to come forward, along with all the leaders.

"Riley has something to say, and then we'll pray for our travelers heading to Jackson. Riley?"

"Thank you, Pastor, for everything. And you kids, you all did a marvelous job!"

Everyone showed their gratitude with hoots, callouts, and an applause that might have gone on forever if Riley hadn't quieted them down.

"I know it's cold, and I'm sure I heard some tummies rumbling out there, so I won't take but a moment." Alejandro walked up to Riley and whispered something in her ear. "Are you sure? You don't have to…" Alejandro nodded his head yes.

Riley looked out at all the people standing before her and found Lupe. She was standing next to her mother in tears but managed a smile once Riley made eye contact.

"Well, it seems our last slot has been filled by Alejandro. Thank you, Lupe and Alejandro. Okay, so sorry, where was I? Um, I know all of you are now aware of my love of our Founding Fathers. George Washington said it best when he said,

It is the duty of all "Nations" to acknowledge the providence of Almighty God, to obey His will, to be

grateful for His benefits, and humbly to implore His protection and favor.[5]

John Adams agreed by stating,

The safety and prosperity of "Nations" ultimately and essentially depend on the protection and the blessing of Almighty God, and the "National" acknowledgment of this truth is...an indispensable duty which the people owe to Him.[6]

"I'm sure you're thinking we are in no way a nation, but you're wrong. Though we are a mere 128, we are a nation. The faith of your leaders is abundant, and the prosperity of our lives depends solely on the protection and blessing of the Almighty God. We as your leaders will not forget that. Neither should you. It says in 2 Corinthians 4:8–10:

We are afflicted in every way, but not crushed; perplexed, but not despairing; persecuted, but not forsaken; struck down, but not destroyed; always carrying about in the body the dying of

---

[5] George Washington, "A Proclamation" printed in *The Providence Gazette and Country Journal* (October 17, 1789), p. 1. See also George Washington, *Writings of George Washington,* ed. Jared Sparks (Boston: American Stationers Company, 1837), Vol. XII, p.119, "Proclamation for National Thanksgiving."

[6] *John Adams, The Works of John Adams, Second President of the United States,* ed. Charles Francis Adams (Boston: Charles C. Little and James Brown, 1851), Vol. IX, p. 169, "Proclamation for National Thanksgiving on March 23, 1798."

Jesus, so that the life of Jesus also may be manifested in our body.

"I know at times it seems we are at the very bottom of some imaginary barrel, but we're not. Yes, we have been afflicted, but we aren't crushed! We've been struck down, but we haven't been destroyed. I know some of you have told me that at times you feel God has forsaken you, but look around. We're alive! We're safe! These are not phrases to be used if one is forsaken. No, I would go more with the word *blessed*. Mr. Miller said something to my family before we left Park City. He said we were acting like a bunch of doomsday preppers. Maybe so, but we aren't underground somewhere scared out of our minds. We are alive, free of fear, celebrating Christmas! This is our gift from God! Enjoy it, feast on it, you and I have not been forsaken! And if by chance I die tomorrow, I die free and happy because those of you that God has so graciously set in my path. We are seeing firsthand God's protection, and I, for one, will acknowledge that truth. And more importantly, I am grateful for His benefits. I acknowledge His providence and will continue to humbly implore His protection and obey His will. Now let's go and enjoy the rest of our Christmas day!" With that, Riley stepped down with cheers of gratitude from everyone.

The pastor prayed over the leaders, as well as the men and women traveling to Jackson. When the prayer was finished, he clapped his hands together, saying, "Let's eat!"

This Christmas was everything that Riley had hoped it would be—one she hoped she could remember forever. Once civilization and the difference of opinion set in, secularism would be back in a frenzy. For now, she relished the moment of nothing but God and His people on the day of Christ's birth. Riley caught a glimpse of Alejandro and ran to catch up with him.

"Hey, Alejandro, hold up!" Riley said slightly louder than she intended. Once she got close enough, she asked, "How's it going?"

"Very nice service you think, Jefe? Very nice. You teach me about Founding Fathers?"

"Oh, sure, they're quite inspirational, which has helped me to move forward. And as for the service, it was truly a blessing! But eh, Alejandro, you have a big job here. With the birth of the Senora O'Hara's baby and the rest of the animals, don't you think that your time here might be better spent than with us in Jackson?"

"Ah, no, Jefe, Mr. Zane have cows back home. He say he take good care of Senora O'Hara and other animals. No problem. Lupe say I go with you so you no starve."

"What? I'll have you know I can make a mean pasta!"

"*Si*, only pasta?"

"Well, no, but with a recipe, I can cook anything and am quite good at it too, I might add. I just can't remember recipes off the top of my head."

"Lupe right, you starve!" he laughed.

Riley chuckled at that. "Augh! Okay. Thanks, Alejandro. I'll find Lupe and give her a big hug."

She latched on to Alejandro's arm, spun him around and gave him a big hug. She released him and said thank you again.

With the feast in full swing, Riley found her ever-growing family sitting at a table together. She spent the entire meal with them, enjoying all the different conversations that were bouncing all over the place—which at times made it hard to concentrate on any one subject. She relished the chaos and didn't want it to end.

Riley was stuffed, although she was quite pleased, knowing she would be indulging herself once again with this fabulous food at dinnertime. Once they all had their fill, games were pulled out and played. Riley knew all this interaction going on around her would have never taken place before the virus. Not that Riley was pleased about the virus; it was just the intimacy of the community she loved that came about because of it. It gave her a great deal of comfort, knowing that when they were in Jackson, this interaction would still be going on.

Her mind drifted toward Gauge. What bothered her the most about his situation was that he was eight and at a camp filled with fifth and sixth graders. She couldn't understand what an eight-year-old was doing there. She thought this would be a good time to find out by speaking to a couple of the camp leaders. She looked for the pastor and saw that he was coming her way.

"Hey, Pastor, I loved the service this morning. You put a lot of work into it, and I just wanted you to know how grateful I am."

"Thanks, Riley. Most of the credit goes to Jasper and Barbra, they did all the work, and of course, the children. But you're welcome."

"Changing the subject for a minute, but have you seen Greg or Maggie? I need to talk to them about Gauge."

"Gauge? What's the matter with him?"

"Nothing. I just thought it was odd that an eight-year-old was at a camp with a bunch of fifth and sixth graders. I'm curious as to why he was at the camp with them, that's all."

"Eh, Riley, Gauge wasn't at the camp. Maybe you and I should have a talk." Riley was confused, and Pastor Scully could see it in her face. "Mind if we go somewhere private to talk?"

"Uh, sure, the corral is peaceful now. We can take care of the animals while we talk."

Senora O'Hara, as Riley liked to call her now, was huge. Alejandro felt she would be giving birth to her foal in the next month or two. Riley took it upon herself to check on her regularly now. She had hoped the baby Clydesdale would arrive before they left, but she knew it wasn't possible. As they entered the corral area, Riley went to work, cleaning out the stalls. Riley's interest was piqued about

Gauge, but she let the pastor gather his thoughts and waited for him to speak.

"The day we heard the gunshots, some of the men decided to see for themselves what was going on. By the time the men arrived, the shooting was over and the buildings were totally engulfed in flames. They found Gauge just outside one of the burning buildings, screaming for his mother and father. They said he was trying to go back into the building. They stopped him by picking him up and taking him to safety. On their way back to the church, they found Scott. Both were covered in soot from the fire. We all knew they had barely escaped the burning buildings. Neither of them said much about it. That was, until you spoke with Scott. The only thing Gauge said prior was that his mom and dad were inside along with his little sister."

"How awful! I don't get it. Why did he ask me to help him find his parents? He told me he wanted to go home. Again, this morning, he asked about them, and I had nothing to offer him except a hug. Poor kid. Levi is a year younger and is fully aware that his family is dead. He talks about them, he talks to Gauge about them. Do you think the trauma is too much for him, that he's blocking out the truth?"

"I can't answer that. What I can tell you is, when he came to us, he knew his family was dead. He said they were dead. His words, not mine. Would you like me to speak to him?"

"No. I'll do it. But thank you for letting me know. This will help me start a dialog with him."

As they moved from one group of animals to another, they talked about all the things that transpired today—just everyday things that didn't push Riley's emotions one way or another. But her mind had a wicked way of circling around, bringing her back to thoughts she tried so desperately to push aside. When they were done, they walked back to the party. Riley thanked Scully one more time before parting. Riley's mother was walking toward their cabin when Riley caught up to her.

"Hey, Mom, have you seen the boys?"

"Which ones? We have so many now," Victoria smiled.

Riley gave her mother a huge smile and said, "Yes, indeed, we do, but I'm looking for the two that need supervision, Gauge and Levi?"

"Ah, well, those two do need a great deal of supervision, they snuck the last of the pie and got caught. Sara sent them to the cabin. I was just going to check on them."

"Thanks, Mom, I got it. I need to talk to them anyway about something else. By the way, just how much pie did they get into?"

"One full one. They ate the whole thing! I'm sure you're going to be up all night with them and their sore tummies. Sara said they looked a little green."

"Good grief! Okay, thanks, Mom. Tell Sara thank you for me."

Riley rushed the rest of the way to the cabin.

What she found wasn't as bad as she had anticipated. The boys were playing with the dominos building something. When they saw their mother come in, guilt washed over their faces. Riley bit the inside of her mouth to stop herself from smiling.

"Hey, you two!" Riley said in the sternest voice she could muster. "I need to have a word with you. Let's go have a chat in your grandparents' room."

Levi took a quick glance over to Gauge and Gauge to him, then both set of eyes were on Riley.

"Now, please. Get moving."

Levi and Gauge did as she asked. Once inside, she asked them to take a seat on the floor, which they did. Their tail ends were protected by the floor from any spankings they thought they were going to get. It gave them both some comfort. Riley saw that they had relaxed a little as she took the only chair in the room and sat.

"First off, you two will have kitchen duty every day after lunch and dinner for a month because of eating the pie."

Both boys groaned.

"Can't you just give us a spanking so it's over with?" Levi asked.

"Shhhh!" Gauge said.

"No, I can't, because those ladies worked hard to prepare the food for everyone, and you both not only took without permission but also took someone else's portion. That was very rude and selfish at the same time. Both of which requires a longer punishment. Oh, and just to let you know, around here when you get in trouble, the punishment is always going to be work. And since I know how much you two love to do dishes, that will be your punishment."

"Oh, boy," Levi muttered, slapping his forehead with his hand.

"Blah, blah, blah," Gauge muttered with his head down.

"Hey, if you would like, I can make it until I get back. Your choice?"

"No! Sorry, Mom," they said in unison.

"Really? Am I the one you need to apologize to?"

"No, ma'am."

"I'll trust you to find the ones you need to apologize to, and do it! Today! Oh, and I'm telling Sara no desserts for either of you for two weeks."

Levi again slapped his small hand up to his forehead. "Phooey! Okay."

"Geez, no dessert? That's not fair," Gauge said, now looking directly up at her. "Okay, I promise."

"Okay, now that's out of the way, Gauge, I need to ask you something." She paused for a second, gathering her thoughts. "What happened to your parents? I know you know. I need you to tell me what happened to them please."

Gauged swallowed hard, fighting back tears.

"It's okay, I'm here with you," Levi took Gauge's hand in one of his and put the other around his shoulder.

"Gauge, honey, it's going to be okay. Once you get it out, all of us can help you. You asked me this morning about them and were wondering if they were safe. I told you I didn't know, but you do, don't you?"

Gauge's eyes welled up with tears now. He couldn't hold them back anymore.

"Yes," he said in a low whisper. "They're dead. They died in the fire." He wiped his nose but kept talking, "My dad gave me something to drink, and I fell asleep. The smoke woke me up. My dad was sleeping, so I yelled at him to get up. His eyes opened, but he didn't move. I pulled on him, but he just lay there with his head on the table. Someone yelled at me to run, so I just ran outside. The bad man was there, laughing. I thought he was going to hurt me, but he saw something that scared him, and he ran away. Some man picked me up and carried me to the church. It was Scott that told me to run. Scott broke his arm in the fire, I think."

Riley was down on the floor with the boys. She pulled Gauge into her arms and held him tight.

Levi was patting his back whispering, "It's okay, my family's dead too."

Riley pulled him into the fold of her hug, nearly crushing them both. Neither of them seemed to care; they just held on to her. Riley pulled back, kissing them both on the forehead.

"I love you both so much, and I want you to understand, you both have a very important job to do now." They had a puzzled look on their face, then she said, "Your families will live on because of you. As long as you live, a part of them lives too. It means you are going to have to follow all the rules and do what your sisters and your grandparents tell you. You stay safe, you stay alive! Do you understand?"

Both of them nodded their heads then said, "We promise."

Levi then turned the table on Riley, telling her, "You stay safe, and you stay alive." He whispered to her with both of his tiny hands cupping her face.

She pulled them in so that all their heads touched, "I promise."

* * *

Because everyone pitched in to get the place cleaned up, it didn't take long to have the evening meal put away. Most of the people from Mercy drifted back over to their lodgings. Riley was surprised that she was alone as she put the last of the dishes up. Neither Lupe nor Alejandro was trying to take care of her. She sighed in relief and put a pot of water on the stove to boil then went down into the cellar to find some tea bags. She thought that a nice cup of hot tea would be a great way to end an already-perfect day. While in the cellar, Riley found some store-bought cookies and took them with her back upstairs. She chuckled at herself for thinking they were "store-bought cookies" when they were more like "store-looted cookies." Just as she was coming up the last step, she heard the door of the kitchen open. It was Anderson and Allen.

"Hey, Boss, how's it going?" Allen said as he closed the door behind him.

"Hi, guys, if you are here bearing bad news, it better be life-threatening, otherwise, I don't want to hear it."

"We're not always the bearers of bad news, are we?"

"Allen, anytime you start the sentence with *boss*, it's bad news."

"Can't two blokes come and have a nice conversation with their favorite Sheila?"

Riley smiled. "If that's the case, tea or coffee?"

"Gads, tea is for wimps!" Allen grunted. "Definitely coffee. Thanks."

Riley playfully rolled her eyes at Allen. "Anderson, I know you're no wimp – coffee?"

"Sure, thanks," Anderson answered. "Today was pretty magnificent. For that matter, the last couple of weeks have been jammed with excitement! A wedding and babies. Today Christmas – there's no beatin' it."

Riley had the cups on the counter with the sugar and goat's milk. She did enjoy the last couple of weeks, and yes, they would be hard to beat. She poured the water through the coffee filter and watched it seep through the other end. Once that was done, she used the remaining water for her tea.

"The only thing I think will come close to it is our moving to Jackson."

"My wife and I were talking about that last night. With the new additions to our family, the extra room will be much appreciated. Not to mention just having some of our privacy back will make me happy. Don't get me wrong, I love my cabinmates, but having my own house again will be nice."

"I'm living with a bunch of men. There's nothing more that needs to be said there," Anderson grinned.

Riley was lost in thought about what they would find once they arrived in Jackson.

"I wonder what's out there? In Jackson, I mean? I wonder, what we'll find? It's hard to believe we are a week away from leaving here. I have my lists made for the trip, and I'm guessing the two of you do too. We'll go over them tomorrow."

"Eh, no, like an actual, handwritten list? No, no, I don't. It's all in my head. Anyway, Sheilas make lists, not blokes!"

Anderson honestly had nothing. He was just going to grab his bag with his clothes, a gun, and step into a truck to leave. Now he was reconsidering that and thought he should make some effort to seem more prepared.

"You're a big dummy, Anderson!" Riley said, laughing. "I'll give you one of mine, and you will take care of everything on that list. How's that for pulling the boss card on you?"

"Ah, well, your lack of delegating is one of your greatest weaknesses. Glad to be of some assistance to you in that area, Boss," Anderson replied back playfully.

"Okay, it just registered. Call me slow, but did you say new additions to your family, Allen? Who are you adopting?" Riley asked.

"Lisa and I are adopting the twins, Jayden and Jordon, as well as their good friend, Ethen. Tina and Kate hit it off with the boys right away and are excited to have them as a part of our family. How about you, Anderson? Why don't you take a few of those boys under your wing and raise them as your own?"

Anderson's demeanor softened as he took a moment to choose his words carefully.

"If, indeed, the world is dead, then there will be no chance of my going back home. With that said, I'm forever grateful that I'm here with all of you. But if the world is not dead and Australia's borders are opened once again, then I am heading home. The kids couldn't come with me, and it wouldn't be fair to them. With all this talk of God's intervention, it gives me hope. But if God has other plans for me, well then, I can only hope at some point, those plans include me going home. But the here and now is what's important."

"Anderson, man, I'm sorry, I wasn't thinking," Allen apologized.

Riley added, "I'm sorry too. I forget sometimes you have a daughter out there. It's hard, wondering if our loved ones are safe. All the what-ifs never fully go away. I'm selfish and don't want you to ever leave. I'll truly miss you. However, I hope and pray that you'll be able to find your way home one day. I hope I will be a part of making that happen for you."

Riley understood the pain of not knowing and knew it would never go away, no matter how many years passed. Anderson was a terrific friend, one that she trusted wholeheartedly.

Allen stood up abruptly and went outside. Anderson and Riley glanced at each other; then they heard the generator start up. The door flew open with Allen coming in on some important mission. He passed the table that Riley and Anderson were sitting at, walked right up to the radio, and pulled the cover off. He slid out a chair and sat down.

"What 'ya doing, mate?"

"I'm going to wish someone out there a Merry Christmas," he said as a matter of fact.

"Ah, well, it is Christmas, mate."

Allen turned on the radio and picked up the mic, causing it to squawk, making Riley cringe. He adjusted the knobs. A faint voice was heard along with static. He fiddled with the knobs some more but couldn't get the voice to come in any louder. Allen went back outside to check the antenna, which helped some with the static. He came back in and picked up the mic.

"Hello, anyone out there. Over."

No one answered.

Allen tried again, "Merry Christmas to anyone out there from the people of Calumet and Mercy. Over."

Again, there was nothing.

Allen glanced over his shoulder at Riley then shrugged his shoulders, as if saying, "Well, I tried."

"Hey, hey, we hear you! Hello, you still there? Hello!"

Allen was leaning back on the back two legs of his chair and nearly fell over. Riley wasn't sure if she should laugh or be concerned for the distressed voice coming over the radio.

"Yes, still here. Over."

"Oh, man, you're the first voice we've heard in weeks. I'm so glad to finally hear someone else's voice."

"Yeah, we're the same. Can you tell us what's going on? Have you seen or heard anything? Over."

"Only what we've been going through, and that's enough!"

"What do you mean, what's been going on? Over."

"We were in Atlanta, but the city was crazy, and no one in their right mind would stay, so we got out. What the virus didn't wipe out, the gangs did. And these gangs aren't the ones from before the virus, these are just regular people going nuts and thinking they're kings or something. On the road heading north, we were chased by slave traders, and how we managed to get away from them, I don't know. It's terrible out there! We're still trying to make our way north."

"I'm sure I don't need to tell you to stay out of the cities. They're all the same. Stand by please."

Anderson was waving his arm around, trying to get Allen's attention.

"I don't know much about American history, but if someone has taken it upon themselves to bring slavery back, we're in big trouble."

Riley whispered as if the people on the radio could hear them. "Ask them where they are. If they ask about us, tell them something vague like in the Rockies, maybe further south, or something."

"My name is Allen. How many are in your group? And can you give me your location without telling me where you are precisely? Over."

"Yeah, I'm Lee Chen, and there are nine of us. We made it to Kansas and are safe for now. You said Merry Christmas from the 'people of,' how many in your group? Um, over."

"We are 128 strong. Over."

"You're kidding! And no one's sick? You wouldn't want to add nine more to your group, would you? We're tired of doing this alone. Eh, over."

Every scenario was the same, Riley thought. They would have to meet them in Jackson. It was too dangerous to have them come here to Calumet, and they had no time to spare in meeting them elsewhere. In order to help these people, they would have to do it in Jackson. There was no other way but to announce it over the radio, which in turn would announce it to the rest of the world. Prior to the virus, it would have taken them two days to get to Jackson from really anywhere in Kansas. However, time had changed, and it would take longer for Lee and his group to get there. With the weather now wreaking havoc with anyone wanting to travel, it would be near impossible to drive during the day and worse at night. It would hinder their travel, causing them to slow down. Adding to that were the unknown elements that could cause them even more delays. Riley guessed it could take them three to five days to get there, and that was being generous. It would more than likely take them longer. She didn't want them getting to Jackson first. Riley was fairly familiar with Jackson, although she had no idea what was waiting for them there. If they found any locals still among the living, they needed to be the ones to negotiate their admittance into town. Having someone blast into Jackson first, announcing 128 people were heading their way, would not help their case. Riley considered the risk of telling the world, or what was left of it, where they were heading. She wanted people to come, but not until the place was ready and not until they were sure they had it secured for everyone, especially for those already in her charge.

Once again Riley leaned in to Allen and, in a low voice, said, "Ask them how long it took them to get to Kansas. Also if they have enough food for about two weeks. Oh, ask if they have a good map of the Western US."

"Sure." Allen asked the questions that Riley requested.

"It took us a little over a week to get to where we are now. We can move pretty fast. But the food is a problem. There's a convenience store

not far from here, so I'll go see what I can find there. We just about lost everything trying to get out of Atlanta but then lost the rest running from those crazy slave lords, or whatever you want to call them. And as for the map, we have one." There was a pause, then, *"Oops, over."*

Allen eyed Riley. "What do you want me to say?"

"Tell him that we will make radio contact with him the day after tomorrow at 6:00 in the morning. That will give us time to get a plan laid out and get people here ready to leave earlier. We have to be in Jackson before them. Tell them if they have to move, move toward Wyoming, and give them nothing more. But if they can stay, they need to stay put until our call. We'll map something out for them and control the way they come into Jackson. Hopefully."

"Leave early? Oh, man, my wife isn't going to be happy about that. Okay," Allen conveyed the message. "Our boss wants to know if you can hang tight where you are. We need to work out a plan to get to you. We're good at this, so you're just going to have to trust us and do your best to stay on the path we lay out for you. Can you do that? Over."

"Yeah, I think we are safe here. We'll wait for your call. Thank you, thank you for everything. I wasn't aware that it was Christmas, but you just gave us the best Christmas present ever. Merry Christmas to all of you, too. Over."

With that, Allen shut the radio off, got up, and went back outside to shut the generator off. When he came back in, he sat down with Riley and Anderson.

"We should talk to your dad to see what he thinks. He's familiar with this area better than anyone and might have some insight on which way we should bring them in. And with that said, I need to go home and give my family the bad news. Eh, when are you planning for us to leave?"

"The twenty-eighth, around 9:00 in the morning. We'll need the daylight to get out of here ourselves, weather permitting, of course. Can you have all the vehicles ready by then?"

"Yeah, Boss. I probably shouldn't say this, but they're ready now. We just need to load them up and leave."

"Great! Let those going from Mercy know the date has been moved up. Tomorrow the council gets together to devise a plan for these people."

Riley got up, taking the cups over to the sink, and began washing them. Anderson told Allen to go ahead, that he would help Riley put things away.

Anderson had some concerns and needed to voice them, "This slave thing, what do you make of it?"

"I don't know, but I don't like it at all. I know it's going to become a problem for us at some point, but right now, we keep our focus on Jackson. And if this slave thing is widespread, which I hope it isn't, we need all the people we can get. I've also been thinking about the military bases. I hope that the military locked them down before this got too out of control because whatever you want to call these people, if they get into one of those bases, we'll be no match for them."

"Wow! I'm glad I'm not inside your head, Boss. Your mind is going all over the place. I never even thought about that, but you're correct. We've a lot of work ahead of us. Are you aware of any military bases in Wyoming?"

"Yes, a few, but I wouldn't know where to find them. There is one around or in Cheyenne that I'm sure of. And if the movies or books have any truth to them, then there are top-secret ones somewhere in the Grand Tetons, but where, I don't know. You know, something like Cheyenne Mountain in Colorado. Although that one isn't so secret anymore. So once Jackson is secure and our people are settled, our first journey out will have to be Cheyenne to find one of those bases. Lee can be our eyes and ears while he heads our way. I wish Benjie was on the radio again. He was a flood of information. I hope and pray he is okay. We need him back on the air soon."

"Riley, it makes me sad to say this, but I don't think I'm going home anytime soon."

Riley knew how much pain he was in. He was oceans away from his family in a world that had just gotten much bigger. It was hard enough for her being here without her husband, but it would kill her to be away from her kids. That kind of separation would carry a pain she didn't think she could bear.

"I'm sorry, Anderson, I truly am."

CHAPTER 16

Riley and Ken got up early and walked together to the kitchen in the hopes of getting the fires started before the radio call this morning. They could see light coming from the kitchen window, and neither of them could imagine who was up this early. When they opened the door, they were surprised to see all the members of the council already there. The doc was even there, which really surprised Riley. Her days were filled with kids sick from colds to tummy aches; three new babies and one on the way; one broken arm, thanks to the slick ice; and the two new additions to her own family, not to mention her brother who still couldn't get around. Lyle handed Riley and Ken each a cup of coffee as the three of them sat down together.

The atmosphere was relaxed due to the casual conversations that filled the room. The smell of breakfast made Riley hungry. She had tried to eat her dinner last night but couldn't get much down. Now she was hungry again. She thought it was odd how much she was eating, yet still she lost more weight. She chalked it up to the hard work of daily life in the mountains as well as the stress. She was happy about going to Jackson early just to get moving again. Waiting a week would have been nice just for the mere fact of being with family longer; however, her mind couldn't rest, and she knew it was the looming trip to Jackson that was causing the restlessness.

As she scanned the room, she wondered if she was the only one that was truly ready to go. Her thoughts were interrupted by Shauna, who brought two plates of food over to Riley's table and set one in front of Riley and the other in front of Ken, then took the empty seat next to Riley.

"Thanks, Doc. I was getting hungry just smelling the food."

"You're welcome. I couldn't sleep much last night with all this excitement. Your dad thought I should come up here for the call. I was grateful for the invite. We haven't heard anything from the outside world for so long. Don't get me wrong, I know it's bad, but just to have something positive for once is nice."

"You do remember you're a part of the council and don't need an invitation?"

"I know. I'm just not used to the new position yet."

"Everyone must have been anxious to be here so early," Riley commented.

"Yeah, you could say that," Lyle joined in the conversation.

"Are you ready to be in charge of this place?" Riley asked.

"You're going to be hard to emulate, Boss, but yeah, I'm ready. And we'll be ready when you call for us to come your way."

Riley laughed at that. "Thanks, Lyle. I hope that call won't take too long and that we can all be reunited quickly."

Lyle nodded in agreement. "Not much longer, and we can get this day started."

* * *

"Everyone is here, and the call is only a few minutes from now, so we may as well get started," Ken interrupted everyone as he stood up. "Okay, everyone, listen up. We have laid out a route that should take Lee's group north so they will arrive from the north side of town. It will take them longer, but it will give all those heading to Jackson plenty of time to get there. We're going to have them call us every night at six, however, those of you going to Jackson won't be getting the updates unless someone can find a radio. That's something I hope you can do right away so we have communication with one another."

"Riley has already committed to making that our number one priority when we arrive," Allen stated.

"Good, then this is going to be a sit-and-wait game for those of us here. Please remember that if you can. Not hearing from you is going to cause a lot of stress for those of us staying here," Ken reminded them.

Norman came in with the rumbling of the generator following him until he shut the door behind him. He walked over to the radio, pulled the cover off, and sat down in front of it. Everyone was quiet as he flipped the switch on. Static was the only thing coming from it. He turned to Allen.

"They have a rapport with you. Do you want to do the honors?"

"Ah, sure."

"Here's the directions to give them." Norman handed Allen a sheet of paper.

"Thanks."

Allen sat down and picked up the mic. "Lee, come in. Over."

There was nothing. Allen waited a few seconds and then called for Lee once more. Still nothing. Allen had a worried look on his face. He called out once more for Lee.

This time there was an *atchoo* that came through the speaker of the radio.

"*Hello, atchoo! Sorry, hello?*" It was a young woman's voice they heard sniffling and sneezing.

"Yes, we were calling out to Lee, is he there? Over."

"*No.*" Sniffles. "*Atchoo! Sorry about that. No, he's not. This is Lucy! I'm his sister. He's left to, atchoo, try and find some medicine for me.*"

"Lucy, are you sick? Over."

"I don't feel good, but we haven't been around any dead bodies in a while and then we only saw them through wind—atchoo—through windows. Whatever this is, it's killing me, though. Atchoo!"

"Allen, let the doc talk to her please," Riley ordered.

"Sure." Allen got up, held the chair out for Shauna, and handed her the mic. "Just hold this down to talk and say 'Over' when you're done talking."

"Oh, okay. Thanks." Shauna sat down with the mic in hand. "Lucy, this is Dr. Shauna Nelsen. Can you tell me your symptoms? Like do you have a fever, sores in or around your mouth, or anything off with your eyes? Over."

"Atchoo! Like a real-people doctor? No, no fever. Just a headache. My eyes itch and are watery. I have a horrible sore throat, and my nose is runny except at night, it gets stuffy. No sores in the mouth. Um, am I supposed to say over? Eh, over."

"Yes, on the doctor and saying over. When did this start? Over."

"Atchoo!" Sniffles. *"When we got here. Over."*

"It sounds like allergies to me. Where have you been sleeping? Over."

Lucy was chuckling now, *"In a feed store on hay, atchoo! Over."*

Everyone in the kitchen was relieved and started laughing. "Might I suggest you not sleep on hay anymore? Over."

"Thank you. Oh, my brother is—atchoo—back. Over."

Shauna handed the mic back to Allen, who took over the conversation with Lee. Riley listened for a little while then felt her part of all this was over, so she decided to go back to the cabin. She said her good-byes to her father and a few others before she left. It was windy this morning, which brought the chill factor up a notch, but Riley thought it was still going to be a gorgeous day. It was still dark when Riley left and walked back to her cabin. Goliath came bounding around the cabin to the cabin door, barked, and then scratched at the door. The door opened to let him in then closed again. Just as Riley reached for the handle to let herself in, the door flew open.

"Wow! That scared me," Riley said, laughing.

"Sorry, I let Goliath in and saw you, but it didn't register," Annie explained.

"That's okay, I'm in now." All of Riley's kids were up, dressed, and waiting for her. "What's going on?"

"Nothing, we were talking about the trip tomorrow," Becca said.

"Ah, yes, it seems to be the hot topic of the day. That and Lee's people. Well, I'm glad to be moving forward myself," Riley said as she moved to the couch, taking a seat next to Becca.

"I'm going to be honest, I'm nervous. If we stayed the full week, I might have talked myself out of going," Becca confessed.

"You know, you don't have to go. If you feel at the last minute you can't do it, then it's okay, Becca. No one will hold it against you," Riley explained.

"I know, but I'm going. I'm putting my big-girl britches on and going. However, I'm sure I'll be fine after the first round of puking. Maybe the second. Seeing a virus-infested body is going to be hard. Moving them, even harder."

"I'm not looking forward to that part. However, I'm ready to get out there and start making a difference," Kota chimed in.

"Listen. Annie, Landon, Bram, and I have done this before, and I can tell you it's never the same. It's never easy looking at a lifeless body, but we are going to put them to rest and hopefully not die in the process. My hope is that we'll find survivors, and they'll let us join them. The dead aren't going to bother us. I just hope there aren't any hostile people waiting for us."

Jesse, Kota, and Becca didn't know what to say. They never thought about anyone hostile being there. Their concerns were mostly the dead. Becca, frightened now, was staring at Riley.

"Do you think there might be people there that would want to hurt us? I mean, not everyone can be crazy?"

"I'm sorry, Becca, I can't lie and say no. If I recall correctly, when we met you, a man was going crazy all over you and Anderson. If crazy is waiting for us, we'll take care of it. I'm not worried. We have a large group going." She paused for a moment then said, "I'm not planning for us to drive right through town blazing our horns. We'll send in scouts first and have a good look from afar before we make our grand entrance. We'll take it easy and slow, I promise," Riley assured her.

"I do feel safe with you. Whatever you tell me to do, I'll do. I'll just be doing it with an upset tummy, I'm sure." Becca gave a weak smile.

"Before we even drive into Jackson, there is a cabin-like hotel right off the road that takes us into Jackson. That's where we're going to stay first—that is, of course, if no one is dead inside any of the rooms. We'll unload everything, get settled in, then map our way into Jackson."

Riley made it sound simple, but Becca knew it wasn't going to be. But she liked the way Riley's mind worked. She wasn't like any woman she had ever met. She wasn't an aggressive person, yet she had no problem taking the bull by the horns and tossing it aside. She was the calm in the middle of a storm. Becca knew that her chaotic life was calmed by Riley's impenetrable composure. She would follow her and knew that whatever awaited them, Riley would tackle it and at some point control it. Jackson would be theirs, one way or another.

"Isn't there a high school there somewhere by that hotel you're talking about?"

"Yes. We won't go there. I have a feeling that is where they set up a triage if too many people got sick. The doc said they would always use schools, town centers, or sports facilities if they needed them for temporary medical needs. If that's the case in Jackson, I would imagine the school is what they used."

"So we're not looking for bodies right away?" Jesse asked.

"Nope. The first thing is to find the police station in the hopes of finding a radio or a ranger station maybe. The radio is our top priority when we get there. Then the living, then the dead."

"You think people living there just left the dead where they lay? That's a bit creepy, don't you think?" Kota asked.

"Ask Pastor Scully. They didn't go anywhere for months. He wouldn't even let the kids go outside to play, they were so afraid. I bet whoever is still alive is locked in somewhere afraid to venture out," Landon answered.

"Okay, you guys are giving me the creeps! Someone say something positive. Please," Becca pleaded.

"Okay, how about this. All of you boys get your hair cut short, and we girls get a trim. We want to look nice for our first meeting with our new neighbors," Riley said cheerfully.

Becca laughed, "Okay, I just happen to be pretty good with scissors. Who's first?"

The guys moaned briefly but did as she asked. Becca found the scissors while Annie pulled a chair over to one of the windows to have better light. One by one, the boys got their hair cut short. Bram poured fresh water into the basin, and the young men found their razors and shaved. When they were done, they all looked very handsome and, more importantly, presentable. Riley thought of the older men and told Becca not to put her stuff up, that she would be back with more. Riley got the last of the eleven men making the trek to Jackson in line to get their hair cut too—even Mr. Miller, who, to Riley's surprise, was happy to be getting a haircut. Becca was right; she did an excellent job on all the hair. When the men were done, Riley and Annie sat down for their haircuts. Not as short, but since this was the first haircut for either of them in almost eight months,

Becca cut several inches off. Becca's locks of hair were amazing, which made Riley slightly nervous to be the one cutting her hair. Becca said to just go for it, so she did. Riley was pleased with the end result, as was Becca.

With the soon-to-be travelers' new, clean look, everyone went off to tend to the last-minute packing. Riley took Gauge and Levi out for one more ride on Duke, as her chores were all done. They only went up to the top of their little peak and looked out into the valley below. It was still breathtaking, even now completely covered in snow. She and the two boys talked a lot about everything but nothing of any great importance.

As they headed back, Levi asked, "Will this be our last time seeing you?"

"I hope not."

"We'll be all grown up when we see you again, won't we?"

Riley laughed. "No. I'll be gone only a few months, not a few years. You'll still be little squirts sneaking pies and cookies, I'm sure."

"Ha, well then, Landon is a little squirt, because he is always sneaking cookies!" Gauge chimed in.

"Mmm, is that so? I know who will be doing the dishes in Jackson after every meal."

Both of the boys laughed.

"I'm not sure I would be laughing because as soon as he finds out you both squealed on him, he'll get you for it. I think I hear a tickle fest coming on. Yep, you'll really be laughing then."

"Whoops," Levi said, smiling back at his mother.

Gauge took it upon himself to get the tickle fest started. That was the signal for Riley to put Duke in a gallop, which immediately quieted the boys.

They rode back to the corral, and once Duke was settled, they all headed for the kitchen to play a game. Riley found Sara and Jena drinking hot tea, in a deep conversation. They both looked up as Riley pulled the seat out and sat down.

"What are you two talking about?"

"Are you kidding? We're talking about people leaving tomorrow, of course. That's all anyone can talk about," Sara said.

"We're going to miss all the rowdy boys around here. It will be incredibly quiet," Jena added.

"A good time to kick back and read a book. Uh, maybe not, since our selection of books is—well—zero, I guess. You'll figure something out, I'm sure." Riley knew the girls would have plenty to keep themselves busy. "I haven't had much time with the two of you, and I feel bad about that. But I want you to know how proud I am of both of you, especially for stepping up to take care of the boys, plus Rachel and Timothy. You're taking a tremendous load off both Becca's and my mind in doing so."

"It's okay, Mom, I'm kind of attached to all of them now anyway. We'll be fine and ready to head to Jackson when you call us to join you. Jena and I were just saying how nice it will be to have our own bedrooms again with a real mattress to sleep on."

Riley couldn't wait for that either. The air mattress had taken its toll on her, and she, for one, was ready to rid herself of it.

"Me too. I'm going to make myself some tea. You two need anything?"

They both shook their heads no. Riley got up to make her tea when a sudden thought swept through her mind.

Jackson should be here very soon—the middle of spring, if not before. The time had passed by so fast that it was hard to believe the New Year was just around the corner. She smiled at the thought of her husband and their seeing each other again. She grinned. She took a quick glimpse around; this time, the thought of her husband was a little more private. If Martin was there to ask her 'if those were clean thoughts she was having,' her answer would have been an embarrassing "no," which made Riley laugh at herself.

"Jackson, please hurry and get here, I need you terribly," she whispered.

* * *

The back roads they had to take to get to Highway Eighty-Nine were horrible, even treacherous at times. A few times, Allen scared Riley so badly that she almost asked him to let her ride in one of the other vehicles behind them. Being in the lead truck with the plow was killing her nerves. Allen had to make a road most of the way to Highway Eighty-Nine leading twenty people in five vehicles, all trucks and all with snow chains on them, through the snow. Allen thought to grab them at the hardware store just before they met Scully. The bed of each truck was full of supplies for them – food, weapons, tools, protective gear, and anything else they thought they would need immediately.

Once they made it onto Highway Eighty-Nine, the outline of the road was easier to see, and Allen just plowed their way right down the middle. Riley had actually hoped to find it already plowed to indicate someone was alive and moving around, but it wasn't. The small towns they cut through were quiet, without a trace of any tracks anywhere. When they finally made it to Hoback, Riley was relieved. They had gotten through the worst of it and thought they might make it to Jackson in another hour. Even though the truck with the snowplow moved faster on this road than the back roads they had just left, they still weren't able to drive very fast. But nonetheless, Riley felt they were making good time.

The rest of the way to Jackson was quiet. However, as they got closer, there were more abandoned vehicles in and on the side of the road. They had seen a few here and there, but nothing like this. The occupants of every small town in the area with no hospital must have flocked here. Riley remembered the sign at the clinic, "Go to Driggs or Jackson." She wondered if the road leading to Driggs was littered with as many vehicles? Allen had to move a few of them out of the way for them to pass. The closer to town, the denser the vehicles. At one point, Riley thought they were going to have to walk the rest of the way in. They finally found the reason for the traffic jam. Large cement barriers were in the middle of the road, blocking the entrance into town. They couldn't even see the "High School Road" sign.

When Allen stopped, he and Riley got out of the truck. Allen moved around to Riley's side and followed her over to one of the snow-covered vehicles. She took her arm and wiped the snow away on the vehicle closest to her. Terror ripped through her as she jumped back from the gruesome sight of the frozen bodies inside while Allen turned his head away in shock. They both recognized the disease-in-fested bodies from the description Shauna had given. These people had stayed in their vehicles rather than go back home. Riley walked to another one, and saw the same thing. Her heart ached for these people as she slowly moved to another vehicle, once again finding the owner and their the family dead – the entire family! Riley hit the car with her fist and spun around. Anger was flaring inside of her. How could they just stay in their vehicles with all the hotels around here? What happened here? She was near tears when Allen cut into her emotions.

"Boss, it will take some time, but we can move them," he said quietly.

Riley looked quizzically at him. "Move them?"

"Yeah, move the cars. I can just push them to the side and make a way for us to go in."

"Oh, yeah, sure. Sorry. I can't believe this. There are children in this car. I mean, why would they stay?"

Riley was shocked, and Allen could hear it in her voice. The rest of their group had gotten out of their trucks, but none looked into the vehicles. Watching Riley's reaction was enough for them.

"What do you want us to do, mate? How can we help to make this go faster?" Anderson inquired.

"For the most part, the vehicles are frozen in place. Grab the shovels, and start digging them out on the opposite side. I'm going to be pushing them with the plow. That should help some. We'll push them down the incline here. We'll have to deal with the bodies later on at some point. I don't want to make a mess of them if I can help it."

"Do you think any of them died because of the virus, or were they just scared?" Becca asked Anderson.

"That I couldn't tell ya. One thing's for sure, whatever drove them here was enough to keep them here. Right, mates, let's get the folks moved to the side."

The process of moving vehicles was arduous work and seemed like it took forever. The next part was to move the cement barriers from the road. With sheer determination and brute force, they moved them. Once the road was cleared, they wasted no more time returning to their trucks so they could get moving again. There were still cars abandoned on the side of the road, but they ignored them and made their way to the hotel that Riley thought would be a good place to make their first base. They were in luck; the parking lot had only one car in it. Allen pulled in next to the car, practically buried in snow, which was in front of the office. The others parked in front of the cabin, got out, and trudged through the snow over to the office to meet up with them. Allen found the tire iron and brought it with him, just in case the door was locked. He tried the knob, but it didn't budge. He lifted his arm with the tire iron, but Riley snatched his arm to stop him.

"What if someone's dead in there?" Riley looked back at the group. "Everyone, please stand over there. Landon, would you grab a couple of masks for Allen and me, please?"

"Sure, Mom."

Landon ran over to one of the trucks parked in front of the cabins, reached into the back, and took out a large bag. He ran back, set the bag on the back of Allen's truck, and got out what he needed. He gave them to his mother, then stepped back as his mother had instructed.

Allen smashed the window and put his hand in to unlock the door. He went in first with Riley following. The office had a large sitting area with the counter set further back. There were two large vending machines: one with snacks, the other with sodas. Behind the counter was a door, which was open. Allen went into the back room to have a look.

"No one's here. I found the key programmer, though." Allen opened the drawer just below it and pulled out a stack of key cards. "We're in business! Just need some power so I can get some keys made."

"I'll leave that to you."

Riley walked to the back room and picked up the phone. No tone. She looked around, not really looking for anything in particular. Opening the drawer to the desk, she found a phone book, the yellow pages. She took it out, shut the drawer, and walked back outside with the others. Riley scanned the sky, and what little sun there was, was being blocked out by the clouds. She heard the hum of the small generator running, then a yell, "It works!"

Riley found her way over to the room they were able to open. Allen put his mask on along with some gloves before he pushed the door open. It was empty. Riley was also surprised the room looked ready for their next guest to move in—which today would be them.

"How is it you're able to get the door open with no electricity?" Riley was puzzled.

"Each door has a battery in it, much like a key fob we use to unlock our car doors," Allen explained.

"Brrr. It's freezing inside. Any chance we can have heat tonight?" Becca had her arms wrapped around herself, shivering.

"I'm okay with hooking up the generator for a little while, Boss, if it's okay with you? I won't leave it on all night. Just long enough to knock the chill out for everyone."

"Thanks, Allen, that would be great. But first let's get the rooms opened up. Everyone has roommates. No one from this point on goes anywhere without four or more people. Make sure you always have your weapons with you at all times. We'll pick teams later on tonight once we are settled. Oh, Allen, I found a phone book."

With that said, she smiled at Annie.

"You've got to be kidding?" Annie laughed.

* * *

Morning came too soon for everyone. Becca was shivering when she climbed out of bed. She was happy to be sharing a room with Riley, Annie, and Keri. The only other girl on the trip was Tamera, who shared a room with her father. She thought it odd how either of them ended up on this trip. Becca had asked Riley about it, which made Riley laugh.

All she said was, "Bram."

It was Annie who had filled her in about Tamera and Bram's infatuation with one another. Because Tamera was nineteen, she could sign up, so she did, which angered her father. When Tamera didn't budge, suddenly, Martin's name was on the list. Annie told Becca that she felt Tamera was elated when her father came, even if it was only to chaperone her and Bram. Becca chuckled to herself.

"What's so funny, Ms. Becca?" Annie's voice came out from under the covers.

"Oh, I was just amused by the whole Tamera-and-Bram situation."

Riley disclosed Tamera's father's dilemma, "Martin is having a hard time letting his little girl go. Not that she can go anywhere, really, but you get my meaning."

"Yes, I do. Martin looks like he could rip Bram's throat out. With that said, Bram is not someone I would want to mess with. All those boys are rock-solid, and none of them less than six feet. Even some of the big men seem small in stature when standing next to them."

"Yeah, but they're all little softies, even Martin. I know for a fact Martin likes Bram because Bram has been very respectful to both him and Shauna. Finding young men today like that…well, in the past, was hard to come by. Bram's father died when he was young. Now with only his sister and mother, he understands Martin because that is how he wants the women in his house to be treated. He's a great kid. On this trip, Martin is going to find out just what kind of a man Bram is, and I know he's going to like what he sees," Riley said.

Becca sighed, "If I was ten years younger, I would be all over them like syrup on pancakes."

"Ms. Becca!"

"Well, you know, Kota and Jesse aren't that much younger than you."

"Mother!"

They all laughed. "How about you, Keri, any interest in our boys?" Becca asked.

Through the covers, Keri said, "I used to have a thing for Tony, but now he and Carson are like brothers. Greyson's kind of cute, though."

"Oh, yeah, he is!" Annie said.

Riley looked curiously at her daughter.

"What? It's okay for Ms. Becca to look but not me?"

Riley could only smile at Annie.

"Do we have to get up? It's so cold," Keri was still buried under the covers, not moving.

Riley got out of bed and flung the covers off of her and Annie.

"Whoa! That's mean, Mom!"

"Then get up, and let's get a move on. The day awaits!"

"Nothing living awaits, it's too cold! Please just a few…" Annie stopped when she realized her choice of words probably wasn't the best to use. All the women in the room were quiet. "Mom, I'm sorry I didn't mean it tha—"

"It's okay, I knew what you meant."

With that, all the ladies were up and moving around. Allen had set up an outhouse for the women inside one of the other rooms. It felt very odd and open when using it, but nonetheless, all the women were grateful for his thoughtfulness. Even with no running water, it was nice to have.

Some of the men were up, helping Alejandro with breakfast. They had a nice fire going that everyone huddled around. It felt good to have something warm in their bellies. Once they had everything put away, they huddled together again to hear what the plan was for today. Last night, Anderson, Allen, and Riley had worked out what the best course of action would be. They decided they would split into two groups: the first group would walk along the west side at the base of the mountain starting at South Park Road. This would give this team an excellent view of all the businesses along Broadway, which was the main road into town. The second group would take the bike path on the east side and follow it to Snow King Avenue. They would be cutting through neighborhoods, but it would also take them into the back of town and not the center. Their goal today was to find the police station or a ranger station if, there was one in town. They would be on foot from this point on. The little radios that Ken always carried in the Chef Wagon had about a twenty-five-mile range, which would allow the groups to communicate with one another. Simply having the ability to communicate with the other group gave Riley a sense of security. The only thing Riley didn't like was that Bram and Landon couldn't be in the same group because they were the best marksmen out of the twenty people in the group. She let Anderson decide which teams they would be on. Bram's group consisted of Tamera, Martin, Jesse, Carson, Tony, Keri, Jasper, Anderson, and Kevin—which would take the road that led up to South Park Road and then to the base of the mountain. Landon's group had Riley, Annie, Becca, Nate, Alejandro, Greyson, Mr. Miller, Kota, and Allen—which would take the road leading to the bike path around the back side of town.

The air was cold with no sun to warm them, but Riley knew they would warm up soon enough with the long trek ahead of them. She longed for the day of not being cold again. She had hated living in the desert and griped about it all the time to Jackson. She wanted to move someplace with all four seasons that was cooler. Well, she got her wish. She just wished it was with electricity. Jackson hated the cold. That brought a smile to her face because once he finally joined them, she would have to listen to him complain about the cold. It took Riley's group awhile to get to the bike path. They passed a few buildings and homes, and all was quiet. The path was peaceful. By the time the night sky gave way to the morning sun, the beauty around them gave them comfort. The sounds of nature didn't seem so scary anymore. The creek running along the path added to the serenity around them. Allen had checked in a few times with the other group, and all was well. By the time they crossed the bridge and had the cemetery up the hill on their right, they were all pretty tired. Walking through the snow was worse than walking in sand. They stopped to take a short break when, out of nowhere, a dog started barking. Actually, what they heard was several dogs barking.

"Now there's a familiar sound we haven't heard in a while," Riley said to no one in particular.

Allen had the binoculars out and scanned the area. He tapped Riley on the shoulder and handed her the binoculars, pointing in the direction he wanted her to look. She saw it too: a light coming from a window.

"Someone is home, and they have pets. Get on the radio, and tell Anderson we are going to make contact with our first resident. That we'll get back to them as soon as possible."

Allen did as she asked. The group walked laboriously through the snow a few blocks when they came to the house in question. Allen and Riley were the only two to go up to the door. The others kept an eye on their surroundings.

Riley took the lead while Allen kept an eye out from the porch. She knocked on the door. The dogs inside the house went crazy barking. Riley could hear a woman inside telling the dogs to hush.

The door opened with the woman saying, "What do you want, Morgan? I told—" She was shocked to see a stranger's face staring back at her. "Who the blazes are you?"

"My name is Riley, and this is my friend, Allen. We're not sick, and we aren't here to hurt you or anyone else for that matter."

"Well, you could have fooled me with all that hardware you're carrying. What do you want? The town is closed, or can neither of you read?"

Riley thought the male version of Miller was bad enough, but the female version was worse.

"We're here seeking refuge. Are there many people alive here in Jackson?"

"What part of the town being closed did you not understand? Now go on, get out of here!" The door slammed shut.

"Well, that was rude," Riley said as she pounded on the door again, which drove the dogs crazy once more.

"What do you want? Now go away, and leave me in peace!"

"If you shut the door again, I'll have Allen here blast a hole in it with his shotgun." Riley was stern and knew neither she nor Allen would do such a thing, but this woman didn't, and Riley needed answers.

"So much for not harming anyone, young lady! Morgan isn't going to like it, knowing you've come into town. He'll probably shoot you himself—that is, if he had any kind of backbone," the woman said with no feeling whatsoever.

"Let's do this one more time. I'm Riley, and this is Allen. You are?"

"Pamela. Not Pam, it's Pamela."

"Okay, Pamela, who's in charge, and where can I find them?"

"That would be Morgan and his goon, Donald. Those two idiots couldn't lead a parade down the street if they wanted to. Bunch of losers!"

Yep, a female version of Miller. She couldn't wait for the two of them to meet.

"Where can we find them?"

"Well, the two of them like to pretend they're the mayor and sheriff of this ghost town. They're probably down at town hall. Let me get my coat, I want to get a load of their faces when they see you yahoos walk in their door."

Once Pamela stepped outside of her house, she was surprised to see a much larger group waiting there. Allen was on the radio, telling Anderson about their meeting with Pamela. Anderson said they had just passed through Kerns Meadows Park, had found their tracks, and were heading toward them now. Pamela had a wicked smile on her face, which Riley thought was funny. The woman was going to like watching this meeting more than she was letting on.

"Just how many people are with you?" she asked.

Riley didn't mind letting her know. She would find out in a few minutes anyway. "Twenty."

"Oh, boy, and are they as armed as the rest of you?" Pamela knew the answer to that without even asking, and Riley knew it.

"Absolutely, and we're all well trained to use them."

"Well, I figured that. I'm not an imbecile! Personally, I hope that young lady there with her bow will shoot an arrow right up Morgan and Donald's a—"

"Anderson's here!" Landon yelled.

"Man, that was fast!" Allen conveyed what Riley was thinking too.

"That was fast, Anderson. How is it you guys are here? What happened to walking the west side of Broadway?" Riley questioned.

"We were at the bridge on Broadway next to the park when you said you saw the house with lights and dogs. I thought it best we join you," he said almost out of breath. "We ran the whole way. Who's this Sheila?"

"Everyone, this is Pamela. Please don't call her Pam. She's agreed for selfish reasons to show us the way to the town's fearless leader."

"I never said he was fearless. As a matter of fact, he's going to wet himself when he sees all of you, and this I can't miss!"

Pamela started down the street, turning at the first corner. They walked five blocks before turning right. Town hall was in their sights. They could see the lights were on, which meant they were using the backup generator. Pamela marched right in the front doors without a second thought. They, however, did not. It was a small building with a clock tower in the front. Anderson stayed outside with everyone except Landon, Riley, Allen, Mr. Miller, and Kevin. Once inside, they saw Pamela standing in the middle of the large foyer with three men standing inside talking to one another. The talking stopped when Riley and the others walked in.

"Who the…" one man started to speak until Pamela interrupted him.

"These are my new friends. This is Riley, and well, I can't remember all their names now, can I? They're here to take the town over, boys! They have the building surrounded, and there's nothing you can do but surrender!" Pamela said with glee in her eyes. She was truly enjoying herself.

"What?" a very large man said.

Riley held her hands up to stop all the commotion.

"That's enough! Pamela's right about two things, and that is we are friends and the building is surrounded, but not for a hostile takeover. I'm Riley, and this is my son, Landon. These are our good friends, Allen, Mr. Miller, and Kevin. There's a total of twenty of us here. We thought it best not to invade your offices all at once with everyone."

"What are you doing here? The town is closed to travelers!"

"I'm sorry, I didn't get your name?"

"The fat one there is Morgan, the bald fart is Donald, and the last of the stinkin' morons is Robert," Pamela said as she introduced them.

"Now, Pamela, I've just about had enough of your…" Morgan didn't get to finish as Riley jumped in.

"Okay, Morgan, we need to talk. Is there somewhere we can speak privately?"

"Um, sure, right this way."

Riley turned to Allen, "Tell the others it's okay to come in now please."

"Got it, Boss."

The building was cozy. Not hot by any means, but it was warmer than outside by a long shot. Riley chose not to sit but instead wandered around the very large office. Morgan sat down behind the desk and waited for Riley to start the conversation, which she thought was odd. He had to have a million questions, but instead, he sat there, watching her. She was sure Allen's callout to her as *boss* didn't slip past him. She took a long look at Morgan, making him uncomfortable as he squirmed in his chair. She smiled at him briefly then looked out the window. Once Riley was satisfied where the control in the room lay, she stood in front of the desk, looking down at the large man in the chair.

"How many people are alive in this town? Do you know?"

"Well, of course, I know! Thirty-eight. I'm aware of about forty in Wilson and about that in Teton Village."

Riley was sure he was lying about Wilson and Teton Village. "Okay, so you have thirty-eight in town here, and I'm going with the assumption you have no idea how many people are in Wilson and Teton Village. No one here has the guts to go check, except maybe Pamela."

Morgan grunted, "Why, I…"

"Here's the God's honest truth. I have 128 people. No, wait, with the nine coming and the three newborns, that brings our total up to 140 people. In that group, we have a doctor, a pastor, a mechanic, a large machine operator, a builder—okay, well, we have two of those—ranchers, children, moms, and dads, along with the elderly, and we are looking for a safe place to move to because in the last few months, our numbers have outgrown our living space. I need you to understand we are coming here. This town…well, this town is officially opened for people seeking refuge. The country is not what it once was…It's beyond scary, and people are dying, not because of the virus but because of the evil dwelling inside man! We have brought people into our fold that have been tortured, raped, and kidnapped. We're done with trying to survive, we're all ready to get back to living, and this town…this is where we're going to do it!"

Morgan was flabbergasted. The look on his face was the look Pamela was hoping to see.

"Well, I'm sorry, but it's not up to you. We have people here to think of. You can't just barge in here and take over our homes." Morgan was standing now, clearly agitated. "I'm sorry I have to say no!"

"I'm sorry too. I want to call a town meeting. I want to talk to everyone and let them decide. You clearly aren't the voice of everyone in this town. I want to meet them. If I have to drive down every street and announce it, I will."

"What gives you the right to do this? You have no right whatsoever!"

"What gives me the right is 140 people that are in my care. And once your thirty-eight hear what I have to say, I guarantee they'll want to be a part of our group. Looking around here, you've done nothing. Have you even cleaned out the bodies of the dead?"

"What? No, of course not!"

"Well, what did you think was going to happen when all the snow melts and the bodies thaw out? You haven't given much thought to anything like that, have you? Have you even been on the radio listening to what's been going on outside of this town? Have you? Pamela was right about you. You're not fit to lead a parade down the street!" With that said, Riley walked out of the room, slamming the door behind her.

Everyone in the foyer heard the yelling, so there was no need to replay it back to any of them.

"I'll be happy to gather the people if you'll loan me a few of your people," Robert said. "And just so you know, the ol' coot over there is my grandmother."

"Humph, killjoy!" Pamela squawked at him.

Everyone except Morgan and Donald laughed.

"Okay, everyone, you know what you have to do. Let's get a move on. Carson, Keri, Landon, Annie, and Tony, please go help Robert with notifying the neighbors of the meeting. Tell them to just come on down here as soon as you notify them, okay? Donald, will you be kind enough to show Allen here where the radio is? We need to call home. The rest of you should start knocking on doors. If there's no answer, look in windows. Remember, red is 'no entry, body found,' green is 'all clear'. There were nine thousand residents here. My only hope is they weren't all home when the outbreak started. Pair up in groups of five, and be safe. A one-block radius for now, please." Riley then turned her attention to Morgan, whose mouth was still opened, "I would appreciate it if you would give me all the information as to where they put the sick when the hospital was full."

Morgan collapsed in the chair next to him. Donald had fallen in with Allen immediately, and Robert helped with the task of gathering locals. Now he was supposed to give her whatever she needed. He was completely blown away by the way these people just came in and took over, totally ignoring his authority. Pamela was enjoying his demise.

"Well, this is too much joy for one person to experience in a lifetime," Pamela said with a grin. "They used the fairgrounds. But I'm telling you, more than half the town is in there. The hospital filled up in a week. That nasty beast of a virus blasted through this place like a crazed child hyped up on sugar. That dimwit of a sheriff of ours put a stop to people coming in from neighboring towns, but by then, it was too late. Those of us that survived this did so only because we didn't leave our homes until about two months ago. Robert got fired from his job because I wouldn't let him go back to work. It didn't take a rocket scientist to know this town was doomed with all the lamebrain tourists that blast through here all year long."

Riley and Anderson looked at one another. Neither of them heeded the telltale signs either. The government and the CDC didn't convey the truth, so they didn't take it seriously until half of the United States map was covered in red, indicating the infected areas. Playing the blame game wasn't a direction Riley or Anderson wanted to go. Right now, they needed to do what they intended to do. Riley didn't like the way she had handled her meeting with Morgan. She didn't want him to feel they had come in and taken over, even though that's exactly what they had done. She would need to fix that, but for now, she needed to focus on her people as well as Lee and his group. She would gladly embrace all the survivors here, adding to their community, if they would all agree to it.

"Thanks, Pamela, for all the info. That helps a lot."

"What do you plan on doing with all the bodies?"

"Is there a crematorium here in town?"

"Ha, you had me fooled, I thought for a minute you were an intelligent woman. My mistake!"

"Well, we have to start somewhere. The more logical solution is to dig a big pit, build a bonfire, and toss the bodies in. It just seems a little heartless, even knowing they won't care. But my compassion can't get in the way of doing the job of cleaning the town out of its dead." Riley turned around to see if Morgan had pulled himself together. "So my next question is, where is a good place we can dig that hole and dispose of the bodies, someplace where we can remember them, like a memorial of some kind?"

Morgan rubbed his face with one hand then stood up. "There's a place. It's beautiful. Peaceful. I take it that large machine operator is in the group with you?"

"That would be me. I'm Kevin." Kevin extended his hand.

Morgan hesitated then accepted it. "We have the equipment, we just didn't have anyone to operate any of it. We were going to start in the spring or summer," he said in a noncommittal voice.

"We are going on the assumption that the virus is dormant right now. If you wait until spring or summer, that might be too late. We're here now because of that. There are twenty of us. Working in pairs, we could easily take care of five hundred bodies a day, but as always, in all things, it possibly won't move that quickly. But we'll start with the hospital first. Then we'll take care of the fairgrounds. That will leave one team to continue checking homes," Riley explained.

"Hey, Boss, got ahold of Calumet, and everything is okay." Allen was now standing in the foyer. "They were extremely happy to hear from us. Lee is having problems with the snow. I told Ken just to bring him in the south side. I would like to get some of the men and work day and night clearing the roads, first clear all of the vehicles then clear all of the snow. We'll start from our hotel and work our way into town, if that's okay with you?"

"That would be great. Thanks, Allen."

"I'm glad to see your intellect came back, young lady. You just might be able to lead that parade after all," Pamela declared.

* * *

With the survivors of the town now inside, town hall was crowded. Donald brought chairs in so people had a place to sit. When word was out that strangers had entered the town, curiosity outweighed fear, and the survivors came at once. Riley gave everyone a minute to get situated before she started the meeting. As Riley surveyed the room of people, she liked that it was a nice mix from old to young. They would be a great addition to the people waiting back at Calumet and Mercy. She hoped they would feel the same.

Riley started the meeting with introductions and then told the story of the people of Calumet and Mercy. She left nothing out about what they had seen in the course of their six months in the mountains and about what they had heard over the radio. She explained the reasons they chose Jackson to make their home and about their thoughts on the virus dormancy in the winter and why it was imperative they clear the town of bodies now instead of later. While she spoke, there were shocked looks, whispers, and even gasps. When she was done, she asked if there were any question or concerns.

"These people just marched in here and took over the place," Morgan said. "They corralled all of you here as if they already owned the place. I don't believe them. The United States is a civilized country, and the horror stories are just that—stories! Now, I vote they all leave and don't come back!"

"Oh, poppycock Morgan! You're just mad because someone smarter than you came in with a plan. You're acting like your stupidity is something to be shared! You need to sit down and listen to Riley. Not one person here has left this town, so no one knows what's out there. Don't expect anyone here to agree with you because that would make them wrong too!"

"Now, Pamela, that's enough!" Morgan was getting angry.

At this point, Kota walked up to the front of the room, which made Morgan step back a few inches.

"Hi. I'm Kota. I'm the one that was tortured along with Jesse over there."

Kota took off his jacket and then started to pull up his shirt. Riley put her hand on his shoulder to stop him.

"It's okay, I got this."

He pulled it all the way off and spun around for the townspeople to see. Gasps went around the room with heads turning so as not to look.

"What Riley has said is true. Good, decent, once-hardworking Americans are becoming—as I heard someone say—their own worst nightmares. This is real. Shoving your heads in the sand isn't going to change what's going on out there."

Kota was done. He didn't put on his shirt until he walked all the way to the back of the room. Morgan was furious now.

"They're using smoke and mirrors, folks! You can't believe this! We need to tell them to leave! They need to leave now!"

One of the men in the back row stood up. "If they leave, who's to say someone else won't come here and just take what they want? At least, these people are asking. And what about the food? She's right about that. Food will go bad, and then what? I'm no farmer, I'm a river guide. Morgan, for crying out loud, you were a banker. Did anyone ever think to get on the radio? Did anyone listen to what was going on out there?"

"Listen, folks, I know this is a lot, however, we need an answer now. There are people that have been chased by the worst of people on their way here. They are tired of doing this alone, and honestly, I don't blame them. If we pool our resources together, then we can make this a place for survivors, a place to live again. We'll have to reeducate ourselves so we can live in this new world of ours. Our community in the mountains has managed to do this on a small scale, so I know it will work here if we join forces. I know we can thrive, but you need to vote now."

One by one, the survivors of the town stood up and said yes. It was unanimous, all except one: Morgan. Even Donald agreed to have Riley and her people stay. With the vote in, the next items on the agenda were getting the hole dug and the streets and sidewalks cleared of snow. Then the ugly task of clearing out the bodies of the dead could begin.

CHAPTER 17

In the days that followed, everyone came together with a common goal: to put Jackson back together. Part of the town began to look lived-in again. Allen and some of the young men used the town's massive snowplow to clear the roads. It took all day and most of the evening to clear the main street and shovel its sidewalks. Salt was spread out on both the street and sidewalks as a final touch. Then they plowed the streets of the living residents, giving them easy access to town square, the library, and the town recreational center. Kevin focused on the hole that needed to be dug. He took a crew with him to the area Morgan said they should dig. Riley didn't realize how much preparation went into digging a hole, but it took them three days of planning, mapping, and clearing the area before they even began to dig. Alejandro was in charge of the kitchen and food, which was where most of the women were working. Riley had never felt that a kitchen was only for women, especially since her husband was a far better cook than she. It wasn't easy work, either. Alejandro worked the women hard to get the restaurant, which was to be used for the community kitchen, up and running. There was a simple reason why all the women chose to volunteer to work in the kitchen for the day. It was the only inside job available, and none of them wanted to work out in the cold. Even Riley jumped at the chance to work inside. When the generator was turned on for the restaurant and the lights came on, there was a huge sigh of relief from all the ladies. A group of them went on a shopping spree in the local grocery stores. They took the pickups Riley's group had brought and loaded them up with everything they could. The residents of Jackson loved the idea of a community kitchen but they loved Alejandro's cooking even more. Even Pamela was impressed.

Riley's group moved into another hotel that had cabins north of Broadway. Any one of the twenty could have their own room if they chose to. It was funny that only the men wanted separate rooms. The women's need for company and a sense of security kept them in pairs. Riley and Annie stayed together, while Becca and Keri became roommates. Martin wasn't about to let Tamera out of his sight, so they continued to share a room. Becca even went as far as to pull an "Alice Crawford" by decorating both of the girls' rooms with pretty blankets and pillows that she found in one of the shops. This made the rooms cozy and nice to come home to each night.

The day had finally come when the dead had to be laid to rest. It was decided to take care of those in the hospital first. Morgan was adamant about not helping. He wasn't going anywhere near the disease-infested dead! That was when a few of the locals realized Morgan had no intention of ever removing any of the bodies. However, they were stunned when they heard it would be Riley and Anderson going in first to deal with them. They had heard Riley's people call her "boss" numerous times, even seen them run things by her, getting her approval before doing something they felt needed to be done. They understood the chain of command within the group. What they didn't understand was, why the leaders of the group were going in to test a crazy theory that was potentially life-threatening. Mr. Miller was the one that took it upon himself to explain it with six simple words: "Do you want to do it?" to which all promptly replied no.

Allen, who was furious, told Morgan that this was the reason he was not a leader, that Morgan was an idiot for thinking his going to town hall every day made him one. Riley had to calm Allen down. She knew his anger stemmed from his not being able to take her place. So for the first day, Allen paced back and forth down the street from the hospital, watching from a distance as Anderson and Riley carried out bodies. Food was brought to them daily. It was left at a designated location, some distance away from the hospital. There was to be no contact at all with Riley and Anderson for five days.

Day one of entering the hospital was scary even for Anderson. Riley could feel his eyes on her as they walked the halls. She freaked out a few times over a simple noise or the sight of one of the gruesome bodies, which caused him to jump too. The bodies were horrific to look at and at times made them gag. It was all they could do to hold it together so they didn't get sick. Although the smell was terrible, the freezer-like atmosphere helped. They only surveyed half of the first floor when Riley made a decision.

"Um, I'm done looking, it's all going to be the same. Let's work from the front door and work our way down the hallway. I'm not sleeping in here with any of these bodies. I'm not that tough!"

"Sure, Riley, you're the boss. I'll get the bags."

"What! And leave me in here to wait! No way, I'm coming with you."

Anderson couldn't help but chuckle at her as they both found their way back to the truck. Anderson grabbed a small bag and tossed it to Riley. Then he reached in and took the two larger bags, filled with duct tape, from the back seat.

They had one truck with a large trailer attached, a second trailer on standby, gasoline, three large metal barrels, and wood. Riley's small bag was full of small items—like flashlights, knives, rope, and so on. Each barrel had a fire blazing in it. With everything ready to go outside, they made their way back to the hospital, carrying their bags with them. Taking the first steps back into the hospital was difficult for Riley. She found herself hesitating when she put her hand on the door.

"You know, Anderson, I won't think you ungentlemanly if you go first."

"Ha, you won't eh?"

"Nope, not at all. After you."

Riley could see Anderson's eyes smiling back at her. Being covered head to foot, his eyes were the only thing visible through the full-face mask.

The first body in the hall was that of an elderly man. They wrapped his body in linen, then duct taped it so the linen stayed. They carried him out on a gurney and rolled him over onto the trailer. One down.

The first floor took most of their day. Once a body was removed, everything in the surrounding area was burned, even the mattresses. All the medical equipment was put into one room.

They found three nurses that had given up their lives to tend to these people. Riley thanked God for people like them. The world was a better place because of the sacrifices they made on a daily basis. This time their bodies couldn't fight back; they just weren't immune. Riley was sure she wasn't immune either, which drove her thoughts back to the job at hand.

It was late in the evening when Riley stopped, put her back against the wall, and slid down, landing on her bottom with her legs out in front of her. Anderson was a little more graceful at sitting when he took a seat next to her.

"Not a bad day's work. I reckon we'll finish up the upstairs pretty fast and be done tomorrow. Whaddaya think?"

"Uh, not my thoughts at all. Have you seen those stairs?"

"Ah, well, I've an idea for that, but you're not gonna like it much."

"I'm listening."

"You can get the backup generator going and then use the elevator."

"Oh my gosh! Get into the elevator with the dead?" Riley's eyes were blazing at him with horror. "I know I've seen a lot so far, but seriously, I'm not desensitized to this!" Riley didn't flinch when looking at him.

"Well, it's a thought. You can always put the body in and run down the stairs to meet it at the bottom." Riley heard him chuckle.

"And just where will you be while I'm putting bodies in the elevator and running down the stairs?"

"Ah, well, that's the great part, isn't it? I'll be disposing of the bodies into the pit."

"Ugh! You're kidding, aren't you? What happened to teamwork?"

"Well, this is teamwork. You tend to business here while I tend to business out there. We'll get done faster…I think."

Riley turned to him again, "You think? You're not kidding at all, are you?"

"Nope. They're all dead, Riley. They're not going to hurt you."

"Good grief!" Riley said as she leaned hard into the wall. "Thanks for that, Anderson."

"No worries; glad to set your mind at ease."

"Ugh! Elevator it is then!" Riley snarled at him. "I'm going to start washing down the room we're sleeping in with the disinfectant. Care to join me?"

With that, Anderson stood up laughing. He extended his hand, offering to help Riley up.

"Let's get to it then. I'm ready for some shut-eye."

Riley opened all the windows on the bottom floor to allow it to air out while they worked. It took them an hour to scrub down the room to Riley's satisfaction. Instead of stopping there, she moved into the hallway. She sprayed it down, then mopped the floor. She let the spray set on the walls and ceiling. Anderson looked around and couldn't believe how clean the place looked. There was nothing left anywhere, not even at the nurse's station. All the books, files, and anything else they could burn was tossed into the fire. They sprayed the desk and cabinets with the solution that Shauna and Martin thought would kill anything and everything: bleach! Once done, they walked outside. Before Anderson and Riley stripped down to their regular clothes, they sprayed each other down with the solution. Afterward, they tossed everything into the fire except their masks. Those they cleaned, then changed out the filters, and let dry. Riley saw Allen standing next to a fire at the boundary line and waved. He waved back. With the bodies on the trailer covered with a tarp and tied down tight, day one was done.

* * *

Riley received a note with breakfast from Annie and Landon. They wrote how proud they were of her, that they loved her and hoped that she was safe. She wondered what they would think of her riding down an elevator with a corpse. Anderson, what a deserter! Her thoughts moved back to the first task of the day—the generator. She wasn't sure where the stupid thing was. The basement! Dadgum you, Anderson! He could have at least helped her turn the stupid thing on instead of leaving right after he ate breakfast. Frustrated, she took two gas containers with her as she had no intention of making more than one trip down there.

It was dark in the stairwell, so she jammed the door open with a screwdriver, turned on her flashlight, then crammed it into her armpit. She grabbed both gas containers and slowly made her way down the stairs.

"Father God, I'm so sorry for ever watching those zombie shows on TV. Please don't let me die of a heart attack down here from my own imagination," Riley whispered to herself.

She knew she just needed to find the electrical room and hoped the generator would be there. What she found at the end of the stairs was a long pitch-black hallway. Riley set the gas containers on the floor so she could shine the light down the hallway. There were several doors, and of course, they were all closed. Riley sighed. She hated horror movies, and at this very moment, she felt like she was in her own, personal one. She could feel her blood being pumped through her body at a rapid pace.

"Ugh, just go already!" she told herself, "There is no reason to delay the inevitable."

Her feet moved gradually beneath her. The floor crunched with every step. The first door had the word "BOILER" stenciled on it. She didn't open that door. Reluctantly, she continued down to the next door, which said, "MAINTENANCE."

"Good grief, it would have to be the last door at the end of the stinkin' hallway," Riley whispered aloud to herself.

Then she inhaled a deep breath as she shone the beam of light down at the last door at the end of the hallway. She took the last few extra steps required, placing her in front of the door.

"There's nothing behind the door except mechanical equipment, Riley. Just open the door, and walk in. No biggy," she said as she continued to coach herself into her next move.

She wiped her gloved hand on her protective suit, then reached for the doorknob. She heard the click and pushed the door open a little. Riley's heart was pounding so fast she thought it was going to burst out of her chest. She pushed the door open as wide as she could, shining the light all around the room.

"Good grief, Riley, you're scaring yourself to death!" she said out loud. "Thank goodness, they labeled everything for us dummies."

She moved as quickly as she could to the generator. It was huge. The light beam fluttered all over it until she found what she was hunting for. She unscrewed the cap to the gas tank then shone the light into it. Empty. Riley sighed as she made her way back down the hall to the gas containers she left by the stairs.

"Shoot! The cap."

Riley went back, placed the cap on the generator, carelessly spun around, and slammed into something hard. The beam of light shone on something big, causing Riley to throw the flashlight at it.

"Aauugghh!" Riley screamed.

The flashlight bounced off the figure and hit the floor, spinning to a stop.

"Ouch! Riley!" The voice was familiar.

"Seriously, Anderson! What are you doing down here? This place is haunting enough without you creeping around scaring the bajeebees out of me!"

"I think I've peed on myself." Anderson was serious. "Geez, I felt bad about leavin' ya here to do this and thought I would come back to give ya a hand."

"Now you feel bad?" Riley had her mask off now, frustrated. Then she began to laugh. She bent down to retrieve the flashlight and she hit Anderson's head as he was coming up with it.

"Yow!" Riley's hand went to her face. She felt moisture just above her upper lip. "I think I have a bloody nose."

"Right! Riley don't move," Anderson's voice was concerned.

The beam of light went jostling down to the end of the hall then whipped back around, heading in her direction. This time she moved out of his way as he passed through the door.

"Here, hold the torch for me, would you?"

With Riley's free hand, she aimed the light at the tank. The tank took all the gas from both containers. It had plenty of room for more, but what they had would have to do. Riley reached up and put the cap back on. Anderson took the flashlight and found the breaker box. He shut off all the nonessential power—like air, refrigeration, and all the downstairs rooms. How he knew what to shut off, Riley didn't know. He flipped some switches on the generator then pulled down on a large lever. The humming sound was nice to hear, but it was even better when the lights popped on. Anderson took off his mask, took Riley's face under the chin, and lifted it.

"Eh, yeah, a bloody nose and possibly a bit of a shiner."

"I think I have it stopped, but I need to clean my face before I start my trek up and down those stairs."

"Yeah, look, I'm truly sorry about all this, Riley. I shouldn't have left you in the first place."

Riley laughed. "I'm okay. A little bloody nose never killed anyone. Just having you help with this made my day much easier. I can handle the rest, honestly, I can. Go do what you need to do. Just don't goof off, and get back here as fast as you can. This place gives me the creeps." Then she really started to laugh, "So you had the pee scared out of you, did you? Serves you right!"

Anderson began to laugh too and said, "Yeah, I did. I'm going to have to change. You sure you're all right?"

"Absolutely. Now go before I change my mind."

"Right, I'm off then."

They took the stairs back up together, parting at the top. Riley looked up at the stairs leading to the second floor. Anderson was watching her.

"They're all dead, Riley."

Riley glanced over at him then back up the stairs. Not saying a word, she took one step at a time. Anderson watched her for a moment, smiling at her, then left to tend to his chores. When Riley arrived upstairs, she was relieved to find only a few gurneys with bodies on them in the hallway. She hoped the bulk of them would be found at the fairgrounds. Riley took her first client, prepared him for transport, then pushed him to the elevator. She punched the button and waited for it to arrive.

When the doors opened, Riley had to stifle a scream. "Good grief, lady! You scared the bajeebees out of me!"

There was a dead woman on the elevator, just sitting on the floor. Reluctantly, Riley entered the elevator to move the woman's legs over so she could push the gurney in. All the while, she was trying to talk herself into riding down in the elevator with them. However, in the end, she just couldn't do it. She pushed the first floor button, jumped out, and took off down the stairs. Once the door opened, Riley latched on to the gurney and pulled it halfway out. Before she went any further, she knew she needed to take care of the woman on the floor. With the gurney stopping the elevator door from closing, Riley took off upstairs again to grab some sheets. She found where the sheets were stored, snatched a stack of them, and ran back down the stairs. She pulled the gurney out so she could get into the elevator and tend to the woman. Then she quickly pulled the gurney partially back onto the elevator to keep the doors from completely closing. It was annoying to listen to the doors trying to close then open again. Riley worked fast to wrap the woman for transport to her final resting place. Once done, Riley shoved the gurney out of the way. Tugging on some of the loose sheet at the feet of the woman, Riley dragged her out of the elevator. She hauled the woman down the hall and left her just outside the entrance to the hospital. She went back to retrieve the patient still on the gurney and, with no effort at all, pushed it to the exit out to the other trailer. Riley would have to wait for Anderson to move the woman, so she stayed where she lay.

Riley was two hours into her work when Anderson returned. She was extremely happy to see him. "I'm so glad you're back. Are you all done at the pit?"

"Yeah. Allen and some of the men had the wood and coal all set to go for me. How about you?"

"With no resurrections occurring, it's gone pretty smoothly. The hallways weren't cluttered with people upstairs like they were down here. However, there are quite a few I couldn't move as they weren't on a bed or a gurney. I only managed to get half of them wrapped."

"No, worries. Shall we?"

The day was long and arduous. They worked through lunch and well into the afternoon before they stopped for a break. Everything had been set ablaze that needed to be, bodies packed on the trailers were ready for transport, and now the only thing needing to be done was to take the bodies to the pit. Anderson and Riley had shed all the protective gear and were eating their lunch in chairs they brought with them. It was cold, and the sky was overcast, but both were very happy to be outside, having the worst part of their job over with.

"I think the doc's going to like her new facilities. It's a nice building. We can finish cleaning it up tomorrow," Riley said.

"It will have to be deep-cleaned before anyone can move in, but yeah, I think the doc will be pleased."

"I think I've officially lost all my fat and gained twenty-five pounds of pure muscle in each of my legs today while running up and down those stinkin' stairs. My legs are still throbbing."

Anderson smiled. "Ah, well, what doesn't kill you will make you stronger. You ready to get these fine folks over to the pit? I would like to spray down the upstairs before it gets too dark. Allen was supposed to leave more gas for us by the pit. Let's hope he did. I'm happier to have the lights on in the hospital than not."

"You and me both," Riley said as she stood up.

Riley looked up at the street where they had put a boundary line and saw Morgan standing there watching them. Anderson saw him too.

"What do you think is goin' on in that bloke's head?"

"Envisioning our deaths, I'm sure."

"Ah, well, that's comforting. By the way, how do you feel?"

"Me? Um, fine, actually, I feel great. You?"

"Spiffy! Not even a sniffle."

"Well, like you said, what doesn't kill you will make you stronger. When we walk out of here alive, Morgan is going to hate us even more," Riley said.

"Oh, he'll hate me, all right, when I have him suit up for the fairgrounds. That lousy fat pi—"

"Anderson, the pit awaits us. Shall we?"

CHAPTER 18

As the sun rose on the sixth day, Riley and Anderson took a look around at the job they had done. The hospital was spotless. They had wiped down all the medical equipment; light covers had been taken down and cleaned along with the bulbs and the light fixtures; metal tables and chairs had been saturated with bleach; anything made of wood had been burned; and even the elevator was scrubbed to perfection, Riley thought. Once the cleaning process was underway, both Anderson and Riley shed the protective clothing but continued to use their gloves and masks. But as they stood there now, they were proud of all they had accomplished in their short amount of time at the hospital.

"Let me go downstairs and shut the generator off, then let's get out of here," Anderson said as he moved toward the stairs.

"You want company?"

"Nah. You and I don't mix well down there. Just be a sec."

Riley smiled as her hand went up to her nose. It wasn't broken, thank goodness, but it was still sore. The lights went off as she stood there, letting her know Anderson was on his way back up. She could hear him bounding up the stairs fast, and then he flew through the door as if someone or something was chasing him. As the door slammed behind him, it startled Riley.

"Something get your nerves all in a tither there, Anderson?"

He laughed. "Forgot the torch. Couldn't see my hand in front of me, which was a bit creepy."

They had worked hard for the last five days but now were all smiles as they walked out the hospital doors for the last time. Loud cheers came from the direction of the boundary line as they came out. Annie took off running to her mother. At first Landon was going to stop her but then he remembered it was okay. He and Bram jogged over to his mother and Anderson with the rest of the town following behind them—that is, everyone except Morgan. Annie gave her mother a huge hug, and Landon and Bram both fell into the hug, crushing both of them. Anderson was inundated with words of congratulations, slaps on the back, high fives, and even the occasional "atta boy." Neither of them was showing any signs of being sick, not even a sniffle. The first part of their mission had been successful. Now everyone was going to have the honor of partaking in the cleanup of the fairgrounds, even Morgan.

Allen got Riley and Anderson caught up on all the news of Calumet and Mercy as well as Lee and his group. The first thing Riley wanted to do was to speak to her parents and kids, who were still in Calumet. She and Anderson walked over to town hall to make the call home. She spoke to her family for about thirty minutes then turned the radio over to Anderson. Her next task was to eat. Annie, Landon, Bram, Kota, and Jesse all joined her on her walk over to the kitchen. The sun was out, which felt good on Riley's face. The kids talked the whole way to the kitchen, informing her of everything they had done. Riley was happy for all the chatter and absorbed everything they told her. Coming around the corner and seeing the snow-covered town square, Riley felt completely relaxed and ready for a hot meal.

Once inside, Riley couldn't believe how great the restaurant looked and how wonderful the food was. None of their meals had been hot while working in the hospital. At best, they were cool, leaning toward being cold. Riley sat down to eat with Annie, Landon, and Kota. Becca came in a few minutes later and took the seat next to Annie and joined in the conversation. With all the laughter and voices engulfing her, Riley felt as if she had come home from a long trip. Once done eating, Riley stood up and meandered over to visit with people at other tables. She enjoyed the conversation she had with them. She found Morgan sitting alone in the back corner, watching her. She made her way over to him and took a seat.

"So, Morgan, something is on your mind. Out with it."

He cleared his throat before he spoke, "You're pretty proud of yourself, aren't you? Waltzing in here, taking command. How do you know the signs of the virus will show in less than five days? You probably just killed us all!"

Riley was calm. "Do you remember the man they called patient zero for the United States, Craig Blakely? Well, he had a roommate, and within three days of Blakely coming home, the roommate was sick. He died two days later. Six days and showing no signs of any kind, I would say we're good." Riley thought about the rest of his comments. "You were never going to clean out this town, were you?"

Morgan put his head down. "No. Not me, personally. I was going to wait for..." he didn't complete his thought.

"Morgan, you're fully aware no one is coming? If this is all of Jackson's survivors, why would you think the rest of the United States did any better? You haven't been thinking clearly."

"I've lived here for the past forty years. What? You've come here to visit how many times? This is my town, not yours!"

Riley's temper was rising. "Wow! Talk about walking off the beaten path, what does it matter that you've lived here for forty years and I've only come here to visit! The bottom line, you were never going to do anything about the dead. You seem to forget as a public servant, you work for the people of Jackson, not for yourself. These people thought you had a plan, which you didn't! Look at them, Morgan! Look at them!" Riley was standing now, waving her arms out in the direction of everyone in the room—all of whom were watching and listening to them. "These people deserve a chance to live again. What you had them do was hide! Personally, I'm sick of hiding, of surviving! I'm ready to get out there and live again! If these people want you as their mayor, I'm good with that. You can sit at your desk all day long in town hall, flipping through papers of no importance, waiting for phone calls that aren't coming, or you can man up! Be the mayor these people deserve and put this town back together." Riley was more calm now, and instead of yelling, she drilled her finger into the table for emphasis on what she was about to say to Morgan, "You decide what you're going to do. I didn't come here to point out your flaws. I came here to get this place ready for 120 people that are relying on me. And whether you like it or not, they are coming."

Morgan was enraged but said nothing. He just stared at Riley.

A gentleman from the front of the restaurant stood up and said, "Excuse me, Bo-Boss and Morgan." Everyone's attention was now turned toward the man speaking. "Um, none of us voted for anyone, I mean, you, Morgan…you just stepped in and made yourself comfortable. In the past week, we have done more living than we ever did in the previous six months with you as our so-called leader. I'm sorry, Morgan, but the boss is right. She set the fire under us, even went into the hospital without asking any of us to do it for her. She knows what's been happening to the world outside of here, when we don't even know what's going on in Wilson or Teton Village. I'm ready to put this to a vote now." The man looked to Riley and then continued, "Sorry, Boss, your people are excluded from this vote."

Riley understood, as did the rest of her group.

"Who's in favor of Morgan being mayor, raise your hand."

No one in the room raised their hand, not even Donald or Robert.

"In favor of, I'm sorry, I only know you as Boss or Mom."

"It's Riley." She smiled, slightly embarrassed.

"Okay, who's in favor of Riley?"

Riley was uncomfortable with the methodology being used to vote, but she needed this town and hoped the people of Jackson needed her. Looking around the room, it seemed all were in favor of her.

Pamela stood up, facing Morgan. "I'm in favor of you helping these people with what they need. I have to give it to you, Morgan, you do know the town. However, putting you in charge is like putting a lamb in charge of a pack of wolves, and that's just plain cruel. So don't leave here sulking. Help this woman, for that matter, help all of us, like you should have done months ago!"

Morgan was angry, but he took a deep breath and thought for a moment.

"Whatever questions you have, hopefully, I'll have the answers to them."

"I have one," Nate said, standing up. "The electric and water company, where are they?"

Clearing his throat, Morgan answered Nate. He even offered to show Nate when he was ready to go. Riley said, "He's ready now." Nate agreed. The room settled down as people went back to eating or just visiting with one another.

Riley turned to Morgan and held out her hand, "Friends?"

"Sure...yeah, okay," he said begrudgingly as he shook her hand.

Riley headed for the door and saw Anderson standing with Allen in the entryway. They both glared at Morgan as he walked past them, leaving with Nate.

"Jerk," Allen said as Morgan passed.

"Be nice, boys, we need to make this work for all of us," Riley said.

"I have no respect for that man! None at all," he continued.

"Ah, well, the mayor here is right. However, we do need to keep an eye on that one."

"Oh, no, you don't!" Riley said, waving her finger in Anderson's face. "Don't you dare call me mayor! I'm just getting used to this 'boss' thing! Don't you dare change my name again!" Riley said, half playing and half serious.

"Ah, well, now that was a butt-chewing like none other, Riley. A mayor's kind of butt-chewing," Anderson laughed.

"Sorry, Anderson, that was a mother chewing out a child, and frankly, I'm quite good at that." Riley paused for a moment, then smiled and continued, "Being a mother, that is, not the 'butt-chewing' part."

Both of the men laughed, and then Allen said, "Then I think you're a woman of many talents, Boss, and they have just increased by one!"

Riley shoved Allen into Anderson, laughing as she passed him, walking out the door saying, "Ha-ha, funny, Allen!"

* * *

Riley, with the volunteers from Calumet and Mercy as well as the volunteers from Jackson, tackled the mess at the fairgrounds. The rest of the people led by Morgan took on the job of sweeping through one of the nicer hotels on Broadway close to town square. This is where they would house everyone from Calumet and Mercy. From then on, it would serve as a place for anyone new needing sanctuary. Morgan still refused to move any of the dead, which didn't surprise Riley.

The system used for clearing the bodies from the fairgrounds was broken into three groups: Those that wrapped the bodies, those that moved the bodies onto the trailers, and lastly, those that delivered them to the pit. Once all the bodies were removed, the cleaning process would take place. The problem was the large number of people that were on the fairgrounds premises. Pamela wasn't kidding when she said that more than half the town had been taken there. They even used the stables, but because of the way the bodies were stacked there, it led Riley and the others to believe the authorities must have used that area for those who had died first. At least they had been wrapped. Becca took one look at the bodies in the exhibit hall and ran outside, vomiting. Then as if the first round wasn't enough, she was sick again. Annie was doing her best to hold it together and did pretty well until the sight of a dead baby sent her running outside with Becca. It took them all a few minutes to gather their composure. Anderson and Riley walked in and started the process of covering bodies. That gave some relief to the rest of the workers. Anderson offered to take care of all the children and infants; there was an audible sigh of relief from everyone, even Riley. But there was nothing anyone could do about the smell. In the arena, someone had had enough sense to lay large tarps on the ground so the bodies weren't in the dirt. It was difficult to decide where to start. Riley wasn't even sure they had enough protective suits to last them the duration of the cleaning process. They would have to work hard to get this done before they ran out of suits. She hoped another trip to the hardware store would be fruitful and they would find more suits and gloves.

Again, it was arduous work. Everyone was ready to quit by nightfall, but no one did. The need to finish the work outweighed their exhaustion. It seemed with each day, the team would start earlier due to the nightmares that plagued their minds. Allen had the lights on so they could work through the evening and well into the earlier hours of the morning. There was a never-ending fire in the pit that lit up the night sky. The smell coming from the pit was awful, and there was no place to go to get away from it. Even those not working at the fairgrounds had to endure the smell.

By midafternoon, on the third day, Morgan got as close to the fairgrounds as he dared to summon Riley. Before Riley could meet with Morgan, she had to discard her suit and gear, then wash up, before heading over to him.

"There's a problem with your friend Lee. They're stuck and can't get any further."

"Where are they?"

"On the Twenty-Six, just north of here, somewhere around Moran, I'm guessing. The snow is too much especially now since the storm the other night dumped all that new snow."

"Let me get Allen on it. Thanks, Morgan."

"What do you want me to tell them?"

"Tell them you and Allen are on your way."

"Me?"

"Yes, you. Or you need to suit up and help here. I can't spare anyone other than Allen. Anyway, you know the area."

Morgan stared at her like she was insane but said nothing. Riley went back, found Allen, and gave him the news. Allen grinned when she told him Morgan was going with him. She wished she could be the fly on the wall for this one. But there was too much work to be done at the fairgrounds. As it was, it took them a week to empty out the entire fairgrounds then another week to clean it. What mice were found were killed, and traps were scattered throughout the fairgrounds in the hope of catching the ones they might have missed. Riley gave everyone that worked the fairgrounds two days off. During that time, Riley met the Chen family—which consisted of Lee, Lucy, their mom, their dad, an aunt, an uncle, two brothers, and a friend of Lucy's.

Allen said Morgan griped the whole way there and then was pretty boastful to everyone about how *he* saved the Chen family.

Riley laughed at that then told Allen that Morgan, along with his pride, would be going to Wilson and Teton Village to check on people there. Allen said he would be happy to go with Morgan just to make sure he did his job. Riley had no doubt that Allen would.

* * *

Teton County housed not only the Jackson Hole skiing area but also all of the Grand Teton National Park. It also included less than 50 percent of Yellowstone National Park with the combined total equaling almost 4,200 square miles of land and water. Riley knew they wouldn't be able to cover all of the area before spring; although she felt they could at least have the neighboring towns completed before summer. Wilson was a small town northwest of Jackson and Teton Village just north of Jackson. Before the search began of the private residences in Jackson, Riley sent a small team to check out both places. If someone was still alive in either of those two towns, they became top priority. Allen would lead a team into Wilson and Teton Village with his choice of 10 people that would accompany him. The stipulation was that out of those ten, Morgan had to be included, which he was not happy about. The rest would stay to work on the houses. In Wilson, 74 people were found alive; however, there were only 16 survivors in Teton Village. Riley was relieved when all 90 people agreed to live in Jackson. Allen said that most of the people were terrified when he and his team found them. However, it took very little to persuade them to come back to Jackson with him. Once Allen had them all settled into the hotel, they were eager to help in any way possible.

The residences that were clean, with beds made, no dishes in the sink, no laundry anywhere, etc., were to be marked with purple paint on the door. Those homes more than likely didn't have someone residing in them at the time of the outbreak and could be moved into immediately. The homes that were cluttered but had no occupants more than likely had someone infected living in them during the time of the outbreak. However, they probably were part of the mix at the fairgrounds or hospital. Those homes had to be gutted and everything burned; then the entire house sprayed and scrubbed. This is where Mr. Miller shone. He was given his own team of 10 people to do the refurbishing of the homes. The body disposal group went in first—not only to remove bodies, but also to gut the homes if needed—then Miller's group went in. Miller took detailed notes of each house, so there were no mistakes as to what needed to be done to them. All the locals were involved in this process, and with almost every home they went into, someone had known the occupants that had lived there. For many, it was hard to see their friends' homes gutted and belongings burned, leaving no remnants of them. The entire group took one square block at a time. They began the process of clearing the houses on January 25 and finished on May 9. They would spend the summer refurbishing the homes. Anderson felt each family should have its pick, and those would be the ones done first. There was no disagreement from anyone; however, one stipulation was made, and that was that everyone needed to be in the same neighborhood purely for safety reasons. Again, no one fought the issue.

When they were on the last block of homes, Allen called Calumet to relay the good news. Once Ken announced the news to everyone in Calumet and Mercy, they couldn't pack fast enough. People were ready and very excited to have a chance at a new start in this new world the virus had created.

The most amazing sight was the day that family and friends from Calumet and Mercy pulled into town square. To be reunited once again brought more joy than any of them could have imagined. Gauge and Levi blasted past everyone and flew into Riley's arms, knocking her flat on her bottom. Riley could do nothing but laugh.

After everyone was settled into the hotel, Alejandro—who now had Lupe by his side—had a feast waiting for them at the kitchen. The meal was fantastic, as always. After they were done eating, Sara showed her mother all the pictures on her phone that she had taken of the boys while Riley was gone. The pictures were an added bonus for Riley since the boys had grown so much during the four months they had been apart.

Riley stood up. "Can I have everyone's attention please?"

Riley waited for the room to quiet down.

"Thank you. First of all, there are no words that can express how wonderful it feels to be reunited with our family and friends. There's not one of us that didn't miss you."

Cheers and whistles were so loud Riley had to wait for the noise to die down before she began again.

"To all of you from Wilson and Teton Village, we are so grateful for your support and even more grateful you decided to make your home here with us in Jackson. And last but not least, by any means, to the locals, thank you for taking a chance on us, allowing us to come to be a part of your community. Thank you for working so hard to make Jackson livable again. We still have a lot of work to do, but for now we'll take a few days off to enjoy our families and friends. Also, take some time to get acquainted with the new members of our community. Before we get started on that time off, I need to say one more thing. Those of you that have been with me from the beginning know what it is that has driven me. Those of you that haven't need to simply look around you. It's family. It's that simple. Every step that has been taken has been taken with God's guidance. I told you awhile back that we were not at the bottom of an imaginary barrel, that God had not forsaken us but had clearly blessed us. Look around you, we are 268 strong, and we have God to thank for that. I can…"

Rrrring, rrrring, rrrring!

Riley stopped talking and looked toward her table, where Sara's phone was lying and now ringing, as did everyone else in the room. Sara had forgotten about it after her mother had looked through all the pictures. Everyone was so shocked by the ringing that no one moved. It took Riley a second before she stepped back over to the table, slowly picked it up, then answered it.

"Hello?"

ABOUT THE AUTHOR

Larissa Self grew up overseas and returned to the United States enrolling in college where she received an electronics degree. She worked for several years before she decided to become a full-time mom. Today she lives in Southern California with her husband and four children.

CPSIA information can be obtained
at www.ICGtesting.com
Printed in the USA
FSHW021335070619
58824FS